Honor dicta...
but lou...

MW00753352

"What lady of my birth would marry any man on such insulting terms?"

"One who doesn't have a choice."

Carissa rose, scowling, from her chair. "Don't be silly! You are completely overreacting! You know where to find me if I should ever tell a soul about your secrets. Then we can talk about marriage—"

"At that point, it's too late."

"Marriage is not the sort of thing that's meant to be handed down as a punishment. Besides that, we barely know each other— and what we *do* know starts with the other's flaws! Tonight, I caught you arranging an adulterous liaison, and, believe me, I have *no* desire to marry a man who doesn't see any particular problem with that! For my part, we both know I'd quickly drive you mad. I snoop in other people's business—"

"And you're a voyeur. Stubborn as hell, to boot. Typical redhead."

"You're no angel, yourself!"

"No, I'm not," Beau lustily agreed. "Nor do I have any plans of reforming."

By Gaelen Foley

MY SCANDALOUS VISCOUNT
MY RUTHLESS PRINCE
MY IRRESISTIBLE EARL
MY DANGEROUS DUKE
MY WICKED MARQUESS

GAELEN FOLEY

My Scandalous Viscount

AVON

An Imprint of HarperCollinsPublishers

This is a work of fiction. Names, characters, places, and incidents are products of the author's imagination or are used fictitiously and are not to be construed as real. Any resemblance to actual events, locales, organizations, or persons, living or dead, is entirely coincidental.

AVON BOOKS
An Imprint of HarperCollins*Publishers*
10 East 53rd Street
New York, New York 10022-5299

Copyright © 2012 by Gaelen Foley
Bonus chapter copyright © 2013 by Gaelen Foley
ISBN 978-0-06-207593-2
www.avonromance.com

First Avon Books mass market printing: October 2012

Printed in the U.S.A.

10 9 8 7 6 5 4 3 2 1

Truth will out.

—Old English Proverb

My Scandalous Viscount

Chapter

1

$\mathcal{S}$ome people in this world (fools) were happy minding their own business.

Miss Carissa Portland wasn't one of them.

Seated between her cousins, the formidable Denbury Daughters, with their governess, Miss Trent, snoring softly on the end, she trailed her dainty opera glass slowly over the capacity audience of about a thousand souls in attendance that Saturday night at Covent Garden Theatre.

To be sure, the little dramas, comedies, and farces playing out among the Quality present were far more intriguing than anything happening on the stage.

Besides, knowing everybody else's secrets in the ton seemed the safest way to guard her own.

Perusing the three gilded tiers of private boxes, she scanned along at a leisurely pace, while the lenses of other ladies' opera glasses winked right back at her.

Fluent in fan language, as well, she watched for those coy signals a lady could discreetly send her lover.

Hmm, over there. Lady S——, sitting with her husband, had just flicked her fan in an arc to Colonel W——, who had come with the fellow officers from his regiment. The uniformed coxcomb smiled slyly in receipt of the invitation. Carissa narrowed her eyes. *Typical tomcat male. She'd better be careful with him.* Drifting on, she picked out the subjects of other various rumors here and there: the jeweled countess said to be dallying with her footman; the political lord who had just sired twins on the mistress he swore he didn't have.

From opposite ends of the theatre, two branches of a feuding family glared at each other, while on the mezzanine, a notorious fortune hunter blew a subtle kiss to the heiress of some encroaching toadstool who apparently owned coal factories.

Tut, tut, poor man, she thought when her casual spying happened across the sad figure of a cuckolded husband who had just filed a crim-con case against his wife's seducer.

Well, the demireps preening in their box and putting their wares on display in low-cut gowns seemed more than happy to comfort him.

Hmmph, thought Carissa.

All of a sudden, her idle scan of the audience slammed to a halt on a particular box, second tier, stage left.

A gasp escaped her. *He's here!*

At once, her foolish heart began to pound. *Oh, my.*

Encircled in the lens of her dainty spyglass, there he sat, lounging in his chair, his muscled arms folded across his chest . . .

Staring right back at her.

A wicked smile slowly crept across his face, and just

to confirm that, oh, yes, he saw her ogling him, the handsome hellion sent her a cheeky little salute.

She let out an almost feline hiss and dropped her lorgnette onto her lap as though she had been burned.

She vowed not to touch it again—at which the audience let out another wave of rumbling laughter.

Oh, bother. She shifted in vexation in her seat and looked around uneasily. Of course, they weren't laughing *at* her, though she probably deserved it.

Devil take him, that rogue's glance made her feel like one of the demireps.

To her own dismay, Carissa Portland had secretly become fascinated by a libertine.

Again.

Where this weakness in her came from, this shameful susceptibility to a well-made man, she quite despaired to guess. Perhaps it was her auburn hair to blame.

Redheads were notorious for their more passionate nature. Probably hogwash, she admitted, but it sounded as good an excuse to her as any.

What *his* excuse was, well, he didn't bother making one. A golden demigod striding the earth like a wayward son of Aphrodite didn't have to. Charming, quickwitted, unbelievably handsome, with a smile that could have melted ice floes across the Nordic Sea.

Sebastian Walker, Viscount Beauchamp, could have got away with murder if he fancied. He was the Earl of Lockwood's heir, known to the ton as Beau.

They had been introduced some weeks ago by mutual acquaintances: Her closest friends, Daphne and Kate, were married to his fellow Inferno Club members, Lord Rotherstone and the Duke of Warrington. So they moved in the same circles, and, of course, she'd heard his reputation. He had lived up to it in spades with her not long ago. The scandalous beast had actually kissed her.

In public!

She had made the mistake of stopping him when he was in a hurry on his way somewhere. She had been leery about confronting him, but she had needed a simple answer to a very serious question: *Where the dash has everybody gone?*

Both Daphne and Kate had been missing from Town for weeks without explanation. This was totally unlike them.

Because of Lord Beauchamp's friendship with their husbands, she was sure he must know something. The aforementioned husbands had also disappeared, supposedly on some hunting trip to the Alps.

But Carissa was starting to doubt everything she thought she knew about her friends. Everyone in their set had been acting so mysteriously before they had vanished. It was all very upsetting. She had no firm information (maddening!), but clearly, something was afoot. She did not understand why she had been excluded.

The truth was, frankly, it hurt.

Thankfully, she had received a letter from Daphne at last, confirming she was safe, but her friend's verbiage seemed deliberately vague. And so, with relief had come even greater annoyance.

Why on earth were they keeping her in the dark? Didn't they trust her!

In an effort to get answers, she had cornered Beauchamp in a safe (so she thought) public place. But when she had delayed him too long with her, as he put it, "nagging," the gorgeous brute had simply snatched her up in his arms and put a stop to her questions with a lusty kiss.

As if she were some wanton trollop on the corner!

If it had not been raining . . . if he had not shielded them from public view with his umbrella . . . she was sure the scandal would have been so calamitous, she'd have hanged herself by now, or (more fashionably) drowned herself in the Serpentine.

Well, the blackguard clearly did not understand the first rules of decent behavior. Though he certainly knew how to give a woman one hell of a kiss.

She put him and the whole discomfiting episode out of her mind with a will, redirecting her attention toward the stage. The evening's program had begun with a concert of Vivaldi's exuberant "Spring," followed by a mediocre tragedy called *The Grecian Daughter.*

The comic afterpiece, *The Fortune of War,* was the one everyone had been waiting for. It was the latest bit of hilarity by the popular Mr. Kenney, a notable wit of the day and founding member of the gentleman's club, Boodle's.

Though the play lacked Mr. Kenney's beloved recurring character, the rascally Jeremy Diddler, the crowd seemed to be enjoying it.

Waves of laughter washed over the audience as the characters bantered back and forth across the stage. Carissa did her best to pay attention, but from the corner of her eye, she was acutely aware of Lord Beauchamp.

When the curtain whisked closed briefly for the stagehands to change the scenery, she could not resist another cautious peek in his direction.

Her curiosity instantly perked up as she spied one of the orange-sellers stepping into his box to deliver a message to the viscount. Carissa saw him take the little note and read it while the orange-girl waited for her coin.

Well, Carissa had no choice. Her innately nosy nature compelled her. She snatched her opera glass from her lap and lifted it to her eye just in time to see the smoldering look that gathered on his chiseled face. Lord Beauchamp glanced across the theatre with a suave nod, acknowledging the sender: Carissa zoomed her opera glass in that direction, too, trying to follow his gaze.

To no avail.

Whoever had sent him the note was lost amid the crowd.

Indeed, it could have been any of Society's highborn harlots wanting to take her turn with him tonight. Scowling, she searched the tiers across from him. Honestly, she did not know if she was more vexed at Beauchamp for having all the morals of a blood stallion, or at herself, for being jealous at how free he was with his meaningless affections.

She swung her opera glass back to the viscount to see what he'd do next. Beau turned to the orange-girl and asked for something; she handed him a pencil.

While he scrawled his reply, Carissa memorized what the orange-seller looked like: a tall, weary lump of a peasant girl. Then the libertine handed her his note along with a coin and sent her off to deliver his answer.

As the orange-girl disappeared through the small door of his private box, questions gnawed Carissa. Who was he involved with these days? Of course, she knew there were many women around him as a rule, but was there any one in particular?

And why do you care? her better sense inquired.

I don't know. Do I need a reason?

Yes, it answered.

She shrugged, refusing to admit to anything. *I just want to know because—because I want to know!*

Suddenly, she was seized with a wicked inspiration.

Why, she could either sit here festering on it, burning with curiosity about which feckless female meant to hurl herself into his clutches tonight, or *do* something. And go find out.

After all, as a lady of information, she had long since discovered that orange-girls . . . could be bribed.

Right.

Instantly rising from her chair, she excused herself with a whisper. Miss Trent awoke with a disoriented jolt, while the Denbury Daughters rolled their eyes. Which was the spoiled beauties' response to most things, actually.

"What are you doing?" Lady Joss, age nineteen, complained at her.

"I have to go to the ladies' lounge."

"Can't you just hold it?"

"No."

"That's disgusting," Lady Min, age seventeen, opined.

"Sorry." Dismissing her cousins' perpetual irritation with her, she slipped out of the Denbury box and closed the little door behind her.

At once, Carissa swept off down the third-floor hallway, her slippered feet pattering busily in the quiet.

She had to find and intercept that orange-seller.

She knew she should not care who Beauchamp would be bedding tonight, but everything in her had to get a look at that note. Seeing it with her own eyes, she reasoned, would surely help remind her that gorgeous rakehells like Lord Beauchamp were nothing but trouble. They chased after pleasure and did not care who got hurt.

She should know.

On the other hand, in all fairness, she supposed, she had to admit there sometimes seemed to be more to him than just charm and charisma. And broad shoulders. Lovely muscles. Mesmerizing eyes the color of seafoam that danced when he laughed, which was often, a rugged jawline, and extremely kissable lips . . .

She shook herself back to the task at hand, hurrying on. Indeed, physical appeal aside, he had actually done a few interesting things in his life.

Using her usual methods, she had managed to ferret out a number of odd tidbits about him, including some highly colorful exploits in his past.

Of course, his origins came from a lineage as excellent as her own. His mother, Lady Lockwood, had been a great beauty of her day, indeed, still was, now in her fifties. His father, the Earl of Lockwood, was said to be a brusque curmudgeon who did not often come to Town but preferred the "huntin', shootin'" life of a country lord.

She did not know where Beau had spent his childhood, but as a young man, he had gone to Oxford, studied Greek and Latin, and excelled in his classes without having to try—so she'd heard. Too smart for his own good, according to her sources, he had been easily bored and had occupied himself with carousing and all manner of wild adventures. And even from his youth, there had been women.

An indecent number of women.

But apparently, the lusty young aristocrat had his heroic moments, too. On one occasion, at age twenty-one, according to the rumor mill, he had been heading home in the wee hours after a long night's revelries, when he had come across a lodging house on fire.

Whether the whiskey he'd been drinking all night had made him foolishly brave, or if he was always like that, she could not say. But he had rushed into the burning building and rescued everyone inside before the fire company could even get there.

He'd saved some twenty people's lives.

Not long after that, his father, the earl, had made him a Member of Parliament for one of the pocket boroughs he controlled. He had thrust the post upon his son so he might gain experience to help prepare him for one day taking his seat in the House of Lords.

Little had the earl expected the young MP to stand up and outrage the leaders of both parties with his fiery idealism, his blistering reproaches, and his regrettable refusal to compromise.

It was nice to know he had not always been a cynic, she supposed, and that he had a sense of civic duty despite his many romantic peccadilloes. By the time he had resigned his post a year later in angry disgust and returned to his rakehell ways, he had made enough political enemies to last a lifetime.

These, in turn, got their revenge on the bold young viscount in due time, when word got out that he had fought a duel against some hotheaded rival for the favors of one of Society's highborn wantons.

Beauchamp, universally acknowledged as a crack shot, had not deigned to kill the man who had challenged him but had wounded him. As a result, his opponent had to have his leg amputated below the knee, and unfortunately, he had turned out to be the nephew of a Cabinet minister.

Of course, there were rules on the books against dueling, but as a courtesy to the upper class, who lived and died by honor, these laws were almost never enforced.

Unless one had enemies in high places.

The bureaucrats had come down on Beauchamp like a hammer, claiming they must make an example of him to teach other young Englishmen that they could not simply go around shooting each other.

It was all Lord Lockwood could do to keep his merry scapegrace son out of Newgate. Instead, after a very large fine and damages paid to the now-one-legged hothead, the handsome young duelist had been sent off, unsurprisingly, to travel. Sow his wild oats abroad, as it were. He was given some post loosely attached to the war effort, she'd heard, but on his father's insistence, was generally kept out of harm's way, well behind the lines.

It was rather hard to imagine that one staying out of trouble, she mused, but somehow the war had ended, and here he was, back again, unscathed.

Rumor had it he had now returned home for good.

Of course, he was scarcely back in England three months before he was in trouble again.

She wasn't sure yet what the hell-raiser had done this time, but she had first caught wind of his latest scrape while snooping in her uncle's study.

She knew that her guardian, Lord Denbury, and his cronies in the House of Lords kept each other informed about the goings-on in their various committees. One of these parliamentary briefs sent to her uncle had revealed that Viscount Beauchamp was under investigation by a secret panel from the Home Office.

No details were given beyond that.

It was altogether perplexing—and just another piece

of proof that, behind that sunny smile, he was one beautiful, bad seed.

Hurrying down the empty stairwell, she pressed on to the mezzanine level, glancing here and there, hunting for that particular, weary-looking orange-girl.

Muffled dialogue from the stage and swells of laughter from the audience poured through the walls from the play in progress. Mr. Kenney was obviously killing them with his famous sense of humor.

Carissa had no time for mere entertainment, however, bustling down the mezzanine corridor, all business.

"Can I help you, Miss?" one of the uniformed attendants whispered as she passed.

She shook her head, gave what she hoped looked like an innocent smile, and hurried on.

It would not do for anyone to discover this secret method of hers for gaining information. Glancing into her reticule to make sure she had a few coins for the bribe, she whisked along the curve of the mezzanine hallway where it hugged the back contour of the closed auditorium.

As she came around the bend, she finally saw the orange-girl she was after, but she ducked into the nearest curtained alcove with a gasp. Someone had beaten her to it!

Ever so cautiously, Carissa peeked around the edge of the alcove. *Blast it, who's that? He stole my plan.*

Then a chill came over her as she studied the man talking to the orange-girl.

He was beautiful, black-haired, and windblown, as if he'd just come back from his travels; and from his muscled body to his dark scowl, he looked decidedly mean.

Her mouth went dry as she watched him bribe the

orange-girl for a look at the note some lady, perhaps *his* lady, had exchanged with Beauchamp. Carissa's heart pounded. *Oh, Beauchamp, I hope you didn't sign your name.*

They never did, on those clandestine notes.

Surely he was too smart and experienced for that. But if he *had* made that mistake, she feared the rakehell might be headed for another duel. It looked as though she might not be the only one feeling jealous tonight.

Huddling behind the curtain of the alcove, she watched in trepidation as the handsome, black-haired man read the note and scoffed.

A snort of cynical laughter escaped him. He shook his head with a bitter smile, then tautly asked the orange-girl for another piece of paper, which she gave him. He crumpled the original note in his fist and stuffed it into his breast pocket.

Then he wrote back another message of his own.

With a dark look, he handed his note to the orange-girl, laying a finger over his lips, as if warning her to secrecy.

He slipped a paper bill into her hand and sent her on her way. Still unaware of Carissa, the stranger watched the orange-girl hurry off, his arms akimbo, his feet planted wide. Then, with a cold smile, as though satisfied his trap was laid, he pivoted on his heel and stalked out of the theatre.

Carissa eased out of her hiding place a moment later, dread tingling through her body. *Oh, Beauchamp, you're being set up.* She scarcely dared imagine what might happen to him if he went to meet his *femme du jour,* whoever she might be. He could be killed!

Once more, Carissa was in motion, hurrying after the orange-girl to stop her from delivering that note, which was naught but a piece of treachery. Beauchamp might be a bad, decadent libertine, but she was not about to let anyone murder him!

Rushing after the orange-seller into the quiet side hallway that backed the row of private theatre boxes, she skidded to a halt.

Too late!

The lump had just stepped through one of the narrow doors, halfway down the row. *Oh, no. What do I do now?*

Heart pounding, she glanced around uneasily.

Merely standing there, unchaperoned, in a part of the theatre where she did not belong was something of a gamble.

Having missed the orange-girl, the thought of venturing into Beauchamp's box to try to warn him—to risk being seen there by the other snoops in the audience—made her blood run cold. She could not afford in any way to become an object of gossip herself.

She already had too much to hide.

With that, she realized the intelligent thing to do was to abandon this mad quest immediately, go fleeing back to her seat, and pretend she had seen nothing.

But a man's life could be at stake.

And although he was entirely exasperating, the world would be a darker, duller place without him. Come to think of it, perhaps she could turn this little twist of fate to her advantage . . .

Oooh, she mused. *An exchange of information. Yes! If he'll tell me where Daphne and Kate went and what the deuce is going on, then I will tell him what I saw. That's fair, is it not? If he refuses, then maybe the rogue deserves what he gets.*

Unsure what to do, she crept toward the door to his

box, then stopped. He was probably reading the false note even now, getting drawn into the trap.

She stood there, torn and hesitating, as another little problem with all this occurred to her. If she tried to warn him what she'd seen, he'd realize she had been snooping into his personal affairs.

He'd notice she was jealous, and then, oh, then he'd laugh his head off and taunt her like a schoolboy—and then, never mind the jealous husband, she would murder him herself, wring the rascal's neck.

At that moment, before she had quite made up her mind what to do, the little door to his theatre box opened and the orange-girl scampered out.

Right behind her, the rogue himself emerged, tall and princely, en route to his assignation.

He stopped the second he saw her and, at once, his eyebrows arched high.

Carissa stood frozen, staring at him, tongue-tied.

She knew she was caught; he flashed a wolfish smile that made her want to shriek with mortified fury and run away. But she held her ground with a gulp while the orange-girl rushed off, leaving them alone in the dim, quiet hallway.

Close enough to touch.

"Well, my dear Miss Portland," he purred, trailing his gaze over her in thoroughly male appreciation. "What a very pleasant surprise. Was there something you, ah, . . . wanted?"

Chapter

2

$\mathcal{D}$espite the usual carefree smile that he wore like a Carnival mask, Beau had walked into the theatre this evening in a dark and nasty mood, feeling very alone in the fight.

He was under enormous pressure, on edge, and angry as hell over all the body blows the Order had taken over the past month. Their handler Virgil's death; Drake's escape and possible betrayal; his fellow agents Nick and Trevor's disappearance; and now the bloody Home Office probe into the Order's clandestine working methods.

Fed up with it all, he'd come to these rich hunting grounds seeking his usual remedy: a willing bed partner to distract him, replace his frustration with a few hours of physical bliss.

Give him that, and he'd be right as rain by morning.

But when he stepped out of his theatre box, he forgot all about the wanton duchess who had propositioned him. For here was a far sweeter morsel, the inimitable Miss Portland, staring at him like the bad little kitty that ate the canary.

He could not explain it, but something about the chit made him laugh. She always seemed to be up to something, and for some reason, he found that adorably amusing.

Even now, the mere sight of her standing there brightened his mood, as always. He could not account for it; he always seemed to go slightly stupid when she was around. Couldn't stop smiling like the village idiot mooning over the harvest queen.

He fought back a grin. *This'll be fun.*

"My dear Miss Portland," he greeted her with an air of gentlemanly gravity, knowing how much she preferred his friend, the grave and gentlemanly Lord Falconridge to him. "What brings you over to my end of the theatre this evening? Surely I dare not hope you came all this way just to see my humble self?"

She tilted her head and gave him a long-suffering look.

"If so, of course, I am your servant."

"Hmmph. Maybe," she admitted, lifting her chin as she folded her hands behind her back.

His eyebrows shot up. "Really? And you even admit to it? You usually run the other way whene'er you see me."

"Can you blame me?" she retorted lightly.

Beau just stared.

God, when he sensed her feminine interest in him, it was almost more than he could stand, holding himself back. He felt his nether regions clamoring for her and forced himself to look away. But it was true. Out of all the women in this theatre, actresses and demireps included (too easy), Lord Denbury's niece was the one he most would've wanted to get into his bed.

Unfortunately, this was just a fantasy, for his brother warriors had already taken care to describe what would happen to him if he trifled with Daphne's innocent little friend.

In general, he feared no man, but these were Order agents they were talking about—three of them, as well trained, and being a few years older, even more experienced than he. No, he really did not fancy getting his face smashed in by Rotherstone's fist, or his ribs cracked by Warrington's boot, to say nothing of what Falconridge might do to him, considering the elder-brotherly fondness the sandy-haired earl had hatched for the petite lady of information. Jordan Lennox, Lord Falconridge, recently married to his boyhood sweetheart, was the easygoing type who almost never got angry, but when he finally did, it was too late. You were already dead.

These seasoned, slightly older agents, well aware of Beau's seductive tendencies and his heated notice of Daphne's friend, had wrested from him a grudging promise not to touch her. Never mind the fact he was rather sure the feisty, little fairy queen wanted to be touched.

Ah, well. That didn't mean he couldn't look.

She wore a simple silk gown of pale spring green, and he had a fleeting fantasy of peeling it off her lithe body. But lucky for her, he'd already made up his mind not to act on his lust, quite apart from Rotherstone's friendly death threats.

The fact was, Carissa Portland was a nosy little gossip with a passion for digging up secrets while he was a spy charged with keeping them for the Crown.

A girl like that was trouble. Trouble he didn't need. He had plenty of that on his own.

"So, what can I do for you?" he murmured, leaning his shoulder into the wall.

"Well." She bit her lip and dropped her gaze, peeking at him from beneath her lashes as she hesitated. "To start, you can tell me who you think you're off to meet."

"I beg your pardon?" he exclaimed in surprise.

She just looked at him.

He laughed softly, folding his arms across his chest. "And what business is it of yours, exactly?"

"None," she said with an idle shrug, avoiding his gaze. "I'm just curious."

He regarded her skeptically. "How do you know about that, anyway? Were you watching me?"

"I have eyes."

"And a nosy little nose," he agreed, tapping her on the tip of it. "But I prefer your lips. Tell me," he added in a confidential murmur, leaning closer, "have you thought about that kiss as frequently as I have?"

"Beauchamp!"

"Portland."

She gave him a dubious smile, seemingly in spite of herself, and leaned against the wall beside him.

"No," she replied at last. "I haven't thought about it at all." Her smooth ivory skin filled with a scarlet blush.

Beau gazed at her in fond amusement. "Too bad. I thought you might have come to get another."

"Hardly." With a stern glare, she moved away, putting a safer distance between them.

"Very well, then, I don't have all night, girl. Why are you here?"

She did not answer at once but considered her words

carefully. "Whoever it is you think you will be meeting tonight, I'd advise you not to go."

"Why?" He crooked a brow at her with a playful leer. "Have you got a better idea?"

"Oh, stop it. I'll tell you why—just as soon as you tell me where Daphne is."

Beau groaned and slumped against the wall. "Please don't start that again. I thought Daphne wrote to you."

He knew for a fact she had, for he was the one who had asked Rotherstone's lady to do so.

"Yes, I got the letter—and I'm grateful for it. I know you had something to do with that. But still, it was awfully vague. Look, I know something's going on, and *I* know *you* know what it is. Now you can either tell me what's afoot or—"

"Or nothing," he interrupted. "I cannot."

"Why?"

"Because. Your friends are safe. That's all you need to know."

She shoved away from the wall, lifting her elegant shoulders in a shrug. "Very well. Your choice. Good evening, Lord Beauchamp." She started to turn away.

"Hold on, you." He captured her elbow gently to stop her from leaving. "What were you going to tell me?"

"Hmm?"

"You know something I don't?"

"Could that ever be possible?" she taunted.

"Hmm, smarty. Come now. Out with it. I acknowledge, you're an expert on Society gossip. Do you know something about my companion for the night that I should be aware of?"

She scoffed and pulled her arm free from his light hold. "You want me to just tell you when you'll give nothing in exchange? Oh, but I suppose you expect every woman you meet to be a fool for you and do whatever you say!"

"It would be nice," he said with an arch shrug.

She leaned closer. "Ha!"

Then she gasped when he captured her with a smile. "Shall I kiss it out of you, then?" He pulled her closer, and though she scowled at him, she let him draw her nearer willingly enough. His pulse leaped at her acquiescence. "You're looking rather beautiful tonight, I daresay."

"Flattery will get you nowhere. Especially when you're on your way to a tryst with another woman! You're an interesting man, Lord Beauchamp."

"Ah, come, what's wrong?" he cajoled her in a sensuous murmur. "Are you jealous, you little darling? Is that why you're here? To stop me from paying attention to somebody else?"

She pulled away with a huff. "Truly, your ego knows no bounds."

"Well, I don't see why you care. You've made it plain that you don't like me."

"I don't!"

"Of course not," he said with a mild wince.

"I just don't want to see you get hurt," she conceded with a wary frown. "You should be more careful."

"Of what?"

She looked at the wall with a shrug. "Oh, I don't know . . . Any number of dangers might await you on these silly assignations if you you'd stop and consider the risks."

"Such as?" he prompted in worldly amusement.

"What if she has the French disease?" she whispered.

"What if *I* do?" he countered.

She gasped in horror. "Do you?"

"Riddled with it. I'm only jesting!"

She smacked him on the arm, and whispered, "That's not even funny, you devil!" Then she pointed at his theatre box. "Why don't you stay out of trouble and go watch the play?"

"It bores me. Just like it bores you, I wager. Besides, this woman has promised me pleasures you cannot imagine," he said in a challenging tone, just to see what she would do.

She glared at him, her green eyes shooting sparks. "Such pleasure, my lord, often leads to pain."

"Which has its charms, as well, on occasion. What are you trying to tell me, poppet?"

"Where is Daphne?" she insisted.

He scowled at her, looked at his fob watch, and pushed away from the wall. "Sorry, have to go."

"Fine, then! Go! But did it ever occur to you that this lady of yours might have a husband?"

"Don't they all."

"It's called adultery!" she whispered.

"You're concerned for my immortal soul. How sweet."

"And your body!"

"Really?" he murmured in fascination.

"I didn't mean it that way!" she shot back, flustered.

He laughed softly. "My chef could light a flambé off your cheeks, love."

"I am only trying to keep you out of scandal!"

"But I like scandal. It gives you little gossips something to do."

"I am *not* a gossip!"

"Sorry. Lady of information. But I suppose you are quite right. You are innocent, and I am altogether wicked. I ought not go corrupting you," he said sar-

donically. "So I shall take my leave of you, fair lady—
though I remind you, it was you who came looking for
me. I bid you a fond good night, and apologize for offending your delicate sensibilities. Then again—this is
just a suggestion—but if my depravity offends you, you
could always try minding your own business." He sent
her a wink. "*Au revoir.*"

"Ugh! Beauchamp."

He paused with his back to her, a devilish, knowing smile curving his lips. "Yes, my dear?" He pivoted
slowly. "Was there something else you needed?" he
asked in a tone of deliberate innuendo.

She threw her hands up at her sides. "Why are you
so impossible? Do you ever think of the heartache you
must cause these women?"

He scoffed, ignoring a twinge of conscience. "They
jolly well know not to take me seriously. You should
learn to do the same."

She whirled away from him. "Fine, then, go! And I
hope you learn your lesson," she said under her breath.
"You deserve whatever you get."

"And you deserve a halo, I suppose," he shot back.

"What's that supposed to mean?"

He scowled and looked away, irked that he had let her
get to him. "Never mind."

"No, what are you implying?" she insisted.

He looked askance at her. "You may fool the ton,
Carissa Portland, but I'm afraid you don't fool me.
Look at you, standing there, so ripe for the plucking."
He moved closer. "Why do you come and torture me,
hmm? Why can't you leave me alone? What is it you
want me to do?"

She stepped back, turning three shades redder than
before. "I beg your pardon!"

He trailed a smoldering stare over her delectable body. "You need a good, sound kissing, for starters." His mouth watered as his stare consumed her breasts, the nipples nigh poking through her gown, just begging for his touch. His blood stirred with want. "Oh, yes. It's abundantly clear you're interested. But you're waiting for me—to do what, exactly? To force you? That's one game I don't play," he informed her in a low tone. "Either you come to me of your own free will, or not at all. But until you decide which it's going to be, run home to your nursemaid, little girl. Go on. Run and hide from me again, just like you do every time we meet. Yes, I have my faults, but at least I'm not a hypocrite. If you're afraid of what you feel, that's your affair. But don't come here pretending all you want to do is scold me. Believe me, I'm happy to satisfy your curiosity and my own about how it would be between us whenever you're ready to ask. But until then, I need a woman, not a little girl. So, if you'll excuse me, love, I have an appointment to keep, with someone who is very much—a woman."

That's what you think, Carissa thought, furiously aware that it was in fact a *man* who waited for him.

A man who was going to give the scoundrel the thrashing that he very much deserved.

Rude, proud, horrid beast! How dare he?

Shaking her head, cursing under her breath as he walked away, she savored the thought of that blackguard getting his just deserts. Every blow he'd take to that handsome face tonight was entirely his own fault. He deserved it.

Some people in this world insisted on courting disaster. But she was done trying to save him, the devil.

She had dropped him enough hints. Whatever happened to him next, he had only himself to blame.

She stayed rooted to her spot, clenching her fists, watching him march out of the dimly lit side hallway. When he disappeared, she stamped her foot and muffled her mental shriek of wrath to a soft, ladylike "Oh!"

He was the most infuriating creature on the earth!

Trembling in her mortified indignation, she was furious with herself for allowing him to perceive her attraction to him.

And her jealousy.

She must be mad to feel anything but loathing for that arrogant lecher. The way he'd looked at her! He might as well have undressed her right there in the hallway. She was outraged—and shamefully aroused.

She felt naked from the way he had stared at her body and the bold, ungentlemanly things he had said.

More alarming still was the fact that he apparently saw through her virtuous charade.

Recalling her own falseness, she promptly realized she had better get back to her seat.

It would not do to have her cousins asking her why she had taken so long going to the ladies' lounge. It would be even more awkward if the solicitous Miss Trent took it upon herself to come and find her, making sure she was all right.

How would she explain herself if the governess found her nowhere near the part of the theatre where she had said she'd be? Such lies would not be tolerated by Uncle Denbury. Not after The Incident in Brighton.

Her strait-laced, proper uncle watched her like a hawk, fully prepared, she suspected, to toss her out on her ear if she strayed again. One mistake, the family had been prepared to cover up, thanks to her innocence and youth, and to the dubious influence of her blithe, worldly, glamorous aunt Josephine, who had taken over the job of raising her after her grandparents died.

Aunt Jo was the Earl of Denbury's sister, older than he by a couple of years though she would never admit it and certainly didn't look it, with the lavish care she took of her hair and her complexion.

She was always dressed in the first stare of fashion and could still get away with telling her many male admirers that she was only thirty-three.

After The Incident, there had been such a row between Aunt Jo and Uncle Denbury that sometimes Carissa still had nightmares about it. She wished she had not taken it upon herself to eavesdrop on that particular occasion.

She shuddered as she hurried out to the mezzanine to make her way back to her seat before anyone noticed her overlong absence.

Hopefully, her cousins were distracted by Mr. Kenney's ribald jokes. With any luck, Miss Trent had fallen back asleep.

Out in the mezzanine, Lord Beauchamp was not in sight. Carissa picked up her skirts to avoid stepping on them in her haste and rushed back to the stairwell up to the third tier of the theatre. All the while, the family fight of a year and a half ago echoed in her mind, now that she had been reminded of it.

There was no use complaining about the fate she had been dealt, her parents dying, then her grandparents. Loss was a familiar phenomenon by now. She had learned to try at all times to anticipate the next blow before it came.

One of the best ways she had found to do that was never to risk getting too close to anyone—a lesson doubly well learned after how she had been betrayed.

She was still sickened by the memory of how she had disappointed her relatives and humiliated herself. She could still hear Uncle Denbury thundering at his sister.

"How could you let this happen, Josephine? You were responsible for her! If you weren't going to watch her, you should've let me and Caroline take her years ago! But no, you had to take Ben's daughter for yourself. Our little niece, and I agreed since you had no children of your own. You weren't supposed to treat her like an adult, Jo! She was just a child!"

"Oh, Edward! Loosen up your stays, you old woman. Every girl gets kissed at her age. It's part of growing up."

"More than kissing happened, Jo, as you know full well! The little bastard got the payment he wanted from us to buy his silence, and now he's nowhere to be found. He's fled to France or Italy, from what I'm told."

"It does not signify," Aunt Jo had shot back mildly. "I'd never let my niece marry such a useless prop even if we could find him. Oh, he's pretty enough, and not too badly born, but he's a fool. Fancies himself the next Lord Byron! That's why she fell for him and his tousled curls and his idiotic poetry, I warrant."

"One only wonders how many other young ladies this Benton has deceived," the earl had growled. "If he ever laid a hand on one of *my* girls—but *I* would never let that happen. This disaster is to be laid at *your* feet, sister. You've failed our brother, leaving her ungoverned. Indeed, she has followed your example to the letter! The chit is too naïve to realize that what a widowed lady of forty-three can get away with is forbidden to a debutante. Badly done, Jo! You've all but ruined her."

"I've done nothing of the kind! We can keep it a secret—and that's a low blow, bringing up my age, you shit. Do you think I wanted this for her? I love Carissa as if she were my own!"

"Your own what? Lapdog? Your fluffy little cat? She's not a pet, Jo! She is not a toy, as I've been telling you since the child was six years old! She's not an accessory made to match one of your gowns, to be picked up and coddled when you remember her, then forgotten when you're too busy with your social calendar."

"How dare you criticize me? I've done the best I can to raise her—I'm not her mother! Well, she's turned out better than your pair of spoiled harpies!"

"You insult my daughters?" he had bellowed. "No more, Josephine! I will not stand for this. Your foolishness has done enough harm to our niece's life! I'm taking Carissa to London, and that is my decision. I'm her legal guardian, so perhaps I am ultimately to blame. She only remained with you on my permission, which is hereby revoked!"

Brother and sister had not spoken since.

Carissa hated having been responsible for such a monstrous family row. Aunt Jo had flounced off on a long Grand Tour, while Lord Denbury had duly brought Carissa up to Town.

After a stern dressing down that had put the very fear of God in her, he had installed her in his home as a lesser member of his family, under his protection, just in case any more seducers drew a target on her chest.

But he had kept her secret, and as she hurried up the stairs, Carissa understood full well that another misstep off the straight and narrow path would not be tolerated.

She'd be tossed out into the street or maybe sent to

a nunnery. To this day, her uncle eyed her with private distrust and disapproval. Her only grace was that he had not told a soul, not even his own wife, about what had happened in Brighton. To be sure, Lady Denbury would not have allowed her into the house if she knew. She would not have wanted Carissa contaminating her own daughters.

Only three people in the world besides herself knew her shame—her aunt and uncle, and the lying cad who had deceived her. She prayed every night Roger Benton had not told anyone about how he'd succeeded with her. That had been the arrangement: a sum of gold in exchange for his secrecy. A nice little nest egg so he could continue his artistic pursuits. No one wanted to pay for his stupid rhymes, after all. He was no Byron.

No wonder she was shaken that Lord Beauchamp had seen through her mask of purity, she admitted to herself. As she reached the top of the stairs, she vowed for the eighth or ninth time in as many days that she would not be going near him again. And her vow held—until she reached the little door to the Denbury theatre box, where she paused uneasily.

He's going to die.

If she went through that door, returned to her seat, and pretended nothing had happened, she might well end up with blood on her hands.

His blood.

Another loss. And this one would be her fault, because, owing to anger and pride, she had chosen to say nothing when she could have spoken up and warned him of the danger.

Blast it, she should have told him plainly what she had seen, not because he deserved it, but because it was the right thing to do.

She closed her eyes. *Oh, Lord, what have I done?* Had she no conscience? She glanced back woefully toward the stairs, then bit her lip in indecision. *What is there to decide? His life could be at stake. You must go after him.*

Warn him, like you should have done before. At least you have to try.

She just hoped she wasn't already too late.

Chapter
3

*W*hat an utter headache of a female!

Who did she think she was to take him to task for his lack of morals—his mother? Actually, his mother was worse in that department than he, Beau mused as he stalked across the wide, opulent lobby of the theatre, still fuming.

He really did not need that mere slip of a girl pointing out things he preferred to gloss over, like the ugly side of the haut ton's favorite sport: infidelity.

Indeed, he knew firsthand how it devastated families, having watched it tear his own parents apart.

He did not like thinking about it. He pushed it out of his mind. It was just the way of the world, and to protest it would be to admit how badly it had hurt him as a boy.

To say nothing of how it had hurt his father.

Trust your mates and your horses, lad, an embittered Lord Lockwood had once told his eleven-year-old heir, in trying to explain why Mother would live in Town from now on by herself. *Care for a woman, and she'll rip your heart in half. You want loyalty,* his father had advised him, *get a dog.*

Bloody hell, he did not even feel like sleeping with that duchess anymore, but stubbornly, it was a matter of principle now. He was not about to let that vexing redhead win. With a growl under his breath, he strode into the hallway off the lobby, heading for the discreet back exit.

Thrusting Carissa Portland out of his mind, he fixed his thoughts on the night's rendezvous. The deliciously sinful Duchess of Somerfield would be along shortly, then they'd leave together as planned.

At the back door of the theatre, Beau paused and from long-paranoid habit, bent to slip his pistol out of the ankle holster concealed beneath his trouser leg. He moved the weapon to the back of his waistband, where it would be in easier reach if needed but still concealed beneath his coat.

Then he laid hold of the door and pushed it open, stepping out into the alley, where she had told him to meet her. They'd take her carriage from there, and go wherever she pleased—if they made it that far. The carriage itself would serve, for all he cared.

The cool night air washed over him as the door closed behind him. He welcomed its calming chill, trying to shake off his frustration with Carissa.

What was it about her? Why should he even care what she thought of him?

He took a step into the alley, but before his eyes could adjust to the darkness, a stealthy black shadow detached from the wall to his right and suddenly slammed into him, driving him back against the door.

Beau barely had time to react. The figure came at him, grabbing his right arm as he reached for his gun, as though anticipating his movement. The moonlight flashed on the silver blade pressed flat against his neck as a voice spoke: "Good evening, Sebastian."

"*Nick?*" Beau froze in stunned recognition, making no attempt to fight back. He stared in shock at his long-missing brother warrior. "You're alive!"

He was instantly released. "Sorry, old boy." Nick let go of him, brushed off his coat with a no-harm-done motion, then he stepped back warily, letting Beau come away from the door. "Wasn't sure what you might've heard about me. Had to make sure you didn't come out swinging."

"Swinging? I thought I was coming out here to get laid."

Nick grinned. "Well, don't look at me." The tension began easing from his face.

Amazed laughter broke from him. Beau clapped him in a bear hug, his throat tightening with emotion. Joy and relief clashed with shock inside him. "Jesus, man, where the hell have you been? We've had no word of you in months. Are you all right?"

"I'm fine."

"*Are* you?" Beau stepped back and studied him. Though he was overjoyed to see his boyhood friend alive, he could not shake the feeling that something wasn't right.

Nick looked scruffy and a bit unkempt, with a few days' beard roughening his jaw and his black hair grown long and rather wild. But all in all, he seemed none the worse for wear.

Beau shook his head. "What happened? Where's Trevor? Why haven't you been in contact?"

"Trevor's safe, don't worry," Nick assured him. "He got shot in Spain, but he's recovering."

"Where?"

"Back of the right shoulder. Bullet punched through and broke his clavicle, but I got him out of harm's way and have been looking after him ever since. He'll be fine."

Beau glanced around the alley. "Is he here?"

"No, best to keep him out of trouble in his current state."

"What kind of trouble are you expecting?" Beau sent an uneasy glance around the alley. Might they soon have company? "Were you followed?"

"I don't think so. Listen," Nick said darkly, "I heard about Virgil."

The reminder of their handler's death jarred him. Beau gave him a somber nod. "Rotherstone's team is abroad right now. They're going to get the son of a bitch who killed him."

"Do we know who did it?"

"Niall Banks," Beau answered.

Nick raised his eyebrows. "Malcolm's son?"

"Well—yes and no. Turns out there's a good chance Niall was actually Virgil's own son, not his nephew."

"What?"

"Believe me, this revelation took all of us by surprise. Turns out Virgil and his brother were both in love with the same woman years ago, or something like that." Beau shrugged. "So, Niall could've been fathered by either one of them."

"Damn," he said.

"Aye. We captured Niall while you were gone, and hang me if the old man and his supposed 'nephew' didn't look exactly alike. Never saw that Highlander so out of sorts."

Nick shook his head.

"Unfortunately, we've got more trouble on top of Virgil's death," Beau continued in a hushed tone. "Drake Parry, the Earl of Westwood—you know him?"

"Know *of* him."

"Seems he's turned against us. His team was killed in Germany. He was captured. Tortured. The Prometheans addled his wits so badly we think they may have turned him into one of them."

Nick looked taken aback at this.

"If Rotherstone can't catch him, they're going to have to put him down."

"Well, that is the standard protocol, isn't it?" Nick murmured cynically as he dropped his gaze.

Beau nodded. "I've been waiting for word from Rotherstone to let me know if they've dealt with Niall or Drake yet, and when they're coming back. Right now, all I know is that when they return, we'll have the memorial service for Virgil up in Scotland." Then he shook his head again, still shocked to the marrow to see his friend alive, standing there, unscathed, in front of him.

He had been bracing himself for weeks now for the worst. "I was half-convinced we'd be holding services for you and Trevor, too. Man, it is so good to see you."

"You, as well. Sorry for putting you through all that. It couldn't be avoided."

"What the hell happened?" Then he clapped him on the shoulder. "Why don't you tell me over a pint? I take it my lady friend isn't coming," he added dryly.

Nick smiled. "No, she's not."

Beau snorted. "Thanks for the message, you bastard."

"Anytime."

"So, you want to go sit in a pub, or Dante House—"

"Can't. I don't have much time." Nick seemed awfully restless, glancing over his shoulder again.

"All right," Beau said cautiously. "Give me the abridged version, then. Where've you been? I've had every asset in Europe on the hunt for you and Trevor."

"I know. That's what I wanted to talk to you about." Nick turned and gave him a hard stare. "I need you to call off your dogs, Beauchamp."

"Pardon?"

"Stop looking for me."

"Well, obviously." Beau furrowed his brow. "You're standing right in front of me. You're back."

"Not exactly."

"What do you mean?"

He gave him a hard look. "I'm done. With the Order. I want out," he said. "I'm not coming back."

"*What?*"

"I quit. I've done my service. I think I'm entitled to have my own life now," Nick said coolly. "War's over. Napoleon's done for. Prometheans all but crushed. It's time for me to move on, and I trust you'll stay out of my way."

"Move on?" Beau echoed in disbelief, even more stunned at such talk than he had been at finding Nick alive. "Is that what you came to tell me? That's it?"

"Aye. That's it."

"Hold on," he ordered, grabbing Nick by the shoulder as he started to turn away. "You know bloody well that isn't how it works. You're not 'done.' You took the vow. The Order is for life."

"Says who? Virgil? He's dead." Nick looked down at Beau's hand grasping his coat. Then he shook his head.

"No. I've given enough for King and country. I can't do it anymore. I just want out."

"Nick, you can't mean this."

"Oh, but I do!" he retorted. "It's time for me to start looking out for myself. Not all of us were born with a silver spoon in our mouth, Beauchamp."

"Oh God, Nick." The blood drained from his face. "You got into trouble at the gaming tables again."

"We all have our vices. Don't try to play the saint with me! You of all people. You and your women. But no matter. I've found a solution. There are people out there willing to pay large sums of gold for a chap with my talents." He held up his gun and smiled.

Beau stared at him in shock. "You've turned mercenary?" A new thought gripped him. He stepped toward Nick more aggressively. "*Where* is Trevor, exactly? He'd never go along with this. However disillusioned you may be, he would never quit. What have you done with him?"

"Now, now—"

"I swear, if you've harmed him, so help me—"

"Nothing is going to happen to Trevor as long as you call off your dogs," Nick replied in an oh-so-reasonable tone. He held his stare in warning. "Just let me go, Beau, and forget we ever had this conversation. Write me off for dead in the Order's casualty rolls for all I care. It's not like anyone's going to miss me."

"Nick! Write you off for dead?" He was so astonished at what he was hearing, he could barely speak. "Have you lost your mind?"

"My shirt, is more like it. You should mark me down as fallen." He nodded. "It'll be easiest that way."

"I'm not going to lie to the Order for you! Look, if it's a matter of money, I can lend you—"

"No! Thank you—but no. No more of your charity, generous as you are. You were always a true friend to me, Beauchamp. That's why I came to say this to your face."

Beau's heart slammed in his chest as he stared at Nick in disbelief. "What, that you're a traitor?"

"No, I'm not a traitor, I just want out," he answered wearily.

"We're all tired, Nick, believe me. But this is so close to being over. If you could just wait—"

"It's no use. I have to go." He turned away.

"I'm afraid I can't allow that." He cocked his pistol and aimed it at his friend, ignoring the anguish of having no choice but to do so.

Nick looked back at him, glanced at the gun, then met his gaze with a hard, challenging stare. "You really want to do this, brother?"

"I keep my vows," he said quietly.

Nick sighed and stared up at the sky. "Beau, Beau. You always were the true believer, weren't you? Bloody flower o' chivalry. We were only boys when we were recruited. What choice did we ever have?"

"The Order is our heritage. And our duty."

He laughed softly and looked at the ground. "You are so amusing. God." He shook his head. "I don't have time for this. Good-bye."

"I'll shoot you if I have to."

"Don't you get it? None of this is worth it. You weren't there, Beau. When Trevor got shot, I thought we'd lost him. Fortunately, he's strong, and he survived. But the moment I saw him get hit, that was the last straw for me. Do you think those bastards farther up the chain of command give a damn about what happens to any of us?"

He swallowed hard. "Nick, we need you in the fight."

"Sorry, I guess I'm just not as selfless as the rest of you. I'm only in London on a job. Tell the others whatever you deem best, team leader. I'll stay out of your way, and theirs, if you'll stay out of mine. Maybe I'll go off and live on an island somewhere once I've made my fortune," he added with a rueful half smile. "If I hear anything new about the Prometheans in my travels, I'll be sure and send you word. In the meantime, I don't want the Order following me, sending snipers. I'm keeping Trevor as collateral to ensure they don't."

"I want to see him first."

"You can't. I'm afraid you've got to trust me."

"Trust you? After this? Maybe you're bluffing! You're the great gambler, after all. How do I know he isn't dead?"

"Ah, you know me well enough to tell when I am bluffing, Beauchamp. I've told you the truth. He's alive and well. Not happy," Nick conceded, "but he'll stay unscathed as long as the Order leaves me alone. Otherwise, he may never get to see his little fiancée ever again."

Beau could not bring himself to believe Nick would really hurt the third member of their team. Trevor was like a brother to them both. But this whole episode had caught him so completely off guard that at the moment, he wondered if he could even trust his own judgment of the situation, especially when, deep down, some of the things that had disillusioned Nick resonated with him, too.

God knew, he understood exactly how Nick felt. He just chose to ignore those feelings, along with so much else in his heart.

"Please don't do this, Nick," he said evenly, summoning every ounce of calm, reassuring authority he had ever possessed as team leader. "It can still be fixed. Whatever's happened, you know you have my help. I am your brother, and I always will be. Just tell me what you need. Money I can loan you. Influence. I'll go and talk to the Elders with you—"

"Enough! I fight my own battles, and I'm sure as hell not dragging you down with me. Do you think I want it this way? It's how it has to be. I should've taken this option long ago. It suits my nature, the mercenary life," he said with a grim smile. "I take work when I want it. Turn it down when I don't like the look of it. Every job's at my discretion. No one's giving me orders. I make up the rules myself. You should join me, Beau. You really should. Not that you need the money, but it's a hell of a lot of fun."

"Jesus, Nick."

"I'm still working on Trevor, but I think he's comin' 'round. He's getting pretty bored down in the cellar."

"Cellar? Damn you—"

"Relax. He has everything he needs down there."

"So he's your prisoner. Your best friend, who saved your bloody life several times, as I recall. Your hostage."

"More like my pension, for years of faithful service. Life insurance, mate." He nodded. "Well, we mercenaries aren't very nice chaps at all, are we? Not like you valiant Order knights."

Beau shut his eyes for a second, in a cold sweat. *This is a nightmare.* The worst part was that he had never seen it coming. Of all the horrific fates he had imagined in the dead of night, trying to dream up some logical explanation for their disappearance, this was one he never would have guessed.

On the other hand, Nick had always been a rebel, even by Order standards, and was without a doubt the fiercest member of their team. Beau was the leader; Trevor was the brains, the strategist, the planner. But Nick had always been the ablest assassin.

A bloody nightmare.

Nick's gaze flicked to Beau's pistol pointed at him. "I am going to go now," he said. "I'll give Trevor your regards. Don't worry, I'll release him once I'm clear. You take care of yourself, Beauchamp." He hesitated. "It's been an honor serving with you." He nodded in farewell, then very deliberately turned around and began walking away.

"Stop!" he barked. "You're coming in, Nick!"

"No, I'm not," he replied, though he did prudently pause, lifting his hands.

"Don't make me shoot you—"

At that moment, the theatre door right behind Beau suddenly opened, bumping him in the back. He stepped forward to catch his balance, and his first thought was that Nick had expected trouble; he must've brought along some mercenary colleagues for assistance. Beau's reaction was instantaneous; aiming for the leg, he pulled the trigger.

Nick cursed and reached down, grabbing his thigh. But as a well-trained agent, his counterattack was equally swift. He fired back as Beau whirled to meet the new arrival in the doorway.

Beau heard the shot and cursed as Nick's bullet sliced across his biceps. But the bullet kept going to graze the new arrival, too.

No mercenary henchman.

Knife already in hand, Beau stopped himself from attacking.

Carissa!

Her face went white as she lifted her gloved hand and touched the right side of her head.

Nick cursed.

Time seemed to stop as she looked down at her white satin glove, smeared with blood.

Then she lifted her gaze uncomprehendingly to his; Beau stared back at her, aghast.

"Ugh," she murmured. Her eyes rolled up into her head, and she crumpled.

Beau caught her as she fainted, but glancing over his shoulder, he began cursing like a sea dog.

Nick had disappeared, and the girl of his dreams lay unconscious and bleeding in his arms.

Chapter

4

*C*arissa awoke to darkness and the sensation of speed. She was in a rocking carriage. The clatter of hooves and wheels racing over uneven cobblestones made her head pound harder. Suddenly, terror gripped her innards because, beyond that, she did not know where she was or what had happened. The side of her skull felt like it was on fire.

Struggling to orient herself, she began panicking all over again to find her usually busy mind a blank. When she started to rise, strong arms stilled her.

"Shh, lie back," said a silken whisper by her ear.

"Beauchamp?" It was only then that she realized he was holding her, keeping some sort of cloth pressed against the side of her head.

"I've got you, sweeting. Just lie still. It's going to be all right," he assured her, but she heard the tension in his voice.

His arms felt wonderful around her, so protective—

but as she wondered why they were speeding through the dark streets in a carriage, she remembered abruptly.

That bang the moment she had opened the theatre door to go and warn him. She had been shot! In the head.

By a bullet meant for him.

"Am I going to die?" she mumbled.

"No, sweet, of course not," he assured her. "You're going to be just fine." The strangled tone of his voice wasn't very convincing, however. She rather thought he was trying too hard to sound calm. "I'm going to take care of you, I promise. You just need to relax now. Stay calm. Hold still and let me keep the pressure on the wound, or you'll only make it worse."

"I'm scared," she whimpered.

"I know, sweet. But you've got to be brave for me just a little longer. We're almost there."

"Where?" Struggling to keep her eyes open, she saw through the carriage window the black silhouette of twisty spires in the moonlight, shrouded in fog. She gasped and tried to sit up.

The Inferno Club!

"No! I can't go in there!" she cried frantically—or so she thought. In truth, her voice only came out as a mumble.

"It's all right. You'll be safe—"

"No decent girl goes in there. I'll be ruined . . ."

"Shh," he whispered again, giving her a reassuring little squeeze. "Sweetheart, you've got to trust me," he whispered. "Trust me."

"Ugh." Her pounding pulse and struggles made the blood seep faster from her wound, as he had warned. She felt it trickling hotly past her ear and down the side of her neck, and the sensation was so sickening, so horrifying, that much to her chagrin, like a blasted ninny, she passed out once again.

*B*eau cradled her in his arms, trying to keep her from being jostled about as they approached the Order's headquarters. His heart was pounding with utter dread.

He had seen plenty of men get shot in his lifetime. He'd been responsible for more than he had any care to count. But that was completely different from seeing blood coming out of Carissa Portland.

In point of fact, he was in an unheard-of state of terror for an agent rigorously trained to fear nothing.

Beyond that, he was furious.

I'm going to kill Nick for this.

And if Carissa lived, he might just kill her, too, for snooping around after him and getting herself shot.

Maybe now the chit would learn her lesson!

You see, Father? You see why I don't get married? he thought angrily. Find one blasted girl he really liked, and he ended up getting her shot. *This is why I just bed them and keep my distance.* Was that so hard to understand?

He paid no attention whatsoever to his own wound. He'd had worse. She was the one who mattered, and in the dark, with all that long, thick hair of hers, he couldn't tell yet how badly she was hurt. But his luck . . . *argh.*

Her head was bleeding a lot, but that's what heads did in his experience, he attempted to assure himself. A lot of blood was never good, but when it came to head injuries, blows that produced no blood at all sometimes turned out worse. The person just fell asleep and never woke up again.

If heaven showed mercy on a sinner like him tonight, her wound would turn out to be nothing more than a gash like the one on his arm.

He chose to believe for now that the bullet had only grazed her. Until he could look at her in the light, dig through her luxurious auburn tresses down to her scalp and clean the wound, and determine how bad an injury they were dealing with, he clung to the hope that it might not be as bad as it looked under all the blood.

Or it might be worse.

One thing was certain: At this moment, he could understand with crystal clarity why Nick wished to quit.

In this moment, with his carriage pounding through the dark, foggy streets of London, his driver whipping the horses to gallop as fast as they could, he could quite happily go live a country life as boring as his father's.

Aye, forget the spy game and all its illicit thrills.

He'd become a dull, old, pipe-smoking, gentleman farmer, with no more pressing cares than deciding which breed of sheep to buy next spring.

"Hold on. Fight for me, girl," he murmured to her, as they careened toward their destination. "You've got a hell of a lot of fight in you. I know. I've seen it. Come on, now. Stay with me, love . . ."

Thank God, his carriage jounced to a halt at last in front of Dante House. Going there was a reflex for him whenever there was trouble, and with his own survival training in battlefield medicine so that he could keep himself and his team alive on their missions, he knew he had everything that he needed to care for her properly.

If her wound was beyond his ability to handle, the Order always had two or three good surgeons ready to come to the agents' aid at a moment's notice.

His driver promptly flung open the carriage door; Beau gathered Carissa up in his arms with a cold sweat beading on his brow and long-forgotten prayers streaming through his mind. She had to be all right. She had to. He could not bear for any harm to come to her, especially when it was his fault.

She could not die, moreover, when his last words to her had been so rude and improper, propositioning her like a thoroughgoing blackguard—when the truth was, deep down, she made more sense to him than most of the people in London.

He lifted her smoothly from the seat, which was now also stained with blood, and carried her out of his town coach. "Door," he ordered.

His coachman ran ahead of him to fling wide the black wrought-iron gate, then raced again to the front door of Dante House. Beau strode up the front path with Carissa's limp body dangling from his arms.

"Mind the dogs," he said to his driver. "Wait here. I may want you to go for the surgeon if this is beyond my skill. Otherwise, I'll need you on hand to assist."

"Yes, my lord." His driver pushed the front door open, and as Beau stepped in, immediately, the pack of vicious guard dogs rushed around to greet him.

He kicked the door shut and roared at them in German to shut up. The black-and-tan beasts sat and cowered.

"Gray!" Beau bellowed.

The old butler came running while Beau carried the senseless lady of information into the nearby parlor and laid her down carefully on the couch.

He realized he was shaking. *Jesu,* what was wrong with him? He'd been hurt worse than this himself over the years and had never reacted so badly.

But this was different. She was an innocent. A civilian. She had no part in this. She was just a girl.

The butler rushed in. "Sir?"

"The lady's hurt."

"You brought her here?" he cried.

Beau glared at him but only realized then that, inexplicably, he had, perhaps, panicked a little.

Well, it was too bloody late now to sit around and try to think up another plan! "Damn it, man, she needs help! Fetch hot water and bandages. And bring lamps, candles. We need more light in here. I'll get the medical bag. Go! Keep the dogs out!" he added. "The smell of blood might set them off."

"Yes, sir—your arm!"

"Never mind that. Hurry!" he ordered, yanking off his elegant, ruined coat.

Gray whisked off to do as Beauchamp had ordered, dutifully shutting the door behind him to prevent the fierce guard dogs of Dante House from coming in to bother them. Beau felt sorry for the beasts. Poor creatures barely knew what to do with themselves ever since their master, Virgil, had been killed. Lud, he wished the old man were there right now.

With the thought of the agents' gruff, Scottish handler, who had dealt with more gunshot wounds and broken heads than he could count, Beau flinched. He did not think he could stand another loss right now of somebody he cared about. He was already haunted enough. How the hell was he going to explain this to Rotherstone, anyway?

No, I didn't seduce the girl, of course, but I'm afraid I got her killed. Sorry, old boy. Your wife's going to have to find a new best friend. He swallowed hard. *No.*

She had to be all right. He bent down to smooth her
forehead gently. *So pale.* He clenched his jaw. "Hang
on, sweet. I'll be right back. You're going to be fine,
I promise." *And then I'm never letting you out of my
sight again, you dear little pain in the arse.*

Unsure where that possessive thought had come
from, he tore himself away from her, strode over to the
bookshelves, where he grasped what looked like an ordinary bookend in the shape of a small bronze statue,
and twisted it.

At once, with a mechanical click, the hidden door
disguised as one of the built-in bookcases popped away
from the wall. Beau went and pulled it open.

Pausing, he glanced over his shoulder at Carissa
one more time. She was still out cold. Then he slipped
inside the secret passageway and ran to get the medical
bag.

*C*arissa was having the strangest dream. It was
lovely and terrifying at the same time, a feverish mix
of blood and sensuality. She dreamed that Lord Beauchamp was gently letting down her hair, loosening her
gown, untying her stays so she could breathe more
easily.

His hands on her were warm and sure, and when
she dragged her eyes open and met his stare, his own
blazed hotly into hers. "It's all right," he whispered, as
she panted and clung to him in fear.

"Trust me," he breathed again, his hand at the side
of her neck, cupping her nape, melting her protests.
She closed her eyes, giving in. But why was he always
saying that?

Trust *him*? It was such a silly thing to say, coming from a libertine.

She felt him pressing warm wet cloths to her head, then heard him wringing them out, bloody rags, in a bucket of water. "That's good. Good girl," he whispered.

When she looked again, she whimpered at the sight of her own blood, reddening the water. "I don't want to die, Beau."

"You're not going to die," he said calmly, sounding much more certain of that now than he had in the carriage. "I'm happy to say the bullet only grazed you. You need a few stitches, then you'll be all better. Did you ever get stitches before, sweeting?"

"No!" She cowered from the needle. "Does it hurt?"

"Just a pinch. Nothing compared to getting shot, and you've already withstood that like a trooper."

She cringed again. He caressed her cheek, holding her gaze with stalwart confidence in his blue eyes. "Don't worry. I'll have you sewn up in a trice."

"Wait, *you're* going to do it? Where's the surgeon—"

"I can do it."

"Are you sure?"

"I've done stitches loads of times, including on myself. It's nothing. Just close your eyes and let me work, all right? The sooner we close this cut, the better off you'll be. This will stop the bleeding. Now, relax. And trust me."

"I wish you would stop saying that." She let out a low, unhappy, and dubious little moan, but she cooperated as he tilted her head so he could get started.

Then, by the blaze of the lamps and candles everywhere, she noticed a long lock of her hair lying by some scissors on the table. "You cut my hair?" she protested.

"Just the smallest bit! Well, I had to! It was in the way. I promise, you won't even be able to tell. If you don't like it, I'll take you to the best milliner's shop in London and buy you any hat you want. Now, can we please get this over with?"

She closed her eyes again. "I hate you."

"I know, love." She could hear the smile in his voice, feel the dangerous warmth of his charm. "Now, be still, or I'm going to kiss you again. Just like that day in Whitehall."

She smiled faintly, forgetting to scowl; then she peeked at him with one eye, and he flashed a roguish half smile at her. But when she saw him holding the needle over the candle flame to purify it, she went woozy again.

Ugh, needles and bullets, all in one night!

He took hold of her head. She squeezed her eyes shut, but somehow stopped herself from squirming away, realizing he was only torturing her like this in order to help her.

Then he got down to business, holding the torn ends of her skin together and piercing both with his needle.

"I've decided," he remarked in an idle tone as he worked, "that when all this is over . . . I am going to find you a husband."

"Oh, really?" she muttered, aware that he was talking to distract her from his work on her wound.

"Mm-hmm. You need someone looking after you, I daresay. Some nice, safe chap to hold the leash."

"I'll give you a leash," she muttered.

"Some good, solid, sensible fellow who'll stop you from following every impulse like a harebrain. Why did you follow me? Just to snoop? Haven't you ever heard what curiosity got the cat?"

"Not to snoop," she mumbled. "I was coming to save you."

"Save me? What are you talking about?"

"I saw him. I saw the man. And I didn't warn you. I'm so sorry . . ."

"Oh, there, darling, don't cry. I forgive you."

"That's why I came over toward your theatre box tonight. I wanted to trade information, but you wouldn't. You were so stubborn. What kind of viscount are you, anyway, that you know how to make stitches?"

"You should see my fancy embroidery."

"Is this really the time for a joke, when a person has been shot?"

"That's the perfect time for a joke, in my experience. I have a good one for you. This toad goes into a tavern—"

"I have blood coming out of my head!"

"Yes, but not nearly as much as I'd feared. Believe you me, I'm thrilled about this. Delighted. You have no idea how happy I am right now that this wasn't worse."

"Worse?"

"I thought I was going to find the bullet lodged in your old noggin, but I'm happy to say, your clever brain's untouched by all the fuss. It only grazed you. You were incredibly lucky, to be honest. An inch lower, and it could have taken off your earlobe and scratched your pretty face. Or worse. Which I don't care to think about. And I don't recommend you think about it, either."

She cringed. "So, what about the toad?"

"Right. So, the toad hops up onto a stool at the bar and orders a pint . . ."

He continued with his inane little story, but as endearing as she found his effort to comfort her, Carissa could not pay attention to a joke when the man was coolly stitching her scalp back together.

She squeezed her eyes shut, determined to bear it through. Ultimately, she succeeded in distracting herself at last by reliving the pleasant memory of his kiss that day.

"Hang on, sweet. One more. We're almost done. You're doing well. There we are . . . Done."

"How many?"

"Lucky seven. Luckier than you realize." He pulled the needle through one last time, then proceeded to tie the end of the thread into a knot. "Good show, my girl. Now you are officially—a soldier."

And now, if you will excuse me, I believe it's my turn to pass out. Beau took a swig from the nearby bottle of brandy to steady himself after that ordeal, then offered it to her. "Go on, take it. It'll help dull the pain."

Her smooth brow puckered in slight disapproval, but she accepted the liquor warily and tipped it to her lips.

Beau gazed at her in soul-deep relief. She was alive. She'd be fine.

Finally, he could exhale.

Only now he began to notice the throbbing in his arm. It hurt like hell. He took the bottle back from her and took another large gulp of the fiery spirits.

The brandy warmed him to the belly but not as much as the sight of her, milky-skinned and tousled, with the bodice of her evening gown loosened and her long hair spilling free over her bared shoulders.

Everything in him hungered to ravish her.

He refused to believe that even he was that depraved, after all she'd been through. Yet, oddly, he felt closer to her now, as if the night's mess had bonded them in some strange way.

Filled with a protectiveness toward her the likes of which he had never known, the urge to claim her for himself stormed through him. He looked away, took a fresh rag out, and spilled a little brandy on it.

"Last step," he murmured, pressing it to her stitches. That done, he leaned down and kissed her forehead, letting his lips linger at her hairline.

As he closed his eyes, he said a prayer of thanks that she had been spared. "You were very brave."

"Well," she said uncertainly, "the toad helped."

"You're a toad," he told her fondly.

"No, I'm not, you are."

"But if you kiss me, I might turn into a prince."

"We both know you're already a prince."

"I think someone's a little woozy from blood loss." He pulled back. "Do you want to see your stitches?" He offered her the hand mirror he had brought along in case he needed Gray to hold it for him to focus the light or to give him a better angle on his work.

She glanced reluctantly into the reflection. "How about that," she murmured, peering at them. "Lord Beauchamp," she said hesitantly, "I think you saved my life." Then she shuddered and looked away.

Probably so.

"Now for the bandage, then you'll be done." He stood to wrap her head. She sat obediently, watching him as he wound a fresh white strip of bandaging around and around her head, hatband style. "Too tight?"

"No, it's good. Thank you."

He tucked the end of the bandage under, then offered her the bottle of brandy again. She did not argue but took it from him and helped herself to a swig.

Beau sat down again, reached for a fresh rag, and dipped it in the clean bowl of warm water. Then he reached across to her and gently used it to clean the dried blood off her skin, dabbing, wiping tenderly.

She did not object.

At length, she let out a sigh, lay back on the couch again, and closed her eyes. "I'm going to be ruined now, aren't I?"

"Why would you think that?"

"Dante House. Wicked Inferno Club. Ruined. My uncle will throw me out," she mused aloud. "I'll have nowhere to go . . . tossed out in the street."

"Come, that's not going to happen. Your uncle may be a stern bit of stuffing, but he doesn't strike me as a cruel man. Besides, no one needs to know you were ever here unless one of us tells them."

She eyed him dubiously. "How's that?"

"Well—" He rinsed the rag out again, then stroked it down her shoulder. "How good a liar are you?"

She started laughing, wearily, cynically.

He was intrigued. "What is it?"

"Oh, I'm a very good liar—when I need to be. Don't you worry about that." She took another swig of brandy.

He arched a brow. "All right. Then we'll make up some story, and no one will be the wiser."

"Do you really think we can get away with this?"

"Of course." He studied for a moment. "First, I have to know. Why didn't you warn me I was walking into a trap?"

"I said I was sorry. You were a beast. You know you were! I thought at last you'd finally learn your lesson about dallying with all these married women. But then I felt guilty, so I followed."

He eyed her ruefully. "You are a piece of work," he said.

She settled back against the cushions. "So, who was he? The jealous husband, I mean."

"Oh, that wasn't a jealous husband."

She blinked. "No? Who was it that shot us, then?"

He snorted. "That was my best friend. You'd better give me that brandy."

She looked at him in astonishment.

Beau shrugged and took a swig from the bottle, which was dwindling fast.

"What did you do to him? Why did he try to kill us?"

"Why do you blame me? You just assume I did something wicked? Did it ever occur to you I'm rather a good chap?"

He did not wait for an answer, but she was thinking it over.

"Trust me, if Nick had wanted to kill us, we would be dead. He's frightfully good at that sort of thing. On that note, if you'll excuse me, I have to tend my arm."

"Your arm?" she echoed. Then she gasped loudly. "Why didn't you tell me you were injured, too?"

"Er, because you were unconscious?"

With a stricken look, she pressed her hand over her mouth.

After all the inconvenience she had caused him this night, he took some amused satisfaction in the soulful contrition that crept into her big green eyes.

"I'll be fine," he said, as she lowered her hand slowly from her lips.

"You should have said something! I didn't realize you were hurt!" Staring at the torn flesh of his arm, she began to turn rather green around the gills. "Would you like some help?" she offered with a gulp, nonetheless.

He laughed. "No, thanks. I can take care of myself."

Relief flashed across her face. "Are you sure?"

"Gray can help me if I need it. That's the butler. Call him if you need anything."

"Oh—well, then—if you're sure."

"Get some rest, Carissa. You lost a lot of blood. You must feel like the very devil. Let me dress this wound," he said, nodding down at his arm, "then I'll take you home."

"All right." She sank back against the cushions.

He dimmed the brightly lit room so she could relax. He blew out a few of the candles and turned down the oil lamp; then he picked up a few of the medical supplies and turned to go.

He would have to remove his shirt in order to tend his arm, and this was one young lady whose sensibilities had already been put through enough for one night. She did not need a bloodied, half-naked man in front of her, as well.

"Lord Beauchamp?" she murmured, as he headed for the door. The sound of his name on her tongue heated him better than the brandy.

He turned back. "Yes?"

"Thank you for saving my life," she said earnestly.

He dropped his gaze. "It was my fault you got shot in the first place."

"No, it wasn't. The fault was my own. If I had warned you straightaway about seeing that man switch the note, this never would've happened. But I was too proud, too stubborn. I hope you will forgive me."

"I'm just glad the bullet only grazed you," he replied, looking into her eyes.

She offered him a tentative smile, which he returned. The gaze they exchanged warmed him to the core. A little abashed, he nodded farewell and started once more to leave.

"Um, Lord Beauchamp? There is one other thing."

"Yes, Miss Portland?" He glanced back over his shoulder.

"You were right," she admitted. "I was a little jealous."

"Aha!" he said with a knowing grin that spread from ear to ear. With a roguish chuckle, he took his leave of her. *I knew it.*

$\mathcal{W}$hen he had gone, Carissa closed her eyes and tried to rest. But now that the worst had passed, and she knew she was going to live, her curiosity returned with a vengeance.

Dante House!

She couldn't believe she was inside the legendary gentlemen's club where the men behaved like anything *but* gentlemen. Too jittery after her brush with death to relax, she sat up slowly on the couch and looked around.

Lying there like some wilting violet was not quite her style, after all. Bad enough she had fainted like a ninny—no doubt Lord Beauchamp was never going to let her live that down.

In any case, she had not been *quite* as unconscious as Beau had believed when he had returned with the physician's bag, stepping through the odd doorway concealed behind the bookcase. She had a notion to get a closer look at that.

Glancing over to make sure no one was coming, Carissa took a deep breath, then gathered her strength and stood. Still wobbly but feeling much better, all in all, she steadied herself. Perhaps the brandy he had given her had gone to her head, but the sensation of his hands on her persisted. The way he'd taken charge so expertly with her clothes and her hair had her feeling most improper. Likely it was the influence of this wicked place that encouraged bad thoughts of yielding to temptation.

Well, she wouldn't be here long, she told herself, and honestly, how many decent young ladies ever got the chance to find out firsthand what really went on in this scandalous den of iniquity? Why, as a lady of information, it was practically her duty to have a look around so she could tell Daphne and Kate about their husbands' club.

And so, Carissa set out to snoop.

Well, the décor was certainly garish, she noted. Red velvet furniture, black leather—Lud! Tiptoeing across the room, she had questions in abundance. Why did they have secret doors and such vicious guard dogs? Why did Lord Beauchamp know what to do in a medical emergency? And why, out of all the jealous husbands he had cuckolded, was it his best friend who wanted to kill him?

So many mysteries . . .

As she headed across the parlor toward the bookcase that he had opened like a door, she caught a glimpse of herself in the mirror and was rather aghast at what she saw.

Drying blood down the side of her gown made her

look like the madwoman in some Gothic novel. But she was even more shocked by the impropriety of her appearance.

Her loosened bodice was slipping off her shoulders; her stays were untied, her hands ungloved; her hair hung freely to her waist, as only her maid and her family members ever saw it on the rarest occasions!

Egads, the man had more or less undressed her.

Maybe it was an everyday occurrence for him, making free with a lady's person, but she was scandalized by his handiwork. Of course, his chief handiwork on her had been the stitches in her head, and without them, she supposed she would still be losing blood.

Taking a step toward the mirror, she stared at the bandage wrapped around her head, morbidly amazed.

Why, I look like one of Welly's troops on the march home from fighting Boney. Wide-eyed, she shook her head at her reflection. What on earth was she going to tell her uncle?

Miss Trent and her cousins must be beside themselves by now, wondering what had happened to her.

Or maybe not. She glanced uncertainly at the clock on the wall. *What time is it, anyway?* A quarter to midnight. The play would be ending soon.

Her head began to pound as she wondered how to explain this to her family. She braced herself on the back of the nearest gaudy chair, then closed her eyes until the wave of dizziness had passed.

No, she couldn't think about that right now.

In a little while, she told herself, she would come up with some clever explanation to account for her absence and her shocking appearance. For now, she had only a small sliver of time to investigate the mystery of that secret doorway before *he* returned.

The knight of the needle.

She giggled, blood loss and brandy making her silly. Hastily retying her stays, pulling her gown up, and fastening it as best she could behind her back without the help of a maid, she went over to the bookcase and studied it, tapping her lip as she tried to figure out how it worked.

She experimented by poking around at a few of the books and knickknacks on the shelves, but nothing happened until she laid hold of an unobtrusive bookend—a small bronze head of some past king.

The clue came when she tried to pick it up; it wouldn't move. It was attached to the shelf, and that didn't make any sense.

Then she found that she could twist it: The bookcase clicked forward from the wall. She drew in her breath and gripped the edge of it, pulling it open slowly, fascinated.

It was heavy, disguised in front with shelves full of real books, but it swung forward like an ordinary door.

Carissa peered into the darkness beyond, her heart pounding. A dark passageway about two feet wide led off into the inky blackness in both directions.

Oh, I cannot wait to tell Daphne about this!

She dashed back to fetch the oil lamp, turning it up to its full illumination. Then she held it up into the darkness and leaned in to have a look.

A secret passageway stretched in both directions. She peered this way and that, a frisson of excitement tingling down her limbs. *I wonder where this goes.*

She glanced over her shoulder at the closed parlor door. No sign of Beauchamp yet. He must be sewing stitches on himself, poor man. Then she paused to gnaw her lip a bit in guilt to know that no one was helping him the way he had helped her.

Oh, well, she quickly concluded, shrugging to herself. He seemed supremely self-sufficient, not the sort who'd want a woman fussing over him.

More importantly, he would be back at any minute. If she wanted to continue exploring—which of course she did—this would likely be her only chance. She took a deep breath. *Just a peek.*

Ever so cautiously, she stepped through the mysterious open doorway of the bookcase, leaving it open behind her to avoid any mishaps.

Unfortunately, she hadn't stopped to contemplate the workings of hidden weight-triggered mechanisms, and as soon as she placed her weight on the first floorboard past the threshold, the bookcase-door swung shut behind her.

And locked.

She whirled around with a gasp to find herself entombed inside the wall. With a gulp, she lifted the lantern, trying to find the latch or whatever to open the thing again.

She spied a simple handle like that on a drawer. But when she pushed it, the bookcase wouldn't budge.

"Come on!" she whispered, trying to jiggle it free, but nothing happened. Lifting her lantern higher, she scanned all around the door and noticed above her eye level an odd little brass plaque set into the wall.

It had a dial in the center with numbers encircling it like the face of a clock. Her eyes widened, and her heart sank as she realized what it was. A combination lock. You had to know the code. "Oh, no. No, no, no!" she whispered, her fingertips alighting on the center dial—

but she stopped herself from turning it and yanked her hand away.

She might only trigger some other bizarre mechanism. *Calm down,* she ordered herself, dry-mouthed.

This passageway obviously led somewhere. She'd follow it and find another way out. *Yes.* Then she could sneak back to the parlor and resume her wilting-violet pose on the couch, and he'd never be the wiser.

Very well, she thought, nodding to herself. She wasn't sure which way to go, as the passage stretched both to the right and the left. With a shrug, she opted at random for the left, summoned up all her determination, and set off, lifting her lantern high. The flickering glow cast an eerie light in the close, narrow space. Carissa took comfort in knowing that while she might hate the sight of blood, at least she wasn't claustrophobic. With each step forward, she grew more intrigued than scared.

The smell inside the walls was damp and musty with age. Having seen Dante House from the outside many times before whenever she had traveled along the Strand, she knew it was one of the row of ancient Town mansions that sat beside the Thames, a relic of the Tudor period.

Now inside the walls, she could feel the weight of its great age, and could only wonder at all the upheavals in London the house must have witnessed over the centuries. It groaned like it was haunted.

Cobwebs fluttered in the draft.

The secret passage turned and twisted like a labyrinth, trying to trip her up on uneven steps, taking her up and down ladders, offering branched paths here and there that left her wondering which way to turn.

It was all a delicious mystery—like Beau himself— but she knew she did not have much time to explore and had not yet come across an exit. The inky black maze seemed to distort her sense of time and sense of space, as well, so it was hard to judge where the deuce she was inside the house, let alone how many minutes might have passed. Maybe ten? At the same time, she was trying to hurry and not to tax her strength too much after her ordeal.

When she came to another dark intersection, she debated whether to go to the right or the left or straight down on the ladder that descended into empty space before her. If she did not have the lantern, she thought, she'd have stepped into that hole and broken her neck.

She held the lantern over it, trying to see what might lie beyond the darkness; but biting her lower lip, she decided that there was only one way to find out.

Climbing carefully onto the ladder in her long, bloodstained evening gown, she hung the lantern over her wrist and gripped the top rung. Then she began her descent, laughing to herself to think of any club member who might happen to see her like this. She might well be mistaken for some macabre lady ghost haunting the old building.

Reaching the bottom of the ladder, she stepped off into another wood-planked passageway, but here, she could feel a slightly stronger draft floating past her cheeks. It made her lantern flicker.

She cupped her hand before the flame. "Don't you even think about it," she breathed. But the threat of losing her light did not deter her from pressing on into the darkness, smiling in spite of herself.

What would Beau say if he knew what she was up to?

Ahead, her lantern's glow revealed an opening. "What's this?" she murmured softly.

A little room opened up before her, perhaps twelve by twelve, but she furrowed her brow to spy its main feature: a gaping hole in the middle of the floor. At nearly ten feet in diameter, it took up most of the room.

Why would they want a giant hole in the floor?

Mystified, she lifted her gaze and saw a sturdy rope hanging down from the ceiling, with thick knots at regular intervals. The knotted rope descended into the center of the hole—like a ladder, she thought—but it was out of reach unless you took a running leap.

Of course, if you missed or did not hold on tightly enough, you'd fall, she mused. *What on earth?* Cautiously walking over to the edge, she peered into the hole, wondering what was down there. She must be at the level of the house's deepest foundations, she thought, for beneath the mighty wood timbers, she now saw stone.

The hole appeared to burrow straight down into the limestone. But why? If they wanted to put a simple cellar beneath the house, why make it accessible only by a treacherous rope ladder? It was too intriguing.

She held her lantern out over the hole, trying to see down. There must be something down there that the men of the Inferno Club did not want anyone else discovering.

Her spine tingled. She hoped it wasn't something sinister. But if it were ordinary or harmless, then why take all these precautions to keep it hidden? She remembered how the Home Office had been speaking to Lord Beauchamp about something . . .

Oh, God. What if there was something criminal going on here? *What if there are, I don't know,* she thought, *dead bodies or something down there?* She swallowed hard.

It suddenly struck her that she must have been completely out of her head to attempt this. There was harmless, ordinary snooping into gossip, then there was serious, wish-you-never-found-out-about-it prying into matters that were better left alone.

Indeed, not even *her* outsized curiosity streak was strong enough to make her consider risking a leap onto that rope-ladder to see what was below. Especially since she would have to put down her lantern even to try it. Without light, she could get lost inside this labyrinth forever, she thought—and at that moment, right on cue, an uprush of clammy air suddenly snuffed out her lantern's flame.

She lurched back from the hole with a horrified gasp, lost her grip on the lantern in the process, and dropped it. She heard it clatter to a stone floor many feet below. Her heart pounding, she found herself staring blindly into utter darkness. *Oh, dear Lord. How am I going to find my way back?*

She could not see *anything,* but at least she had the sense to back away from that hole. When she felt the solid wall behind her, she breathed a shaky sigh of relief. *Right.*

Her first task was to find her way back to the ladder. Turning ever so cautiously, she felt her way to the corner of the passageway down which she had come.

Panic snagged at the edges of her mind, but she managed to keep it in check as she groped along down the narrow passageway and found the ladder at last. Willing herself to stay calm, she started climbing, rung by rung.

This, at least, was easily done.

At the top, she now had another choice to make: right, left, straight. Well, she had come from the passage straight ahead and had not located any exits that way. She stared in one direction, then the other. With a shrug, she decided to try going to the right.

As she made her way along the narrow passage, this had all become a lot less entertaining. The darkness closing in on her felt oppressive; the stuffy air choked her. Her head began to throb again. Her stitches burned.

Worst of all, the darkness began to play tricks on her mind, filling her imagination with dire thoughts.

She almost felt as though the house were alive; it did not want her there, an intruder. She had the sense of countless crawly things all around her in the darkness, and the absurd fear whispered through her mind that once in, she was never getting out . . .

Just when panic welled up into her throat, she turned a corner—and saw a light ahead. *Oh, thank God.* She approached silently, drawn to it like a moth.

The dim light ahead became a softly glowing oval on the wall of the dark passageway.

It did not look large enough to be a door of any kind. Indeed, she did not know quite what it was until she reached it and looked at it . . . through it . . . into a dining room.

Fascinated, she realized she was staring *through* what appeared to be a typical convex wall-mirror, with twin candle sconces attached to either side. Every upper-class home had them; the curve of the glass helped amplify the light. But you could not normally see through them!

She marveled at the brilliant invention with no idea how it was made, though as a lady of information, she knew she had to have one. A spying window disguised as a mirror!

The dancing flames atop the candles were obviously the light source that had drawn her. Then, peering through the treated glass into the room, she beheld Lord Beauchamp.

Shirtless.

Tending to his wound. *Oh, my.* She stared.

The man was utterly beautiful.

No wonder the scandalous hussies of the ton couldn't leave him alone. A mild swooning sensation made her feel light-headed, but she assured herself it was only due to blood loss. Still, she barely blinked, staring at his magnificent body with only a hint of guilt, safely hidden behind the glass.

Perhaps it was just as well for her morals that whatever treatment had been applied to the mirror to render it transparent had also darkened the glass a bit. Her view was slightly veiled, as if she were gazing through brown bottle glass. She could see line, but not much in the way of color . . . and, truthfully, that was enough of a visual feast. The shape of his broad shoulders. The muscled swells of his chest, his brawny arms. Sleek waist. The breathtaking sight of his chiseled abdomen. To be sure, all that was quite enough without adding to it the true, warm tones of his skin, the jade blue seduction of his eyes, and the angelic gold of his hair.

But she jerked herself out of her dazed staring, for she could also *hear* through the mirror, and the conversation in progress was most intriguing.

"I can hardly believe Lord Forrester shot you!"

She leaned forward to see who had spoken.

An aged butler with a gaunt, unsmiling visage marched into view, bringing the viscount a writing set.

The butler stepped around the large guard dogs lying on the floor and placed it on the table near Lord Beauchamp.

Egads, she thought, staring at those panting beasts sprawled on the floor, their big, fanged mouths drooling as they panted. She'd be lucky not to get eaten if she ever managed to find a way out of this labyrinth.

Beau, meanwhile, had shrugged. "Well, but how can I be angry? The man's like a brother to me. I'm just glad he's alive." He winced as he doused the wound on his arm with a slosh of brandy. She was relieved to note that the bullet had only grazed him. "I got him, too. In the leg. Obviously, neither of us really wanted to hurt the other. It's the girl's doing, frankly."

Carissa frowned.

"She hit me in the back with the door. I thought Nick had brought reinforcements. She's lucky I didn't accidentally kill her, thinking I was being attacked from both sides."

The butler nodded. "Well, a leg wound should slow the baron down, at least."

Beauchamp nodded. Drying the wound with a fresh rag, he dabbed blood and liquor off his arm. "Anyway, that's why I'm not angry. You must know what I've been thinking all this time, Gray, though I refused to say it aloud."

"Indeed, my lord. We all feared the worst," the old fellow agreed with a sympathetic look.

"Now that I know he and Trevor are alive, that's all that matters."

"Do you mean to tell the Elders?" the butler asked with a nod toward the writing set.

"Certainly. Just not . . . yet."

"Sir?" he countered in surprise.

Elders? Carissa wondered.

"Gray, they won't understand," he said with a frustrated glance. "They'll put a price on his head, just like they did with Drake. I'm not sending assassins out after my best friend. I'll tell them everything, *after* I've got all this sorted out."

"After?"

"After," he repeated. "And I'm counting on you, Gray. I'm going to need your silence and your cooperation. You'll be as loyal to me as you were to Virgil, I trust?"

Carissa watched the scene unfolding in confusion. To be sure, this was far more intriguing than the play at Covent Garden Theatre.

The butler, Gray, meanwhile, had folded his hands behind his back and fixed the rakehelly viscount with a skeptical stare.

"You sound very sure about this."

"Nick is confused right now. That much was obvious." He shook his head. "I have to help him. I can make him listen to reason, I'm sure of that. I just need to track him down."

"What about the girl? She's compromised you, sir."

I've compromised him? she mentally retorted. *I daresay it's the other way around!*

"I'm aware of that, believe me. Of course, I'm sure I've compromised her, too. And you know what the worst part is? Her uncle is the bloody Earl of Denbury. Highest of high sticklers! I wish like hell that Rotherstone and his team were here."

Carissa furrowed her brow in confusion at Beau's mention of Daphne's husband. Lord Rotherstone was involved in this somehow? *Team?* she wondered, increasingly bewildered.

"I mean, I don't see why Falconridge had to go with them. He shouldn't even have gone on that mission, not with his injuries."

Mission? Carissa tilted her head. *I thought they were on a hunting trip.*

"It's been over a month since he killed the assassin," Gray replied. "I'm sure he's doing fine."

Carissa's eyes widened. *Assassin?*

Gentlemanly Lord Falconridge? The paragon of the universe, the wonderful, scholarly earl she most would've loved to have for an elder brother had *killed . . . an assassin?*

"Well, he should have stayed in Town. Unflappable as he is, he'd have been perfect for dealing with Ezra Green. Better than I am at it, anyway."

"If the Elders did not think you equal to the task, my lord, they would not have hesitated to give it to someone else."

"Thanks." Beau exchanged the rag he'd been pressing against his arm for a long strip of bandage.

He began winding it around his biceps and finally tucked the end of the bandage under like he'd done it a hundred times before. "I've got to take Miss Portland home."

"Very good, sir." The butler gave a cordial nod, but then hesitated, lowering his head with a worried look. "My lord, do you really think Lord Forrester has betrayed the Order?"

Order?

Beau let out a sigh and shook his head. "I don't know, Gray," he admitted. "I know Nick would never work against us." He shrugged. "He said he just wants out, and truthfully, after tonight, I can't say I blame him.

When I saw that girl get hit—" A murderous look hardened his face. His big body bristled, but he shook it off.
"He's lucky he didn't hurt her."

Hullo, a bullet scraped my head.

"Hell, after the night I've had, I rather hate the spy
life myself."

Her jaw dropped as he reached for his shirt, and all
the puzzle pieces flew together in her mind. Her eyes
were as round as moons, her heart thumping. Her
mouth hung open in the darkness; she covered it with
both hands, staring with the greatest astonishment of
her life.

But there was no mistake. Her ears had not deceived
her. Lord Beauchamp was a spy, the Inferno Club a
front for some sort of covert ring. Daphne's and Kate's
husbands . . . and even dear, chivalrous Lord Falconridge!

How can this be? She did not know. But it was. All
that she had overheard left no doubt on the matter.

No wonder Dante House had all these mysterious
passageways! Her heart pounded like it would burst
right out of her rib cage with her excitement at this trea-
sure trove of secret information.

She had never heard one rumor in Society that ever
came close to anything like this.

As for the "hunting trip" to the Alps that Lord Rotherstone, Lord Falconridge, and the Duke of Warrington
had gone on—well, now, there was a half-truth!

So much else about her friends finally made sense.

Even the Home Office investigation. Of course!

Surely it had to do with their spy stuff, not with Beau
himself. She suddenly furrowed her brow, wondering
if this was the real reason why Daphne and Kate had
disappeared from Town.

Beau's exchange with the butler had made it clear that trouble was afoot. Perhaps the agents' wives had simply been sent off somewhere for their own safety.

Of course!

That's why Daphne's letter hadn't made any sense! That's why Beauchamp had refused to give her any details. She saw it clearly now. Daphne must not have been allowed to reveal where she and Kate were. *Oh, of course! Of course, of course.* Carissa pressed her hand to her heart, filled with the greatest relief, indeed, joy, to understand at last that her friends were not excluding her. She had been half-convinced they had turned against her. But she *knew* she hadn't done anything to offend them!

She closed her eyes as her doubts about Daphne's friendship dissolved. She repented for ever having doubted either Daphne or Kate. She hadn't been rejected, after all. God, how she had agonized over the fear that her friends had somehow found out about The Incident in Brighton and were ostracizing her for her lack of moral fiber—and for concealing her secret from them.

As for Lord Beauchamp, she looked at him, also, with new eyes.

At least she understood now why he knew how to make stitches. And why he had gone "traveling" all those years abroad. Why he trained his iron body so hard. Not for vanity's sake. Not to entice his lovers. But for the practical reason of being ready and able to fight for his country.

Inside the dining room, he started to put his shirt back on, then looked at the blood all over it, and sighed, tossing it away. "Would you get me another shirt, Gray?"

"Right away, sir." The butler bowed and withdrew.

Beau pulled the candle closer and took out a sheet of paper from the writing set. Carissa gazed at him, savoring her new understanding of the mysterious fellow, when all of a sudden, she felt an odd tickle crawling up her arm.

She reacted automatically, flinging the spider off her arm with a small, girlish shriek of revulsion.

Silencing herself too late, she pressed her lips shut, grimacing, while frissons of cold disgust continued running through her. All motion in the dining room had stopped.

The butler had paused midway to the door.

Lord Beauchamp was staring at the mirror.

The guard dogs lying on the floor near him had perked up their ears. One growled, rising from the floor.

The others began bristling, as well.

"I say, did you hear something, my lord?"

"Indeed. One moment, Gray." Beau's face hardened as he pushed away from the table and began stalking toward the mirror. "It would seem we have an intruder."

Carissa froze, wide-eyed.

Bare-chested, he came up to the glass and stared into it, silent for a long moment. She shrank back, though she doubted he could see her. A scowl formed on his face.

"Carissa?" he chided in a deep, disapproving rumble.

She held perfectly still.

His stare intensified, boring into hers mere inches away though she prayed he could not really see her through the glass.

He folded his arms across his chest. "I know you're in there."

She squeezed her eyes shut, mouthing a curse.

"Answer me," he ordered.

Blast! Heart pounding, she did not know what to do, especially since she still had not managed to find a way out of this stupid maze.

There was no telling how he'd react to her intrusion, but she was sure she was in trouble now.

She had not crossed any ordinary rakehell. She had just disobeyed a man she now was rather sure was a spy for the Crown.

Cursing herself for being a snoop, she folded her arms across her chest. *Very well.* Best to get it over with.

"I'm here," she admitted.

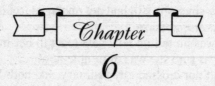

Chapter
6

"*O*f course you are," he said in a fresh wave of exasperation with her.

Gray looked at him in alarm.

Beau glared at the mirror. "I thought I told you to rest."

Her glum voice came from behind it: "Sorry."

He folded his arms across his chest, more outraged than he permitted to show on his face.

Just. Bloody. Perfect.

"What are you doing in there, Carissa?"

She heaved a sigh. "I'm stuck." He could hear the frustration in her muffled reply. "I'm stuck inside the wall!"

Gray shut his eyes and clapped a hand to his forehead.

One of the dogs trotted over and jumped up to place his paws on the console table beneath the mirror, his nose twitching for the scent. Beau pushed the animal away with a reassuring mutter before it started barking.

"Would you please get me out of here?" she insisted. "I can't find any way out of this stupid maze!"

He scowled at his own distorted image in the convex mirror. "Maybe not. Maybe I should leave you in there. 'Teach you a lesson.' What do you say to that? A taste of your own medicine, darling?"

"Lord Beauchamp, please! I know I shouldn't have done it—"

"No, you shouldn't have," he agreed.

"Just let me out of here. I can explain!"

"What, that you're a perfectly brazen little sneak?"

"Fine words, coming from a spy," she retorted.

Beau paused at the confirmation that she had heard plenty, indeed, and oh, yes, Gray had been exactly right.

Bringing her here had compromised his cover, along with that of all his fellow agents. In short, bringing her here had been a mistake. He looked away with a curse. *What the hell am I going to do with her now?* What a fool he had been, to assume the chit might actually do as she was told!

She must have seen his murderous expression. "I'm not going to tell anyone," she offered in a solemn tone.

"Ah, that makes me feel so much better!"

"You have my word!"

"The word of a girl who's already told me she's an excellent liar!"

"Oh, please, don't be a beast to me again, I beg of you! Let me out of this maze, then you can yell at me all you want. Please. It's dark in here and my head hurts and there are—disgusting spiders."

"Serves you right," he muttered, but the contest was settled. She took the prize for the most vexing female on the earth.

He sent the butler a taut nod. "Take the dogs into

another room. If anyone here's going to bite her, it's going to be me."

"Yes, sir." Gray did his bidding, but shot him a glare of reproach as he grabbed the collar of the pack's alpha dog. A look that said clearly, *This is your fault.*

Beau scowled back, well aware of that.

He could have throttled himself for bringing her here—a known gossip! But what the devil else could he have done with her? Left her bleeding in the alley? A civilian? A girl?

Yes, she *had* been nosing into matters that were none of her affair, but one of the Order's chief mandates was to protect the innocent.

It wasn't as though he could have brought her into the theatre to tend her with half of high society in the building. Hardly a covert maneuver.

Then he would've had to explain to the bureaucrats as well as the ton gossips why someone had tried to shoot him outside Covent Garden Theatre.

And why he had been alone with Carissa Portland in the first place. Indeed, her political uncle would certainly want to know the answer to that. That was all he needed. The Tories angry at him, along with the radical-leaning Whigs, who already wanted to shut the Order down.

With the investigation under way, Beau did not need any added attention right now, nor did he wish to make an enemy of the powerful Lord Denbury.

Perhaps he could have taken the chit to his house to tend her wound, but it was farther across Town, and with her losing blood like that, every moment had counted.

Well, no good deed was left unpunished, he thought, his pulse pounding. When Gray had led the dogs out and pulled the door shut behind them, Beau stalked across the dining room.

As he headed for the fireplace, the most disturbing thought of all plagued him, a nagging suspicion at the back of his mind that in some strange way, he had done this foolish thing on purpose, bringing her here.

Not just for practical reasons.

A fleeting doubt whisked through his consciousness, that maybe, just maybe, some perverse, desperate devil in his head had taken over in that moment of panic when he'd seen her bleeding, driving him to react from emotion instead of his usual logic.

It wouldn't surprise him—since this was Carissa Portland they were talking about, and what a smiling, happy dunce he usually turned into when she walked into a room.

Maybe the long-denied heart in him had seized upon this chance to show her the truth about him and his life, or at least to wave it under her nose, knowing that she, of all people, would take the bait and do exactly, well, what she had ended up doing.

Because she was in it now, whether she liked it or not. Even as his brain told him this was a calamity, his heart brimmed with the eager possibility that maybe now he'd find relief for the loneliness.

Maybe, if she knew the truth about him, he could finally be known and have a real connection to a woman.

Beau hated the whole idea of admitting to himself that he was lonely in the first place, and even more so, that his own impulses could have tricked him.

The notion was too threatening. He scoffed at it and threw it out, assuring himself he was not *that* great a fool. Still disturbed, he walked over to the white marble fireplace, glancing up at the massive, Renaissance-era chimneypiece.

Twin candelabra sconces were set into both ends

of the mantel. He reached up to the one on the right
and grasped the middle candlestick holder, twisting its
brass base until he heard a mechanical click.

Heavy gears churned beneath the floor, and suddenly,
the bricked back of the fireplace rotated open.

He ducked under the mantel and stepped over the
coal basket, leaning into the narrow space beyond.
"Carissa! Down here!" he called sternly as he stepped
through, into the secret passageway.

In short order, she came bustling around the corner,
groping her way through the pitch-blackness. "Oh,
thank you, thank you, thank you!" she exclaimed, hurrying toward him. "You are an angel of mercy! It's so
dark in here!"

"That's to deter people who don't belong," he answered dryly. Virgil had made the agents memorize
the labyrinth years ago, so they wouldn't need light to
negotiate its passages.

"Sorry!" she mumbled in a defensive tone as she ran
into him, clumsy in the darkness. He steadied her by
her arms as she put her hands out blindly to catch herself when she tripped. Her palms landed on his bare
chest; she yanked them back with a soft gasp.

Not that he had minded. Indeed, the shock of her
touch sent a thrill of awareness running along his every
nerve ending. "You all right?" he murmured, acutely
aware all of a sudden that he was half-naked, and they
were very much alone.

"Yes," she forced out in a slightly breathless voice.

Well, he'd never had sex in the labyrinth before. He
thrust the rakish thought away and gestured toward the
back end of the fireplace. "It's just through here. Mind
your head." He offered his hand to assist her.

"Thank you." As she placed her fingers lightly atop

his, the touch gave him another jolt of pleasure—which he ignored. He had been quite stupid enough around her already.

What the late, great Virgil would've said about his blunder Beau did not care to contemplate, but he was sure none of the more seasoned agents on Rotherstone's team would have let this happen. There'd be hell to pay when they got back.

Meanwhile, Carissa stared at the open slab of brick that made up the secret doorway and shook her head. "Fascinating," she murmured as she bent down to venture through it.

His lips twisted at her wonder. Did she think this was a game?

Nevertheless, he remained silent, steadying her as she lifted the hem of her long skirts and carefully picked her way over the coal basket. When she was safely through, straightening up inside the dining room, he followed her.

Then he shut the doorway behind him by twisting the candlestick the other way. The hidden fireplace door rotated shut.

She stood a few feet away, brushing the cobwebs off her arms and checking herself, he gathered, for spiders.

Beau pressed his lips together, refusing to smile. "What are you doing?"

She rushed over to him. "Do I have any spiders in my hair?"

He eyed her, sorely tempted to play a very boyish prank—one she thoroughly deserved. But when he glanced at her hair and saw the blood matted in her auburn tresses, he was reminded anew of all she had been through tonight, and resolved to treat her gently.

Of course, he was going to have to put the fear of
God in her to make her grasp the need for secrecy.

"No," he murmured. "But I'm afraid you've got a
bigger problem than spiders at the moment." He took
hold of her elbow and steered her to the nearest chair.
"Sit down, Miss Portland. You should not be up walking around."

And you should really put a shirt on, she thought
nervously, as he guided her to a chair beside the wall
and pressed her down into it.

She could not stop staring at his body. The raw, masculine beauty of his physique was overwhelming at
such close range. He stood before her, as completely
unself-conscious as the Greco-Roman marble male
nudes that he so much resembled; hands on his hips,
he seemed to be gathering his thoughts on how to deal
with her.

She had no suggestions.

Indeed, she could barely think at all, watching the
candlelight play over the hard, chiseled torso right in
front of her, his charming navel at about her eye level.
The flames' warm illumination teased her with the
urge to touch and explore the velveteen smoothness of
his skin.

She doubted the renowned libertine would have
minded, even as cross at her as he was. But she was
hardly mad enough to try, though, especially now that
she knew she was dealing with no ordinary rakehell
but a spy.

In the next moment, he stepped closer, grasped the
wooden chair arms, and lowered himself to a crouched
position before her.

Thus corralling her in her seat, he stared into her eyes, his own, piercing blue and full of suspicion. "You've been a very naughty girl, Carissa."

She swallowed hard.

"Why were you eavesdropping?" he demanded in a low tone.

"I-I told you, I got lost. I couldn't find a way out."

"You also told me earlier that you happen to be a good liar. So I know now not to take you at your word. But I'm warning you, I want to know the truth. How much did you hear?"

She blanched. "All of it."

He lifted his brows inquiringly.

"I heard you talking to the butler and I-I figured it out. I mean, I don't know exactly, of course, but I realized . . ."

"Yes?" he prompted, staring at her.

"You're some kind of secret agent," she fairly whispered, barely able to contain her excitement. "I can't believe it! And so is Lord Rotherstone and Lord Falconridge and the Duke of Warrington? That's what this place is—your headquarters?" She glanced around breathlessly at the room, but Beau did not answer the question.

The club's large dining hall was quiet, dim, and empty, but for them. Only now did she notice the strange mural painted on all four walls above the wainscoting, like twisted visions born of fever. She stared, realizing the scenes depicted the travels of Dante through the various circles of Hell—flames, devils, monsters, and all.

He still hadn't responded, but she took his silence for confirmation.

He was looking at her very strangely.

"Finally, it all makes sense," she said in a conspiratorial tone. "That's why Daphne and Kate had to leave Town, isn't it? You've got some kind of trouble. Is that the reason for the Home Office investigation?"

"You know about that, too?"

She tucked her chin demurely and gave him a guilty little smile. "Was that friend of yours a secret agent, too, the one who shot us? Is he a traitor?"

"Carissa."

"Is that why you went traveling all those years, for this career? You don't have to worry," she hastened to reassure him, "I can keep a secret. I'm not going to tell anyone."

"No, you're not," he agreed.

She frowned at the steel in his eyes and the chill that had come into his voice. "You're angry. Well, I suppose you would be. I deserve it, I know. Truly, I am sorry. I realize I shouldn't have gone snooping like that, but how could I resist! You know my curious nature. Someone in your line of work ought to understand, of all people. A secret passage? It was too intriguing!"

"As I said to you earlier tonight, don't you know what curiosity got the cat?"

She gazed at him in dismay. "You're not going to forgive me, are you?"

"No."

"Why not? Was it so bad, what I did?"

"There are consequences for your actions, don't you understand that?" he exclaimed, anger flashing in his eyes.

"Consequences? W-what do you mean?"

He just glared at her; his silence made her even more nervous. "What are you going to do to me?"

"Not half of what I'd like to," he growled.

"Fine! Stay angry at me, then—" She tried to rise from the chair, only to be pressed down again by his firm hand on her thigh.

She went very still.

If his hand on her leg were not unnerving enough, the hard look in his eyes sent a chill down her spine.

She began to understand at that moment that she might be in very serious trouble, indeed.

"People have been killed for the information you now possess, Miss Portland," he informed her in a low tone.

She decided with a gulp that while she usually disapproved of his free use of her first name, under the circumstances, she vastly preferred him calling her Carissa.

"Miss Portland" sounded almost like a veiled threat in this moment. Emphasizing the distance he suddenly wished to put between them.

She searched his cool blue eyes with a fist of fear wrapping around her heart. "I told you, I'm not going to tell anyone. You must believe me." She flicked her tongue over her lips as her mouth went dry. "Well, you must at least admit I am as loyal as any Englishwoman—!"

He just looked at her, a veritable Stonehenge of a man. Silent, enigmatic, hard.

Her heart pounded with the sudden fear that she might never get out of here alive, after all. Maybe she'd seen too much! Maybe that hole with the rope had been a dungeon cell for visitors who went snooping . . .

She gulped. "If your purpose here is really serving your country, then surely you must acknowledge I'd never do anything to jeopardize the security of England."

He lifted his chin slightly, but his flinty eyes gave away nothing; he merely let her continue to squirm.

"Do Daphne and Kate know about all this?" she asked, trying another hopeful tack. "They must," she answered her own question, her heart pounding. "Well, there you are, then! If you can trust my friends, then obviously, you can trust me just the same!"

His answer was a snort. "The only reason we trust the other ladies is that they are married to our agents, Miss Portland. Do you comprehend me? They have a very strong, personal interest in their husbands' survival, so we are generally confident we can rely on them to keep their mouths shut. This status does not apply to you. Besides," he added, "they aren't 'ladies of information.'"

"Well—that is true. But I am trustworthy!"

"Trustworthy?" he exclaimed, finally showing a little emotion—namely, outrage. "Ha!"

"What? I am, too—trustworthy!" she insisted in wounded indignation.

"What an absurd claim! You're nothing of the kind."

She harrumphed.

"Everything you've done tonight refutes it." He swept to his feet, an angry demigod looming over her in his half-naked wrath. "How could you do this, Carissa? I only brought you here to save your life! I cannot believe even you would go this far! I save your life, then turn my back on you for one minute, and this is how you repay me? Go trespassing where you don't belong? What are you, a child? Can't you ever leave well enough alone?"

She drew breath to respond, but when she parted her lips, no words came out.

Hang it all, the man was right.

She shut her mouth and lowered her head, well and truly scolded.

"What are you going to do with me, then?" she mumbled after a long moment. "Am I going to be arrested or something?"

"No, you're not going to be arrested, you meddling little nit. There's only one thing I *can* do with you," he grumbled. "It's obvious. We have to marry."

"*What?*" She looked up at him, wide-eyed.

"Consequences," he said in satisfaction, folding his muscled arms (one bandaged) across his chest, an irked Adonis.

"Marry?"

"It's the only way I can personally make sure you keep your mouth shut," he declared.

She gaped at him for another few seconds, then finally closed her mouth, shut her eyes, and pressed her fingers to her forehead.

Her skull was pounding once again; indeed, her head was spinning from his tyrannical solution.

She strove to keep a calm, soothing tone, though panic simmered just beneath the surface of her voice. "Don't you think you're being, oh, just a wee bit excessive, my lord?"

"Too bad."

"You don't want to marry me any more than I do you!"

"It does not signify. I made a mistake in bringing you here, and now I've got to pay for it."

With a stunned scoff, she looked at him in astonishment. "What lady of my birth would marry *any* man on such insulting terms?"

"One who doesn't have a choice."

She rose, scowling, from her chair. "Don't be silly! You are completely overreacting! You know where to find me if I should ever tell a soul about your secrets. Then we can talk about marriage—"

"At that point, it's too late. The damage is already done. I can keep you in line more effectively when you're by my side. Under my roof. Following my rules," he added darkly.

"Now, hold on one minute," she protested, backing away. "Marriage is not the sort of thing that's meant to be handed down as a punishment. Besides that, we barely know each other—and what we *do* know starts with the other's flaws."

"So?"

"Think about it! Tonight, I caught you arranging an adulterous liaison and, believe me, I have *no* desire to marry a man who doesn't see any particular problem with that! For my part, we both know I'd quickly drive you mad. I'm a very flawed person!"

"You don't say."

"It's true! I'm cowardly. I snoop in other people's business—"

"And you're a voyeur," he added with a cool, taunting smile. "Stubborn as hell, to boot. Typical redhead."

"Well, thank you," she retorted. "But you're no angel, yourself, I'll have you know."

"No, I'm not," he lustily agreed. "Nor do I have any plans of reforming."

"Well, that settles it, then. We would never suit."

"Then I suppose we are both destined for a life of misery, because I am marrying you."

"No, you're not."

"Yes, I am."

"Oh, come on, Beauchamp!" She stamped her foot in growing alarm, for she could already feel herself losing this battle. "Half the ladies of the ton would die of heartbreak if you ever took a wife! Mass casualties! They'll be stabbing themselves in the street!"

"Not my problem," he said with a devastating twinkle in his eyes that seemed to call her bluff.

Carissa gazed wistfully at him.

Ah, bugger. If she were honest, she had been half in love with the scoundrel for weeks, never mind her disapproval of him.

How could she pass up the chance to make him her own? He was likable in his temperament, he was physically irresistible, and, in practical terms, the rogue would be an earl. Marrying him could turn out to be a good thing for her, though, to be sure, it had its risks.

The question of what sort of life she might have married to a spy was rather terrifying if tonight was any example.

On the other hand, she could get out of her uncle's house, where she had lived like a poor relation for the past year and a half. As an orphan, she had been passed around among her relatives, rootless, with no settled home where she truly belonged. She'd never had that.

This could be her chance to be the mistress of her own household, and no one could ever hand her off again.

As to her shameful secret, she thought, staring at the floor, surely, if any man could ever understand about her fall from grace, it surely would be Beauchamp, sinner that he was.

"Well?" He waited.

Not that he was really giving her much choice.

Carissa stared at him, her heart in her throat. This match could quickly become a disaster for them both, since he was only doing it to keep her quiet.

His talk about heavy-handed rules sounded as if she would be worse off than if she had married the stupid poet.

But what else were they going to do? She had already

spent nearly two hours alone with one of the most renowned seducers in London.

No young lady's reputation could withstand that.

She should be glad he was willing to marry her to save her good name, in addition to saving her life. Lord knew she did not wish to subject her uncle's family to another brush with scandal . . .

"Carissa, I want an answer." He folded his arms across his chest with a bit of a glower on his face. "Will you cooperate, or do I have to drag you to the altar?"

Her heart pounded.

"You don't have to drag me," she forced out in a strangled voice. Then she cleared her throat and drew herself up to face her future husband. "I accept."

His blue eyes narrowed slightly in satisfaction. "There. Was that so hard?"

She dropped her gaze, feeling woozy again from blood loss, or perhaps more from the fact that she had just agreed to marry a spy.

Beau reached for the clean shirt the butler had brought him, lying on the nearby table.

She wrapped her arms around herself, feeling a bit of a chill. "Do you know what time it is?"

He nodded toward the longcase clock by the wall. "Little after midnight."

The play would have just ended about a quarter hour ago. She pondered the implications of her failure to return to her seat. Her cousins, their governess would be frantic.

She was not looking forward to what came next.

He pulled on his bloodied coat. "Come," he ordered, watching her with a wary eye. "I'll drive you home. Let's go tell the family our happy news."

Chapter
7

*B*eau was just a little bit in shock at how difficult it had been to get the stubborn chit to say yes.

It had not escaped the notice of his ego that she had vehemently turned him down at first. Ungrateful puss! Did she think she was going to get a better offer from somebody else?

Well, he supposed, perhaps, that in the terms that he had used, it had hardly been a proposal to make a lady swoon. Still! He was Sebastian bloody Walker, by God, the future Earl of Lockwood. He was by all accounts a brilliant catch. Didn't she know how many females of higher birth and greater beauty were chasing him on any given day?

This one, he could not begin to figure out. Each time he thought he had unlocked the secret mechanisms of her knotty female brain, she spun about in a new direction and went clicking and whirring off like some ingenious little automaton wrought by Merlin himself—for the purpose of driving men insane.

His male pride harrumphed. He supposed all that signified, however, was that at least he had procured her for his bride.

Neither of them said much as he drove her home to her uncle's. He expected they would find the earl's house in an uproar over Denbury's missing niece. He was not looking forward to this meeting. Soon he pulled his horses to a halt outside the elegant town house on a garden square. They sat for a moment in the moonlight. The street was very dark.

Beau gazed at the glowing windows of the Denbury mansion, then he glanced over at her; he could tell by the nervous look on her pale face that she did not relish going in there, either.

She turned and met his gaze. "Here we are."

"Ready? You remember what you're going to say?" he murmured. They had discussed it before leaving Dante House.

She nodded.

"Don't worry. It'll be fine," he assured her softly. "How's the head?"

She touched her bandage with a self-conscious look. "Not too bad."

"Let me see." He reached over and turned her face to see if any blood was coming through the bandage, but there was no stain, no seepage. "I think you're in good shape."

She smiled wryly in the darkness. "You owe me a hat."

"Right," he agreed with a rueful nod. "Right, then. Let's get on with it."

They walked up to the front door, exchanged an un-eager glance, then Carissa stepped in first, with Beau right behind her.

The activity in the house resembled that inside a chicken coop invaded by a fox. There were such squawks and cluckings and hysterical flappings-about of all the female inhabitants, the likes of which Beau had never seen.

Lady Denbury was beside herself; the governess was crying; the two famed termagants known as the Denbury Daughters were bellowing at the maids.

All of this chaos only intensified when the women saw the bandage around Carissa's head and the blood on his coat. How could the old man bear it? Beau wondered, but when Lord Denbury himself came striding through the hubbub, the three of them fled into his study alone, and the earl shut the door. Whereupon, they jointly presented her powerful uncle with their excellent cock-and-bull story.

Side by side, they told the stern, patrician chairman of countless parliamentary committees how Carissa, feeling ill in the stuffy theatre, had stepped outside to get some air. She explained how she had been harassed by a few of the skulking footpads who lurked in the square across the street after dark.

Then Beau explained how he, while waiting for a "friend," had heard her cry for help and rushed out to save her. But in scaring off the unsavory thieves who had been trying to snatch her reticule and her necklace—if not worse—one of them, while retreating, had turned and fired a pistol at him.

"As you can see, it hit me in the arm." He nodded down at the torn and bloodied sleeve of his coat, proof that what he said was at least approximately true. "I was shielding your niece, but Miss Portland wanted to see what was going on—"

"Naturally," her uncle muttered, raising an eyebrow at her.

"When she peeked out from behind me, the bullet grazed the side of her head. As I told her, she's very lucky. She could easily have been killed."

"So, you brought her to a surgeon?"

"No, sir. There was no time to find out. I tended her myself."

"*What?*"

"She was already unconscious, and, I must say, there was a lot of blood. From my service in the war, I am well versed in tending these kinds of wounds. But I had to take her to where I had the necessary supplies on hand and the space to work without a theatre full of gossips looking on."

"So where exactly did you take my ward?" he exclaimed.

"Dante House."

Lord Denbury groaned, hiding his face in his hand. "Fortunately, I soon found the bullet had only grazed her," Beau continued. "She needed a few stitches—as did I. As soon as I had her all bandaged up, I brought her here. I can assure you, sir, nothing dishonorable happened. You have my word on that. Unfortunately, we both know the ton won't see it that way."

"Quite." Denbury lifted his head from his hand and eyed him warily. "As you are a gentleman, I trust you know what this means."

"I do, sir," he said firmly. "That's why I'm here. I can provide your niece with a good life, and I see no reason why she'd be unsuitable for me."

Carissa and he exchanged a cautious glance.

"Your family name is most august, and besides, my father is getting on in years," he continued. "He has spoken to me on several occasions about his desire to see the future of our line secured."

Lord Denbury's angry expression changed at the mention of Lord Lockwood. "Yes . . . I know your father well. A solid man. His friends miss him in London. You should tell him so."

"Thank you, sir. I will," Beau murmured, lowering his gaze.

Lord Denbury looked askance at Carissa, studying her for a second. "Is this match amenable to you, as well? Despite his reputation?" he added dryly.

She kept her head down with a meek air that Beau found surprising. "It is, my lord," she answered.

He began to nod. "Very well, Beauchamp. If you are a true son to Lockwood, I cannot withhold my consent. Especially under these rather dubious circumstances. I daresay the two of you make quite a pair."

"Thank you, sir," Beau replied, flashing a smile and ignoring the fact that it probably wasn't a compliment.

*C*arissa watched the two men congratulate each other over a handshake and a glass of port, and with that, her fate was sealed.

And so it began.

The wedding preparations, starting with the marriage license.

The few days it took for the Archbishop of Canterbury to issue the special license so they could marry quickly brought on a whirlwind of activity, both parties scrambling to arrange all for the impending union.

Uncle Denbury was put in charge of the venue, while his wife took charge of the flowers, the music, and the cake. Beau went hunting for a ring and ordered his domestic staff to make everything ready for the arrival of the new lady of the house.

Carissa, meanwhile, fled to her favorite modiste's shop, where she begged to see whatever formal gowns the famed seamstress might have on offer, anything that could be made ready within a few days. Haste was necessary to try to stay ahead of Society gossip. They wanted the marriage to be a fait accompli before the ton started asking questions.

The savvy woman proved her savior, emerging from her sewing room in the back of the shop with an almost finished satin ball gown. It was a luscious creation in a very delicate pale pink, barely a blush tone, soft enough not to clash with her red hair.

Given the occasion, the modiste suggested adding white lace trim with seed pearls. Carissa eagerly assented, then sought out the rest of her ensemble. Her gloves and kid slippers would be white; her chemise would be the finest linen, and underneath that—as she supposed her bridegroom would discover on their wedding night—white silk stockings held up by rose-ribbon garters.

Giving the seamstress all of two days to complete the alterations, Carissa then turned her attention to the task of moving out of her uncle's house.

It took the remaining two days to pack and organize all her clothes and books and possessions, even with the help of several maids.

Her cousins watched all this with little comment. They seemed oddly subdued about her leaving. Having complained about her since the day she had arrived, no doubt they'd be glad to be rid of her, she thought. But seeing their slightly elder cousin truly going off to start a new life with a husband, it appeared to sink into the girls' minds that they would soon be doing the same in the normal course of affairs. They became strangely clingy to their mother, and Aunt Denbury must have been thinking the same things, because she did not question it but drew the girls to her bosom for frequent hugs and occasional kisses on their foreheads.

Carissa refrained from comment. She wondered what her own mother would have said about her future husband. Of course, she had been a toddler the last time she had seen Mama alive. She shrugged off painful memories and focused on the task at hand, organizing a second trunkful of her personal effects.

She did not wish to seem ungrateful, but in truth, it would be a relief to escape her uncle's house. After fifteen years of being fobbed off on different relatives, she could not wait to have a real home of her own, at last.

Though a small bud of hopeful excitement was slowly unfurling in her heart at the prospect of having a settled place forever where she really belonged, her optimism mingled with ever-growing apprehension about her wedding night.

Now that sharing a bed with him was a certainty, only a matter of time, she found herself gnawed by countless fears over all the diverse ways he might react to the revelation that he had married a nonvirgin.

What if he turned out not to be as understanding as she hoped?

Indeed, what if he was furious? He was a warrior. What if he became violent? He could kill her as easily as a gnat. Very well, he probably wouldn't kill her, she admitted. But what if he threw her out? Annulled the match? Divorced her? Shamed her in front of all the world?

Frightening specters of this sort kept her awake those three nights before the wedding day, tossing and turning in her bed.

She dared not tell him ahead of time. Then he might back out of the match, and the rumors had already begun to percolate in Society, all because Cousin Araminta had leaked the news to her best friend. The rumor clock was ticking. It was like some infectious fever that took a certain number of hours to gather strength before the full sickness exploded in the host.

Maybe she should strive to fake her way through her wedding night, she pondered, staring at the ceiling. Just somehow try to brazen it through.

Not all girls bled their first time, after all. Aunt Jo had told her so when they had first had that excruciatingly awkward Talk.

But could she ever fake innocence well enough to trick a spy, a man who'd had more women than a sultan with his harem?

And did she really want to start their marriage by deceiving him? He was only marrying her in the first place because he didn't trust her to stay silent about the Order.

On the other hand, if she chose honesty and told him all, then he might decide he had married a woman he'd never be able to trust and simply shut her out.

But he can trust me, her heart insisted as she lay awake that night. Her fall had been naught but girlish gullibility. Was it really so important to dredge up all that unpleasantness?

And good Lord, as a spy, what might he do to Roger

Benton if she recounted her sad tale of how she had been seduced? Not that she cared if Beau rearranged the poet's face, but she did not intend to send her new husband off immediately into another duel.

Oh, come, she reasoned with herself. Why did she really have to bring it up at all? It was in the past. Everyone had secrets, and she was quite sure Beauchamp was never going to tell her all of his.

Her worries persisted into the next day as she finished packing the last trunk to be sent over to her new home. She pressed down its contents to make it all fit, then fastened the brass latches.

Dusting off her hands, she called for the footman to take the last trunk down to the carriage.

Just as he took it out, Aunt Denbury bustled in, back from her wedding-related errands. The cake from Gunther's had been ordered. She had procured the services of a harp-and-flute duet to play for the ceremony. A few flower bouquets would also be ready for tomorrow—with only one problem. With barely twenty-four hours to go, they still did not know *where* the wedding would take place.

Then, that evening, Uncle Denbury marched in wearing a rare, broad smile, the sort that said he had just saved the day. He called them together and announced to his family and the bride that he had pulled some strings, then he awed them with his news. Thanks to a sizable donation, they had just been granted permission to hold the wedding in no less a magnificent spot than the Lady Chapel inside Westminster Abbey. This was his wedding gift to them.

Carissa hugged him for his kindness, but was still in shock over everything when the next day came.

The grand event.

After all that flurry of frantic activity, it had all come together in the last minute as if by magic.

Now that the hour toward which it had all been building was at hand, time seemed suspended in the stained-glass serenity of the chapel.

The harpist and flutist played; the flower bouquets perfumed the air; her gown fit splendidly, and as she stared solemnly through the white veil draped over her head, she saw that at least, in this moment, she had nothing to be ashamed of as a highborn bride worthy of a future earl.

Society might raise an eyebrow at their marrying in haste, but everything was proper in the end.

Presently, the wedding was already half-over. Perhaps now she could start to focus on the marriage itself. Whatever happened, she vowed to herself, she would do her best by him. Beauchamp wasn't perfect, but neither was she. Just as her uncle has jested, they were a pair.

An earnest welling of emotion overtook her heart as they stood hand in hand before the altar. She stole a nervous glance at the handsome viscount by her side.

How heavenly he looked, tall and proud and noble in his dove gray coat, like a golden angel visiting earth in the guise of an English gentleman.

His white cravat fairly gleamed with perfection; the longer edge of his pale silk waistcoat peeked out beneath his gray jacket's neat cutaways—baby blue and silver pinstripes. His trousers were white, his shoes black. And his white-gloved hand supported hers as the vicar read to them from II Corinthians.

"Love is patient. Love is kind . . ."

She knew the passage well; her mind wandered.

Despite the beauty of their setting, she could not deny that it was rather lonely for a wedding.

The only guests were Uncle and Aunt Denbury, serving as witnesses, and their children. Lady Joss still looked bemused by it all. Araminta covered a yawn. Miss Trent wiped away silent tears yet again, while the future Lord Denbury, her uncle's ten-year-old son, young Horace, fidgeted and scowled at having to don his stiff Sunday clothes in the middle of the week. *Little monster, that one.* Carissa wished that Daphne were here. And also Lord Falconridge, of whom she had grown especially fond.

She wished at least they might have waited for Aunt Jo, who had been summoned from Paris. She should be here in a few more days, but Lord Denbury said it was just as well. He did not dare give his worldly sister the chance to come gusting gaily onto the scene as she was wont to do and say some outrageous thing that would scare the groom away, or worse, snatch him up for herself.

There seemed to be no danger of that, however.

Beau stood his ground beside her, listening intently to the reading. She wondered if he was already regretting this. When she stole another sideward glance at him, she found him smiling. Just a touch of softness around his lips.

Anxiety and sheer agonizing infatuation made her every muscle clench. *Dear God, please don't let him notice anything amiss tonight! I can't bear for him to hate me.*

At her wits' end after three days of worry, she had thrown up her hands and more or less decided to try deception. She did not want to do it, but with spy trouble afoot, he had enough to worry about without also having to fear that he had inadvertently married a harlot.

After all, if he thought that of her, would that not give him carte blanche to continue his libertine ways instead of behaving like a proper husband? She had already been jealous of his liaisons with other women before there had been any talk of marriage. If he resumed such pursuits after they were wed, she really did not know how she would endure it.

So she had decided that tonight, she would play the innocent—which shouldn't be hard, since she had only done it once, anyway.

If he voiced any suspicions about her afterward, she would rebuke him for a scoundrel and a knave to dishonor her with doubt and accusations. Why, she could throw a fit of hysterics worthy of Araminta, if it came to that.

Her original thought, that she might be able to trust him with her secret, faded into darkness the more the hour of truth drew near.

"Love keeps no records of wrongs . . ."

The wise old vicar glanced at Carissa as if he somehow knew his words were going into one ear and out the other.

She looked askance at him, this dangerous, charming man who was about to become her mate for life, and wanted one simple thing with all her heart.

For him to love her.

 $\mathscr{F}$ illed with tender protectiveness toward his bride, Beau stole a sideward glance at her, delighted all over again by her loveliness. She looked radiant today, and he could hardly wait to get his hands on her tonight.

At last, he would have the right to enjoy her as he pleased, with the full consent of God and man.

He regretted the fact that none of the people he would have expected to come to his wedding were on hand, but it was no use complaining. Virgil was dead. Rotherstone's team was off in Europe, and Nick and Trevor were God-knew-where.

While his bride had been feverishly making her wedding preparations, he had done the same and more, namely, marshaling every resource he had left to put all London assets on the watch for Nick.

The baron had no family for Beau to get in touch with, but he had covered the legal and financial angles. He notified banks and solicitors in case Nick tried anything tricky with whatever money he had been paid for his nefarious deeds. Beau had also put out a query on Nick's whereabouts with a particular Bow Street officer who sometimes helped them sniff out clues.

Likewise, he had activated his web of informants in the gambling hells and taverns Nick had always favored. He had also alerted the gunsmiths they had used in the past that he wanted to be told immediately if Nick came in. Hell, he had even put the blackguard's former tailor on notice.

No doubt, Nick had holed up somewhere that he would be impossible to find, but with a hundred pairs of eyes on the lookout, he soon wouldn't be able to drink a pint in London without Beau's knowing about it, where and when.

Yet, still pained by the betrayal of the friend he had always expected would be his best man, he put Nick out of his mind and focused on the ceremony.

The vicar asked the great question.

Smiling, Beau glanced at Carissa; maybe it was time he took a new best friend. He laid his hand over her fingers, which rested lightly on his forearm. Then he looked forward again and gave the priest a proud nod. "I do."

$\mathcal{W}$hen they returned to the Denbury home, Carissa could not stop staring at the ring on her hand.

The deed was done, their mad pact cemented.

The slim golden band on her finger was startling proof that the two of them had actually gone through with it.

She was Lady Beauchamp now.

It was all a little overwhelming. How ironic it was in hindsight, that two people so expert at keeping secrets should have so swiftly concluded that this was one they couldn't keep—their unsanctioned time together inside Dante House. Maybe deep down, both of them had really wanted this but had been too cowardly to admit it. All she knew was the day had the disconnected quality of a dream, a swirling mix of unexpected happiness—and the sudden recurrence every now and then of her own, private agony about tonight.

Scarcely able to believe that the beautiful man beside

her was her own, she teetered between amazement and terror, that it would all fall apart in the blink of an eye. Shame still lurked in the hidden corners of her heart ever since Roger Benton had robbed her of her innocence.

If Beau figured it out—if he asked—should she maybe just tell him the truth? She could not stop watching him, trying to read him, looking for any sign of what she ought to do.

Of course, he quickly charmed her relatives though not perhaps her uncle. Aunt Denbury and Miss Trent were in awe of him. Even the little monster warmed up to him; the brotherly air he adopted soon cut through Araminta's shallow flirtations and even thawed the hauteur of the elder sister, Lady Joss, by talking to her about the racing colt that the famed equestrienne had chosen for her father's stables.

Though it was only just the family, they had an elaborate dinner—which Carissa barely touched—followed by the splendid wedding cake with champagne. The vanilla almond cake from Gunther's was an artful confection of seven layers, with fluffy white icing and marvelous sculpted flowers.

Then came the exchange of gifts, starting with her teary-eyed aunt's contributions to her trousseau. Among these treasures were a silver tea service that had been passed down in her family, and a bolt of ravishing Brussels lace for tablecloths or whatever else she might need to make her new home more her own.

Miss Trent gave her the latest book of essays on wifely virtue and another on managing a great household.

Araminta gave her a green Paisley shawl; Joss gave her a fabric-covered blank journal for a diary and a writing set. Horace presented her with a gift obviously supplied by his father, a small painting of all of them together that had been done years ago at Christmastime.

She hugged them all, taken aback by their rare display of warmth. Either they had cared for her all along more than they had ever shown, or were doting on her now from guilt, realizing that they could have made her feel a little more included all along. Now that she was leaving, perhaps they felt a belated touch of regret.

Or, the cynical side of her observed, maybe this show of affection came from a more practical awareness of her new position in Society. But she pushed the uncharitable thoughts away. They did not belong here now. Whatever was causing her relatives to be so kind to her on this, her wedding day, she was not about to question it, merely grateful and quite touched.

Then her husband of about three hours turned to her with a roguish smile. "Well, my lady, would you like to see your gifts from me?"

"Of course."

He stood, took her by the hand, and pulled her up from her seat, holding her gaze. "Come with me."

"Where are we going?"

Mischief danced in his blue eyes. "Oh, you'll see."

"Where's he taking her?" Cousin Horace echoed.

"Join us," he invited her kin in his usual easygoing way. "I'm sure we'll all be very interested to see her reaction."

"Beauchamp, what have you done?" she murmured as he led her to the front door.

He opened it without a word, gesturing to the world beyond as he held it open for her.

Carissa looked at him in puzzlement, then lifted the

hem of her skirts and stepped out. Sunset had set the western sky afire; the leaves of the tall plane trees in the garden square caught the light and glittered as if gold coins were growing on every bough.

Following her out, Beau lifted his fingers to his lips and let out a piercing whistle in as common a fashion as some Billingsgate fisherman or burly mail-coach driver.

Little cousin Horace, much impressed by this feat, instantly tried to copy him, but Aunt Denbury brushed the boy's hand away from his mouth. "Don't do that, Horace."

"Close your eyes," Beau said to Carissa. "Go on!"

She did, and blocking out all sights made her more aware of other senses, like touch: his gentle, steadying hand on the small of her back.

And hearing . . .

The clip-clop of horses' hooves and carriage wheels approached. A curious smile tugged at her lips. "Who's coming? Have you brought someone to see me?" Then all of a sudden she gasped. "Have you brought Daphne?"

He harrumphed. "No."

The sound stopped.

"Now open your eyes."

She obeyed.

Halted at the curb, she beheld a gorgeous coach-and-four. The liveried coachman tipped his hat to her. "Milady."

Her jaw dropped. Wide-eyed, she spun to face her husband. "For me?"

He grinned. "Now you can travel in style."

"Oh—Beauchamp!" Amazed, she covered her mouth with both hands and looked at it again.

The rich cherrywood of its sleek chassis had been polished to a high gleam. The brass fixtures fairly sparkled—and the horses! The snow-white pair in black harness had been adorned with red plumes on their heads for the occasion.

"Jamison will be your driver," Beau informed her, gesturing to the coachman. "He's been with my family a long time. I trust him implicitly."

Carissa nodded to her new driver. "Pleased to meet you, Jamison."

He bowed, beaming at her. "Felicitations, milady."

"It's beautiful, Beau. Just beautiful," she echoed in lingering disbelief, turning to her new husband.

He tapped her on the nose and playfully leaned closer. "Just so you're aware," he added in a conspiratorial tone, "I've given Jamison strict orders to keep you out of mischief when I'm not present. Given your penchant for getting into trouble, I don't intend to let you go gadding about Town willy-nilly when I'm not there to keep you out of trouble. If you ask to be driven to any destination that I might deem unwise, I've given Jamison discretion to refuse until you've checked with me first."

"Oh, really? So you've set your man to spy on me?" she murmured with a pointed look.

He smiled serenely, his face close to hers. "Rather irksome when the tables are turned on one, isn't it, my dear?" He took her hand. "Come. There's more."

"More?" she exclaimed.

He marched back into the house, tugging her after him.

"Oh, yes. We're just getting started. Hurry, love. We can't stay here all night. If you take my meaning."

Her eyes widened at his murmured innuendo.

When they arrived in the drawing room, three boxes tied up with ribbon bows had appeared on the low table in front of the fireplace, along with a large, mysterious, mound-shaped object concealed under a square of blue silk and, likewise, adorned with a ribbon.

"All this is for me?" she exclaimed.

"You are the bride, aren't you? Start with this one." He pointed to the silk-draped object. "Hurry," he added, glancing at the mantel clock. It was a couple of minutes before six.

"Don't be so impatient, Lord Beauchamp. Honestly," her uncle muttered.

Carissa inspected the odd-shaped present, then turned to her bridegroom in skeptical curiosity. "What's under there?"

"I'll never tell. Go on, open it. Don't try to lift it, though. It's too heavy. Just take off its clothes."

Her cousins shrieked at his mischievous whisper. Aunt Denbury's eyes widened; Miss Trent choked; the earl scowled. Suppressing laughter, Carissa gave him a warning look that scolded him to behave. Then, pink-cheeked from his flirting, she did what he suggested. As she untied the ribbon, she realized that never in her life had anyone made such a fuss over her. It really was bizarre.

Taking hold of a corner of the silken square, she glanced at him where he sat in the nearby armchair; he stared back at her like a man at a card game, his face revealing nothing. He rested his chin on his fist.

Then she whisked the silk away and gasped in amazement at the ornate, gilded, vase-clock sort of a thing built in layers. The bottom was a sturdy wooden pediment ornamented with flower garlands and medallions. Above that was a small pastel painting of what looked like the main pavilion at Vauxhall, and above that, there sat golden figurines of four musicians with their instruments.

"It's beautiful," she said, staring at the mystery. "But, um . . . what is it, then?"

"Hold on thirty seconds, and you'll see."

She turned to him, brow furrowed. "Why is that?"

"I know what that is!" Horace announced, stepping closer. "It's an automaton clock!"

And right as the hour struck, the clock came to life with a single, melodious chime.

A great whirring and clicking gathered from inside its wooden mechanical housing. The chimes turned to music, the gilded players striking their instruments, their tiny arms working to produce the little, tinkling, music-box melody.

At the same time, a tiny placard popped down in front of "Vauxhall" that said: *Dance*.

On this command, painted figures of waltzing couples only as tall as her pinky finger emerged from the side of the vase and began revolving across the front of the Vauxhall painting and back into the other side. She counted ten different pairs of little painted dancers, each clothed in the first stare of fashion.

The girls exclaimed in wonder as the next feature clicked into motion—a miniature Cupid flew out of a tiny golden door and began circling above the dancers, bobbing up and down mechanically with his bow and arrow, as if looking for a target.

"Oh, how perfectly delightful, Lord Beauchamp!"

"It's a marvel!"

They all clapped when the little show was over. The musicians stilled their bows; the dancers retired until the next set on the quarter hour; and Cupid flew back into his hiding place.

"Do you like it?"

"I do! Thank you so much, you dear man. It's magical," she told him with a warm gaze.

"You forgot to read the inscription on the back," he added softly.

Mystified, Carissa stepped around the corner of the table to view the back of the musical automaton clock. She leaned closer to read the small brass plaque attached to the wooden base. She saw he'd had it engraved.

Flowing script letters recorded their names and the date of their marriage, and then in plainer block font beneath this, she read the inscription: To MY SWEET CARISSA. DANCE WITH ME FOREVER. YOUR LOVING HUSBAND, BEAU.

Her heart fluttered as she read it a second time. Speechless, she went over and hugged him.

When he drew her into his arms with a low, fond laugh, she kissed him fervently on the cheek. *I think I'm going to like being married to you.*

As she pulled back, he captured her face between his fingertips and gazed, smiling, into her eyes. His lack of a droll comment filled her with exquisite, trembling hope that he actually meant every word of that romantic inscription and that it was not just his usual, droll hyperbole.

Maybe he *wasn't* just marrying her in order to make sure she didn't spill his secrets. Maybe he truly cared.

When he chucked her gently under the chin and told her to continue opening presents, she could not find her voice. His generosity and the words engraved on that splendid clock had practically melted her into a puddle of honey on the floor. "Go on," he urged, nodding toward the other boxes. "I'm not done spoiling you yet."

The dreamlike feeling returned as he awed her yet again, with a beautiful opal necklace made small and delicate enough not to overwhelm her petite stature. So much of the Renaissance-Revival-style jewelry so popular was too much for a lady of only five-foot-one. Miss Trent helped put the necklace on her, and they all admired her while he beamed with husbandly pride.

"I had a feeling that stone would look perfect with your skin."

The smolder in his eyes was growing stronger as she kissed him in thanks, this time a cautious peck on the lips. His fourth present, thankfully, lightened the mood. She knew he was up to something when he set the largest of the three pasteboard boxes on her lap. It was wide and tall, circular in shape, but for its size, it felt lighter than it looked.

She pulled off the ribbon, then lifted the lid. And promptly burst out laughing as she lifted out the most hideous bonnet the world had ever seen.

"What? You don't like it?" he exclaimed, pretending hurt.

"It looks like a drowned peacock on top of a rat's nest!" She laughed uproariously, as much in release of nervous tension as with real humor.

Her relatives were silent; politely baffled, they knew not how to react. They could not imagine why the man would give her such a thing—or why she'd laugh—but it was a private joke between the two of them.

The promised hat.

The moment was seared in her memory from that night at Dante House, when he had promised to take

her to the best milliner's shop in London and buy her
any hat she wanted if she'd just hold still and let him
make the stitches.

His way of apologizing for having to clip a little of
her hair to clean the wound. "Well done! You are true
to your word, my lord!" she declared.

"Put it on. I want to see how beautiful you look."

She did, presenting herself with a flourish.

"Gorgeous," he declared.

"Oh, but, cousin, you can't wear that in public!" Araminta burst out, unable to help herself.

"She's right," Joss agreed sternly. "It's horrid."

Carissa laughed harder. "No, it isn't! It's all the kick."

"She's just jealous," Beau said knowingly, folding his
arms across his chest with a sly nod.

"Don't be jealous, Min. You can borrow it anytime
you like!"

"You two are mad," Uncle Denbury muttered.

"The Batty Beauchamps," little cousin Horace suggested.

"Hmm, I rather like that," Beau replied. The final
gift proved a return of his cheeky humor: the perfect
gift for a lady of information.

He waited for her reaction as she opened the box and
carefully brushed aside the tissue wrapping to discover
the next bit of jeweled frivolity he'd bought her.

Nestled in the tissue paper, she found a diamond-
encrusted opera glass, so she could snoop in style.

She looked at him in adoring amusement, not knowing whether to laugh or to shake her head at him in
chiding.

He grinned, apparently knowing what this gift meant
to her. Acceptance of her foible. Affection for her
anyway, in spite of her being a . . . gossip.

There, she could admit it.

Then it was time to go, leaving as a resident of her uncle's house for the last time. It was oddly difficult, even though she was only moving a few blocks away. She'd still be in Mayfair.

Amid the cycle of farewells, she was still nervous about the wedding night ahead. He must have known she would feel that way, which was why he had looked for props to make her laugh to help dissipate the tension.

The touching realization of his kindness also helped put her at ease. If she could just get through their first time with all its uncertainties, then she had to believe everything would be all right. Besides, in her heart, she knew the truth: This man had long since seduced her.

All that remained was to consummate the match.

Chapter 9

A married man. Fancy that. Beau was quiet, musing in the carriage on the fact that his rakehell days were done.

He would've thought a part of him would bemoan the close of his career as a seducer, but he found himself glad to put old ways behind him. All it had taken was finding the right woman. He glanced over at his new bride beside him. Hand in hand, they rode in companionable silence after their long, eventful day. Studying her, he noticed that she looked a little apprehensive about tonight.

Touched by her innocence, he smiled to himself. He'd soon dismiss her maiden fears. He lifted her hand to his lips, kissing her knuckles to give her silent reassurance.

She sent him a grateful smile.

"It's been a good day, hasn't it?" he murmured.

She nodded. "I think it all went well."

"I'm glad you liked your presents."

"I have something for you, too." She turned to face him. "I just didn't want to give it to you in front of everyone."

"Oh, really?" he teased her with a playful leer.

"It's nothing improper, you rogue," she said with a grin. "Though I did buy something special to wear for you tonight." She bit her lip shyly.

"You did?" He sat up straight. "What color?"

She laughed. "You'll see soon enough."

He moaned.

She studied him in amused affection. "You were wonderful with my uncle's family. Thank you for that. They can be difficult to manage at times."

"So can we all." He paused. "Will you miss them?"

"No, they're just a few blocks away. That is far enough," she added archly.

"Then why were you looking so somber a moment ago?"

She let out a sigh and shook her head. "I was just wondering what the gossips will make of all this. What do you suppose Society will think of our hasty marriage?"

He leaned back against the cushioned squabs with an idle shrug. "Who cares?"

She looked startled. "Well, I do, for one!"

"Why?"

"I don't like people to gossip about me. What?"

He eyed her skeptically. "Nothing. It's just, well, it's a little late for that now, don't you think?"

"What do you mean?" she exclaimed.

"Putting the speed of our 'courtship' aside, you will be a countess, dear. I'm afraid being the subject of talk and observation comes with the coronet. Especially when it's me you married."

She stared at him.

"Don't worry, I'm sure you are equal to the task."

"I'm glad *you're* sure," she muttered. "Don't you know what people are going to think?"

He couldn't help smiling. "You're the expert on such things. Enlighten me."

"That improprieties took place between us—you being you. That this hasty marriage was necessary—if you take my meaning!" She pointed to her stomach.

"Oh, nobody's going to think that, and even if they do, they'll see they were wrong when no little Junior arrives before the requisite nine months."

"Yes, but in the meanwhile, I don't relish being the subject of rude and indecent speculation."

"Very well, if anyone gossips about you, you come tell your husband, and I'll shoot 'em."

"You're not taking this at all seriously."

"No."

"But of course not. You're not the one whose name will be dragged through the gutter. Mine will!"

"Why on earth do you think that?"

"Because you could've had anyone!" she exclaimed. " 'Why would he pick her?' That's what they're going to say. No one will be able to make sense of it!"

"Are you daft?" he asked indignantly. "Look at you, Carissa! You're beautiful! Clever. Charming. You're perfect for me." He sat back again, scowling mildly at her. "*You're* the only one who seems to think it strange that I should want you."

"But you didn't," she replied, holding his gaze in challenge. "You were forced to marry me because I snooped in Dante House, remember? Your only purpose was to keep me quiet."

He stared at her. "You still think that's the only reason, even after what I had inscribed on the automaton clock?"

She tilted her head, searching his face for a long moment. "You puzzle me."

"You think too much. Relax a little, love." He gave her cheek a fond caress. "I'm not going to let anyone say anything bad about you. In the meanwhile, I suggest you try not to let the silly gossips bother you so much. Whatever they say, it's really quite meaningless, believe me. After all, you know who your true friends are. Their opinions are the ones that matter. And they are going to be very happy for us."

She was silent.

He looked at her intently. "Surely you are not so entirely untrusting that you even doubt your friends?"

She stared beseechingly into his eyes.

"You doubt *me*?"

"No—I doubt myself," she admitted.

Trailing his gaze over her lovely face, he saw the distress in her green eyes and tried to understand. "You doubt that you deserve affection?"

"No, it's not that. It's just—if I rely on it, if I let myself need anyone . . ." She struggled with her words, dropping her gaze. "Every time I've ever let myself depend on someone, they disappear. That's why I always try to rely only on myself."

"Carissa," he said softly, "I'm your husband now. You can count on me. Do try to get used to that fact, all right?"

She conceded with a nod, but a wary smile tugged at her lips.

"Now put all your cares out of your mind, my lady! These are my orders, as your lord and husband. It's your wedding day! Be happy!" He seized her about the waist and pulled her onto his lap, planting a loud kiss on her cheek just as the carriage rolled to a halt.

"You're mad," she chided in a soft, breathy tone right before he captured her mouth for a more serious sort of kiss. The light caress of his lips evoked a dreamy sigh from hers that told him he had succeeded in chasing away her fears, at least for the moment. The silken stroke of her tongue gave him a tantalizing taste of what was still to come tonight, while the thrill of the chemistry between them heated every inch of his body.

Then his servant came and got the carriage door.

As the man put down the step, Beau gave her a smile. "Welcome to your new home." He got out, straightened his coat, and called cheerfully to his butler: "Get the door, Vickers!" Then he turned back for his bride.

When she appeared in the open doorway of the carriage, he swept her into his arms and carried her over the threshold.

"Welcome home, my darling," he was moved to whisper as he stepped into the entrance hall. He felt like she needed to hear it.

Her embrace tightened around his neck as she returned his kiss. Then he set her down and steadied her while she blinked back tears of emotion. As she regained her composure, he began introducing her to the entire domestic staff assembled there to welcome the new lady of the house.

Under the rule of the ever-capable butler, Vickers, the domestic staff numbered about twenty in all, not including the outdoor gang of stableboys and gardeners. The footmen wore their full Lockwood livery for their master's wedding day, gold brocade with peacock blue; the maids were dressed in their best uniforms, with starched white aprons. They bowed and curtsied to her, presenting her with flowers and a few small gifts.

Beau was quite pleased with how his household made her welcome. The staff were always wonderfully efficient, but more importantly to him, they were a cheerful bunch. He had never been one to tolerate a rudesby under his roof. It was one of his greatest needs in life to have a happy home; therefore, any troublemakers or dark clouds were soon sent packing. Those who passed muster and remained appreciated their situation, for he was a generous master and treated his people well.

As a result, they were devoted to him and took pride in their work, especially in their frantic preparations over the past week in readying for his domicile for the new Lady Beauchamp's arrival.

When he had introduced everyone, they then embarked on a tour of the house, for he was determined to make his bride feel at home. His town house was not vast like the mansion, Lockwood House, which he'd inherit when his father died. Obviously, he was in no hurry for that day to come. Besides, his present dwelling suited him well. It was equal parts elegant and snug; it was convenient in every respect, and with minimal upkeep, it gave him no headaches when he had to travel for long periods of time. He just hoped it was grand enough for Carissa.

He got the impression there were a lot of marriageable young debutantes out there who would have insisted on something more magnificent. Beau had no desire to move.

Years of roaming the Continent like a nomad made

him grateful for the stability of having one set address to come home to.

Showing her first the rooms on the ground floor where they had entered, he opened the door to the anteroom off the entrance hall. With its rows of bookshelves and its bay window overlooking the street, he generally used it as his study, and the likeliest place for receiving business callers when he had meetings.

Next, he led her down the corridor, past the foot of the grand staircase, to the formal dining room. Every candle had been lighted: He had wanted the room to sparkle so she would be impressed.

He glanced at her and saw he had succeeded. Her eyes shone in the candlelight. Good, he thought, relieved to escape the disruption of noisy, dusty home renovations to suit his lady's tastes.

Moving on, he led her toward the back of the house to the well-appointed kitchen. Cook had made sure not a crumb had been left on the floor. Carissa admired the very modern cooking range and declared she had no idea how to use it. Mrs. Tarleton assured Her Ladyship she would explain all about its many features if she wished.

"Some other time," Beau replied, playfully tugging his viscountess along toward the back door at the far end of the central hallway. He took her outside for a peek into the garden and beyond that, the mews, where her new carriage had been stored.

Turning her around, he steered her back toward the entrance hall, then led her up the stairs to the main floor. Along the way, she admired the statuary niche above the landing where the staircase switched directions.

They came out at the top of the stairs, across from

the formal drawing room, with its chandeliers, ceiling medallions, and light blue walls. He showed her how the pocket doors could be rolled back to join the drawing room to the music room, creating one large space for entertaining.

She seemed pleased and stepped through the opening into the music room. She glanced at the pianoforte and asked him if he played.

"A bit," he answered. "You?"

"A little," she replied with a modest smile.

They moved on. At the back of the main floor lay his favorite room in the house—a cozy, cheerful parlor, or morning room, with an informal dining table and chairs. A bow window overlooked the garden. Carissa ran her hand over the plump, stuffed couch before the fireplace, then glanced around at all the thriving plants, a faint smile on her lips.

"This is where I usually eat my breakfast," he informed her. "Assuming we'll be doing that together in the future, pick a seat to be your designated chair."

She chuckled, looking them over. "This one. So I can see out the window."

"You'll have the morning sun in your face. It comes in this way."

"Well, I shall enjoy the view. And if it's too strong, I'll take the one across from it."

"Very well," he said sagely. "Now that that important business is all sorted, we'd best move on. The night is waning," he added, delighting in her blush at his innuendo.

Beau was encouraged, for Carissa seemed pleased by everything so far. As they left the parlor, he pointed out the closed door to the servants' stairs across the hall.

"The female servants' quarters are on the fourth floor

of the house," he explained as they wandered on. "The footmen have their dormitory in the basement level, along with the wine cellar and the scullery and such. I'm sure you'll see all of that eventually if you care to inspect it."

She nodded but seemed content to pass on that for now. Once more, to the main staircase they returned.

Beau could already feel his blood warming as he showed her up to the third floor, where the bedchambers were located. He escorted her along the corridor, where empty spaces waited to be filled with children.

"These two bedrooms could be for either the boys or the girls, and at the front of the house could be their nursery, or their little schoolroom," he explained.

"How many?" she inquired, smiling as she turned to him, rosy-cheeked at his talk of their future offspring.

"At least two of each," he answered firmly.

"You've got everything figured out, haven't you?"

He dodged the question with a twinkle in his eyes. "And so, my lady, that concludes your tour. Any questions?"

She shook her head, holding his stare. Neither of them could look away.

"It is a snug, efficient place. That's why I bought it. Of course, we won't be here forever," he added. "When my father passes on, we shall inherit Lockwood House. It is five times the size of this place."

"This is more than enough for me."

He gazed into her eyes, warmed by her approval. "I hope you will be happy here."

"I know I will," she whispered with a small catch in her voice.

"Good. Then, you have one more room to see." He took her hand and led her to the last room on their tour.

When she stepped over the threshold into the dim, welcoming space, Beau glanced back and nodded a silent dismissal of the servants who had trailed.

Vickers and a few of his underlings had followed in fascination of their new mistress, eager to be of use and to hop to it if they were needed, or if she found anything to be out of place. Even Beau did not know how anxious they were to see their beloved, kind master settled in life. Then he shut the door and joined her in his, or rather, their bedchamber.

Carissa had crossed the room to her traveling trunks, which had been brought over from her uncle's house but were not yet unpacked.

She knelt before the smallest leather trunk, lifting the lid; he could see that she was searching for something. "Here it is." She lifted out a small object about the size of a book; it was wrapped in a square of silk and tied with a ribbon bow. She brought it over to him. "I made it for you myself. Here."

"Well, this is very thoughtful of you." He took it from her with a smile, intrigued. "You didn't have to give me anything."

"Of course I did, it is our wedding day. Careful!" she warned. "It's not entirely dry yet."

He furrowed his brow in curiosity, and even after he had unwrapped it, he was not sure of what exactly he was looking at. "Hmm." He carried it closer to the light, then examined the little pasteboard box by the candelabra's glow. She had covered its surfaces with small bits of paper sealed into place with varnish, and decorated it here and there with bits of colored glass.

Upon closer inspection, he discovered that the paper was actually taken from bits of newspaper clippings that had been written about his various exploits over the years and had appeared in the *Times* or the *Post*.

"It's a secrets box," she murmured as she joined him by the table. "You see, I've known more about you for a while now than you realized. Good things. I guess you could say I, um, made a few inquiries about you here and there."

"Why?" he asked, smiling.

"You're going to make me admit it?" she exclaimed.

"Aye."

"Very well! I was more interested in you than I had let on."

"There, was that so hard? But I have a confession, as well. I was interested in you, too."

"You were?"

"Couldn't you tell?"

"I . . . ." She stared at him, wide-eyed and blushing.

"Speechless?" he asked wryly.

"I would have never dared presume—!"

"Well, your friends' husbands threatened to thrash me if I touched you. Even so, I couldn't seem to help myself."

"Lord Rotherstone threatened to thrash you for my sake?"

"And Warrington, and of course, Lord Falconridge. They're very protective of you."

"How sweet!" She beamed at the revelation of her friends' concern. "Well," she said, laying a hand on his chest. "I have a husband to protect me now. But back to the matter at hand. Let me tell you what your present means."

"I'm all ears."

"This is my way of saying how much I admire you

for all you've done. How proud I am to be married to such a man. You've done so many interesting things in your life, and I'm sure you'll do many more. I realize most of them have to be secrets, but there's no harm celebrating the ones I'm allowed to know about, is there? Most of all, this box comes with my promise that your secrets will always be safe with me."

He shook his head in wonder at her sweetness. "I adore it. And I adore you." He set the box on the table and turned to her, taking her face between his hands. He kissed her on the forehead, his lips lingered at her brow. "Thank you, darling," he whispered.

She tilted her head back to gaze up earnestly at him. "I realize our marriage had an unconventional start, but I want you to know that I'm sincere, as well, and I intend to make you happy."

"You've already been doing that for weeks without even knowing it," he whispered, then he gathered her closer and lowered his head to claim her mouth. She slid her arms around him, parting her lips as he deepened the kiss.

*C*arissa could feel his heart pounding against her chest. She clung to him, dizzy with desire.

Even her long-standing anxiety over this night began to fade in the gathering heat of her passion for him, the hunger she had tried so long to ignore. Indeed, it was hard to remember her fears at all when his clever fingers started plucking at the buttons on her gown.

His wandering hands distracted her, making her forget everything but this moment.

"You are wearing far too many clothes," he informed her, breathing heavily. "Something must be done."

She gave him a game half smile.

His wet lips gleamed in the candlelight. "Turn," he whispered. "I'll help you with your gown."

She obeyed, then stood quivering while he unfastened the buttons down her back. Soon, she felt the coolness of the air licking at her skin, his fingertips trailing down her spine.

When he had unbuttoned her dress down to her hips, his hands came to rest on her shoulders; she trembled violently as his lips played at her nape. He kissed her neck over and over while his hands gently pushed her puff sleeves down off her shoulders.

This was nothing like her experience with the poet, she thought dazedly, absorbed in sensation. She could barely remember that cad's name at the moment, nor had she any desire to. He'd been rushed, awkward, selfish.

Beau was the opposite of that and completely sure of himself. She could feel it in his every touch. His air of confident command was an intoxicating aphrodisiac. Without a word, he freed her arms from the sleeves, and still standing behind her, slid her gown down her body. His hands followed the fabric down the curve of her hips until she stepped out of the pool of blush-colored satin on the ground. But he was not through with his task yet.

When she turned to him, he captured her chin and tilted her head back, capturing her lips for another leisurely kiss. His fingertips trailed down her throat and chest, then he slid his palm down her waist to her petticoat tapes. "Back to business," he whispered.

She watched in deepening excitement as he diligently untied them. He sank to his knees and took his time with the task of working her petticoats down her body as well.

Carissa's chest heaved as she now stood before him wearing no more than her stays, her stockings, and chemise. He was on eye level with her breasts. "Turn," he rasped once again. She pivoted slowly, his hands on her hips all the while.

When she stood with her back to him, he unlaced her stays with an almost tender motion. The rigid garment was cast aside. "And turn," he murmured again, barely audible.

Carissa swallowed hard as she obeyed, slowly pivoting to face her husband.

He studied her in silence, a storm of passion darkening his chiseled face. Still on his knees, he trailed his fingers down her arm, making every inch of her tingle. He was studying her as rapturously as she had stared at the musical clock. "You are so beautiful," he whispered.

"I'm glad you're pleased," she forced out in a shy, strangled mumble.

"Such white skin, such sweet freckles." Here a kiss, there a soft caress, all the way across her collarbones, from one shoulder across her chest to the other.

She trembled with yearning and bit her lip and waited in agonized pleasure to find out what he would do to her next. When his warm hand cupped her breast through the thin white muslin of her chemise, she went still. But it was his right; she did not object.

He leaned closer and kissed the valley between her breasts through her light covering. "You're incredible," he breathed, "elegant, delightful, . . . sweet from head to toe."

Then he slowly stood up, kissing his way up the center of her chest as he rose. Carissa tilted her head back, her toes curling as his kisses explored the crook of her neck. His playful lips closed on her earlobe, with a warm little bite that made her giggle. She leaned against him, weak-kneed with desire. His arms cradled her, then he began removing the pins from her hair.

Before long, her long locks had tumbled free around her shoulders. "You have no idea how long I have been wanting to do that," he whispered with a roguish twinkle in his eyes.

"Now you can do it whenever you like," she told him with a breathless smile.

"I am a lucky man." He tugged the knot of his cravat loose.

She reached up with trembling fingers and helped him untie it. In the midst of her wifely task, she got caught up in staring at the beautiful architecture of his Adam's apple. With his cravat hanging loose about his shoulders, she found a whole new appreciation for his soft, sculpted lips, the rugged line of his jaw, and the sweep of his seductive throat. At length, she came back to her senses and got on with her task, reaching up to push his handsome coat off his shoulders.

Holding her stare, he unbuttoned his waistcoat and tossed it aside. She slipped his suspenders off each of his shoulders with a caress, while the deep V of his shirt fell apart, revealing his bare chest.

Instantly, she was agog at his masculine beauty, but her gaze homed in on the necklace that he wore: a small, manly cross on a rugged silver chain. She reached out and touched the small, Maltese cross of white enamel in a steel frame. Then she met his gaze in question.

His eyes smoldered with blue flame. "The insignia of the Order."

She absorbed this in fascination, then let the little

metal cross fall against his chest once more. He leaned
down to kiss her.

She returned his kisses eagerly, and while his arms
wrapped around her waist, she stroked his lovely
chest. He reached for the placket of his trousers after a
moment. Still kissing him, she could feel the backs of
his knuckles brushing against her stomach as he unfastened it. The sensation filled her with wild, impatient
hunger. He pulled back just long enough to lift his shirt
off over his head with a sweeping motion. She drew in
her breath at the sight of him. The man was perfectly
luscious.

He cast his shirt aside. "I want more of you."

Carissa could not speak, but he would not have allowed it anyway, his mouth consuming hers. He
wrapped his arms around her. She let her hands go
exploring; her palms traveled over the hard swells of
his chest. She marveled over every warm, chiseled
harrow of his muscled abdomen. The feel of him was
velveteen, and with each moment that passed, his skin
burned hotter.

Beau kissed her passionately, his fingers raking
through her hair. "I want to be inside you." He steered
her gently to the edge of the bed, where he took hold of
her chemise and gathered it around her hips.

"Sit," he whispered.

She did. He sank lower; she spread her legs wider as
he went down on his knees and began to explore her.
The room was filled with their panting as she watched
him.

The drumming of her pulse set the rhythm. He licked
at her nipple through the light muslin while his other
hand squeezed. Carissa moaned, squirming beneath
him. Inch by inch, he slipped her chemise off her

shoulder, freeing her arm from the sleeve and exposing her breast.

She gasped at the hot, damp shock of his mouth claiming her nipple. While he sucked one breast, his fingers played with the other, teasing her nipple, flicking and pulling it, kneading it, until she was on fire.

He switched sides, working the other sleeve down and freeing her other arm while he sucked and played. The sway of his body between her thighs enchanted her though he still merely knelt beside the bed. He teased and caressed her with every inch of his magnificent body. She knew he was doing it on purpose, driving her utterly mad with all his sensual temptation.

She moaned his name imploringly, but he was not nearly done playing with her. With a final pinch of her nipple he trailed his fingertips down the center of her belly until he came to her mound. He pressed her center gently with his thumb, gave it a loving, broad stroke with the heel of his hand, and began pleasuring her with his finger.

A high-pitched sigh escaped her lips as his middle finger penetrated her. Carissa did not know how much she could bear as he knelt beside her, kissing her thighs, tasting her body with his tongue while he pleasured her with his hand. As passion threatened to overtake her senses entirely, she tried to hold back, scarcely wanting him to see this wanton side of her, but he looked at her from across the smooth sweep of her naked body and gave her a devilish, knowing smile. "I need you now."

Kissing her mouth, her chin, her chest, her nipples, he dragged himself back just far enough to get rid of his trousers, also kicking off his shoes.

Carissa stared, amazed, at the glory of her warrior's nakedness. His sleek hips, his muscled buttocks in the mirror behind him, and thrusting toward her face where she lay on the bed, his big, rosy cock, hard and surging. As he took off his pantaloons, she just stared, awestruck. He had strong thighs, elegant muscled legs—even his bare feet were beautiful. He climbed onto the bed, his hands planted on either side of her, his body covering hers.

The feeling of his naked body against hers was blissful. She ran her hands over him, touching him everywhere as he nuzzled her nose with his own, then stared into her eyes, giving her silent reassurance. His Maltese cross dangled over her.

"I want you to tell me if anything causes you the least distress," he whispered. "I want every moment of this to be good for you, for you to know that you can trust me."

Her voice fled at his tender words, reminding her of how she was deceiving him in this most intimate of moments. She hated herself for it but dared not interrupt their joining now. She could not bear to think about her foolish past. He was all that mattered in this moment.

"You all right?" he murmured.

She nodded, took his chiseled face gently between her hands, and pulled him down to kiss her. He obliged heartily, and, slowly, he filled her.

Carissa felt no fear, no pain, which just went to show how excellent he was at the art of seduction. She did not shrink from his hard body penetrating her as he claimed her for his own. She wanted nothing more than to belong to him.

She could feel his heartbeat pounding in time with hers, the delicious weight of him atop her as he began rocking her with tender care. His lusty panting filled her world. She wrapped her legs around him while he linked his fingers through hers, pinning her to the bed. They moved in unison for a timeless eternity, as if they had been made for each other . . . as if this was meant to be.

She knew it was.

"My God, you are delectable," he breathed, rolling onto his back at length and pulling her atop him.

She groaned at the wave of sensation the new position brought.

"You like that?" he observed with a narrow smile.

"I like whatever you like," she answered, flushed and breathless. In truth, she could barely form a thought in the haze of sensual pleasure he'd cast over her.

A light sweat had broken out on them both. She was sensitive and tight, but there was no pain as his hard length thrust more deeply into her passage. She felt completely free with him and thrilled to his every growl and groan, audible evidence of how much he was enjoying her. He moaned her name as she straddled him, braced on her hands above him.

She splayed her palm against his chest. "Are you really mine?" she whispered.

"Goddamn right I am," he ground out, his teeth clenched with pleasure. "Anytime you want me."

His answer flooded her with a burning wave of passion. She leaned down to consume his mouth in a nigh-barbaric kiss. He grasped her buttocks and pulled her down more firmly onto his iron shaft. She gasped at his depth inside her, the size and power of his taking.

He sat up after a few moments; she had to shift her position to accommodate, kneeling across his lap, facing him. With his hands planted behind him, he lifted his hips up and down, giving Carissa the ride of her life. Her eyes closed, her head tipped back in abandon. She clung to his broad shoulders while he drove her on and on toward her climax.

As she looked into his glittering eyes, the pleasure and the sweetness of the life ahead of them took her by surprise with a flood of welling emotion that seemed to come out of the blue. Surely he would think she was a quiz, but she couldn't help it; in the throes of passion in her wedding bed, tears filled her eyes, as if the formidable walls she'd so long built around her heart had suddenly burst wide open.

It was only then, in that moment, that she gave herself to him without reserve. But Beau was too wise a lover to find the tears of her release anything but beautiful.

As though he could sense exactly what was going through her mind, he reached gently for her nape and drew her lips to his while the tears ran down her face.

Her gasps were ragged with more than physical release as his kisses coaxed her toward the quivering brink of climax. Pleasure overwhelmed her from every direction, inside and out; she felt like she was falling, but he was there to catch her in his strong, sure arms.

She cried out, rather a sob, and clung to him with desire shooting upward like a burning star through her body, to her heart, piercing through her very soul.

With the fire of his lips against hers, the shattering realization hit her that love was not lost to her, after all. The betrayal she had suffered had once made her vow never to love again, but she knew tonight she had been wrong. Love's exquisite bond was worth another try.

She embraced him more tightly, barely aware of the cries of pleasure that filled the room as her own, until they faded and Beau moved her slowly, tenderly onto her back. And then, resting on his elbows, he reached his climax, too, with a few hard, deep, and passionate strokes.

He gathered long fistfuls of her hair, winding them round his fingers—as if to wrap himself in her—not hard enough to hurt. He buried his face against her neck, moaning with release. His groans enveloped her, every muscle going rigid while he convulsed and filled her body with his seed. She welcomed it blindly, longing quite to her own surprise for her future as the mother of his children.

As sanity gradually returned, and the slackened weight of him grew heavy, leaden, atop her, she smiled to herself. Following him that night at the theatre—her snooping—had surely been the best mistake of her life. "Oh, husband," she purred at last.

His lips taut with emotion, Beau kissed her brow and wrapped his arms around her. She could still feel him trembling. But he said not a word.

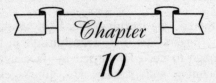

Chapter 10

$\mathcal{S}$ometime later, Beau sat in the chair near the window in the darkness, staring at his bride asleep on the bed. Physically, he was well satisfied, but mentally, he scarcely knew what to make of that experience. The mystery of Carissa had just decidedly deepened.

A kiss told a man many things about a woman, making love to her even more so, and as of this moment, he barely knew what to make of the beautiful stranger he had married.

She slumbered in sated exhaustion, having fulfilled her wifely duties beyond his wildest expectations.

Beau was confused. He was not quite sure what had given it away . . . not so much their physical joining, but perhaps her lack of inhibition. He had reveled in her passion at the time, delighting in her enthusiasm, but afterward, it had begun to make him wonder.

And as the glow of pleasure wore off, reality had

started setting in, questions gathering like storm clouds in his mind while Carissa fell asleep.

Now he sat studying her from across the room, darkly troubled by her failure to mention anything he might want to know about this. Yet at the same time, gazing at her, he had never felt more tenderness toward any creature, more protectiveness.

Staring at her in his bed, he knew that she was right where she belonged, but beyond that, he really did not know what he was supposed to think or feel.

As much as he hated being lied to, though, he could understand why she would try to get away with this deception tonight.

There were many men who would be screaming at her right now and bundling her back to her family in shame.

Whatever his faults, however, Beau had never been a cruel man, especially to females.

Damn it, he was supposed to be a spy. He should have researched her before getting himself into this.

And when would I have had time for that?

It had been a mad scramble from the moment he'd swept her off to Dante House to save her life.

He half feared he had been absolutely played.

But the likelier reality was that he'd let himself be blinded by lust. Every time he had looked at Carissa Portland, he had wanted her. Were there cues he could have noticed if he had not been thinking with his cock where she was concerned?

Then a cold knot of dread formed in the pit of his stomach as he wondered if this shocking, wedding-night revelation was just a taste of things to come.

Good God, what if he had married a woman who'd

prove as unfaithful to him in the future as his mother had been to his father? Would his passionate redhead make a cuckold of him? Was he doomed to walk in his humiliated father's footsteps? Yet how could he, of all people, ever honestly complain, after his own past dalliances with other fellows' wives?

He probably deserved it.

Aye, maybe this was naught but ironic Fate repaying him in kind for his own past as a libertine. He knitted his brow, his jaw clenching in defensive anger.

Very well, so he wasn't a saint. But *he* had never tried to hide that fact from her.

Carissa, on the other hand, had attempted to deceive him, even as she gave herself to him, surrendered. It was bloody low of her. It went to a question of character, in his view. A lack of honesty. A lack of judgment. And a definite lack of respect. Did she take him for a fool?

It was insulting to see she really didn't trust him.

At the moment, he didn't trust her, either.

Beau closed his eyes, rubbed his brow, and after a long moment's fight with himself, decided by an act of will that he was not going to get angry about this.

He was tempted to use his subtle interrogation skills to coax the truth out of her tomorrow. He could easily work on her bit by bit until he had the whole story.

But he recoiled at the prospect of using his spy training on his wife. She wasn't a bloody Promethean.

No. Let her come to him and speak her piece when she was ready. He thought of the automaton clock, and his lavish inscription, and realized the least he could give her was a little time.

Until then—he couldn't help it—he'd be wary of her, too, until she willingly laid her cards out on the table.

He knew it wouldn't be easy for her. She had already said herself that she didn't trust anybody. But forcing her to give him the details, humiliating her with the fact that he knew she was lying, or hurting her in any way was unacceptable.

Sooner or later, he swore to himself, he'd win Carissa's trust.

After all, if there was one thing he was absolutely sure of, it was that she had not meant any harm.

She never did. Not when she had followed him into the alley. Not when she'd got herself stuck in the wall.

The memory of her checking herself for spiders made him shake his head while his heart clenched. *You're a walking calamity, girl. But you're my calamity.*

Besides, it was important to keep this in perspective. Between Nick and the Home Office, he had so many other, larger problems right now, the last thing he wanted to do was to go to war with his wife when they had been married barely twelve hours.

With a grim, uncertain sigh, Beau got up from his seat by the window and returned to join her in their bed—which, he supposed, he had made, so he'd better lie in it.

Settling into his spot, he took her into his arms and held the lovely, maddening creature; Carissa slept on his chest, peaceful as a child.

He kissed her head much too tenderly in spite of himself, even as he noted in surprise how much it hurt to suspect strongly, if not to know for a fact, that she had given herself to someone else before him.

So, he mused uneasily, this was the pain he had caused those other men, casually bedding their women.

Now that the proverbial shoe was on the other foot and he had learned his little bride was not a virgin, he had a life-altering realization, forced to confront the truth of his *own* past behavior. No preacher's sermon could have changed him more than the shame he felt in that moment, now that he truly grasped what he had done to others, as it seemed he was finally reaping what he had sown.

How could he not have seen it before? he wondered. But he had not wanted to see it, carefully blocking the wrongness of it all from his mind as he took his pleasures where he liked and went on his merry way.

But now his eyes were opened, and he was revolted at himself. The great libertine was distraught with contrition in the silence, while Carissa's chiding from that night at the theatre rang in his ears. *Do you ever think of the heartache you must cause these women?*

Of course, he had never meant any particular harm, but he could no longer ignore how callous he had been.

How destructive, in his selfishness.

The usual blithe excuse that everyone did it withered into dust. To be sure, any private doubt about his ability to stay faithful to his wife in the future promptly disappeared.

This small taste of the kind of anguish he had caused his fellow man was enough to put him off the ton's favorite sport forever.

He shuddered and held Carissa closer, fervently glad to be done with that sort of life.

As he lay there, he tried not to let his outraged male pride obsess over the question of who the hell had had his wife before him. *I'll tell you one thing,* he thought as he stared into the darkness. *Whoever he was, if he forced her, he's a dead man.*

Chapter
11

$\mathcal{A}$t breakfast the next morning, their second official day of being married, Carissa stared across the table, trying to read Beau.

His handsome face gave away little. His easy smile was firmly in place. There was only the slightest hint of a shadow behind his eyes, but he was gallant and polite and could not have been more solicitous. She felt the warmth between them and tried to put her fears aside.

He didn't notice.

When he passed the sugar for her tea before she could ask for it, she smiled gratefully but sensed some hidden sentiment behind his calm mask, and her worries persisted. He seemed . . . distant, ever so slightly.

God. Had she been too free with him last night?

But she had wanted to make him happy.

Nevertheless, guilt for deceiving him was making her jumpy—as if she weren't already nervous enough about meeting his parents today. Her jangled nerves left her with little interest in her breakfast, but the morning room was pleasant, filled with sunshine that sparkled off the silver and the pastel-colored china. Beyond the window, a bright spring day beckoned out in the garden.

She told herself for the tenth time that everything would be fine, and just when she had started to settle down, Beau spoke up and scared the blazes out of her. "Before we set out today, I feel I really must warn you about Mother."

She looked up from her barely touched plate in surprise. "Warn me?"

He stirred a bit of milk into his tea, ignoring the morning paper the butler had just brought him. "When you meet her, try not to take it personally if she needles you. The truth is, I'm afraid, she doesn't believe any woman on earth would ever be good enough for me. It wouldn't matter if you were a royal princess. So, if she's hostile, take it with a grain of salt."

Carissa raised her eyebrows. "Very well."

"We'll only stay a few minutes. Pay our respects, let her get her first look at you, then we'll set out for Hampshire."

She shook her head uneasily. "You can't blame her for being angry. I still don't understand why you refused to invite your parents to the wedding."

"Why, so they could ruin it for us with their fighting?"

"To leave them out was barbaric. They'll probably blame me."

"No, trust me, they'll know full well why they weren't asked. We've been through this many times. If they could act like adults around each other, it would be different, but they would've turned it into a spectacle, and God knows what sort of havoc they'd have wreaked."

She heaved a sigh. "So, what should I expect from your father?"

"He won't give you too much trouble. We'll spend a few days in the country with him. I'm eager to show you our family estate."

"I'm looking forward to seeing it." She paused, gazing into her teacup. "It's a shame your parents aren't able to get along. Was it an arranged marriage?"

"No, from what I'm told, they were madly in love early on, but within a few years, they could hardly stand the sight of each other." He shrugged. "I really don't know why, or which of them was the first to start having the affairs." He looked at her strangely. "All I know is that when I was chosen for the Order, it was the last straw for my mother. Father gave his approval, and she never forgave him for it. It didn't seem to matter to her that it was what I wanted, too."

"Hmm."

He seemed anxious to change the subject. "We should get going soon."

She put her fork down, wondering what she was in for today. "I'm ready."

Before long, they were in the entrance hall, where Beau held her pelisse for her. She shrugged it on, then he accepted his hat and walking stick from the butler.

"We won't be long, Vickers," he said, as they headed for the door.

"Very good, sir." The butler opened it for them, revealing not only the bright spring day beyond but a visitor, who had just arrived.

The man stepping down from the carriage had a lanky, narrow frame and a pale face, pinched and haughty. He cut a somber figure like a churchman all in black. He swept off his top hat when he saw them, revealing a shock of greasy dark hair. "Lord Beauchamp! I'm so glad I caught you," he called, striding toward them.

Carissa felt her easygoing husband tense at the sight of him, and this was enough to intrigue any lady of information. "Mr. Green," he greeted their visitor with a subtle edge to his voice. "To what do we owe this honor? Poor timing, though—I'm afraid we are on our way out."

"I only need a moment, sir."

They could not have left then if they wanted to, for the man had parked his carriage at an angle, blocking their own against the curb.

"I've come to return your documents," he said.

Beau stepped forward quickly. "You brought them here?"

"Why, yes." Mr. Green started to offer them to him, but paused and raised an eyebrow. "Is that a problem?"

Beau's mouth flattened to a taut line. He glanced at the carriage. "No harm done, I suppose."

"What is it?" he countered.

"These are sensitive documents, Mr. Green, as you well know. Yet it doesn't appear you've taken the proper precautions."

"I've brought them to you personally, hand delivered. What more can you want?"

"Your word that no unauthorized person has seen them?"

"Of course not!" he said, while Carissa marveled at this exchange and tried to get a peek at those important papers. Their visitor lifted his chin. "I'm not a fool, my lord. I only wished to do you a convenience."

I doubt that, Beau's tense posture seemed to say.

"Of course," Mr. Green continued, "I had another purpose in coming."

"Of course you did," Beau said under his breath.

"I have a question I'd like you to answer."

"Can't it wait? As you can see, my lady and I are on our way out."

"Miss," their visitor finally acknowledged Carissa with a begrudging tip of his hat.

"Mrs., actually," she corrected him with a broad smile, hoping that a whiff of feminine charm might ease the tension between the two men.

Instead, Mr. Green looked at Beau in astonishment. "You've married? But I was not told of this!"

"I wasn't aware I needed the government's permission," he said crisply.

Green's eyes narrowed. "Felicitations, my lord."

Beau turned to her, impatience sharpening his handsome features. "My lady, this is Mr. Green, one of our esteemed MPs."

"How do you do," she said, but the man's faint, reptilian smile left her cold.

"Mr. Green, this radiant creature is my wife, Lady Beauchamp."

Carissa smiled fondly at Beau, while Mr. Green made odd, uncomfortable noises. "A private word with you, my lord?" he inquired of her husband.

Beau said nothing but excused himself from her company briefly with a light touch on her elbow, then he stepped aside to speak privately with their unpleasant caller.

Carissa stepped back into the threshold of the doorway while Beau went toward the waiting carriages with Mr. Green. Pretending to search in her reticule for something, she strained her ears for all she was worth to listen in on their low-toned exchange.

"Don't assume getting married is going to make

you look any more respectable to the committee, Lord Beauchamp. I'm happy for you, of course, but we are not so easily fooled."

"What do you want?" Beau replied tersely. "Why are you here? My next appearance before the panel is a week hence."

Green's belligerent stance eased somewhat at Beau's refusal to flinch. He stepped back a little and adjusted his coat with a nervous tug. "I have a question for you regarding one of Warrington's missions."

Kate's husband!

"What is it?" Beau asked darkly.

"You'll recall how one of the King of Naples' favorite courtiers ended up dead. If the Order gave the duke clearance for this killing, I have no record of it."

Beau scoffed, looked at the sky, and folded his arms across his chest. "You think he just did it for fun?"

Green's anger flashed. "Do you really want to know what I think, Lord Beauchamp?"

"By all means."

"*I* think that you fine gentlemen of the Inferno Club are so drunk with your own power and your own dubious talents that you feel entitled to go running around Europe doing whatever you please, including cutting down anyone who stands in your way. And why shouldn't you? There are never any consequences. The Crown has given you carte blanche."

"Everything we do is in service to the Crown," he bit back.

"Is it? I am not yet entirely convinced. You claim that is the case, and so the Order's long, august tradition would have us believe. But now that we understand how much latitude Virgil Banks let you have, who knows what you might have been doing out there on your own? Or what you might be planning next?"

"Oh, now we are the conspirators? The Prometheans are the threat, Green."

"If they really exist."

"Would you like to see the scars that prove they do?"

"Of course not." Green flicked a distasteful glance over him.

"No? Shall I not offer up my body to the panel, too? You noble inquisitors want to probe everything else about our agents' bloody lives—"

"Just get me the proper documents that show who authorized Warrington to kill the Italian. I want to see the chain of command."

"At your service, sir. It'll take a few days."

"Very well. But don't tempt me, Beauchamp. I'm sure you feel the Order is quite innocent in all things, but that is part of the problem. You don't even see the threat you pose. It's time you all were held to account, and if the Crown won't do it, the House of Commons will, and the Home Office. We are no longer living in medieval days, if you haven't noticed, yet you and your kind still seem to think you are a law unto yourselves."

Beau just looked at him. "Careful, Mr. Green. You are starting to sound like your old mentor."

Green narrowed his eyes and decidedly backed down.

He flicked his gaze toward her. "Felicitations once again on your marriage, my lord. She's very pretty."

How dare you comment on my wife? Beau's glare seemed to say, but to Carissa's relief, he kept his aristocratic indignation to himself.

When the haughty MP had driven away, Beau remained by himself a moment longer, bringing his anger under control. Carissa watched her husband worriedly.

He took a deep breath, squared his shoulders, and pivoted toward the house. Marching toward her, he sent her a distracted smile intended to reassure. "I have to go and put these papers in the vault. I'll be right back."

She nodded, but waiting for him, she was unsettled by all she had overheard. It sounded like little Mr. Green was out for their blood, especially Warrington's. Poor Kate!

She wondered if Daphne and the others knew about this Home Office investigation . . .

When Beau returned, Carissa took his arm.

He laid his hand over hers and gave her a trusty smile. "Come, let's take your new equipage out for a drive," he said lightly, but she saw the worry in his eyes.

The sunshine glittered off its polished brass fittings, and the horses pawed the ground prettily, as though eager to show off their paces, but Carissa pulled her husband closer. "Are you all right?"

"Of course. Why?"

She eyed him dubiously, feeling very protective. "I take it that unpleasant little lizard man is with the investigation."

"He's in charge of it," he admitted with a glum look askance. "Some people should never be given power. They enjoy it far too much."

"I noticed."

"Ah, don't fret, my dear. All will be well. I just have to dance to their tune for a while until they're satisfied."

"If there's anything I can do to help you with him—"

"No."

"Perhaps we could charm him? Invite him to dinner. Expose him to good Society? Make a generous contribution to his next campaign?"

"Er, darling, that's what they call corruption."

"Really?" she exclaimed. "I was only being polite!"

He let out a chuckle and, to her relief, began to relax. "No, it's all right. Don't worry about the 'lizard man.' I've got him well in hand."

"Are you sure? It sounded like he's out for Warrington's blood."

"So, you were eavesdropping again. I should've known. And which of us is the spy here?"

"I couldn't help it! Does Kate know?"

Beau heaved a sigh. "It's not just Warrington they want. The truth is, they're after all of us. It'll be fine," he said, but it didn't sound fine to her. "Territorial squabbles between the Order and various branches of the government have been going on for eons. This is just the latest round."

"Is there anything at all that I can do?"

"Just hold your tongue about it. I mean it, wife," he warned her sternly. "Under no circumstances are you to speak of this with anyone. Not even the other wives. The ladies already have enough to worry about, knowing their men are off on a dangerous mission abroad. The threat was rather severe, which was why we had to spirit them out of London so quickly to stay for a while at one of the Order's secure country estates. It's a beautiful villa, where they are both comfortable and safe, being guarded round the clock by some of our best men. But there is no need to disturb them with all this. Especially now that Lady Falconridge is with child, I don't want her getting a shock."

Carissa nodded soberly, absorbing this.

"I promised Rotherstone and the others that I would look after their ladies. Frankly, I don't want them bothered with any of this until everything's been cleared."

"I understand."

"Good." He lifted her hand and gave it a kiss.

She was silent for a moment, racking her brain for some way she could be of assistance, nonetheless. "Maybe my uncle could help you. I know he'd be willing. He likes you."

"In spite of himself?" Beau flashed a wry smile. "Don't worry, I just have to be patient, answer their questions, and put up with Green a little while longer. I'm sure the Regent will call an end to this nonsense soon. And—when it's over—I'm taking you on a proper honeymoon trip."

"Are you, indeed?"

"Oh, yes. You'd better start thinking about where you want to go. I have to be back for the next round of interrogation in about a week. But it will be nice to escape with you for a few days in the meanwhile."

She leaned against him, rested her head on his shoulder, gazing up at him. "Beau? Who is Mr. Green's mentor?"

"Ah, you heard that, too?"

She nodded.

"While Green was at Cambridge, it seems he was part of a coterie of students devoted to a charismatic don, Professor Blake Culvert. Bit of a firebrand, known as The Prophet. Culvert was already infamous for his Radical screeds, but when he publicly declared his atheism, the university sent him packing. Understandably so," he added with a shrug, "since most of the colleges at Cambridge are supposed to be turning out young clergymen."

She nodded. "Atheism goes against the school policy at Oxford, too, doesn't it?"

"Yes, but Culvert's followers among the students

rioted when their hero was sacked. Not that their disgraced professor has fared too badly since then without his teaching post. Culvert has gone on to write a number of books—outlawed in France, by the way, after what they've been through over there. But I understand his writings and public speeches make him a decent living in England. His occasional arrests on charges of sedition or whatever mischief only seem to help his sales."

She snorted.

"Of all the times he's been arrested, none of the charges against Professor Culvert have ever stuck. He always walks free, but perhaps that has something to do with the fact that so many of his former disciples are now liberally peppered throughout the government."

He said it casually, but Carissa was taken aback as she began to see the scope of what Beau was up against.

"I've heard that Culvert also receives grants and pensions from unnamed wealthy patrons sympathetic to his views. Which is rather disconcerting," he conceded in a sardonic tone. "Who they might be . . ."

"Is Mr. Green one of his patrons?" she murmured.

"No. That would be too dangerous for his political career. Green cut off all ties with his former idol when he went into politics. At least, publicly."

"Ah," she said.

Beau sent her a rueful glance. "I heard that in the election that won Green his seat, his opponent accused him of still sharing Culvert's extreme views. Green disavowed the old man repeatedly and presented himself to the voters as a moderate Whig."

"The people must have believed him."

"Perhaps. He's also very good at the art of slander and character assassination, which is mainly how he defeated his rival, from what I hear. Dirty game, politics."

She absorbed all this with a chill down her spine. "So this horrid little power-crazed bureaucrat that you have to answer to might still be harboring Radical sympathies that he's taking out on the Order?"

Beau sighed. "I have no doubt that is the case."

"My God, doesn't that worry you? He's not even being honest about his real motives!"

He shrugged. "What am I to do?"

"But it's a conflict of interest!"

"It doesn't matter," he said rather vehemently. "He's not going to destroy the Order. Not while I'm there. He can try, but we've been around a hell of a lot longer than these 'modern men of progress' and their shiny new ideas."

"What kinds of ideas?"

"Dissolve the monarchy. Disband the aristocracy. Marriage also is outdated in their circles. Free love is all the mode."

She gave him a sardonic look.

"What?"

"Sounds like what the ton espouses."

"No, no, there is a big difference between the time-honored tradition of adultery in the aristocracy and the Radical notion of free love, my dear. One abuses the sanctity of marriage with idle gallantry; the other rejects it from the outset, along with any notion of chivalry."

"They don't believe in chivalry?" she exclaimed.

"I should think not. They see it as an insult."

"How?"

"In their world, women are the same as men, and neither want nor require any sort of male protection or deference."

Carissa struggled to comprehend such a world. "But

if there's no marriage . . . and ladies are the same as gentlemen . . . then what about the children? And who takes care of the old people? What becomes of the families?"

"Oh, my dear, you are woefully provincial. Haven't you heard? The family is an artificial system of oppression," he replied. "They've got no more use for it than for the Church. Haven't you read the inimitable Godwins, or noticed how poets like Shelley or Blake are always making up their own religions?"

"No one can simply invent right and wrong."

"You can try, if you're arrogant enough. Up is down, right is wrong, women are men, and before you know it, no one needs anyone anymore. Forget civility— the human race will then be free to descend into 'the perpetual war of every man against his neighbor' that Hobbes described two hundred years ago."

"Sounds hellish."

"I know. Yet they think they are building utopia. Bloody do-gooders."

"Lud." Carissa shook her head at his rant, but when the coach rolled to a halt before an elegant terrace, she turned to Beau in surprise. "I thought your mother lives in Lockwood House!"

"Well, that would make it rather awkward when her lovers come to visit, don't you think?"

She winced. "Sorry. I didn't realize it was quite that bad."

He sighed and climbed out of the carriage, then turned back to assist her. "My parents came as close as they could to divorcing without actually going through all the scandal and inconvenience of formal proceedings."

"So, they hate each other now?"

"I don't know," he said wearily. "I always wonder if they could have reconciled their problems years ago if both of them weren't so proud." He avoided her gaze as he shut the carriage door behind her. "If she had tried just going to my father and talking to him, telling him why she was so unhappy, I know he would've listened. He is a reasonable man."

He eyed her meaningfully; Carissa was not sure what sort of hint he was dropping her, or if it was just her guilty imagination.

"If my father ever had the chance to hear her side of the story, if she would've trusted him enough to explain, then who knows how things might have turned out for them? If only she had tried being honest."

He gave her a pensive look, then walked ahead of her to the door.

Carissa's heart was pounding.

Then they went in to see the countess.

Chapter
12

$\mathcal{L}$ady Lockwood's butler opened the door before they reached it, sweeping them into the entrance hall with a polite gesture of welcome. "Congratulations, sir," the butler said to Beau in a hushed tone.

"Thank you, Franklin."

"Lady Beauchamp, if I may, I wish you much joy."

"Thank you so much," she said warmly, blushing a bit.

"Franklin's been an installment here since I was a boy," Beau informed her. "Helps look after the old gel."

"Sir," Franklin chided, fighting a disapproving smile. "May I take your coat, my lady?"

"Perhaps you'd better not," Beau interrupted in a low tone. "Let's not settle in until we see what sort of reception we are going to get."

Franklin gave the viscount a subtle nod. "If you'll wait here, sir, I'll go and see if she'll receive you."

"Here's hoping," he mumbled.

Franklin bowed, then ascended the stairs to inform Her Ladyship they had arrived. Beau put his hands in his pockets and paced across the entrance hall as they waited. Carissa checked her reflection in the pier glass. She turned to him. "Do I look all right?"

"You are always beautiful," he said. "But you should've worn the hat I gave you."

She grinned.

Franklin returned with a look of relief. "Her Ladyship will see you now."

"Huzzah," Beau said under his breath.

Carissa shot him a look as they climbed the curving staircase, trailing Lady Lockwood's stately butler.

When they reached the drawing room, Carissa hung back a little, letting him go first. Beau swept off his hat with a gallant air as he breezed into his mother's drawing room. "Good morning, Barbara!"

The beautiful blond woman sitting by the fireplace did not smile back. "Well, if it isn't my traitorous son."

"Pleasure to see you, too," he said brightly. "I've brought someone to meet you."

"By all means." As the bristling countess stared at her, Carissa searched her brain for every lesson Aunt Jo had taught her about standing up for herself before the haughty denizens of Society.

Though her knees felt like rubber, somehow she kept her face serene, reminding herself she had every right to marry Beauchamp. It was not *she* who had sought the match, after all. He was the one who had insisted.

"Mother," Beau introduced her softly, "this is my wife, Carissa."

Carissa gave her new mother-in-law a most respectful curtsy. "My lady." Having made this show of deference, she cautiously lifted her gaze.

The countess rose slowly from her chair. Heart pounding, Carissa felt like she was watching some sort of glacier-dwelling dragon rising to devour her. At that moment, it was easy to envision the disruption this grand, terrifying lady would have likely brought to their wedding day. On the other hand, she certainly saw where Beauchamp got his looks. "Barbara" was as blond and beautiful as he.

Lady Lockwood regarded them with a haughty lift of her eyebrows. "So, the two of you have come to apologize? You humiliated me in front of Society," she accused her son. "And you let him do it, whoever you are," she added with a frosty glance at her new daughter-in-law.

Taken aback, Carissa glanced at Beau.

"Mother," he chided, a soft edge of warning to his voice. "You know precisely why it had to be this way. You are proving it now, confirming my expectations."

She huffed. "You grow more like your father every day. No consideration for anyone but yourself! I hope you know what you're in for, dear," she said to Carissa. "The Walker men are infamously selfish."

"Please do not abuse my father's name in my hearing, Mother. The fact is, I was not going to let the two of you ruin our wedding day."

"It was a very small affair, Lady Lockwood," Carissa sought to assure her. "We meant no offense. Lord Beauchamp was only trying to be kind to me since I am an orphan. He thought it would pain me if he had his parents there while I did not."

Lady Lockwood took her measure, scanning her from head to toe. "You are the Earl of Denbury's niece?"

"Yes, my lady. My father was the earl's younger brother, the Honorable Benjamin Portland."

She flicked her eyebrows and looked away with a dismissive air. "So, you set your cap at my son, did you?"

"Come, Carissa, we've stayed long enough."

"It's all right," she assured him. He had warned her in advance to be ready for a confrontation. "I'm sure Her Ladyship only wants to make sure I am good enough for her son."

Lady Lockwood seemed surprised by her show of pluck. "Our match *was* unexpected, my lady. It came about quickly, but it wasn't quite as sudden as it seems, for Beau and I were friends before we—became involved. In any case, my aunt Josephine, the Comtesse d'Arras, will be holding a reception for us when she arrives from the Continent. We would be most honored if you would attend."

Lady Lockwood gazed at her for a long moment. "The Comtesse d'Arras? Denbury's sister, yes? Formerly Lady Josephine Portland?"

"Yes, before her marriage long ago. Do you know her, ma'am?"

"We were friends at finishing school."

"Really? She raised me!"

"Did she?"

Carissa nodded enthusiastically. "Aunt Jo had no children of her own. Her husband, a French émigré, was well advanced in years when they married. When my parents died, she took me in and raised me as her own—well, after my grandparents became too old to keep me," she amended.

"How did your parents die?" Beau inquired softly. "I don't think I ever heard."

"They went to Ireland in 1800 to celebrate the Unification with some friends in the Irish aristocracy, but their ship went down on the voyage home."

Beau put his arm around her. "I'm so sorry."

"It's all right." She gave him a wan smile.

"So you stayed with your grandparents first?"

She nodded. "They had me for several years. They were already in their sixties. Within a few years, I became too much of a burden to them. I suppose I was rather noisy and rambunctious."

Beau smiled at her.

"It was decided that I should go and live with my aunt Jo," she resumed. "I stayed with the comtesse until a year and a half ago, when I came to London to live with my uncle, Lord Denbury, and his family. They have girls about my own age, and Aunt Jo wanted to do some traveling once the war had finally ended," she said vaguely. "She was not at the wedding, either, my lady, but she'll be here any day now, and when she arrives, we'll have the big reception, and everyone must come. I do hope you will consider attending—"

"Of course she'll come," Beau said, giving his mother a pointed look.

Her Ladyship said nothing for a moment. "Let me know the date, and I will see if I am free. Your father won't be there?" she asked her son.

"I can't promise you that, but you know he hates coming to Town," Beau said with a shrug.

Shortly after that, they took their leave.

Carissa fairly collapsed in the privacy of their carriage. "Lord, I'm glad that's over!"

"Not a bad first foray. She'll come round, I think. Now you have just one last hurdle." He smiled ruefully at her. "Meeting Father. That won't be anywhere near as hard as this. He'd like you better if you were an animal, of course, but above all, he will be satisfied that I've finally taken a wife."

"So, you're saying he'll see me as a broodmare?"

"Yes, but don't take it personally. All women are broodmares to him."

"No wonder your mother objects."

"True. It takes two sides to make a war." He studied her for a moment. "That was an eye-opening story, hearing about your life." He shook his head. "I never knew you'd gone through so much. Passed around like that from home to home. It must have been difficult."

"Well, it's not as if you had it easy, either. At least my parents loved each other. It must have been hard for you, having your home serve as a battlefield."

"It did rather lead me to conclude that only fools believe in love," he admitted.

"You don't believe that anymore, do you?"

He gazed at her intently, as though waiting for something.

Like an explanation she ought to have volunteered.

"Beau?" she asked, growing nervous.

"I am no expert in these things," he relented, "but it seems to me that love goes hand in hand with trust. Don't you think?"

"Yes . . ."

"Do you think you could ever come to trust me, Carissa?"

She nodded, but her mouth had gone dry.

"Good," he whispered. Then he lifted her hand and gave her knuckles a kiss through her glove, a wistful glow in his eyes.

She looked away, her heart pounding. As the carriage rolled on, she was seized with private dread.

Her doubts whispered: *He knows.*

Chapter
13

*L*ater that day, they arrived at the beautiful Hampshire estate where Beau had grown up, and which would one day belong to them. Thick old trees lined the drive, beyond them, rolling green meadows where the earl's horses frolicked. A lulling tranquility hung over the place as they drove up to a fine old manor house of red brick, ivy growing up the walls.

Carissa glanced at Beau and saw how his face had softened gazing at the place, his muscled frame easing, as though, here, he was able, finally, to leave behind the tension of London and all his mysterious responsibilities.

As she watched him greet his father when the Earl of Lockwood came out to greet them, the bond between the two men was immediately apparent. If the son had been forced to choose sides between his parents as a child, it wasn't hard to guess that he had sided with his sire.

In short order, Beau presented his new bride to the gruff, stoic country lord.

The Earl of Lockwood studied, nay, appraised her, like a filly on auction at Tattersall's, his shrewd, skeptical eyes shadowed under the brim of his tweed cap. He was a brawny fellow in his sixties. If Beau had inherited his golden good looks from his mother, it was clear his sharp mind and steely spine came from his sire.

"I'm happy for you both," he concluded gruffly. A man of few words, he reined in his joy to a terse nod. "Congratulations."

As Lord Lockwood turned away, Beau gave her a discreet wink that told her she had met with the old man's approval.

Then they had to hurry to catch up as Lord Lockwood marched off to show her around the estate; Beau followed, rather astonished by his father's display of toleration for a female.

Carissa was relieved, meanwhile, that her new father-in-law saw no reason to reproach them for not inviting him to the wedding. He scarcely inquired about the day beyond the basic facts. Apparently, his son's reasons were understood without much need for discussion.

He had nothing to say when Beau reported their visit to Lady Lockwood. But the tale of her cold reception toward Carissa seemed to make the man all the more determined to take his new daughter-in-law under his wing. As if to make up for his wife's rudeness, he warmed up considerably as he led them around his estate, explaining to Carissa what each of the many farm buildings were, pointing out his most prized horses among the herds.

When they passed a giant oak tree, he stopped to relate a funny childhood story about his son, explaining in his rumbling tones how Beau had climbed some thirty feet up into its branches, then, couldn't figure out how to get down. "No one could find the lad. He wouldn't call for help—of course. Stubborn pride though he was only about eight years old. Finally, one of the servants spotted him. The whole staff was in a panic. His mother ran around screaming for me to get him down, but the pup wouldn't hear of anyone's helping him. Wanted to climb his way down on his own."

Laughing, she glanced at her husband. "That does sound like him."

Beau smiled and lowered his head, looking slightly sheepish after the story. "Well, I figured I got myself into the scrape, I should jolly well get myself out of it."

"And you did!" His sire slapped him on the back, and they moved on. "And you learned an important lesson. Never rely on anyone but yourself."

The earl's words struck Carissa as she drifted after the men, who now went to admire the flock of pure-bred sheep of some breed or other. How often had she shared those same sentiments. But now, since Beau had come into her life, she knew the loneliness behind those words.

It really was a shame his parents could not find a way to be together . . .

No, I'm not going to meddle, she vowed, though the gossip in her wanted to know specifics about what happened between them, and if the breach could be repaired. But no, she warned herself. Absolutely not.

Beau would throttle her. And as the newest member of their clan, she was in no position to pry or interfere. She thrust the temptation to try to help her new family out of her mind and just smiled, watching the lambs go bouncing through the grass.

There was a peaceful stillness at the estate that soon put her in a lazy mood, especially when they walked to the edge of the earl's fishing pond, which was fed by a babbling brook.

She sighed and leaned against a tree, watching the stream flow, like she used to watch the ocean waves tumble on the beach back when she lived at Brighton with Aunt Jo.

Ezra Green and his threats against her husband and the other agents of the Order . . . all her troubles seemed a thousand miles away. Before she knew it, it was time for supper. They returned to the stately house.

"Thank you for the tour," she said, smiling at the earl.

He nodded, and she gave the gentlemen a curtsy before leaving them to enjoy some time as father and son while she went off to dress for dinner.

*W*hen she had gone, Beau glanced at his sire in question, waiting to hear his old man's verdict on his choice of brides. In truth, he braced himself for some caustic remark reflective of his father's general mistrust of the female race. But to his surprise, no criticism came.

His father gave him a nod. "Seems a fine girl. Well done. A good selection. The Denburys always had impeccable bloodlines. She should breed fine sons for the Lockwood line."

"Sons! Good God, Dad, I haven't been married yet forty-eight hours. Let me figure out how to be a husband before I have to learn how to be a father."

The earl laughed. "Bit surprised at your timing, I must say. Rather an odd time to take a wife, with all that's going on."

"Yes, well, it couldn't be helped," Beau admitted.

His father raised an eyebrow. "Already breeding?"

"No! No, she found out about the Order. It's all right, though. I had my eye on her for months before she went snooping into my affairs."

"Snooping?" he asked swiftly. "Sure you can trust her?"

The question pained him though he knew his father only meant in the operational sense.

He nodded. "I'm sure."

"Hmm," Lockwood mumbled, studying him with an all-too-knowing eye. "So, what else?"

"I've had news of Nick and Trevor. They're alive."

The earl stared at him. "Thank God."

"They were delayed on the Continent. Trevor was shot. I haven't seen him yet, but Nick says he's going to be all right. That's all I know for now."

And as much as he dared to share for the time being.

"Well, I am glad to hear it. If there's anything I can do to help, let me know."

"Thanks." He knew his father had been concerned, for his mates had been coming here for holidays and such since they were boys. Especially Nick, who had never had much of a home of his own to return to.

His father sat back in his chair and studied him for a moment. "You do seem happy with her."

He smiled ruefully. "Nonsense, I only did it for you. You've been barking at me to take a wife for years."

"Bah," the earl grumbled, and Beau laughed.

They passed a pleasant dinner, after which, father and son remained at table to have a glass of port.

Carissa retired to the drawing room alone. Waiting

before the fireplace, she stared into the flames and sipped an after-dinner cup of tea until the gentlemen arrived.

At her husband's request, she sat down at the piano-forte and, although the instrument was out of tune, did her best to enliven the atmosphere with a few songs.

Lord Lockwood stared at her almost in perplexity, as though trying to imagine how different his life might have been if he'd ever had a daughter.

At length, it was time to retire for the evening. She thanked their host for the fine meal and the earlier tour of the grounds, then she kissed him on the cheek. "Good night, Lord Lockwood."

"Tut, tut, my girl, it is your right to call me father," he mumbled, startling her with this unexpected mark of favor.

Beau looked surprised to hear it, too. But Carissa accepted his gracious offer and gave his hand an affectionate squeeze. "I will, then. Good night, Father."

It was strange to speak the word. She'd had no occasion to call anyone that in sixteen years. She was truly touched, and when the gruff old lord bowed to her, in turn, she was warmed to think they had already formed a bond.

Then Beau offered her his arm and escorted her up the stairs. The earl watched them go, his hands resting on his hips. "Go get me a grandson," he ordered.

Carissa turned bright red, but Beau laughed. "Believe me, I will do my best!" he shot back.

Soon they were in Beau's private bedchamber. She was still smiling as he helped her undress for bed, kissing her nape like a worldly gallant while unfastening each pearl button down her back.

"Now I see where you get your charm from," she remarked.

"You find my father charming?" he exclaimed.

"Entirely."

"First time anyone's ever accused him of that. Better not let him hear you say so."

"Well, it's true."

"Too bad my mother doesn't share your opinion."

"Well, for what it's worth, I think he's grand."

"He seems to like you, too. And for my part, I couldn't agree with you more. That man has been the rock of my life, truth be told."

"One can see that, watching you together." She stepped out of her satin dinner gown and turned to him. She held his gaze thoughtfully for a moment, pondering that, then went up on her tiptoes to give him a kiss.

He returned it. "What was that for?"

"Do I need a reason?" she asked with a flirtatious smile.

"No, indeed."

When she went to hang up her gown, she could feel his smoldering gaze following her. She soon returned to him and helped him to remove his coat.

"Sorry we left you alone like that after supper," he murmured. "My father is pretty well set in his ways. The evening glass of port is de rigueur."

"I can still taste it on you," she whispered, stealing another kiss from his too-tempting lips. She began unbuttoning his waistcoat in rising desire.

"Father and I will be going out riding early tomorrow morning, just so you know where I'll be."

"Not too early, I hope. For I confess, I've got plans to keep you up late tonight." She held his gaze with a playfully seductive look as she backed toward his bed.

He watched her in fascination.

Climbing into the bed, she pulled the covers back invitingly. When she patted the mattress, Beau came over and sat on the edge of the bed beside her. He wore his usual faint smile, but his pale eyes seemed wistful.

She cupped his cheek in concern. "What is it, darling?"

He covered her hand with his own against his cheek, gazing soulfully into her eyes. "There's something I—" he started, then stopped himself.

Carissa had frozen. She stared at him, wide-eyed. Her whole body had tensed; she felt the blood drain from her face. *Oh, God, here it comes.* "Yes?" she forced out, praying she was wrong, that it was just her guilty conscience.

He gazed wistfully at her for a long moment. Perhaps he saw the dread written on her face, for his veiled expression softened. He cupped her cheek, staring into her eyes. "Never mind," he whispered with a tender little smile. "It's nothing."

"A-are you sure?"

"Yes. Your beauty robs me of my wits. I've completely forgotten what I was going to say. Kiss me," he breathed.

She did, trembling with that near miss as much as with desire for him. She slid her arms around him, hating herself for her deception but vowing that even if she could not give him honesty, at least she could give him this. She was desperate to show him that, whatever she might be lacking in forthrightness, her devotion to him was sincere.

He slipped his hand beneath her hair, his fingers warm and sure. She heard his breath catch as his silken lips parted hers, deepening the kiss.

Her heart pounded with the sense of risk, the closer

she got to him. But the danger was not enough to make her stay away. She caught the lapels of his unbuttoned waistcoat in her fists and drew him closer, helplessly. His clever tongue gliding with hers, his grip on the back of her neck tightened with passion.

In moments, desire of blinding intensity engulfed them both like brilliant, colored flames. No words were needed to acknowledge what they both craved. Her hands shook with her hurry to finish undressing him.

While he caressed her thigh, she pulled his loose white shirt free from the top of his dark trousers and slid her hand up underneath the billow of fabric. She groaned at the beauty of his sculpted abdomen, eagerly running her hand up his heaving chest, reveling in the feel of hot, velveteen skin over iron-hard muscle.

Never in her wildest dreams would she have believed that a man like him could ever belong to her. But he did.

This titled Adonis adored by half the women in the ton was hers to love. The truth glowed in his smoldering blue eyes. It was carved into every chiseled plane and angle of his unforgettable face as he stared at her, hair tousled, blue eyes stormy with desire as he pressed her down slowly onto her back.

She closed her eyes as he moved atop her, his smooth caresses possessively claiming every inch of her. She clung to him, his wolfish panting filling her senses while the moist heat of his mouth adored the tender flesh beneath her earlobe.

"Oh, God, I want you, Beauchamp," she ground out.

He raked his fingers through her tresses before coming up for air from his sport at her neck. A wicked half smile curved one corner of his lovely mouth when she grasped his engorged member and felt it throbbing in her hand.

He watched her, smoky-eyed, visibly pleased as she hurried to unbutton the placket. The trembling of her hands slowed her task, but he waited patiently. Her heart pounded with anticipation.

When she had fully freed him from his trousers, she began stroking his rigid member in her grasp. Beau let out a throaty growl of pleasure and closed his eyes. "You do know just how to touch me." He enjoyed her attentions for a moment longer, skimming a deft hand up her thigh and using the caress to lift the hem of her chemise.

Then he returned the favor, pleasuring her. She was quickly rendered breathless; fevered; aching with desire; undulating with his every skillful stroke while he nuzzled her cheekbone, kissed the edge of her eyebrow, and flicked the corner of her lips with the tip of his tongue.

Dying for him, she turned her face to capture his mouth full on, winding her arms around him. He filled her mouth with his tongue, kissing her with equal desperation; with a smooth motion, he eased atop her. His eyes glittering with need, he guided himself to the dewy threshold of her passage.

She stroked his golden hair and bit her lip with needy impatience, closing her eyes, longing for his taking. She could have wept with relief as he penetrated her. With a soft groan, she took him in her arms and wrapped her legs around him. "Yes . . . please."

"Is this what you need?" he taunted in a whisper, pressing into her more deeply.

"You know it is." She raked her fingers down his smooth, strong back. She whimpered with searing pleasure as he began to rock her. God, she was putty in his hands.

"That's right," he whispered, "give it all to me. I love feeling you melt beneath me, just like this." He gripped her hair and tugged her head back, kissing her throat, pumping harder, faster, more insistently.

She was sure she had died and gone to some lewd heaven. She dropped her arms to the pillow above her head and simply let him ravish her.

Aye, with a dreamy smile, she welcomed it.

Beau linked his fingers through hers and brought her to climax, joining her in a shattering explosion of blissful abandon. The world had disappeared beyond their marriage bed, but as he held her in the spent, panting silence afterward, she felt closer to him than ever, despite the secrets between them.

Indeed, there was no going back now. She looked into the eyes of her wonderful husband and let out a weak, exhausted laugh, half a purr of pleasure.

Slightly sweaty, he gave her a kiss on the cheek.

Her heart was still pounding as she hugged him, but in her heart, she realized that, having started down this path of deception, she was going to have to be careful not to veer off it inadvertently in the future.

She'd have to make sure to keep her story straight because there was no way, she vowed, that she could ever bear to lose him now. She kissed his square chin and glowed as he petted her hair, gazing into her eyes.

"I think I'm falling for you, wife," he whispered.

"And I you, husband," she breathed. Another little lie, for the fact was, she was over the moon for the scoundrel. *God, I've never had a chance like this before, that somebody might really love me. Please never let him learn the truth that could take him away from me.*

In for a penny, in for a pound.

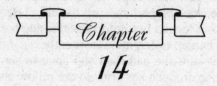

Chapter
14

They returned to London to find that their hasty marriage had become the talk of the town.

Fortunately, the worldly Aunt Jo was back and ready for the gossips. The glamorous comtesse had arrived while they had been out in the country. With her own peculiar magic, she had in the blink of an eye arranged their reception despite having been away from England for a year.

By some additional miracle, Carissa had even succeeded in coaxing her father-in-law to come to Town for the party, and now the grand night of the soiree had arrived.

All throughout Aunt Jo's elegant house near Hyde Park, the candles glittered. The chandeliers cast a dancing light over the jeweled guests, who continued arriving in waves.

Carissa was sure they had come more to see the long-absent Comtesse d'Arras than to celebrate the union of the new Lord and Lady Beauchamp. But, determined to be seen as a credit to her new husband, she presented herself as the future Countess of Lockwood with every ounce of beauty and refinement that she and her aunt's savvy French lady's maid could conjure in her appearance.

Beau, of course, was effortlessly gorgeous, but Carissa's intricate coiffeur alone had taken over an hour to create. She wore a rich, apricot-colored gown that flattered her complexion. A topaz necklace set in gold glittered round her neck.

The ton's arbiters of fashion, who had never really noticed her before, looked her over with their haughty glances and nodded in approval.

Meanwhile, the house resounded with the music of the chamber players, the clinking of wineglasses and fine china as an array of delicacies were served.

Most of all, the rooms buzzed with conversation. For once, Carissa didn't have the heart to eavesdrop on what the gossips had to say. Aunt Jo had firmly insisted that all the worst scandalmongers must be invited and treated with especial honor. Otherwise, there was no telling what unpleasant twists the tale of her marriage would take when they shared it with the ton.

While she kept a serene smile on her face and struggled not to fidget under the inspection of several Almack's Patronesses, her glamorous aunt was a force to be reckoned with.

Knowing that Carissa desperately preferred the role of observer to being scrutinized as the center of attention, Aunt Jo distracted her guests, entertaining all with amusing anecdotes about her life in Paris.

With her vibrant red hair, sparkling blue eyes, and carefully tended complexion, the comtesse enchanted them with her beauty and a lilting monologue about her travels on the Continent.

Elsewhere in the party, Beau also saw the need to lay to rest any idle talk about the cause of their hasty marriage. He unleashed the full force of his charm on the crowd of guests, radiating his own, particular golden glow, like a veritable sun god leaning nonchalantly in the doorway of the drawing room, where he could talk to everyone at once.

Of course, some of the ladies looked daggers at Carissa, but Aunt Jo had said they must be invited. Then they would see with their own eyes that their former rakehell playmate was in love and legally attached.

Their pouts only grew when they heard about all the lavish gifts the romantic bridegroom had showered upon his chosen lady at their small, private wedding.

They had jolly well better get it into their heads that any future dalliance with her husband was naught but a pipe dream, Carissa thought. In truth, she did not like seeing ladies he had shared a bed with here tonight, but since she would not be able to avoid running into them in Society in the future, she supposed she might as well offer the olive branch first, as Aunt Jo had wisely counseled.

She greeted them with dignity in the receiving line, offering her hand and accepting their felicitations while Beau stood by her side.

Across the room, meanwhile, Lord and Lady Lockwood coolly acknowledged each other and attempted to engage in conversation.

"Rather reminds me of the Congress of Vienna," Beau whispered in her ear, watching their tense negotiations over the quality of recent weather.

Real progress was reached when both parties agreed they had seen fine, clear skies for the past week.

Beau and Carissa exchanged a glance; likewise, his parents watched the newlyweds, in turn, and looked wistfully at each other.

Aunt Jo and Uncle Denbury had also resolved their quarrel now that their ruined niece had by some miracle been safely married off, indeed, had made a brilliant catch. At last, with the party under way and everything running smoothly, Carissa took a few minutes alone with their hostess of the evening.

"This was so thoughtful of you, my dear Aunt. They all seem to be enjoying themselves," she ventured, glancing around the drawing room.

"Of course, darling! I told you, just leave everything to me." She put her arm around her with a soft, merry laugh.

"We both appreciate it."

"Not at all. I only wish I'd been here for the wedding."

Carissa offered her a regretful smile.

"As for your new husband, he is just the most adorable thing I've ever seen! I can see why some of these ladies look so sad. Their fun is over. You'll have to watch him," she added in blithe cynicism. "Walk with me, darling," her aunt murmured. "I'm afraid there's something I have to tell you."

She frowned and joined her aunt out on the terrace.

"What is it? Is something wrong?" Carissa asked in concern.

When they had cleared all the guests, Aunt Jo turned to her, standing at the railing. She glanced around, then answered in a low tone. "I spotted Roger Benton in

Paris. I did not speak to him, but he looked even more dissipated than before. Apparently, the poet's finding inspiration these days in the opium dens."

"Oh," Carissa murmured, shocked by the unexpected subject.

"I'm sorry to bring it up like this, but I'm worried."

"Why?" she whispered.

"From what I hear, he's out of money." Aunt Jo searched her eyes grimly. "If word reaches him that you've married a wealthy future earl, I would not put it past him to try to come back to the trough for another payment."

Carissa drew in her breath, her heart pounding. She lifted her hand to her lips, her stomach suddenly churning.

"You haven't told Beauchamp, have you?"

"No," she whispered.

"Good. It is not worth jeopardizing the happiness you've found with him. He obviously adores you."

"Do you really think Mr. Benton would come back for another round of extortion?"

"He's done it once, and with opium addling his wits, making him even more desperate, what does he have to lose?"

"But Uncle told him never to come back to England!" she whispered.

"I know. But that was always the danger of keeping this secret, darling." Aunt Jo shook her head with worry. "It puts us in constant danger of blackmail. But you're not in this alone. You've finally got a real chance at happiness in this world, and after all you've been through, my sweet girl—" She cupped Carissa's cheek with a gloved hand, "I'm not going to let him or anyone else ruin this for you."

She hugged her aunt all of a sudden. "What shall I do?" she breathed in terror.

"Now, darling, there, there." Aunt Jo held her in a motherly embrace for a moment, then took her by her shoulders and gave her a firm look. "It's very simple. If Mr. Benton attempts to contact you again, I want you to get in touch with me immediately. I will help you."

"How?" she asked anxiously.

Aunt Jo shrugged. "We'll simply pay him off again."

"Maybe I should just tell my husband."

"And risk his hating you? You can't trust the male ego, darling. Do you think just because he's had other lovers in the past that he'll see it that way for you? Of course not. Men are complete hypocrites, my darling. They hold themselves to one standard, but for females, it's another set of rules entirely. It's easier just to play the game and spare yourself the heartache. There is a good chance he will never forgive you. If you want my advice, a smart woman knows when to keep her mouth shut.

"But h-he's different. He's not like that."

"You said that about Roger Benton once."

Carissa dropped her gaze, shaken by the news, but after a moment's consideration, she knew that her aunt was right. There was no point in risking the relationship after she had already got away with her deception.

If Roger Benton came back for more money, why, she'd take one of her husband's pistols and shoot him, claim some stranger had tried to break into the house.

To be sure, that would be one way to get rid of the looming black cloud of extortion that threatened to follow her around for the rest of her life.

Well, she conceded after a moment, maybe that was

naught but a fantasy of revenge, but still, she resolved to handle the problem herself, with Aunt Jo's help.

There was no need to burden Beau with this when he already had so many other important things to worry about.

"Are you going to be all right?" Aunt Jo murmured.

Carissa took a deep breath and nodded, squaring her shoulders. "So be it."

Aunt Jo gave her a bolstering look, hooked a hand through her arm, and together they walked back into the party.

"Ah, there she is! I was just looking for my bride." Beau came striding toward them.

Carissa managed a relatively guileless smile. "I was just having a private chat with my favorite aunt."

They exchanged a glance.

"How sweet!" he said warmly. Then he stopped himself. "Are you through—should I go away?"

"No, it's fine. We're done talking," she assured him while Aunt Jo chuckled.

"What did you need, Lord Beauchamp?"

"I think your guests want us to start the dancing now. If the bride is game?" He cocked his head at her with a jaunty look and offered her his white-gloved hand.

Carissa took it and let him lead her to the drawing room that had been cleared for dancing.

Walking by his side through the watching crowd, she felt like she was floating. How had an ordinary girl like her ever managed to snare the likes of him? She couldn't stop staring at him, wretchedly in love. Perhaps guilt was sharpening her emotions, but wound up as tightly as a top, she felt even more enthralled than usual by his every smile, the twinkling of his blue eyes, the glow of the candlelight on his golden hair.

Her prince.

Please don't let me lose him.

Maybe Aunt Jo was right. Nothing was worth risking what they had found. She adored him. *Yes.*

Whatever she had to do.

*T*he honeymoon was over.

Beau could not escape this fact, for when the next day came, he found himself in front of the Select Committee once again. But knowing his little bride was waiting for him at home gave him newfound patience as he sat answering their questions.

The intensity of his feelings for Carissa had exploded exponentially over the past few days. As a result, with the bureaucrats pummeling him with their pointed questions, he was beginning to wonder in the back of his mind if he had done her wrong, dragging her into this life.

He hadn't much choice about the timing of their marriage, but maybe he should've waited until all of this unpleasant business was over. He feared he'd been a little cavalier with her future.

What if Ezra Green succeeded in his witch hunt? Somehow managed to paint the Order as a collection of villains? He did not expect that little lizard man, as Carissa had put it, to best him, but it occurred to him now, rather belatedly, that if all this somehow went to Hell, he'd be taking her down with him. The thought turned his blood to ice.

All the more reason to succeed in his mission and find a way to outmaneuver the insufferable Mr. Green.

In the first hour, Beau addressed the politicians' tedious concerns about various past missions. In the second, he talked about how the Order structured its financials.

After a break, they sat down for the third hour of questioning, and it was then things got more uncomfortable.

With the pressure mounting, having evaded the topic for weeks, he saw that he could no longer dodge Green's questions about where Max and his team had gone.

Beau sat there coolly while the panel was practically screaming at him. If he held out much longer, they might drag him out and lynch him on a lamppost.

"You are duty-bound to tell this chamber where they've gone!"

"It is a sensitive mission. I don't see why you need to know," he said.

"We are not asking you, Lord Beauchamp! If you continue in this vein, there will be consequences!"

"Such as?"

Green swept to his feet. "It is not your place to ask us questions, Lord Beauchamp. Your duty is to answer those which we put to you. Now, tell us where they've gone and why!"

"I don't know!" he retorted.

"You are lying, sir!" Green thundered, his voice echoing in the stark, stone chamber. "We both know that you're holding information!"

Beau stood up as well, fully rising to the challenge. "You're calling me a liar?"

"That is your trade, is it not? Your expertise. You claim you don't know where Lord Rotherstone's team has gone. God's teeth, you can't even tell us where your own men have disappeared to. What good are you? Why are we talking to you in the first place? Did the

Elders purposely assign an incompetent as our liaison? Because you, sir, have done nothing but waste our time! Perhaps you'd fancy a sojourn in the Tower until you remember exactly whom you serve!"

Beau leaned forward, his fingertips resting on the table. "Don't. Threaten. Me."

"Then cooperate. As I was told you would."

He narrowed his eyes, weighing the odds of their actually throwing him in the Tower.

It was rare these days, but it would make a hell of a statement.

Not that the threat really surprised him.

It was where England had traditionally put traitors, after all, and that was the point the panel was trying to make. That the Order had grown too powerful over the centuries—and that power corrupts.

That was the foregone conclusion the self-righteous lead investigator had already made. Now Green was just grasping for any facts that could remotely prove his theory.

Beau saw the time had come to budge, if only a little. There was no way he was going to inform the Inquisition about the possibility of Drake's having turned traitor, let alone the distressing fact of Nick's having hired himself out as a mercenary.

Buying time, he leaned toward his legal counsel, provided by the Order. They conferred in whispers. Beau nodded reluctantly, then sat up straight again.

Green's spiteful stare bored into him expectantly.

Beau lifted his chin. "All I can tell you at this time, Mr. Green, is that Lord Rotherstone's team was dispatched to Germany."

"Lord Beauchamp, you are truly trying the patience

of this chamber." Green heaved a sigh. "To which of the German principalities did they go? You must be more specific."

"Sir, my colleagues are on a very sensitive mission. All will be revealed to the proper authorities once the matter's done. That is how the Order has always worked."

"If you haven't noticed, things have changed, my lord. Now, I'm sure your intentions are the highest," he said with a sneer. "Nevertheless, we must know where they are."

Sorry, Max. Beau suppressed a sigh. "Bavaria."

"Why?"

Beau just looked at him.

"Was it not in pursuit of the man who murdered Virgil Banks?" he persisted.

"No, Mr. Green, the agents only pursued Virgil's killer on grounds of his being the designated heir to Promethean power. The Order has no mandate to pursue private, personal vendettas."

"But Virgil was your handler," he pointed out. "He trained the lot of you since boyhood. The men must have wanted blood."

"Indeed, we all did. Virgil's loss was a blow that all of us still feel to the core. But to lapse into criminality in order to avenge him would go against everything he taught us."

"Very well," Green uttered at length, dragging his hand through his thinning hair as he strove to endure Beau's obstinacy. "Why Bavaria?"

Beau drummed the table with his fingertips for a moment, considering how much he might safely say. At length, he answered slowly and deliberately: "We received intelligence last month about a gathering of the last remaining Promethean leaders, to be held some-where in the Alps."

"But they were supposed to have already been de-stroyed," another committee member exclaimed.

"Was that another lie?" Green prodded.

"A remnant; only the canniest of them survived," Beau said coldly. He stared at them for a moment. "You do not seem to understand how pernicious this conspiracy had become before we carried out the purge just before the battle of Waterloo. The Prometheans were entrenched in the highest echelons of power in nearly every court in Europe. This death cult, for lack of a better word, did not last centuries or grow this powerful by being care-less or advertising who their members were."

"So, you really sent three titled peers of the Realm to finish them off," he drawled.

"Sir?" he demanded, not liking his tone.

"It seems rather reckless. Aren't men of your rank too valuable to waste? Any common foot soldier could have done the job just as well."

"Their rank has nothing to do with it in this case." He shrugged. "They went because they are the best."

"And because it was personal," Green goaded him.

Beau sealed his mouth shut and fought for a moment not to rise to the bait. At length, he said, "If a threat remains, they will put it down. Just as the Order always has—while you slept soundly in your beds."

The panel members exchanged irritated looks.

Then Green glared at him. "When you hear from them, you will notify us. Is that understood? I want to know their findings and to be kept abreast of their progress."

And I want a magic unicorn, he thought, but he merely smiled. "You'll be the first to know."

Chapter
15

$\mathcal{M}$eanwhile, Carissa sat in her splendid carriage as it rumbled along toward a particular bookshop in Russell Square known to be a haunt of Radicals. If the Select Committee was going to investigate her husband, she thought it a fine time to do a little investigating of *them* on his behalf.

What Beau had told her about Ezra Green and his former mentor, the disgraced professor, sounded altogether suspicious. Fortunately for him, he had married an accomplished snoop.

To be sure, her inquiry was taking her as far away from the shallow waters of fashionable ton circles as she'd ever been, into the strange and somewhat topsy-turvy world of London's intellectuals and artists.

As if she hadn't already had enough of poets, she thought dryly. Indeed, the quirky little bookshop a stone's throw from the British Museum must have seemed an odd place to find a viscountess and her maid on a sunny spring day.

Nevertheless, she had contrived to be there, for she had read in the paper that Professor Culvert would be giving a lecture there that afternoon to hawk his latest volume.

As they neared the bookshop, she called to Jamison, her driver, not to stop quite yet but to go a little farther down the street.

If they halted right outside the bookshop, her rather ostentatious carriage, Beau's wedding gift, would be visible through the front window, and she did not wish to draw the notice of all those self-righteous, modern-day Puritans inside.

She knew the type. Of course, they reveled in sin and venality, but in financial matters, they became strangely holier-than-thou. Dilettantes who condemned material possessions, and yet, strangely, always expected others to pay for their bohemian lives—railing against the same aristocratic patrons who kept the duns from their doors.

Carissa shook her head to herself. It was Roger Benton all over again. For the sake of following "truth and beauty," he could justify all manner of lies and ugliness—seduction, blackmail—and yet, he went on blindly writing his nauseating love poems. And wondering why nobody wanted to publish them.

She shuddered with suppressed anger. In reality, that cad did not know the first thing about love. Beau had more poetry in his laughter than Roger Benton had in all his grubby chapbooks.

Gritting her teeth at the thought of her ruiner, she accepted her driver's hand and stepped down from the jewel box of her carriage. With her maid, Margaret, trailing, she walked the short distance to the bookshop.

Heart pounding, she paused to look up at the sign and briefly hoped this wasn't a bad idea. But she was simply being herself—a lady of information—and a loyal wife.

She squared her shoulders and strode in to see all the strange people she and Beau had joked about: the commune folk, the free lovers, the closet revolutionaries. She might have been a little nervous to go among such oddities, but after all, it was only a bookshop.

The lecture had already begun—or rather, the ranting. She entered quietly while an old, white-haired man with a drunkard's red nose and a rumpled tweed coat was tearing into those who'd passed the Corn Laws. She took in the scene with a cautious glance as she proceeded into the shop. A small crowd had collected in the rows of chairs set up near the back, but a few other customers were searching for books to purchase, paying little mind to the speech in progress.

Margaret looked at her in question. The poor maid, like her driver, Jamison, had no idea what they were really doing there. Carissa was unsure if her maid was even literate, but she whispered her permission to have a look around in case she wished to buy any books or magazines for herself.

A clerk approached, eyeing her rather skeptically. "May I help you, madam?" he asked in a low tone.

"Oh, yes!" She flashed an insipid Society smile. "Do you have any Gothic novels?"

He looked down his nose at her, flicking a derisive glance over her fashionable gown, as if to say, *I should have known.* "On that wall, ma'am. The latest from Mrs. Radcliffe just arrived."

Carissa nodded her thanks, shrugged off his cheek, and sauntered toward the shelves containing an array of the Gothic "dreadfuls" that earned such scorn from book clerks round the world, despite the fact these were the books that kept their shops in business. Of course, not even the brisk sales of Gothic novels could compare to the popularity of religious essay collections by leading preachers of the day. But she supposed Professor Culvert and his followers would have mocked those, too.

As she drifted over to the shelves the clerk had pointed out, their location gave her a better view of the lecture in progress.

Professor Culvert was doing nothing to inspire patriotism in English hearts as he almost seemed to praise the Americans for killing three thousand British soldiers back in 1812, in some frontier land called New Orleans.

She pretended to inspect Mrs. Radcliffe's latest spine-tingling tale while she listened to Culvert almost gleefully recounting how England had fumbled that brief war. She could hardly believe her ears. Did he hate his own country? And how could it be, she marveled, that no one in his audience seemed to mind the way his careless talk belittled the sacrifice of the soldiers who had died?

The more she listened, the more distressed she grew to think that one of the so-called Prophet's former disciples held *her* warrior's fate in his hands.

But surely no one took this delusional graybeard seriously, she assured herself. That must be why the Home Office always let him go each time he was arrested. The so-called Prophet was not the sinister villain she had been expecting, but an object of pity, wild-eyed and unhinged, making his stand alone against the world. Poor old fool, he was as mad as the King—whom he no doubt hated, too.

On the other hand, the people who believed him, she mused, maybe they were the dangerous ones.

She let her gaze wander discreetly over the attendees. Disgruntled "Ayes!" came from angry gazetteers with dirty spectacles and ink-stained fingers clenched into fists.

There were half a dozen lost-soul types, tragic *artistes* who looked like they had awoken on the floor of some pub. The only lady in attendance turned out, on second glance, to be a man. Carissa's eyes widened. Why, she had heard of such people, but she had never seen one before.

That she knew of! she amended as she quickly looked away. Beyond these rather more unusual attendees, Culvert's listeners appeared to be from the artisan classes, with a wealthy merchant here and there, judging by his somber dress. There was a Catholic priest, recognizable by his collar, no doubt waiting to hear Culvert's position on the important matter of the Catholic vote. She had heard Uncle Denbury arguing about it sometimes with his colleagues.

A few Dissenters—Quakers, she guessed—in their plain garb ambled in late, but did not sit down, listening skeptically from the back row. They seemed to agree when Professor Culvert expounded on the precept that no man was born better than his fellows. Fair enough. But when he let slip a comment ridiculing God, they shook their heads in offended shock and walked back out.

The priest just frowned, but perhaps decided to forgive seventy times seven.

Deciding she had seen enough, Carissa went to buy the Radcliffe book, but the clerk had hurried over to the author's table to manage the aftermath of the lecture.

The notorious Blake Culvert now sat himself down at the waiting desk to sign copies of his tome for those who wished to buy.

Waiting for the clerk to return, Carissa sauntered closer. She was tempted to go and talk to the old fellow and buy his book herself to better understand the soil from which a noxious flower like Ezra Green might have grown.

But the Radicals crowded round their hero, and soon their questions had him expounding on a hundred new topics.

The man liked to talk.

Standing a little off to the side, she quietly observed, waiting for her turn to buy her "silly Gothic novel." She would throw in a fashion magazine or two just to tweak the haughty little clerk, she thought, but he still paid her no mind at all.

Indeed, it was extraordinary, how she, a young lady of the Quality, a bloody viscountess, seemed to be invisible in this part of Town. The people in the bookshop seemed to have dismissed her on sight as an empty-headed miss because of what she wore. Such enlightened souls!

Impatience overtook her. She was just about to put Mrs. Radcliffe's novel aside and leave when something interesting finally happened. A tall, lanky man with a big nose and the soulful eyes of a kicked dog pushed his way eagerly to the front of Culvert's desk. "Sir!" he greeted him with an air of familiarity.

Professor Culvert actually stopped talking for a

second. At that point, Carissa would not have thought it possible.

He blinked at the man in shock, then quickly lowered his voice and glanced around. "Charles, what are you doing here?"

"Sorry I missed your talk, sir. We had customers who simply wouldn't leave, but Mother finally said I could go."

"Just a moment." Culvert waved off the next man in line with a gesture that asked for a moment's privacy.

All of Carissa's well-honed skills as a snoop went on full alert. The Prophet turned back to the new arrival.

The tall, plain man beamed, seemingly oblivious to the old professor's mysterious ire at the sight of him.

"Congratulations on your new book, sir!"

"Get out of here," Culvert ordered in a hushed tone.

"Oh, it's all right! I only came to tell you my latest scene is almost finished. I hope you'll come down to Southwark and see it!"

"Charles, it was wrong of you to come. You must leave at once. Use the back door. The blasted soldiers they always send to spy on me will be here any moment."

"So?" Charles gave him a knowing smile and lowered his voice. "I have nothing to hide. Do I?"

Nevertheless, he did his idol's bidding, retreating with a dutiful bow.

Hmm. Carissa stared after him, mystified, yet still doing her best to pretend she was minding her own business.

I wonder if I should follow him. But then she shrugged it off. Culvert was the one to watch.

Margaret stared at her when they left a short while later.

"Are you all right?" Carissa inquired.

"Mad, they are!" the maid exclaimed. "What was all that about, milady?"

"I haven't the slightest idea. We should have gone to Hatchard's. Much better service there. Better selection, too."

Beau wasn't home when Carissa returned, and it was just as well, for she wasn't quite sure what to say about her snooping expedition.

Perhaps it would be better not to burden him with this, either. Especially now, poor darling; he'd have spent the whole day in front of the Committee, and would likely need some cheering up by the time he got home.

Telling him where she'd gone would probably not accomplish that. In fact, it would likely have the opposite effect. A savvy married woman learned to choose her battles wisely, after all, and this one wasn't worth it. Why risk a quarrel by confessing to something that had yielded no useful information and would needlessly upset him?

Just forget about it.

Her choice made, she put it out of her mind, along with the small nagging guilt this additional secret created—which was silly, she told herself. Why should she feel guilty when all she was trying to do was help?

Nothing had come of it. So what? She shrugged it off.

Let it go.

In any case, the spring sunshine was so inviting that when she got home, she put on a wide-brimmed straw hat and went out into the garden to relax.

She pulled a chair into the shade and amused herself by happily riffling through a shallow periodical for ladies that she had just bought. With sunlight dappling her skirts and the soft breeze blowing on her cheek, it wasn't long before she closed her eyes and dozed, marveling as she drifted off at how content she had recently become in life.

She was not sure how long she had been resting when she became aware of the sensation of someone watching her.

As soon as enough of her consciousness returned to form a clear thought, she assumed it was her husband.

She had told the servants not to disturb her but to tell Beau where she was as soon as he got home. Expecting him to join her, a dreamy smile curved her lips as a finger trailed down her face.

She slowly dragged her eyelids open. And shot straight up out of her chair.

"You!"

"Relax, Lady Beauchamp. I'm not going to hurt you."

She shrank from him, heart pounding. Sitting there beside her, as calmly as you please, was the black-haired stranger she had seen that night at Covent Garden Theatre.

"Pardon me if I have my doubts," she forced out, sitting up straighter in her chair. "You shot me the last time we met!"

"I wasn't aiming for you, as I wager you are well aware, my lady. Nevertheless, I am heartily sorry for your pains." Beau's "best friend," Nick, gave her a small, ironic bow of contrition.

"What are you doing here?" she demanded, edging back from him in her seat. "What do you want? My husband isn't home."

"My dear Viscountess, you shouldn't tell a man who breaks into your property such a thing. Keep that in mind in future. But, of course, in my case, I already know. It's you I came to talk to."

She eyed him warily. "What for?"

"Well, mainly to offer my congratulations on your marriage. Many a lass has tried and failed where you've succeeded. Do you love him?"

"I beg your pardon!" she exclaimed, turning red.

Dark to Beau's light, Nick flashed a smile that shone like the midsummer moon. "But of course you must. They all do. The question is, does he love you in return?"

"How dare you ask such impertinent questions?"

"Only from brotherly concern. You must tell our lad how disappointed I was not to be invited to the wedding. I'd always thought I'd have stood as his best man."

"So did he, but it seems you were in hiding from the law," she clipped out in reproach. Her gaze flicked down to his leg, where she remembered Nick, too, had been injured that night behind the theatre.

He noticed her glance and gave his thigh a pat. "No worries. I've had worse. I admit, the dashed thing smarted.

"He aimed low; I aimed wide."

"And I nearly got my head blown off!"

"Oh, come, it was an accident! You're fine," he informed her, though a prickly look of guilt passed behind his coal-black eyes. "Very well, I'm sorry! I'll say it again. How many times do you want to hear it? Lord! Women."

Carissa stared at him, thoroughly puzzled by the man.

Though she was certainly nervous sitting here with a man she knew to be a trained assassin and a mercenary, she kept her wits about her and tried to think what would best help Beau.

She knew he wanted to find Nick. Perhaps she could delay him. Draw him into conversation and buy a little time until her husband came home. He should be back shortly from the interrogation. She swallowed hard, shoring up her courage. "You know, Beau thinks that you betrayed him."

Nick heaved a sigh. "Sorry again, but I can't afford to care what Beauchamp thinks. It's not his life, it's mine."

"But he is your best friend, is he not?"

Nick looked away.

"How did he offend you that you'd turn your back on him?"

He rolled his eyes. "I had no choice."

"He hasn't given up on you, you know."

"Of course not. He's Beau. He doesn't give up on anything. Ever."

"You can still resolve this, you know, whatever's wrong. I know he doesn't think you are all bad—Lord Forrester, isn't it?" she ventured, addressing him by his title.

He nodded, verifying his name. "Look, Beau's done nothing wrong, as I told him. I'm the villain here, we're all very clear on that."

"Why did you betray him?"

"Stop asking questions! I have not betrayed anyone!" he retorted, his dark eyes blazing. "I am sorry if they see it that way, but the Order does not own me!"

She lowered her gaze. "Why don't you stay for supper; then you can tell us both what happened and how we can help. I, for one, am very curious to hear how a baron ends up becoming a mercenary."

He raised an eyebrow. "He told you that?"

She shrugged. "Well, I am his wife."

"Which is why I'm here." He eyed her strangely. "You really don't understand what this is right now, do you?"

"Pardon?"

He rolled his eyes. "God, you are naïve. I never thought a rake like him would go for such a dainty little miss, but—never mind. I came because I want you to deliver a message for me to our mutual friend."

"Tell him yourself, he'll be home soon—"

"Would you be quiet and let me finish a sentence?"

"Sir, you will not hush me like a hound dog!"

"Well, stop howling like one, then."

"Nobody's howling. If you want to hear howling, believe me, I can do that—and all the menservants will come running. Is that what you prefer?"

"Lady Beauchamp," he corrected himself with profound politeness. "Will you please tell your husband that I came to see you? Just tell him you and I had a friendly little chat. Tell him I stopped by."

She furrowed her brow. "That's the message?"

He nodded, with a hard look in his eyes.

"Well, that's not a very interesting message, is it?"

"Don't worry," he murmured rather coldly. "He will understand." Lord Forrester rose from his chair and headed for the garden gate.

Carissa stood, casting about for some other way to delay him. "So—you're leaving, then?"

"Quite a gift for the obvious, haven't you?" he tossed out without looking back.

"You're welcome to stay! You don't have to go! Wait, the gate's locked! I can get the key—"

"Don't need it. But that was a nice try to delay me, Lady Beauchamp," he remarked with a sly wink over his shoulder. "Just give him the message." When he slipped out of sight behind a tall, mounded shrubbery, she picked up her skirts and hurried after him.

Blast it, get back here, you annoying man!

She could see why they were friends. They had a lot in common. The swagger, the wit. Aye, she thought, they were both equally maddening. "Lord Forrester! Nick!" she cried, just as he ran a few steps to leap up the side of the brick wall, hooking his hands atop it.

She cursed under her breath as he vaulted over the top and dropped down lightly on the other side. Then he was out of sight, but she heard his running footsteps on the other side of the wall.

Perplexed by his odd visit, she set her hands on her waist. *Well! So, that's that.*

Beau's reaction was sure to be interesting, even if Nick's simple message was not.

Still, the brief visit left her uneasy. It was awfully bold of him to come here, she thought. Then again, she was learning fast that Order agents, even ex–Order agents apparently did not know the meaning of fear.

When Beau got home, she told him right away what had happened, but she was unprepared for his reaction. Which was, in a word, rage.

"*He came here?*" he thundered. "Did he hurt you? I swear to God, if he laid a finger on you—"

"No, I'm fine!" She cowered from him slightly, for she had never seen her easygoing husband act this way before.

"Did he harm you in any way, Carissa?"

"No! He only startled me a little at first. He was amiable enough." She shook her head. "It was the strangest thing! He apologized about the shooting, then congratulated us on our wedding. The main thing he wanted was for me to give you a message."

"What message?" Beau growled.

"It wasn't much," she said with a shrug. "He just wanted me to tell you he was here."

"Did he, indeed," he said in an icy tone. He let out a curse under his breath and walked away in seething fury. "Son of a bitch."

She furrowed her brow, bewildered. "Am I missing something?"

He looked askance at her.

"Tell me!" she insisted.

He scowled. "He was threatening you, Carissa."

"What? No! Surely you are mistaken—"

"No mistake. He did not make his meaning obvious, for he did not want to scare you. I'm glad to see he has at least that much decency left, not to go frightening a woman. No," he said, "the message was for me."

"I don't understand, what does it mean?"

He looked at her grimly. She could see he did not want to tell her.

"Please! If this concerns me somehow—"

"It was a warning," he ground out. "If you really want to know, he was making the point that he can get to you anytime."

Her eyes widened while Beau resumed pacing, nigh shaking with rage.

Oh, dear. She suddenly felt faint. Well, when he put it that way . . . *Gulp.* This was, after all, a man who had already shot her. "You really think he'd try to— kill me?"

"Hard to say. The Nick I know would never harm a woman. I hope to God he's bluffing. But these days, who the hell knows?" He shook his head in brooding fury. "He must be in some damned pile of trouble because he is certainly not acting like himself."

"But w-why would he want to harm me?" she exclaimed, trembling and still shaken by this news. "What did I ever do—?"

"Darling, all you did was marry me. That was your only mistake," he muttered. "This has got nothing to do with you. This is a strike at me. Because I haven't done as he asked and called off my people. In fact, I've put even more pressure on him through watchers and informants since our last little chat. Must have rattled his cage a bit. Still! To come near my wife? I'll have his bloody head for this!"

Beau seemed ready to break the skull off anyone who got too close to him at that moment. The man was literally growling to himself.

"You're scaring me," she mumbled, intimidated by his wrath.

He cast her a baleful glance, then closed his eyes and rubbed his brow, visibly striving for calm. Hands on hips, he took a deep breath and let it out slowly. "I'm sorry." When he opened his eyes again, he had managed to soften his expression. He looked at her with eyes full of regret as he shook his head. "I'm so sorry I wasn't here to protect you. Bloody politicians kept me an hour longer than I thought! But you must know, whatever happens, I will keep you safe. You have my most solemn word on that."

"I know you will, husband." She nodded, approaching him with caution. "And really, no harm done so far. I'm fine."

He drew her into his arms and held her for a moment. She could feel his big body still bristling with fierce, protective rage as he sheltered her in his embrace.

"Normally, I'd send you off at this point to that estate where the other ladies are being guarded round the clock. But Nick's an Order agent. He knows the location of all our safe houses." He kissed her forehead as he brooded on the matter. "No," he murmured at length. "I think right now the safest place for you is next to me. And if he comes near you again, I'm going to blow his head off."

"Shouldn't we seek some answers first? We need to figure out what's going on with him."

"You're right. Information. Vickers!" he suddenly bellowed.

The butler hurried in. "Yes, milord?"

"Ready our things. We're going to France," he clipped out.

"France?" Carissa cried, pulling back from his embrace. "What are you talking about?"

"We're going to get to the bottom of this. I have a few days before I'm due back before the committee. I should have just enough time to get to Paris and back, but we're going to have to move quickly. You're right. We need information. I have no idea what's going on with Nick, but I know someone who will. I need to speak to Madame Angelique."

"Who's that?" she breathed.

"The conniving harpy who corrupted him, I wager. Have your maid pack a bag for you as well. Run along now. There's no time to lose." He nodded toward the staircase, his eyes flinty. "We sail with the tide."

Chapter
16

$\mathcal{H}$ours later, their Channel crossing was under way on a sleek schooner owned by the Order. A fine, strong wind propelled them onward toward the Continent.

Overhead, the black skies were thick with stars, while the moon silvered the rolling waves.

Carissa came abovedeck to find Beau standing at the rails, nose into the wind, in profile to her as he faced the rocking seas, a cool, focused intensity hardening his chiseled features.

The high breeze tossed his hair back from his face and rippled through his long, dark greatcoat. Moonlight gleamed on his black boots and the various weapons strapped to his tall, sculpted body.

He looked formidable and deadly, and yet, still, every inch the gentleman. Gazing at him, she knew he could handle whatever his enemies threw at him.

And she could not believe he was hers.

Feeling her presence, perhaps her desire for him radiating to engulf him, he turned from the sea, and when he saw her, he held out his hand to her to come to him.

Carissa steadied herself. It made her a little nervous to go so close to the edge, but she could not resist.

Venturing out across the slippery, seesawing deck, she joined him at the rails. He gathered her close and put her in front of him so she had a better view of the crashing waves and their plumes of foam.

Keeping his arm around her waist, he let his big, warm body block her a bit from the wind. As he held her, she could feel the restless energy thrumming through him with all that was going on. Her own thoughts were a bit more primal. She leaned her head against him, wondering if it was wrong to want him so much every time they touched.

"Beautiful, isn't it?" he murmured in her ear.

She made a low sound of assent; the continuous swirl of the waves mesmerized her.

"Are you all right after that unpleasantness today?" he whispered at her ear. "I've been worried about you."

"I'm fine," she insisted, caressing his arm to let him know that an Order wife would not be so easily intimidated. "What about you?" She shook her head. "This must be really hard for you. Having a friend turn on you like that."

He fell silent, brooding. Eventually, he shrugged. "At least it's better than thinking they were dead. That was my worst fear before Nick finally showed up that night outside the theatre. But I can tell you one thing. I certainly wasn't expecting something like this."

"Poor man," she said, nestling against him. "You've been carrying so much on your shoulders. And such a hurtful thing, too. A friend whose help you thought you could count on—but he only made your problems worse."

"Yes, well," he whispered ruefully, "I have a new friend now." He kissed her on the cheek.

She smiled, still gazing forward at the passionate, poetic crashings of the water though she was acutely aware of his body against hers.

"You smell good," he remarked as he nestled his face in her blowing hair.

They stood in silence as he pondered his situation a little more. "I guess it's mainly Trevor that I'm worried about. Lord Trevor Montgomery," he explained, "the third man on our team. That's how the Order divides us up, you see. Three-man teams that usually act independently but sometimes coalesce into a larger squad for bigger missions."

"Oh."

"Nick is holding Trevor as his hostage to try to preclude the usual punishment for his defection."

"What's that?"

He paused. "A bullet."

She turned to him and paled. "They'll kill him?" Then she drew in her breath. "They're not going to make you do it, are they? He's your friend!"

He shook his head. "After today, him coming after you like that, I don't think there's any friendship left."

"Don't give up, Beau." Her heart ached for him. She moved closer and hugged him. "Don't write him off yet, especially not because of me. I wasn't even that scared! He seemed like a good enough fellow. There might turn out to be a perfectly good explanation for all this."

"Then why wouldn't he tell me that before?"

"Maybe he's trying to keep you out of it."

He considered this. "When I offered to help him, he did reply that he fights his own battles."

"You see? I wish you didn't have to go through this. But try not to decide too firmly about him until we have the facts. Sometimes, when people do the wrong thing, they have a good reason. Maybe whatever it is with Nick, it's not as bad as it seems."

He rested his jaw against her head. "You're a very sweet person, do you know that? I'm glad I married you."

"As am I!" She smiled at him. He kissed her on the head. "I'm also glad that you let me come with you," she informed him. "I've never been to France before, you know."

"Well, we won't be there long. I'll take you back some other time for a proper holiday, when all of this is over."

"I'd like that." She looked up at him while some crewman called out the hour, eleven, and a few of them made some adjustments to the sails.

The night voyage was risky, but the captain knew the route well; Beau had wanted the cover of darkness for their arrival. The war was over, but after twenty years of blood, the peasants throughout the French countryside were not always quite welcoming, Beau said, to Englishmen traveling alone. Arriving before sunrise would mean fewer eyes to watch and report to whomever on their movements.

"So, where are we going, anyway?"

"You're not going anywhere. You're staying in the carriage."

"Oh, do I have to?"

"Yes, you do, my snooping lady."

"Why?" she protested.

"Three reasons." He tightened his arms around her waist, resting his jaw against her hair. The winds buffeted them both. "It's dangerous. It's full of unsavory characters, and it's not the sort of place that a man wants the mother of his future children exposed to."

His answer left her even more intrigued, but she was sensible enough to accept his firm command on this. "Well, who is this woman you mentioned, then? You can tell me that, can't you?"

"Hmm. Madame Angelique. She's long been a contact of the Order."

Carissa glanced at him in surprise. "Is she a spy, too?"

"Angelique is many things. Mostly a survivor. When the French Revolution broke out, she was the toast of the demimonde. The sixteen-year-old mistress of some duke who went to the guillotine. But she somehow survived the Red Terror. Must've charmed the right men as the winds shifted. Now she owns a grand casino on the outskirts of Paris, part brothel, part gaming hell. She's grown rich and quite powerful, in an underworld sort of way."

"What do you mean?"

"She can get you anything you'd want to buy."

"Indeed?"

"She deals in everything from secrets to weapons to, er, various types of pleasure for sale. She's a sort of banker, too, for loans that need to be kept off the books. Conniving harpy," he growled. "I'd wager anything it was she who helped Nick hatch this brainchild of hiring out his skills as a mercenary. He's already had particular dealings with her in the past."

"What sort of dealings?"

"I'm not sure you want to know. Well, it's not the sort of thing a man discusses with his wife!"

"Well, now!" She turned to him with a mischievous grin. "If the wife happens to be a lady of information, then the husband would be cruel to keep it from her."

"You are too much," he muttered.

"Tell me," she commanded with an arch look.

"Very well." He cleared his throat a bit in reluctance. "As far as I know, Angelique took a bit of a fancy to Nick. She . . . likes Order agents."

"Oh, really?"

"So she let him work off the gaming debts he ran up in her establishment in a fairly simple way."

Carissa's eyebrows lifted. "You don't mean—?"

"Yes, I do," he answered dryly.

"So, the former harlot can now afford to play the wealthy customer?"

"Just so."

"My goodness." She pondered this for a moment. "Poor Nick."

"Oh, I don't think he minded too much," Beau replied.

"I see. So you're saying she's quite beautiful, this Angelique?"

"Not as beautiful as you," he breathed as his warm lips skimmed along the side of her neck. "Speaking of which, we have some time to waste. Come down to the cabin with me."

Enthralled by his whisper, she sent him a coy look from the corner of her eyes.

He took her hand and led her away from the rails, a sensuous invitation in his eyes.

She followed all too eagerly.

*B*y the time they left the boat, Carissa was blissfully worn-out by her husband's ardor. That man, plain and simple, was a stud, she thought, and a nigh-insatiable one, at that.

It was impossible in such a state to be the slightest bit worried about anything they faced. She was thoroughly content, staring at the dynamo she had married as the sailors rowed them ashore, where a few armed men from the Order's safe house in the port city of Calais were waiting with a carriage.

Almost immediately, they were under way again, heading for the mysterious Madame Angelique's establishment.

The roads were not as smooth in France as they were in England because of damage from the war. But despite the bumpy ride, she slept like a babe in the carriage, leaning on the man who had pleasured her so deeply on the ship.

As the horses trotted on through the night, Beau held her, brooding in his own thoughts. She was not sure how much time had passed when he caressed her head to wake her and told her they had arrived.

Sitting up, she was still rather groggy as she looked out the window. Burning flambeaux lined the long drive up to an ancient, towered chateau surrounded by wrought-iron fences and a densely wooded park. The grand gambling hell and bordello had a palpable air of decadence and decay.

"Egads, is this the sort of place your missions often take you?" she asked in a dubious murmur, staring at the building.

"Sometimes." Beau was giving his weapons a final check. Pistols under his coat. A dagger in his boot.

"You'd be surprised at the information you can pick up."

"And the diseases, I daresay."

"You stay out of sight. I won't be long. If there's trouble, do whatever my men tell you."

She nodded. "I will. Be careful, darling."

"No worries." He sent her a little salute with a rakish twinkle in his eyes after what they'd shared, then he headed into the chateau.

Chapter
17

$\mathcal{W}$hen Beau entered the casino, the place was as loud, smoky, and profane as he recalled. He noted with surprise how he privately recoiled. It wasn't so long ago that he didn't even notice, let alone react to the dissipation he saw on every side.

The tables were thronged with well-dressed people throwing their lives away on another roll of the dice. The vingt-et-un dealer shuffled the cards, while the roulette wheel spun. Ladies of the night tempted winners and losers alike with their wares. A sumptuous banquet was on offer in the dining room, where a fountain spouted champagne.

He moved on in search of the establishment's proprietress, passing a dimly lit parlor where a stage had been set up for tawdry theatricals. The whores, male and female, were making a display of exotic pursuits that involved leather bindings and the dripping of hot wax.

Well, Madame Angelique had not survived the Red Terror by being squeamish, he thought, but she was a lady of information on a level that Carissa could never have dreamed of. The Order had often turned to the wily French businesswoman for intelligence. News crossed her premises from every corner of Europe. Of course, only a fool would trust her overmuch, for although her information usually proved reliable, she was perfectly frank about the fact that her only principle in life was cold self-interest.

He spotted her from across the smoky card room in the back: jewels in her dark, upswept hair, her lips painted scarlet. She wore a tight black gown that plunged both in front and back, showing off a body that made it hard to believe she was a little over forty. But Angelique had survived the end of the world as she knew it on her powers of seduction, and so, understandably, had worked hard to preserve them.

Lifting a champagne flute to her lips as she held court, she saw him coming from the corner of her eye.

Beau saw her pause and blanch ever so slightly at the sight of him, and he instantly feared the situation with Nick must be worse than he had thought. For aside from the guillotine, nothing rattled Angelique.

She had masked her momentary lapse of sangfroid by the time he bowed over her offered hand. Jeweled rings winked on her fingers, encased in black satin elbow gloves. "My dear Sebastian," she greeted him.

"*Ma belle enchanteresse,* always a pleasure," he replied, dutifully kissing her on both cheeks.

"Whatever brings you to my humble establishment?"

"Concern for a friend," he countered softly. "We need to talk."

Her wary eyes narrowed. She gave her underlings a
curt command, then turned to him again. "Very well,"
she murmured. "Follow me."

She rose from her chair. Beau tracked her to an intimate alcove hung with red velvet curtains that stank of
cigar smoke. With a gesture, Madame caused a nearly
naked girl to bring him a brandy.

"*Merci, petite.*" Beau took the cup and raised it to his
hostess. "*À votre santé.*" He took a sip to show his trust.
"Excellent."

She gave him a cool smile. "Only the best will do for
my particular friends."

"I expect you know why I'm here."

"I wouldn't dare presume."

He smiled at her. "What have you done to Nick?"

She lowered her gaze, drumming her jeweled fingers
on the table between them for a moment. "It is unwise
to meddle in a friend's affairs, *mon cher.* Someone
could get hurt."

"So, it *was* you who put him up to this."

Her dark eyes flickered, but she must have realized
there was no point in trying to fool him. She shrugged.

"I have no shortage of enemies, and our Nicholas is
so talented in so many ways." The treacherous beauty
flashed a knowing smile.

Beau stared at her. "If he was in debt to you again,
wasn't it enough to let him work it off in your bed, like
before?"

She laughed gaily, but there was a hard note in it.
"You know I have a weakness for you boys. I admit
it. And he is a fierce lover, to be sure. Even when his
heart's not in it," she added cynically. "He doesn't even
mind being restrained, which I recall *you* wouldn't let
me do . . ."

Beau gave her an uncomfortable smile. Another reason why he had told Carissa to wait in the carriage.

He'd give her one thing, though. The harlot knew her trade.

"Nevertheless," she continued, "I have always put business before pleasure. *Cher* Nicholas owes me a great deal of money, I'm afraid. So, I thought we'd try something new."

"So, you decided to get into the mercenary trade?"

"I didn't mean to. But about six months ago, I received some very annoying death threats." She shrugged. "I let Nicholas handle my enemies for me, and he was so efficient at this, that I realized this could be a lucrative new venture for us both. You know I've done guns and artillery for years," she said as she lifted her drink to her lips. She knocked back a swallow and said, "In the past, I've always offered the product. Never the service. It dawned on me—opportunist that I am—that starting with Nick, I could open a whole stable of bad boys willing to work for gold. I have the contacts. I get him work and take my cut as agent—just like I do with my girls. He does the rest, and everyone's happy."

Beau gazed at her while she tossed back a shot of brandy. "You're a hell of a woman, Angelique."

She gave him a coy little nod as a thank-you.

"So, has it been as profitable as you had hoped?"

"Eh, new enterprises are always slow to start. One must be patient. Fortunately, it's a dangerous world out there. Plenty of people need our help. But I have to be choosy about my men. Nick is rock solid, of course. I have yet to find his equal."

"Don't expect you will."

She shrugged. "If they've got the inborn talent, the killer instinct, he can train them. He hasn't much time for that, though. He's just one man, but he's been going at a steady clip since we started a few months ago."

Beau shook his head. "You know this is unacceptable to the Order."

"Nick has quit the Order, Beauchamp."

"It's not as simple as that," he whispered. "He's in over his head. Do you understand the position in which you've put me, and him? He's in England to kill someone. I can't let that happen. I need to know about his current contract."

"You need to mind your own business, darling. This does not concern you. I've already told you more than I should. But you Order men . . . I am powerless to do aught but indulge you."

"Listen to me." Beau leaned closer. "Virgil has been murdered—"

"Yes, I heard. And I am sorry about that. I know how much he meant to all of you."

He paused, waiting for a cluster of people to pass by. "What you don't know is that his death brought unwanted attention to the Order from within the British government," he informed her in a low tone. "We now find ourselves under investigation by the Home Office." He paused, barely able to believe the reality of it, himself, as he spoke. "They're trying to paint us as dangerous, lawless, seditious. Exactly the way Nick is acting."

She stared at him in shock.

It was the first time Beau had ever seen her look surprised. "Absurd!"

"I know. But it's the truth. I told Nick what was happening—he confronted me in London to tell me to stay out of his way," he explained. "When I told him about the investigation, he just shrugged it off. His personal disloyalty to me aside, I am telling you, with this investigation going on, he cannot come into our country and carry out this mission and hope to escape the officials' notice. He's going to get caught, and when they find an Order agent behind the hit, that's all the excuse they'll need for them to hang us all. You've got to stop him. Call it off."

She studied him for a moment. "This investigation," she murmured. "Are *they* behind it?"

The Prometheans.

Not even the powerful Madame Angelique dared to speak the sinister name in her own establishment.

"Not that I have been able to learn," he answered in a lower tone, glancing around. "There is some great gathering of them in Germany right now. Haven't heard a peep from the lot of them in weeks."

"Nor have I." She nodded a greeting to some newly arriving guests but did not summon them over.

"I trust you understand now why you must call off the hit."

She stared at him uneasily. "I would if I could, Beauchamp. But I can't."

"Don't play games with me, of course you can! You must. If it's a question of money—"

"It's not. I have no way of stopping him," she murmured. "I don't know where he is. He wanted it that way. He knows his business better than I do, so I agreed." She folded her arms across her chest with a defensive shrug. "For security's sake, he said we'd cease all contact until the job was done. He'll be back when it's finished for the other half of his pay. Until then"— she shook her head ominously—"I have no godly way of reaching him."

Beau cursed under his breath, unsure if he should believe her. "Then tell me who's the target." Maybe he could come at this from the other end—protect the intended victim, if he could not stop the assassin.

"That's not yet been revealed," she replied. "The client told me to send my man to London, where he would receive further instructions. So I did."

"You're telling me he agreed to do this sight unseen?"

"What should he care? You know as well as I do it is not uncommon for information to be doled out only as needed," she answered, bristling. "Besides, it was more money than either Nick or I cared to turn down."

He raised a brow.

"Eight thousand. Half up front, half when it's finished."

He absorbed this. "That *is* a lot of money."

Damn. This was all sounding worse than he had expected. Beau took another swallow of brandy. His mouth had gone dry with a veritable foretaste of doom. "Well, if you don't know who the target is, what can you tell me about the client?"

She gave him a wicked half smile and countered, "What can you do for me?"

He heaved a sigh. "What do you want?"

"I have some time tonight. It's been a while."

"No, *chérie,*" he said, startled.

"You turn me down?" she exclaimed.

"I'm married."

"No—!"

"Yes."

"No, you're not!" she cried, amazed.

"Yes, I am," he answered, nodding. "That was Nick's mistake, you see. He threatened my wife to try to stop me from coming after him. With that, he went too far. That's why I'm here."

"Threatened your wife!" she echoed. "Well! My first

hired mercenary certainly has a strong commitment to his mission. I'm so pleased."

"It's nice that you can joke about it," he said coldly.

She shook her head at him. "I can't believe you're married." Then she laughed. "So, who is she?" she demanded, and it was about then that one of her hired bullies came over and murmured something in her ear.

Angelique turned to Beau with a look of astonishment. "You brought her here? He says you've got a woman in your carriage. Well, don't be a boor, bring her in!"

"Angelique, leave her out of this—"

"I said bring her in," she snarled. "I want to see her. I must see what sort of woman it takes to land an Order agent for a husband, of all things."

"She's not coming in here. She's a lady!"

"Oh, and what am I?"

"You know what I mean. She is an innocent."

"Really?" Her eyes flickered with bitterness at that word, but she smiled. "Then I truly must meet her. I have never seen one of those!" She turned to her hireling. "Bring Lady Beauchamp in. Through the side door," she added. "Avoid going past the theatre. She is an innocent, after all," she mocked him.

"Fine," Beau muttered, realizing he wasn't going to get anywhere by offending the fierce woman. He still needed answers, and besides, he thought, Carissa could handle it. "I have men guarding her. Tell them I approved it," he instructed her servant.

When the large fellow lumbered off to summon Carissa, Beau looked imploringly at Angelique. "Don't speak of things that would be inappropriate for her. Please. I know life is unfair, but let someone be sheltered in a way you never were."

"You mean you don't want me to tell her how we soaked my bed with our sweat that night?"

He looked away.

"Ah, well," Angelique said at last in a philosophical tone. "I guess I won't be having fun with you anymore. Not for a few years, until you're bored, anyway. Then you'll be back."

Don't hold your breath.

"At least there's still Nick. And how is Warrington? Tell him to come see me. It's rare to find a man who can really put me in my place," she added with a wicked smile.

"I'm afraid he's married, too."

A string of indignant French curses poured from her lips at this shocking news. By the time Carissa was escorted in, staring all around her with eyes as round as saucers, Angelique was in a full French pique.

Beau stood, beckoning his wife over to the alcove.

She looked at him in confusion, paused for a second to stare at Madame Angelique, then warily approached.

"Lady Beauchamp, join us. Congratulations on your marriage. I am so happy for the both of you," Angelique said in a tone as cold and tart as an after-dinner *sorbet*.

As Carissa sat down beside him, she greeted Angelique in fluent French, telling her how pleased she was to meet a respected colleague of her husband's.

Her smooth response took Beau aback and seemed to mollify their annoyed hostess. Egads, the little Society lady must have taken the haughty madame's measure in a glance.

Intrigued by her cool response, Angelique saw fit to interview her. "So! You have married Beauchamp. How ever did you do it?"

"I honestly don't know. He just fell in with me," she

said with an idle shrug. "It's far more impressive what you've built here—with no man to help you! Incroyable."

When Angelique saw that Lady Beauchamp was not an insipid aristocratic miss, after all, and would not be intimidated, but instead, played the polite game move for move with her, she lost interest in her sport.

She gave Beau a begrudging nod of approval and finally divulged the information for which he had allowed his wife to be dragged into this decadent den of iniquity.

"So, if we are quite through with the pleasantries, ladies, please, let's get on with it. Who was the client?"

"May I speak freely in front of Lady Beauchamp?" Angelique inquired in mystified amusement.

Beau gestured for her to do so.

Carissa sat very still, waiting. No doubt all her snooping senses were on high alert.

"Who he came here representing, I do not know, but he was one of your countrymen. He said his name was Alan Mason, but only a fool would fail to use an alias when hiring an assassin."

"What did he look like? Any details you can remember."

"Hmm." She furrowed her brow in thought. "He was rather an odd duck. Tall, thin, in his thirties. Dark-haired, with a mustache. Badly dressed, even for an Englishman."

Beau frowned.

"I took him for a tradesman or solicitor or some such. Not wellborn, judging by his speech—though I suppose he could have been disguising his accent. One thing is certain. He was much too nervous ever to have done this sort of thing before."

Beau considered this.

"I could tell he was out of his depth. He was so nervous his hands were shaking . . . until I plied him with brandy and offered him one of the girls." She tossed Carissa a challenging look.

She didn't flinch. "Did he accept?"

Beau swelled with pride in his little lady of information.

"He accepted the brandy but was in too much of a hurry for the girl."

"Did he say anything about who he was working for?" he pressed her.

"I asked. He would tell me nothing."

"Is there anything else you can remember?" Carissa spoke up.

Angelique gave a very Gallic shrug. "I don't know. I did not like him."

"Why?" Beau clipped out.

She paused in thought. "After we had concluded our business, his relief that it was done, and perhaps, the brandy that I gave him made him bold."

"How so?"

"He started asking me impertinent questions. Personal questions. About the past. The war." Angelique met Beau's gaze warily. "He wanted to hear about the Terror. What it was like living through that. He couldn't seem to help himself. Normally, I would not have tolerated such ill-bred, prying questions—but for eight thousand pounds," she added wryly.

"What sorts of things did he want to know?" Beau persisted. "Names? Dates?"

"No! That was the strangest part. He asked about the details of what it was like to be there. He wanted to know the sound when the guillotine fell. How the crowd went silent, waiting, until the blade rang, and the thump of the head dropping in the basket. And then the crowd's roar." She stared into space for a moment. Then she shoved the memories away with a shudder. "That's what he wanted to hear about. So I told him, as much as I could stand."

Beau studied her.

"When Mr. Mason saw he was distressing me, he stopped his questions, and he actually apologized. Odd. He said he meant no harm, that he was an artist—in his spare time, I suppose. He said he was working on a piece dealing with the Revolution. Strange topic for an English painter, no? Or was he a sculptor?" She frowned. "Come to think of it, I did not ask what sort of artist he was. I was too annoyed." She shook her head again, mystified. "Very odd man."

"And you have no idea who might have sent him?"

"Pah! If he pays in gold, what do I care?" She fell silent. "But I will tell you one thing," she added after a moment. She eyed them shrewdly. "I think somebody sent him into the lion's den and didn't much care if he got eaten."

"How's that?"

"You don't choose such a greenling for your liaison to hire a killer unless you've already decided he is a disposable man. Whoever sent him is probably going to kill him after the job is done. I would," she said. "Now, if you'll excuse me, I must attend to my guests."

$\mathcal{B}$eau and Carissa exchanged a guarded glance as they went back out into the night.

"Sorry," he mumbled ruefully as he walked her back to the coach, his hand on the small of her back. He glanced around over his shoulder, making sure no one was following them. "She wanted to meet you."

"It's all right," Carissa answered. She lowered her gaze to watch her footing over the unequal gravel down the drive. All the while, she fought to keep her mouth shut.

It took almost more discipline than she possessed to refrain from asking her husband bluntly how many times he had slept with that formidable woman. He did not seem too proud of it, but it was obvious he had. A lady of information recognized the small, guilty signs.

Carissa refused to ask the question, though, considering she had no room to talk when it came to matters of virtue. More than ever, her conscience was gnawing at her to tell him everything.

After the wild goings-on she had just observed inside that chateau, she could not believe that Beau would be shocked by anything she had to tell him.

But now surely wasn't the right time. He already had so many other things to worry about, she reasoned. Besides, having kept up her deception since their wedding night, she was beginning to think he'd view the cover-up as worse than the crime. How was she even supposed to bring up such a topic? *Oh, by the way, dear, I know you thought you married a nice little virgin, but I actually had a lover before I married you.*

The thought of it made her cringe. She had better figure it out soon, just in case Roger Benton heard about her match, as Aunt Jo had warned.

One thing was certain—Madame Angelique would have no trouble brazening her way through this situation. Carissa, on the other hand, was supposed to be a gently bred young lady.

As they walked to the carriage, she realized that, yes,

she was rather jealous of that woman, oddly enough, a woman who was also noticeably jealous of her.

It was not the fact that she had slept with Beau that chiefly bothered her. Many women had, she'd been forced to accept. But that was in his past: She was the one he had married. What she was jealous about was how he had talked to Angelique. He had treated her with the respect due an equal, as if she were a man.

The contrast could not have been more marked as he assisted his little bride to the carriage and hovered over her every move with the utmost protectiveness. Lord, did he see her as helpless?

Was she?

If only she had but a small dose of that Frenchwoman's audacity . . .

When she thought of how timid and secretive she had become ever since her fall from grace, how frightened of disapproval, she was angry at herself. Shame had made her sneaky. One thing she'd say for the brazen Angelique—she did not appear in the least ashamed of what she was.

In some strange way, that brazen harlot inspired her.

What would it be like to flaunt the world without a care? What would it be like not to be bound up in secrets? But to demand a man's respect on her own terms.

Indeed, what would it be like if Beau treated *her* like that, as well, instead of always protecting her as though she were a child or a dainty china doll? Of course, she knew, he meant nothing but the best. He was a gentleman; it was how he had been raised, and she loved him for it, but still.

Inexplicably peeved, she strove to dismiss the unpleasant twinge of jealousy. "We'd better get home fast," she remarked, putting it out of her mind as he got the carriage door for her, gallant as ever. "It would seem we've got an artist to hunt down."

"No-ho, my girl," he chided with an idle smile. "You're not hunting anyone. *You're* staying out of this."

"The devil I am." She paused, one foot on the carriage step. "You need my help. Tracking down this kind of information is exactly what I'm good at."

"No," he replied. "I mean it, Carissa. It's not safe. You stay out of this."

She stared at him for a second, hardly surprised by his patronizing answer. Nevertheless, she fought a brief, silent battle with her temper. Then she shook her head, sprang up into the coach, and took her seat.

He gave his men their instructions, then joined her inside. He pulled the door shut, glancing at her. "You're not pouting, are you?"

She sent him a mutinous look, arms folded. "I can do this."

"Perhaps you can, but you shan't." He rapped on the carriage to signal to the driver.

The carriage rolled into motion.

"Why must you treat me like a child?" she asked a few minutes later as they rolled along, the carriage squeaking and rocking over the rutty road. "One would think you'd be grateful for the help."

"I can do it myself."

"You sound like that eight-year-old boy your father told me about, stuck in the tree, refusing to let anyone help him! Well, I'm sorry, the stakes are too high for me to coddle your stubborn pride."

"What pride? I'm trying to protect you!"

"Exactly! Maybe I want a chance to return the favor."

He scoffed. "You protect me?"

"What?" she cried angrily.

"That's absurd."

"How? Why can I have no role in this? Nick threatened *me*. I obviously have a vested interest!"

"I can't have you interfering."

"Why can't you trust me?"

He just looked at her.

She blanched. "I'm an intelligent woman! I can do things! I have skills!"

"And no training. Carissa, you are not an agent. Look, I appreciate your sentiments, really. But I can do this myself. Women have no part in this."

"What were we just talking to?"

"She doesn't count!"

"But I do?"

"You're a lady. Besides, look what happened the last time you meddled!" he reminded her. "We both ended up getting shot. Now, please. Enough!"

"Enough?" She tossed her head in outraged amusement. "Madame Angelique would never let you get away with that."

"Madame Angelique is not my wife. You are, and you will do as I say." With that, His Lordship dismissed her by turning aside to watch out the opposite window.

Carissa huffed, folding her arms across her chest as she leaned against the squabs. But although she did not speak her mind aloud, she was busy hatching a plan.

By Jove, she would make him eat his words, prove herself his equal. She'd show him what she was capable of; and then he would treat her with the same respect he had shown to Madame Angelique.

Sitting there, she decided she would make her coup by figuring out who this artist fellow was, the "disposable man" who'd been sent by some anonymous party to hire Nick.

Better to ask forgiveness than permission.

Stubborn creature, not even an Order agent could be everywhere at once. He needed help, whether he'd admit it or not. The man already had enough to worry about. She would simply lighten the load for him and bring him answers. Maybe *then* her arrogant spy would see that a lady of information could put her skills to equally good use.

Things were rather prickly between them on the boat ride back across the Channel.

But it was just as well that they had headed home.

For when they arrived the next morning, the butler worriedly handed Beau an official-looking letter. The news it brought made Carissa's stomach plummet to the floor.

The Committee wanted to see him.

Now.

Chapter
18

"*L*ord Beauchamp, how good of you to join us."

Beau was getting seriously tired of Ezra Green's sarcasm, but he bit his tongue.

At least they had not found out he had left the country for the past forty-eight hours. "Gentlemen, what seems to be the matter?" he asked in a most amiable tone as he took his seat in the cold, stone, parliamentary chamber.

Green studied him from his elevated seat in the center of the long table across from Beau. "We received news overnight of a most shocking violence that took place a few weeks ago in Germany. Bavaria, to be precise, several miles north of Munich—right in the vicinity where you say your colleagues went."

Beau went very still. "What happened?"

"Mass murder, it would seem. More than seventy bodies were found burned to a crisp inside a large cavern in the Alps." Green could not seem to help his gloating.

He shrugged. "There was some sort of fiery explosion that people reported hearing for miles around. Some villages even saw the fireball. They thought perhaps a firedamp leak had ignited inside one of the old mines up in those mountains," he said. "When the locals went up to investigate, they found dozens of charred bodies inside the cave."

"How unfortunate," Beau said cautiously.

"Hmm, yes. The authorities from Munich were called in to investigate. They're still not sure how many people died in there. For some, there wasn't much left of them to find."

Beau sat there for a moment, tapping his fingers idly on the table. "And how does this concern me?"

"Don't be coy!" Green said scornfully. "We both know your fellow agents were behind this!"

"Do we? Perhaps the villagers were right. 'Twas an accident. A firedamp leak at an old mine. Unless you have some evidence that my agents were connected? Were they seen by the living, found among the dead?"

"Very well, you want to play that game. Who were the dead, you ask? Only some of the most powerful players in Europe. Personal friends of various crowned heads from Rome to Russia!"

"Prometheans," Beau murmured.

"So you say! Though the bodies were burned mostly beyond recognition, the authorities were able to guess at their identities by the personal effects they left behind at the nearby home of a nobleman—Waldfort Castle. Sound familiar?"

Beau clenched his jaw. Indeed, it did. It was the name of the place Drake had gone with James Falkirk.

"The Munich authorities questioned the servants at this castle. One of them finally admitted to the strange goings-on there. She spoke of a raid in which Count Glasse, the castle's rightful owner, was killed. Upon his death, all authority was transferred to an Englishman. I think you know his name: Drake Parry, the Earl of Westwood."

Beau quickly hid his shock.

"Your colleague didn't even bother to give a false name."

"Why should he? The Prometheans had already learned his identity when they captured him. They tortured it out of him, Mr. Green."

"Well, it may interest you to know that soon after Lord Westwood took command of Waldfort Castle, another Englishman showed up there, matching the description of your friend, Lord Rotherstone."

Beau's heart was pounding. So, they got inside. But seventy bodies—? "Were they in that cave?" he asked, bracing himself for the worst. "Do we know if they're alive?"

"I have no idea—and you are missing the whole point!" Green exclaimed. "Don't you see? The German authorities have traced this back to England! We've got scores of the rich and powerful burned to cinders in a cave, and if British agents are found to be behind it, your friends may have just set off a major bloody international incident!"

"What, on the word of a servant girl?" he shot back. "What you people should be asking is what all these bleeders were doing in that cave in the first place. That's the real question! But you don't want to hear the answer to that, do you?" He struggled to check his anger. "We have long known the Prometheans had one of their underground temples in the Alps, but we never managed to find the location. Apparently till now."

"So, you admit the Order was behind this?"

"I couldn't say, but I certainly hope so." Privately, his awe grew as the news of his colleagues' accomplishment sank in. Seventy dead!

The Promethean cult's surviving leaders had been meeting at Waldfort Castle—at least that had been the Order's theory.

If this news was true, it meant that the Order's centuries-old shadow war against the Private was genuinely over, at last.

God, how he wished he had been there!

Instead, he was left with the miserable task of cleaning up the mess their victory had caused.

At least it was a victory.

He asked again: "Did our men survive?"

Green gave him a withering look. "Unknown, but unlikely, especially Lord Westwood. The servant said he led the others into that cave that night. So he could blow them up, it would seem. No questions asked. No proper trials. No due process for any of these high-placed men from countries, some of whom count themselves friends of England. If this is true, once again, our nameless, faceless, invisible Order agents took it upon themselves to act as judge, jury, and executioner."

"The bastards were Private!"

"Private," Green said with a smirk.

Beau stared at him, marveling. "You still don't believe the threat is real, even after all the evidence you've seen?"

But Ezra Green's cold smile informed him the man had already fixed on a single-minded notion of who the real enemy was. And he looked at Beau with a hatred he no longer bothered to conceal. "There will be hell to pay for this, you must understand, Lord Beauchamp.

Not even the Regent can protect your precious Order anymore. Not after this."

"Just tell them it was a firedamp accident."

"Oh, you gentlemen are so very good at covering your tracks. But this time, you've gone too far. It cannot be excused away. This is an embarrassment to our government. I am sorry to inform you, Lord Beauchamp, not even peers of the Realm are at liberty to go committing mass murder abroad."

Beau shot to his feet and slammed his hands on the table in frustration. "You don't even care what the truth is, do you, Mr. Green? This investigation is a travesty, and what your true reasons are for conducting this witch hunt, I scarcely dare to wonder!"

"What is that supposed to mean?" he cried.

"It means the crowned heads you claim are going to be so offended by these deaths are the very ones the Order has just saved! The Regent, the Czar, the Habsburg emperor—they all should be thanking us."

"For what?"

"Securing their lands from a threat they won't even acknowledge until everything's on the brink! Just like you! But why is that, Mr. Green? Why do you brush off this threat? Could it be because you're—" Beau bit back his words, silencing himself from unleashing a truly reckless tirade.

"Oh, do, please, go on." Green rested his chin on his hand and waited intently for him to finish.

The unspoken question hung on the air like a cloud of dark smoke in the chamber. *Could it be you're one of them?*

But even Beau knew that was absurd. If Ezra Green were a Promethean, the Order would have known about it long ago.

No, Green hated them for entirely different reasons.

"Never mind," Beau muttered.

"Good. Now, then, if you are quite through hurling accusations, my lord. When you hear from your colleagues, you will bring any communiqué from them directly to me."

"Why?" he demanded. "What are you going to do?"

Green's eyes glinted. "I am going to have them arrested the moment they set foot on English soil."

"For what?"

"Seventy counts of murder. I don't want to do it, of course, take our heroes into custody," he said. "But I'm afraid it's the only way we shall be able to satisfy the ire of all these foreign powers. At least your fellow peers will receive the sort of trial they never gave their victims."

"Victims?" he exclaimed, then he checked himself, striving for patience. "So that's what you imagine for them. A trial in the House of Lords?"

"Justice demands it."

"Your pride is what demands it, Mr. Green—no, I will speak!" he shouted when another panel member tried to tell him to sit down. "Public humiliation? Then you don't know these men! They'd rather die than be dishonored!"

"Oh, I imagine they'll do both, Lord Beauchamp. Our good English rope is strong enough for noblemen's nooses as well as commoners'. The only question is, are you going to join them on the gallows?"

"Don't your kind prefer the guillotine?" he shot back, but Green merely smiled.

"Trust me, we are going to get to the bottom of this, Lord Beauchamp. In the meanwhile, don't do anything foolish, please. You have cooperated to my satisfaction so far, but if you try to warn your 'brothers' of our plans, I promise you will share their fate." His threat delivered, Green dismissed the panel and marched out of the chamber.

Bloody little martinet.

Beau was trembling with rage. He angrily tugged at his cravat, feeling strangled. If only Virgil were alive to tell him what to do. Surely, the Order's greatest victory could not come at such a cost. They had always been willing to give their lives, but to be cast as the villains in this final hour was a profound betrayal by the country they had given their all to defend.

As he walked outside, still in a daze, Beau vowed he would not let that happen. Drake and the others had just defeated the last of the Prometheans; now it was up to him to save them. But how?

Think. He felt like the walls were closing in. *What would Virgil do?* Hat in hand, he leaned his back against the building and stared up at the blue sky far beyond the towers of Westminster, trying to tell himself he was not terrified or completely overwhelmed.

Finally, his pulse began to slow to normal. He strove to clear his mind. Obviously, he had to get a message to Max, warn him not to come back to England yet with his team.

Provided any of them was still alive.

Unfortunately, because of the investigation, Green already knew about most of the communication channels the Order agents used. But, the more he thought on it, he supposed it would not be too great a problem to send a courier to Madame Angelique.

She could put a few scouts along the French coast to watch for Max and his men and give them the message.

Of course, it might already be too late. If that fire in the Alpine cave had happened a few weeks ago, then they'd be reaching the coast any moment now, and from there, it was not a long journey back to England.

He could station men to watch for the returning agents on British shores, as well, even at the various London docks. But Green, no doubt, had also done that. It would simply be a race to warn his brother warriors to stay away until this was resolved, lest Green have them arrested.

His mind still churning, his mood gone dark, Beau was craving Carissa's presence as he arrived home. He was damned tired, having had almost no sleep last night because of the conditions of their journey. Awful roads and a tossing sea had made sleep elusive, and upon arriving home, instead of resting, he had had to go dashing off to sit through the interrogation.

Now he had visions of his wife sleeping in their bed, catching up on her rest, as well. He couldn't wait to take off his clothes and join her. Nothing was better than feeling her warm, soft body beside him . . . and if more than sleeping happened, he was perfectly happy to go along with that. Just the sight of her tender smile cheered him. Her soft, steadying touch brought wordless comfort after all that aggravation. The way she looked at him made him feel like he could conquer any challenge. Hell, was it so wrong for a man to have an occasional need for his wife's affection and support?

He walked in the door, closed it quietly behind him, expecting that the lady of the house was sleeping.

"Lady Beauchamp is upstairs?" he mumbled at his butler as soon as he walked into the entrance hall.

"No, milord. Her Ladyship has gone out," Vickers replied.

"Out?" he echoed, taken aback. "What do you mean, out?" This was not the answer he wished to hear.

Had he not specifically told her to stay safely inside the house because of the threat from Nick? "Where did she go?"

Before his man could answer, the tinkling chimes of the musical automaton clock went off. Beau gritted his teeth. The dainty tune grated on him at the moment.

"Madam left her itinerary in case you wanted to join her, milord."

"Itinerary?" he murmured, snatching the note out of Vickers's hand in annoyance. As his gaze trailed over her note, he could not believe his eyes.

It was a list of art galleries she had apparently gone to visit. In outright defiance of his stated orders.

Damn her, she must have gone snooping for information about that blasted artist!

Why that . . . nosy little baggage! He was outraged. How dare she so flagrantly ignore her lord and husband's simplest request?

With the latest developments from the panel, the last thing he needed right now was his little gossip of a wife out there sticking her nose in again where it didn't belong, stirring up trouble, asking suspicious questions around Town. The Order already had enough trouble. It did not need the lady of information complicating things further.

Damn it, this was his fault. He should have taken her in hand well before this. In growing fury, his thoughts returned immediately to her wedding-night deception.

He had given her a fortnight now to come forward, he had been nothing but kind to her in the meanwhile, and she still had not owned up to anything. He saw he had made a mistake. He should have confronted her right away, the next morning, for she clearly thought she had got away with her game. Well, he had allowed this, and now he was paying the price. She must see him as a fool.

If she could so blithely flout his specific instructions, then it was obvious his gentleness and patience with her had been interpreted as weakness.

A mistake he would immediately correct.

Beau glanced at the first place on the list, and with a growl under his breath, stalked out the door.

It was time to bring his good lady wife to heel.

𝒞arissa was tired, too, but she did not allow herself the luxury of sleep. If Beau had to suffer, she'd suffer with him. She vowed he would not go through this alone.

Still, either fatigue or all these spy intrigues must be getting to her, she thought as she walked through the art gallery, for she could have sworn she was being followed.

Surely it was just her weary mind or imagination playing tricks on her. After all, Beau was right—she wasn't an agent, she was just a neophyte, jumpy with the quest she had undertaken.

Nevertheless, she was determined to help him. She might be just a gossip, but she knew how to collect information on someone, what sorts of questions to ask— and how to ask them without being too obvious.

Presently, she was working her feminine wiles on the curator of the third art gallery she had visited so far

today, while Beau was detained, being grilled and berated once again by the panel. *Poor darling.* She saw no
reason why she should not get started in the meanwhile
since there was no time to lose if they were going to
figure out who had hired Nick and hopefully stop him
from shooting whoever he'd come to London to kill.

Of course, she realized that Beau might be a little
cross at first when she told him how she had spent
her day. But in the end, she was sure he'd appreciate
her efforts—although, to be truthful, her quest hadn't
yielded much in the way of answers yet.

No matter. She was not going home empty-handed.
She had to find *something* about the artist Madame Angelique had described. It was the perfect way to prove
her mettle to her husband, for she was determined to
make her oh-so-capable spy husband take her as seriously as he did Madame Angelique.

Indeed, she had settled into the decision that she
didn't just want his affection, she wanted his respect.

Oddly enough, her conscience was not satisfied with
this.

*How can you demand his respect when you haven't
really earned it? You haven't even told him the truth!*

But I will, she insisted. *I'll tell him everything, just as
soon as I'm sure it won't destroy our marriage.*

*Not telling him the truth is what could destroy your
marriage, you henwit,* it berated her.

But I can't take that chance. I can't bear to lose him.
Then she shook her head, trying to brush off her mis-
givings. *I must be as mad as half these artists, talking
to myself.*

The most uncomfortable feeling of all was her suspicion that it was not Beau's respect she was truly after
but her own.

There could be something to that, she admitted. To be sure, the fact that she had believed Roger Benton's lies, that she had fallen for that, had thrown herself away on a man who never loved her, that she had been that desperate for love in the first place to willingly deceive herself about his sincerity—for, of course, deep down, she had known he was a bounder—but she had ignored that knowledge, needing to believe.

That foolish self-deception had cost her much of her self-respect. She had never really forgiven herself for it.

And if it cost her Beau as well, she never would.

No, it wasn't worth it, she thought with a shudder.

Finally, after being orphaned, passed from home to home, seduced and betrayed, finally, she had found love. If she had to lie to keep it, then so be it.

Maybe it was best if he never found out.

"So, how can I help you today, Lady Beauchamp?" the curator asked, quite at her service after she had had her maid hand him her calling card.

It still made her giggle inwardly how having a title changed things, when, really, after all, she was still the same inside.

In quite a contrast to the clerk at that bookshop in Russell Square, the tidy little art dealer had dropped everything to wait upon Her Ladyship.

"I am interested in looking at works by English artists who've dealt with the French Revolution as their subject," she told him.

He lifted his eyebrows. "A curious subject, if I may say so."

"Oh, I know!" she answered gaily, playing the blithe ton lady once again, assuming that he kept an eye on the Society column in the *Post*, considering he made his living selling art to the aristocracy. Paintings were always needed for country estates and Town mansions. They made nice wedding gifts for highborn newly-weds, as well. "You might have seen the notice in the paper about the grand soiree my aunt, the Comtesse d'Arras, threw for me and my new husband."

"I did hear something about that," he admitted with a smile. "My humble congratulations to both you and Lord Beauchamp, my lady."

"Thank you. How kind! In any case, I wanted to thank my aunt by giving her a painting. She was married to a French count, you see. She's still got property there, and I know so much French artwork made its way to England for safekeeping during the war."

"That is correct, my lady. Many of the French nobles had to sell their collections to pay their way out of France in order to survive. Very sad. Art and jewelry were the easiest valuables to move to safety while so much of their property was being confiscated by the Revolution."

She shook her head. "It's hard to imagine how they simply took people's homes away from them, where their families had lived for generations, and just handed over the estates and everything to their own supporters."

"Jacobins," the little man spat while her thoughts harkened back to Professor Culvert's speech touching upon such subjects.

Even a Society miss knew that the Home Office was terrified of underground Jacobin sympathizers in England. Such groups were known to exist. The government was always trying to root them out before they tried to start all the guillotine-Revolution mischief here.

"Well, thank goodness for Wellington," she murmured.

"Indeed," he answered heartily. "So, could you tell me, Lady Beauchamp, more about what sort of painting you were looking for? We have quite a number of military portraits and a few battle scenes." He gestured to the wall, where a few of them were hung.

"Do you have anything a bit earlier? Paris street scenes from perhaps the 1790s?"

He considered her request. "I may have something in the back. Let me go and look. May I offer you a chair while you wait, my lady?" He gestured to the elegant seating group in the front corner of the shop, near the sunny bay window.

She smiled at him. "That looks pleasant. Thank you."

He bowed. "I won't be long." He retreated into the back, and Carissa went and made herself comfortable on a Chippendale chair upholstered in pastel blue striped satin.

Margaret followed, but Carissa pointed out the window at the bakery across the street. Even from here, the delicious smells made her mouth water. "Would you go across the street and buy a few muffins for us, Margaret? It's been quite an undertaking this morning, and I find myself rather peckish. Get some for yourself, as well," she added, handing her a few coins from her reticule.

Her maid smiled and bobbed a curtsy, then hurried off on her mission. The little bell above the shop door jangled when she left.

Carissa rested her elbow on the chair arm, propped her chin on her fist, and closed her eyes, hoping that a bite to eat would help her stay awake. With the spring sunshine streaming through the window, she could have drifted off, contented as a cat.

When the bell jangled again a moment later, she was too tired to acknowledge the arriving customer. She heard the door close, then a few footsteps as the person drifted into the shop.

"So, I see you are now a patroness of the arts, Lady Beauchamp," a voice said. "How very aristocratic. I'm impressed."

At the sound of that voice, she drew in her breath and flicked her eyes wide open, sitting up straight in her chair. Staring at the man with dark, tousled curls and flamboyant, if rather rumpled clothes, she shook herself. Surely she had nodded off, and this was but a nightmare.

Roger Benton sauntered closer with a sly smile.

"If you want to pay tribute to the muses, my lady, I can think of better ways to do it than squandering your new husband's money on overpriced paintings."

Her mouth went dry as he approached, bracing his hands on the back of the chair across from her. His gaze trailed over her. "Marriage must agree with you. You look spectacular, Carissa."

"Oh, shut up," she hissed, her heart pounding. "Stay away from me."

"What, no time for an old friend now that you're a viscountess?"

She was nonplussed, nearly too shocked to speak. How dare he approach her this way! Aunt Jo had warned he might try something, but she hadn't expected it so soon.

"I always knew you'd land on your feet," he said as he flicked out his dark plum coattails and took a seat across from her with the practiced ease of a dandy. He struck an elegant pose, crossing his legs, propping his patrician chin on his knuckles. He gave her another forced smile, but she could not miss the change in his appearance.

Dissipation had sent his good looks downhill. He had lost a good deal of weight, she could see. His color was poor, he had dark circles under his eyes, and the puffy lips that had enchanted her were very chapped and irritated, as if he'd had a cold for several weeks.

But it was the glazed look in his eyes that was the biggest change. His eyes glittered with desperation. *What has he done to himself?* she wondered, startled to feel a small measure of pity amid her hatred and revulsion.

"Were you following me?"

"Only in hopes of finally getting my chance to wish you much happiness. You know, I've been reminiscing on the times we shared—"

"Stop it, you vulture," she cut him off in a low tone. "You know I don't want to see your face."

"Oh, that's sad. Well, I'm afraid it's going to cost you for me to go away."

Heart pounding, she glanced one way, then the other, making sure that neither Margaret nor the art dealer were in sight. Then she looked at him again.

"I am sorry," he said politely. "I never thought it would come to this. But the poet's path is not an easy one."

"You're no poet," she whispered.

"Yes, I am. I even wrote a poem for you, my dear. A limerick. Would you like to hear it? There once was a lady in Brighton, a redhead whom little could frighten, till her aunt's disapproval brought on her removal by an uncle whose fortune was titan."

She scoffed and strove for patience, then she shook her head. "Do you know what my husband would do to you if he found out about this?"

"The question is, what would he do to you?"

She stared coldly at him. "How much do you want?"

"Two thousand pounds," he answered evenly. "I think that's fair, don't you?"

She flinched. "That's more than last time."

"The stakes have gone up."

The pity she had felt dissolved. No, she realized, he was a disgusting human being. How could she ever have thought otherwise? "That's a lot of money. It's going to take me some time. I only have five hundred in my personal account."

"Well, I'll take the five hundred now, and I'll give you two days' time to bring me a draft for the rest."

"Very generous of you," she murmured coldly. "You do know that I wish with all my heart I had never laid eyes on you. Don't you?"

"There's no need to be unkind, my dear. Now that I see you," he said with a leer, "you should be grateful that money's all I'm asking for."

Repugnant.

What did I ever see in him? She could not believe she was allowing herself to be blackmailed, but at that point, she would have paid any sum to make him go away.

She supposed at least she should be grateful that he had not showed up at her house. Her hands trembled with fear as she took her bankbook out of her reticule; she lowered her head and used the pen set on the nearby table to write him a cheque that emptied her account.

She handed it over to him.

He smiled and blew on it to dry the ink. "There. Was that so hard? Pleasure doing business with you once again, my lady. You can bring the remainder to me at The Clarendon Hotel, day after tomorrow. Agreed?"

"Go to Hell."

He forced a taut chuckle. "So fiery! I'd nearly forgotten how hotly you burned, *ma chère*. I'll take that for a yes." He folded her cheque and slipped it discreetly into his breast pocket. "Until then." He rose and sketched a bow to her. "Lady Beauchamp."

As he turned to go, the bell on the shop door jangled again.

Carissa thanked God that Margaret had not been here to see this, but when she looked over at the door, she froze in horror. It was not her maid.

Her husband stepped into the shop, those keen blue eyes of his taking in the scene with a sweeping glance.

Roger did not seem to realize who the new arrival was as he strode toward the door, as though eager to get his money from the bank and spend it in the nearest opium den.

But as Roger approached, Beau shut the door behind him and locked it.

He paused in surprise, realizing the danger, when Beau pulled down the shade.

Beau leaned against the door and folded his arms across his chest.

She sat frozen in her chair, staring in disbelief at the nightmare tableau of her girlhood seducer face-to-face with the man she loved. The husband she had lied to.

Roger had suddenly started looking queasy, but he tried to play it off, no doubt hoping his suspicions about the large, blond man's identity were mistaken. "Ah, you're blocking the door, mate," he said in a friendly tone.

Beau fixed him with a dark stare full of impending doom. "Carissa," he murmured in a voice of terrifying calm. "Who is this?"

Chapter
20

$\mathcal{B}$eau had already been to the first two art galleries on Carissa's list. Not finding her at either, he was on his way to the third. He still wanted, with every yard of ground he covered, to throttle the chit for snooping into matters he had specifically told her to leave alone.

In any case, he was driving into the street where his next destination awaited when he saw his wife's maid leave the art shop ahead, heading for the bakery across from it.

He saw the carriage he had given Carissa for their wedding, and told his driver to pull up behind it. Leaving his carriage with the coachman, he had glanced in the bay window of the art gallery as he approached and had seen his wife talking to this man.

For the first split second, his knee-jerk reaction was a chilling thought of his mother's unfaithfulness to his father. But edging closer for a better look at the man in question, he dismissed this passing fear. It would bloody well take more than the likes of that sad, sorry soul to provide any competition for him. No, he realized, something else was going on.

He had glanced at Carissa again, and in the next heartbeat, his well-honed instincts as a spy homed in on the subtle cues that told him she felt threatened.

Her tense posture.

The pallor in her face.

His anger at her for ignoring his orders immediately dissolved as his protective instincts went on full alert.

He had already been in motion to go in and rescue her when he saw her write something down and give it to the man.

He had paused, briefly bewildered. Was she passing information to someone? Had one of his enemies already got to her?

That's when he stepped in.

Presently, he waited for her answer to his question. But it seemed Carissa could not speak.

He directed his next query to the stranger, a thin, slightly dilapidated dandy. "You have some business with my wife?" he demanded.

"N-no."

"What did she give you?"

"Nothing!"

In no mood to argue, Beau shot out his right hand and grasped the dandy by his cravated throat. He lifted his arm just a bit to send the startled fellow up onto his toes to avoid being strangled.

From the corner of his eye, he saw Carissa watching with her hand pressed over her mouth while the stranger struggled to free himself from the grip cutting off his windpipe.

Beau, meanwhile, reached into the fellow's breast

pocket and calmly retrieved the piece of paper he had seen him tuck away there. When he dropped the young man, he stumbled forward, gagging for air and clutching at his neck. "You're mad!"

"Sorry," he said blandly. He unfolded the piece of paper. He wasn't sure what he was expecting, but it certainly wasn't what he saw.

A cheque from his wife's account for the hefty sum of five hundred pounds.

He stared at it, holding his fury at bay and striving to make sense of this. *What the hell—?*

In the financial discussions he'd had with her uncle, drawing up the particulars of their marriage settlement prior to the wedding, Beau had learned that, as an orphan, Carissa had inherited a generous trust fund from her father. The trust fund bestowed on her an annual allotment of five hundred pounds to do with as she pleased, apart from his own dowry settlement upon her for a certain amount of pin money each month.

But why the hell had she just signed over her entire year's portion to this stranger?

He looked from one to the other. "Somebody care to explain this?"

Neither answered, but the excruciating glance they exchanged, indeed, something about the way the two reacted to each other tipped him off that they had once been more than friends.

And the truth dawned. Her lack of virginity on their wedding night . . . The vigilant way she kept watch over the ton gossip . . . He saw now that it was not for prurient interest's sake but because she was keeping watch over her own secrets. He put two and two together with an inward flinch. *So, this was the chap she didn't want to tell me about.*

The stranger then attempted to lie to him.

First, he cleared his throat. "I take it you are Lord Beauchamp. I'm an artist, sir. Her Ladyship just commissioned a painting from me. It was supposed to be a surprise for you."

"Really? And now I've gone and ruined the surprise . . . No, I don't think so," he murmured, but when the shop owner stepped out of the back, he barked abruptly at him, "Leave us!"

Startled, the little man halted in mid-stride—glanced around at them—then shrank back into his office without a word.

Though Beau had a feeling he already knew the answer, he asked the question anyway. "What's the money for?" When he took a step forward, the stranger leaped back, staying out of arm's length.

"Let's be rational about this, Beauchamp! Violence isn't going to solve anything! Besides"—he glanced at Carissa—"you can afford it. What I'm selling is worth at least that price."

"And what exactly are you selling, Mr.—?"

"Benton," he conceded warily. "Roger Benton."

"And you are selling . . . ?"

"Protection," he replied, visibly steeling himself, "for your lady's reputation."

Hardened as he was to the darker side of life, Beau was slightly shocked that the blackguard had just admitted to extortion. How bad was it, whatever Benton had on her?

He looked over at Carissa, longing for her to say something. Anything. But she just stared at him with soulful anguish brimming in her eyes.

The pain in her gaze checked the fury rising in him.

He did not know what might have happened between

them, but it was obvious this man had hurt her, and that was all that mattered.

Everything in him wanted to throw Benton through the window. But he had a better idea in mind . . .

"I see." He drew himself up with a cool stare. "How much, then?"

"Three thousand."

"You said two!" she cried.

He glanced over his shoulder at her with a mocking sneer. "His pockets are deeper than yours."

"Oh, God," she wrenched out, hiding her face in her hands and turning away.

"No, it's fair," Beau said stiffly, like a very copy of her uncle, Lord Denbury. Playing his role with a tense nod, he was, of course, already plotting treachery.

"This is a very serious matter, as we all know how easily rumors get started. Once begun, they are impossible to root out. It isn't worth it. My lady, you will explain your part in this to me later. Mr. Benton, of course I would pay any price to protect my family's honor."

"Very reasonable of you, Beauchamp."

"I am a reasonable man," he said through gritted teeth, "and not unacquainted with the ways of the world. But my bankbook is at my home. If you'll accompany me in my carriage, we shall go there now, and I'll write you a cheque for the full amount. Then you can be on your way—"

"Hold on, now, I am hardly getting into your carriage, Beauchamp. I'm not a fool. And I have no interest in seeing the inside of your home though I'm sure it's splendid," he said with a sneer, looking very satisfied with his own cleverness. "We meet in a public place."

"Very well." Beau gave him a cold stare. "Not everyone is as dishonorable as you, Benton. I was merely trying to keep the matter out of the public eye. But if that is your preference, then I will meet you at, say, The Gray Gull Inn on the docks near Billingsgate. Do you know the place?"

He nodded warily. "I can find it."

"Good. Then, when we have concluded our business, you will never come near my wife again, and you will stay silent on this matter—if you value your life."

"Fair enough."

Beau stepped out of the way from where he'd been blocking the door and unlocked it for him.

Benton sauntered toward the exit, looking slightly relieved to be making a clean escape. He glanced back at Carissa, then paused next to Beau, one hand on the doorknob. "The Gray Gull, in an hour."

Beau nodded, and Roger Benton slipped out.

He stared after him, lifting the shade on the door's window and watching through narrowed eyes as the blackguard hailed a hackney. One stopped for him shortly. Benton climbed in, and as the hired carriage trundled off down the street, Carissa's maid returned.

He opened the door for her as she came cheerfully gusting in. "Oh, Your Lordship, ye found us! Are ye hungry, sir?" She lifted the assortment of muffins wrapped in cheesecloth that she had brought over from the bakery shop.

"No, Margaret. Er, your mistress shall be heading home now. When you get there, would you tell Mr. Vickers to have the traveling chariot made ready? Her Ladyship will be going on a journey—and you will join her. You'll be leaving immediately, this afternoon."

"Beau!" Carissa wrenched out.

He ignored her with a flinch. "This will be a long trip to the country, so pack whatever clothes she might need for a month. You may go out to her carriage now. Her Ladyship will join you in a moment."

"Yes, sir," the maid murmured, hesitating with a somber glance over at her mistress.

But when he nodded gently at the door, Margaret bobbed a curtsy and scurried out to tell Jamison they'd be leaving in a trice.

Beau could hear Carissa crying softly. He turned slowly and met her teary-eyed gaze.

"I'm so sorry," she whispered with shame and grief in her eyes.

He stiffened, threatened by her tears. This was not the time or place for this, and he was not ready to let go of his anger. Nevertheless, raised from his cradle to be a gentleman, he offered her his hand. "Come, I'll walk you to your carriage."

She remained where she stood, struggling for composure. She took a handkerchief out of her reticule. "You're sending me away?"

"You leave me no choice," he replied.

"A-are you going to kill him?"

"Should I?"

She shook her head with a shrug. "I was just surprised that you didn't challenge him to a duel."

"There's no point dueling with a man who has no honor. It defeats the whole purpose." He paused, lowering his head. "I don't want to make any wrong assumptions, since you've provided no information for me to go on, but it seems to me this man would not have the power to blackmail you unless your involvement with him at some point was voluntary?"

"Yes," she admitted in a strangled whisper, lowering her head. "It was the biggest mistake of my life, but he did not—force me."

Beau nodded, feeling strangely numb, as though he were watching the scene unfold from outside his own body. Perhaps his heart was still in shock now that he faced the reality of her deception, but none of it felt real. "You do know that if he had, he'd be dead on the floor at this moment?"

Drying her tears with her handkerchief, she managed a nod.

"That can still be arranged if you feel he deserves it," he added. "The choice is yours. Only say the word, and I'll take care of it. In fact, it would give me great pleasure."

"No. Not for his sake but for yours. It's not worth the risk you'd take, with the panel breathing down your neck."

He could not help his cynical reaction, muttering, "I am touched by your concern."

"Please! I didn't mean to hurt you—"

"Stop." He glared at her in warning, fighting back a wave of anguish. "Not now." He looked away again. "Come. Let's get you home."

She closed her eyes, steadying herself. Clutching her reticule, she glided past him toward the door, head down. But she paused beside him, looking up into his eyes. "You're really going to pay him off, just like Uncle Denbury did?"

"Hell, no," he breathed. "I'm going to pay him *back*."

What Roger Benton did not know was that The Gray Gull Inn was the haunt of an infamous press gang that worked the docks, hunting for recruits—willing or otherwise.

So, instead of going to hand over three thousand pounds to buy the blackmailer's silence, it was the black-mailer himself he went to hand over to the press gang.

When Beau sat down in the sailor's tavern across from Roger Benton an hour later, he glanced over at the group of swarthy sea dogs drinking in the corner. He beckoned them over with a crook of his finger, then he laughed as they surrounded his dandyish companion.

It was too bad Carissa wasn't there to see it as the press gang dragged Roger Benton away, kicking and shrieking, to introduce him into His Majesty's service and fit him with a uniform—the newest recruit for the Royal Navy.

Now he might have the chance to make something of himself, Beau thought in amusement as he bought himself a drink. He was going to need it before heading home, for next came the hard part.

Dealing with Carissa.

There was no use putting it off. Tamping down his anger and frustration, he tossed back a well-earned shot of whiskey, also ignoring the hurt. Then he set his glass down, gathered his thoughts, and returned to the house.

When he arrived, the staff had already packed her bags. Margaret was telling the footmen which pieces of luggage still had to be loaded into the traveling chariot.

"Where is Lady Beauchamp?" he inquired of his butler.

"In the drawing room, my lord."

Beau walked slowly up the stairs and found her sitting by herself in front of the musical automaton clock, waiting for it to chime. Her shoulders were slumped. Her slender arms were wrapped around herself as though she were trying to ward off a chill.

He pushed the door shut behind him with a soft click; she didn't look over.

As he sauntered up beside her, she glanced at him.

He noted her red, puffy eyes and pale face. The sight of her like that wrenched his heart. It made him want to gather her into his arms and tell her nothing mattered, kiss away the hurt of whatever that bastard had done to her.

But she had misused him, and a man had to draw the line somewhere, or he ceased being a man.

Mistrusting his own emotions, not quite knowing what else to do, he joined her in staring at the clock. "Benton won't be a problem anymore," he spoke up at length. "In case you were wondering."

"Thank you," she breathed in a shaky whisper. Then she paused, her head down. "You've known all along, haven't you?"

"That you weren't a virgin? Yes," he murmured cautiously. "Since our wedding night."

"Why didn't you say anything?"

He turned to her. "Why didn't *you*?"

She faltered. "I was frightened."

"Of me? Honestly?" he demanded in a low tone of indignation. "Why? What did I ever do to make you see me as a threat?"

"No, that's not what I meant—I didn't want to lose you!"

"I see." Such an answer was a test for a cynical man. "So you deceived me out of love? Is that your claim?"

"Beau, please. I didn't know how you'd react if I tried to tell you beforehand. If you'd back out of the marriage after we had placed ourselves in a scandalous situation. And then, afterward, after our wedding night when you didn't seem to notice, I didn't know how I could possibly bring it up! I just wanted to leave well enough alone. Then he showed up. And once again, he wanted money. That horrible—parasite."

"Well." He folded his arms across his chest. "I would say your taste in men has greatly improved." He looked askance at her. "At least now I understand why you're obsessed with the gossip."

"If it ever comes out, I shall have embarrassed you along with myself. I can't believe I've been so selfish. I never even thought of the impact on your reputation until after we had married."

"Oh, I'm pretty hard to embarrass," he drawled in a low tone though he could not say why the hell he was making this so easy on her. She deserved to suffer, or at least to grovel, just a little.

She gazed at him with large, soulful eyes full of sorrow and regret. "I was only—with him once. It was nearly two years ago, a youthful indiscretion. I never intended for it to happen, it just did."

"Please, I don't need to know this."

She let out a pained scoff with tears in her eyes. "Am I to tell you or not? You're angry at me if I speak or stay silent—"

"It's not the fact that you slept with him that hurts me. For God's sake, I'm not a saint myself," he muttered, shocked to hear himself admit that anything could hurt him in the first place. He looked at her, at a loss. "It's that you clearly didn't feel that you could trust me. All this time, you thought you got away with it. You really must take me for a fool."

"No!"

"I'm not a fool, Carissa. I was trying to be kind to you. Ever since that night, I have been as patient as I know how to be. Waiting for you to come to me and confide in me. I gave you every opportunity to try me so you could see that I would understand. I wanted you to know that you were safe. I thought surely, if I gave you some time, you'd finally open up to me and see that you could trust me. But you never did."

She started crying softly again, her hand to her lips.

"What did you think I would do, throw you out?" he asked wearily, offering her his handkerchief. "After all the women I've been with? I'm not that great a hypocrite—though I will admit, I was a little disappointed. How could you misrepresent yourself to me?"

"I'm so sorry."

"For what, lying to me or getting caught?"

"I shouldn't've lied."

"No, you shouldn't," he agreed, struggling to remain firm in the face of her tears.

Her emerald eyes searched his beseechingly while the rosy lips he'd kissed so many times trembled with remorse. "My lord, can you forgive me?"

He gazed at her, at his wit's end. "What sort of ogre wouldn't?" he exclaimed. "Please stop! I hate to see you cry. I'm not going to hurt you, Carissa. It's not a matter of forgiving you. Don't you see that? To be honest, I scarcely know what to do with you at the moment. You can't tell me the truth. You don't do anything I say. If you won't trust me, then how can I trust you? And if there's no trust, how are we supposed to love each other?"

"But I do love you! I do love you, Beau."

The way the words wrenched from her for the first time, so passionately, so pained, with tears streaming down her face, nearly overwhelmed him. He stared at her in silence, taken off guard by her fierce declaration. Lovers had said that to him before, but never in a way that had made him believe it, until now.

Until Carissa.

He stepped closer, drawn to her, more desperate than he had ever dared admit for the love she offered, true or false; incapable of one word, he gathered her into his arms, his heart pounding. She trembled in his embrace as he lowered his head and claimed her tender mouth in a fierce storm of need.

Pulling her closer against his body, deepening the kiss as she wound her arms languidly behind his neck, all he knew was that no other woman had ever made him feel such things. He wanted to throttle her at the very same time that he wanted to hide her away in a safe, velvet jewel box where no one could ever hurt her. He yearned to lose himself in her, the oblivion of her yielding body, the tenderness of her heart; and at the same time, just as strongly, like a horse that had never been tamed, he wanted to run from her, but he could not.

She had got inside his soul, and he feared her for it, knowing she could destroy him if she ever left him, for that's what women did. They were not to be trusted. Today was proof of that. His sire had told him so at an early age, and somewhere deep inside, he still believed him.

What the hell am I doing?

It was all suddenly more than he could take. The cold, solitary, all-surviving part of himself that he had never shared with any lover—the part that had let him enjoy a night of bed-sport with whomever, without the slightest risk to his heart—was suddenly clamoring like hell for him to get out of there, keep this woman at arm's length. Before she destroyed him.

He ended the kiss and pushed her away, panting and confused amid the sudden, ironic realization that apparently, he didn't trust anybody any more than she did.

Heart pounding, all he knew was that if he did not get back control of this situation, he was doomed.

"You must go to the country," he ground out, refusing

to let himself become any more pathetically wrapped around her finger.

At least she didn't know he was.

She clung to him, the tears shimmering in her eyes like melting emeralds. "Please don't send me away, Beau," she begged him in heartbreaking, sensuous need. "Don't make me leave you, my darling husband. Not now."

"No." His voice sounded rough and strange even to him. "It's time for you to do as I say and show me you can be a proper wife." He swallowed hard, gently pushing her hands away from his face. "You will go to the country and wait with the other ladies until it's safe. Then I will send for you. You will be quite comfortable there, and safe."

"What about Nick? You said he knows about the place."

"I will send special instructions to Sergeant Parker to apprise him of the situation. It will be fine." He felt more normal when he looked away and put his mind back on business. "Besides, I don't intend to give Nick time to hear about your relocation. I'm going to hunt him down as soon as you leave London. I've got to settle this with him now," he growled, avoiding her stare.

But he could see from the corner of his eye that she seemed to be getting the message. He was putting his foot down. "Promise me you'll be careful."

"Of course."

She jumped with a startled gasp when the clock suddenly chimed.

The two of them were so quiet that the silvery little tune seemed like a din in the stillness of the drawing room.

Beau rested his hands on his waist, pained by a memory of their wedding day and all its hopes. But he told himself this was not the end of the world. Every marriage had its fights. Yet, for some reason, he could not meet her gaze while that little melody played. Every note was slightly agonizing to him at the moment.

"Come. Time to go," he clipped out at length when the song had finally finished. *Before I change my mind.*

"Must I?" she whispered.

"You leave me no choice!" he said rather too vehemently, refusing to be swayed. "Damn it, I have too much else to worry about without you meddling and making everything harder! I'm sorry, but you've brought this on yourself."

She lowered her head. "Then I will go."

Damned right you will. Jaw clenched, he escorted his errant wife out of the drawing room with a light touch on the small of her back. He walked her down the stairs into the entrance hall, where he handed her her reticule, and gently set her pelisse over her shoulders to keep her warm. Then he led her outside to the waiting coach and pressed a light kiss to her knuckles before handing her up.

She went with a true lady's stoic grace and dignity.

It seemed very un-Carissa-like to him, but for all he knew, maybe now that she was free of her secrets and could be real with him, she might turn out to be an entirely different person. Only time would tell. He hoped the real Carissa wasn't too different. He liked her an awful lot just the adorable, maddening way she was, lies and all.

Maybe that was the problem. Maybe deep down, they were too much alike.

As she took her seat in the large and comfortable traveling chariot, she looked back at him through the open door of the carriage, as though half expecting him to change his mind.

Beau refused to. "Write me a line to let me know as soon as you're safely there."

She nodded. "I'm sorry," she whispered one last time.

He stared back at her, torn with regret and the need to keep her out of harm's way. "I know, sweeting." Once more, emotion nearly unmanned him, but he quickly shoved it down, keeping his mind on the facts. "Say," he asked, changing the subject, "before you go, did you happen to learn anything useful about French Revolution artists at those galleries?"

"No." She shook her head rather bitterly. "All my meddling was for naught. It was all a waste."

He frowned, hearing the cold note of self-directed anger and disgust in her low-toned answer. "You were only trying to help," he conceded.

She just shook her head and looked away, her lips a taut line. "Good-bye. Close the door, please. Driver!"

Beau shut the carriage door and said good-bye to Margaret, who had been sitting inside the coach, awkwardly playing deaf and dumb during their exchange, as only the best of servants could.

"All set, Jamison! Keep them safe."

"Aye, milord!" the coachman called, then he chirruped and snapped the reins over the horses' rumps.

Beau stood on the pavement, watching the carriage pull away. He folded his arms across his chest as an unsettling question floated like a dark phantom through his mind. Could it be that part of his reasons for staying silent about knowing Carissa's secret was because it was a way of keeping a safe distance between them?

Maybe he wasn't so bloody noble, sparing her the confrontation all this time. Maybe he had just been sparing *himself* the risk of getting truly close to her.

He breathed a self-directed curse as her coach pulled

out of sight around the corner. Bloody hell. He was a
hypocrite. The thing he hated most, after Prometheans.

Maybe . . . dear God, maybe he was even a bit of
a coward, he thought, cringing. Danger in battle had
never made him hesitate, but no woman before Carissa
had ever had this kind of power over him. Knowing the
jeopardy it placed him in made him downright itchy,
jumpy, restless. Anything was better than dwelling on
this subject.

He thrust all his tangled questions away, turning
back to the house and back to the business at hand.
Marching inside, he threw himself back into the realm
of life where he was master.

He quickly wrote, then coded a secret message for
the Order's team in Calais who ran the safe house—
the men who had picked him and Carissa up on the
coast when they had gone to see Madame Angelique.
*'Trouble in England. Tell Rotherstone and his team to
stay in France until I send for them.'* Short and to the
point. He only hoped that he was not too late.

Then he returned to the docks, not far from where he
had sold Roger Benton to the press gang, to have his
message delivered.

Striding down the quay, he found the old fisherman
he'd hired before to take messages for him across the
Channel; he paid the grubby captain a small fortune
and warned him with the usual dire threats never to
speak of this. The old man agreed. Their bargain made,
Beau waited around to watch the fishing boat sail off
down the Thames.

Then, satisfied, he turned to face the city, his eyes
narrowed as he moved on to his next task, considerably
more challenging.

Find Nick.

*C*arissa was in misery, but the reunion with her friends was a comfort. Daphne and the other wives were shocked by her unannounced arrival at the idyllic country estate tucked away in a remote corner of the Hampshire countryside, a few hours' drive from London. The sculpted gardens and wooded park created a tranquil atmosphere, but the presence of armed guards was a stark reminder of the danger.

The other women made much of her, welcoming her with hugs and tears, then, with cries of astonishment when she told them she had married Lord Beauchamp.

"Why didn't you write and let me know immediately?" Daphne shouted, hugging her in congratulation.

"I wanted to tell you in person."

"Oh, I knew it—I told you he was mad for you!" Daphne released her, but Kate studied Carissa, tilting her head.

"You don't look terribly enthusiastic about it," the

dark-haired young duchess observed, folding her arms across her chest.

"We are in a quarrel," Carissa admitted, and it was all she could do not to burst into stupid tears again. She could not believe the man had made a watering pot of her.

But Daphne fondly took her under her wing. "Poor thing. There, there, dearest. Come in and tell us all about what that rogue has done to you."

"I'd rather not talk about it," she said with a dignified sniffle. How humiliating it would be to admit that she had finally told her husband she loved him, and he hadn't said it back.

Not that she could blame him after what she had done.

She was a liar and a hussy and a sneak, and she didn't deserve him. He might not think that, but she did.

"Well, we're here to listen whenever you need to talk," Daphne comforted her. "For now, you just come and settle in and we will do our best to cheer you up. It's wonderful you've come, just when we were quite beside ourselves with boredom! I've missed your wit. We are going to have fun together here and make the best of it. We are Order wives, after all, and we understand our duty! Isn't that right?"

The other two ladies nodded though they were looking at Carissa rather strangely. She supposed she did not seem at all like her usual feisty self.

Daphne put her arm around her. "Now, then. There are a couple of pretty bedchambers for you to choose from . . ." The blond marchioness escorted her into the beautiful manor house, and the others followed.

Inside, Carissa paused to smile at Mara's adorable

little two-year-old son, Thomas, from her previous marriage. At thirty, Mara, Lady Falconridge, was several years older than the rest of them. She had been widowed before her recent marriage to Jordan, Lord Falconridge.

Carissa did not know Mara as well as she knew the others. Indeed, she had been skeptical of her, not only because the gossips had whispered that she was the mistress of the Regent but because she knew that Mara had broken the wonderful Jordan's heart when the two were barely twenty. But they had recently made up—and more.

Little Thomas clamored for his mama to pick him up. Mara lifted him for a snuggle, then set him on her hip.

"Has Beauchamp received any word from our husbands?" Kate murmured.

Carissa shook her head. "Not that I've heard, sorry." She sighed. "I miss my Beast."

Carissa smiled at the nickname the other men had given ages ago to Kate's husband, Rohan, the Duke of Warrington.

All the men had known each other since boyhood.

"It's hard being apart," Daphne agreed, taking the role of leader, just like her husband, Lord Rotherstone, did with the men. "But they're doing what needs to be done," she declared, flashing a smile. "Besides, I'm sure they miss us even more than we miss them."

Carissa said nothing, knowing her husband didn't miss her at all. He was glad that she was gone.

Then the ladies showed her around inside the house.

Their patient willingness to bear up with whatever sacrifice was required of them completely chastened her.

No wonder Beau was exasperated with her if he was comparing her to model wives like Daphne. *You can't tell me the truth, you won't do anything I say . . .*

Now that she was back among her friends, their bond of shared secrecy among them all as Order wives foremost in her mind, at last, she realized how she had risked everyone's safety by asking all those questions at the art galleries. Dear God, she could have put them all in danger! If she had said too much, if her questions got back to the artist who had hired Nick, then the villains, whoever they were, could trace her to Beau, to the other men, to the women, and even to little Thomas. The danger she had put her friends in sickened her, on top of how she had lied to Beau. *How stupid! How arrogant! How blind.*

She had thought the risk was only to herself, and she had been prepared to face that danger with sufficient courage. But if she had stopped to see the links and for once, not thought of herself as solitary, with no real bonds to anyone, as she had ever since she was an orphaned child—then she would have listened to her husband and not gone snooping today.

It didn't matter that she was only trying to help. She had unwittingly risked the safety of everyone she cared about. What on earth had she thought she was doing, meddling like that? She was not a spy! She had no training. Who was she to conduct an "investigation"?

Just some foolish ton gossip, pretending she knew what she was doing. She buried her face in her hands after the others had left her alone in her assigned bedroom. The servants had brought in her luggage, and the other ladies had given her some privacy to make herself comfortable before supper. *Another blunder.*

She had overstepped her bounds like a little know-it-all on top of throwing away her virginity on a cad and lying to her wonderful husband about it.

She shook her head, disgusted with herself, and utterly depressed. She vowed that henceforth, she'd leave the snooping to the spies. She wanted nothing further to do with all this intrigue, did not even want to discuss it with her friends, which was good, considering Beau had ordered her not to talk about it with them.

At least, thanks to his getting rid of Roger Benton, she would no longer have to monitor the ton gossip. Indeed, she thought, it was past time for her to start minding her own business.

As for Beau, she couldn't blame him if he hated her right now though that tortured kiss had been anything but hateful. She knew she had hurt him, and she ached with sorrow from head to toe because of it.

What would he do now? she wondered. Would he pull back from her forever? Would he punish her by going out to find some other female to satisfy his more manly needs while she was gone? The thought sickened her, but it wouldn't have surprised her. He had not said "I love you" back, after all. She closed her eyes, feeling just awful.

She really did not know where she stood with him right now. But all she could control at this point was her own actions and she decided the time had come to change.

The only way she could redeem herself was to show him that she could obey like a proper wife; she *could* tell the truth, and she *would* accept his rightful authority as her husband. God knew, they had to start somewhere.

She'd take her sentence of being exiled to the country without complaint. Placing her hand on her heart, she raised her head and made a private vow to be a good, obedient, Order wife—like Daphne.

From this moment on.

*T*hat night, Beau wove through the noisy, all-male crowd gathered to watch the prizefights. Ale and blue ruin flowed; the air was thick with the smoke of countless cigars; rough laughter burst from a group where a man had just told his mates a very dirty joke. Most of all, the wagers flew, which was why he had come.

It was as likely a place as any to find his mercenary friend. He had checked in with his various contacts, whom he'd told to keep their eyes and ears open for him for any news of Nick. But his watchers had nothing to report. The bastard was obviously being careful. But since they had been friends for years, Beau decided to check at gambling hells he knew Nick fancied.

Madame Angelique had said Nick had already received a portion of his payment. Knowing him, it wouldn't be long before he was back at the tables.

Beau knew from experience that Nick always turned to the heady distraction of gambling when he was under particular pressure, as now.

When he had heard at one of those gaming hells that Tom Cribb would be fighting tonight in Covent Garden, he knew this would be the place to look.

Nick loved to wager on the milling matches above all, and the English champion was his favorite pugilist. Cribb would be starring in tonight's headline battle.

Beau knew Nick had to be here. He scanned the crowd continuously for any sign of him.

Meanwhile, inside the rails, the intermediate match

would be starting in a few minutes. The meaty pugilists were receiving last instructions from their trainers.

Beau continued on the hunt, privately cursing himself for not telling Virgil long ago about Nick's gambling problem. Every time he had nearly gone to the old Scot about it, Nick had talked him out of it and promised he would change.

On three different occasions, Beau had allowed himself to be persuaded because Nick was like a brother to him and because he wanted to believe. Certainly, he had not wanted some new, green agent replacing his best friend on the team. Nick was a damned fine spy, fearless, lethal.

Not to mention it went against Beau's nature to be disloyal. He had been blinded by his loyalty, perhaps, forgiving to a fault. And now look where it had got them. Aye, he was paying the price for it now—though not as high a price as Trevor was paying. *Hang on, mate,* he mentally told his other closest friend, Nick's hostage. *I'll get you out of this, wherever you are.*

Winding his way toward the bet makers' tables, Beau leaned against a post where he could see the men coming and going as they went to lay their wagers.

Excitement was high in the crowd; loud and boisterous talk filled the air. Everywhere, men were debating the various strengths and weaknesses of the two pugilists about to begin and airing their opinions on the last brawl.

All of a sudden, Beau spotted Nick in the crowd.

Instantly, he was in motion, striding toward him. He had his loaded Mantons at the ready beneath his coat in case his friend needed persuading. He was not above forcing Nick's compliance with a pistol in the ribs.

One way or the other, he was going to put an end to this—and then there was still the matter to sort out of the bastard coming after Carissa.

Beau was very eager to pay him back for scaring his wife. Even Nick knew when he had gone too far.

But highly honed senses must have alerted Nick to the approach of a hostile party.

Beau was no more than ten feet away from him when the black-haired mercenary glanced over his shoulder and saw him coming.

He bolted.

Beau instantly ran after him, pushing through the crowd, while in the ring, the opponents were announced. The boxing fans started chanting for their favorite while Nick did his best to lose him in the crowd.

Beau spotted him just before Nick vanished out the door. He barreled after him. "Damn it, get back here!" he roared as he burst out into the dark, wet night.

Nick slipped around the corner. Beau was undeterred, sprinting after him, leaving the glow of the building's doorway lanterns.

The narrow streets around the place were choked with the parked carriages of all the spectators crammed inside. Beau hunted his quarry through the maze of vehicles, his weapon drawn. When he bent down to glance beneath the endless rows of carriages, he saw running legs.

He chased. "Don't make me shoot you again, you stupid bastard!" he shouted into the darkness. "Stop running like a coward and talk to me! I know what's going on! I spoke to Angelique!" he shouted.

"Your wife is very pretty," Nick taunted from the shadows somewhere nearby.

Beau rocked to a halt on his heels and glanced

around, his chest heaving. He had heard him, but he couldn't see him. He suddenly yanked open the door of the nearest carriage, but Nick was not inside. "Come near her again, and I will forget you and I were ever friends."

"Relax, Beauchamp, I was only making a point."

"What, that you've forfeited all honor?" Beau crept toward an alleyway ahead. "Who do they want you to kill?" he persisted, trying to keep him talking so he could home in on his location.

"Don't know yet. Probably find out soon." Nick paused. "Not that it's any of your affair."

"It's madness, man. You don't even know who hired you. It doesn't smell right, and you know it." He whirled around the corner with his pistol in position, but Nick wasn't there. "Where are you?" he shouted, losing patience. "Come out and face me like a man!"

But there was no answer.

He continued searching, but Nick had slipped away.

Beau cursed under his breath, dragging a hand through his hair as he whirled in frustration, scanning in all directions one last time. Nick was nowhere to be found.

He stopped, took a deep breath, closed his eyes to clear his mind, and pressed his eyelids with his thumb and middle finger. *What now? Think.*

His heart still pounding, fury in his veins, it took but a moment to choose his next strategy. Then he was striding to his carriage. If Nick was going to be difficult, he had other angles to pursue.

There was only one gunsmith in London that the Order agents really trusted to produce the weapons on which their lives so frequently depended.

Hans Schweiber was a Hessian-born gunsmith whose

family had been in the trade for generations. He was one of the primary contacts Beau had first alerted to keep an eye out for Nick, but he had heard nothing back and decided tonight it might be worth his while to stop in and check with the old man.

When Beau walked into his shop half an hour later, Schweiber peered over the small, rectangular spectacles perched on his nose. The rest of the shop was dark, and the weathered gunsmith was alone, working by candlelight on one of his sleek, well-balanced creations.

"Herr Schweiber," Beau greeted him.

"Lord Beauchamp. Thought I might be seeing you soon," he remarked serenely, pausing to change tools.

"Why is that?" he greeted him. Beau closed the door behind him and sauntered in. He found Schweiber's place oddly comforting—the familiar smells of gunpowder and oil, and the leather of the powder flasks on offer.

Hunting trophies and military memorabilia adorned the walls, honored gifts from the highborn hunting fanatics and military officers who revered the Hessian for his skill in making the weapons that had saved their lives.

Schweiber looked over the tops of his spectacles again. "You tell me."

Beau leaned an elbow on the counter, watching the gunsmith work. "You know about my problem with Forrester." He met his gaze. "Has he been here?"

Schweiber stared warily at him. "*Ja,*" he admitted after a moment's hesitation.

"When? Why didn't you contact me?"

"It was only the day before yesterday, and I was thinking it over."

"What do you mean, thinking it over?"

The Hessian shrugged. "He said you were the problem."

"Me?" Beau exclaimed.

"*Ja*. He told me you turned traitor."

Beau looked at him in astonishment, then burst out in angry, cynical laughter. "Oh, that is Nick for you." He shook his head. "Schweiber, surely you didn't believe him!"

"I wasn't sure whom to believe," he said with an unsmiling, German stare.

"And you weren't eager to pick sides," he retorted matter-of-factly.

Schweiber shrugged.

"He didn't attempt to threaten you into silence, by chance?"

"No, no. I'm too useful to get threats even from my most dangerous clients," he said with a low chuckle.

"Well, I can assure you, I am following all the usual protocol. It's Nick who's left the Order's purview. I need to find him before he does something rash. What did he want from you?"

"Sniper rifle." Schweiber put down his rag and eyed Beau with cagey acceptance.

"Sniper rifle," he echoed, nodding. "Did he say anything about the sort of shot he had to make? Ask for any unusual specifications on the gun?"

Schweiber shook his head.

"Did he give an address for you to send the bill to, or where to send the piece when it was ready?"

"No need for me to send a bill. He bought the best weapon I had on hand. He actually paid me up front for it. First time, far as I can remember."

"How novel," Beau said dryly.

"*Ja.*" The old man paused. "It did make me wonder."

"What is it?" he pressed him.

Schweiber gave a guarded look. "He seemed agitated. He was acting so strangely that I told my apprentice to follow him—at a safe distance, mind you. Good apprentices are hard to find. Told the lad not to let himself be seen."

Beau went stock-still. "Where did he go?"

"East End ganglands. The street was unmarked, but Michael can show you the place when he gets back from making his delivery."

"Superb. Well done, Schweiber. Thank God somebody in this city has their wits about them besides me. When do you expect your apprentice back here?"

"Not until tomorrow. Delivery was in Leicestershire."

"Send the lad to me as soon as you see him. Time is of the essence."

"*Ja,*" Schweiber said serenely.

"Thank you, Hans." Beau headed for the door, but he paused before going out. "Your boy was sure that Nick didn't realize he was followed?"

The old gunsmith nodded shrewdly. "Michael prides himself on stealth. Wishes he could become an Order agent."

Beau crooked a sardonic brow at him. "Talk him out of it."

Schweiber smiled and reached for his polishing rag once again.

Beau gave him a slight nod of farewell, then he went back out into the darkness.

Chapter
22

That night, Carissa was sitting around in the drawing room with the other ladies. Thomas was delighting them all, rolling a ball back and forth with each one of them in turn and ignoring his mother's repeated assertions that it was time for the tiny lordling to go to bed.

"He's our entertainment," Daphne was explaining as she rolled the ball back to the tot.

The ladies had had a nice evening supper, followed by a stroll through the gardens at sunset and a half-hearted game of croquet on the green. But the most interesting part of Carissa's introduction to the Order's estate—aside from seeing her friends—was the tour of the property with an explanation of all security procedures from Sergeant Parker.

The Order's trusty warhorse had been assigned as their chief of security, with a dozen more men under his command. The rugged, sun-weathered soldier was much tougher, she suspected, than his stocky, compact frame would suggest at first glance. Parker showed her three different escape routes from her chamber, depending on from which direction any threat might arrive.

He pointed out the several locks on her chamber door; he gave her a loaded pistol to keep in the drawer of the nightstand beside her bed; he showed her the rope ladder stored in her closet if she should need to escape out her third-story window. He then explained the haversack of basic supplies they had prepared for her to grab and go if they should come under attack for any reason.

She was fascinated. The pack contained some money, a water canteen, a small supply of dried foods, a pair of sturdy shoes, extra bullets for the pistol, and a compass.

"Understand, of course, my lady, this is all the last line of defense. The Prometheans have never discovered this place, but one must always be prepared."

"Of course," she had answered faintly though she wasn't quite sure who the Prometheans were.

"Good. Now you'll know what to do if the worst were ever to happen—if we ever came under attack here, and my men were overwhelmed. There's no need to worry, mind you. I've no reason to believe we're in the least danger of that at this time, but these are our procedures, and I'm showing you all this now because the Order believes in being prepared for any eventuality."

She nodded uneasily.

"Now, in this situation, if you hear me or one of my men give you the signal to run, you take your pack, use your ladder, and climb down. Leave your finery behind. You'll want to blend in with the surrounding folk. Lots of jewelry will make it easy to tell which woman's the aristocrat."

"You make it sound as though they would actually hunt me a-and the other ladies?"

"Aye, ma'am. As the wife of one of our agents, you'd be a very valuable hostage."

Oh, dear God, she thought.

"Has His Lordship ever mentioned what you should do if somebody grabs you?" Parker asked.

"No," she answered, wide-eyed.

"Right. Groin. Throat. Eyes. Close range, those are your targets if you can't get to your weapon. Just so you know."

"Ah," she murmured in amazement.

"So, then," he resumed his explanation, "if you hear the signal from me, you go. Don't wait to hear it twice. Flee into the woods and try to meet up with the other ladies but don't wait around. It's important to keep moving. If you become separated from the others, you must follow that stream—you saw it from the garden?"

"Yes."

"There's a path alongside it. Follow that brook downstream about two miles until you come to the coaching inn at the edge of the village, with carriages for hire. We prefer you hire a post chaise and drive yourself if you're up to it. It's better for you to leave the area at once. But if you're not comfortable with that, you can use the gold in your pack to buy a ticket on the stagecoach to London. Either way, get to Dante House as quick as you can. You'll be safe there. Don't talk to anyone along the way if you can avoid it. Have you got all that, milady?"

"Yes. Thank you very much, Sergeant. I daresay our husbands chose the right man for the job."

He had dropped his gaze with a modest smile. "They do their part, ma'am. I do mine."

"Well, I appreciate your dealing so openly with us about it and not simply trying to shield us from the reality."

He smiled ruefully. "Some of these things, I know, are hard to hear and frightening to imagine. But I've noticed in my years of service, ma'am, if I may say so, that Order men don't marry namby-pambies."

She was still musing on her lesson in personal security as Mara captured her son on her lap and tickled him. "You need to go to bed, sir!"

Thomas giggled happily. "No! I stay!"

"What's that you're looking at?" Carissa asked Kate, nodding at the magazine the young duchess was idly riffling.

"*La Belle Assemblée.* It's actually quite silly, but they've got bits about all the attractions of the Season available in London right now. Honestly, I live there half the year and had no idea there was quite so much to do! Now I really appreciate it, after being stuck out here for weeks on end. All these entertaining plays and concerts and diversions right under my nose, and I've never gone to see them."

"Like what?" Daphne asked.

"Kew Gardens, for one. It's open to the public every Sunday, but I have never been there. And Vauxhall."

"You've never been to Vauxhall?" Daphne exclaimed.

"No! I grew up in Dartmoor, remember?"

"You're so deprived!" Mara teased.

"What's wrong with Dartmoor?" Daphne protested. "It's very picturesque!"

"Yes, well, it might as well have been the far side of the moon. There's nothing to do but either read or watch the wild ponies."

"We have got to take her to Vauxhall when all of this

is over," Mara declared. "You'll love it, Kate. Music, fireworks, everything."

"Don't forget the trapeze lady," Daphne reminded her.

"Oh, this one sounds eccentric!" Kate tapped the page. "A waxworks museum! 'The Gala of History.' Have any of you ever gone there?"

"Isn't that in Southwark?" Mara asked.

"Yes! Just on the other side of the river, it says. Have you been there?"

"Oh, yes," she answered wryly. "Unfortunately, I made the mistake of thinking it would be a suitable amusement for my son. And I'm sure it will be. When he's fifteen."

Kate arched a brow, peeking over the edge of her magazine. "Was it risqué?"

"No, it was altogether gory!" she exclaimed. "You and your Gothic novels, of course, you'd probably love it."

Kate sat up straighter. "Really?"

" 'Guaranteed to send a chill down your spine.' They have a sign over the door that promises as much," Mara answered.

Daphne shot her a quizzical look. "And you brought a two-year-old there?"

"It was Jordan's idea! Honestly, we didn't know what we were getting into. There were supposed to be historical figures. I thought it would be educational." She feigned a shudder. "Well, it was a history lesson, all right. All the most horrible scenes from human history on display. Roman Coliseum . . . Spanish Inquisition . . . French Revolution."

Carissa's head shot up.

"The lads would probably love it," Daphne chuckled.

"I carried this little one out screaming," Mara replied.

"Did you say French Revolution?" Carissa ventured, her heart suddenly pounding with an uneasy premonition.

"Oh, yes." Mara rolled her eyes. "Guillotine. Marie Antoinette . . . and a basket of the most lifelike heads."

Kate laughed. "Smashing!"

"I think the artist behind the place must be quite demented," Mara drawled.

"Aren't they all?" Daphne asked.

"Well, this one certainly takes particular glee in scenes of death and destruction."

"Do you know the name of this artist?" Carissa pursued.

Mara shrugged. "No idea. Why?"

"Just wondering," she answered cautiously.

"Would you like to see the advertisement?" Kate offered her the magazine.

Carissa got up and took it from her, carefully scanning the small, square advertisement for the Gala of History Wax Museum in Southwark.

Charles Vincent, Proprietor.

Charles . . . Southwark . . . A memory was taking shape in the back of her mind, but it wouldn't come clear.

Kate tilted her head. "You all right? You look as if you've seen a ghost."

"Oh, come," Daphne teased, "don't be a ninny. I'm sure the scenes of doom aren't that realistic!"

Carissa managed a rueful smile. "It does sound horrid, though. But you're right. Our husbands would probably love it." Even as the conversation drifted on to another topic, her mind whirled.

The memory suddenly resurfaced at her probing.

Yes! The bookshop in Russell Square, with all the radicals, artists, and intellectuals, where she had gone to hear Professor Culvert's talk. The enigmatic conversation she had eavesdropped on after the lecture came rushing back into her mind.

Charles, you should not be here!

Why not? I don't have anything to hide, do I? She remembered the weird smile Charles had given the professor. *"You should come to my place in Southwark and see my latest scenes . . ."*

She hid her shock from her friends, absently rolling the ball back to Thomas.

That had to be it. She could feel it in her bones.

The few painters' names she had collected from the fine-art galleries had seemed unlikely candidates for her quest. The art dealers hadn't been much help though they had tried. Was it possible she had been looking in the entirely wrong place?

But a wax museum . . . ?

Could this Charles Vincent who owned the Gala of History be connected somehow to Madame Angelique's Alan Mason? *What if they're the same man?*

Mara had just confirmed a French Revolution scene at the wax museum, and Madame Angelique had reported that was the artist's area of interest.

Carissa's blood turned to ice water in her veins as a disturbing picture slowly began to emerge. For if Charles Vincent *was* Alan Mason, the artist whose prying questions could unnerve even Madame Angelique, then it was possible to trace a logical line from the French Revolution artist to Professor Culvert . . . back to his onetime protégé, Ezra Green. *No . . .*

Could the head of the panel himself, in charge of investigating the Order, have been the one to hire Nick?

But why?

She forgot to breathe, staring at the floor.

Because it's all a setup.

Her mouth went dry. She was shaking. Ice-cold.

If this was true, that could mean that Ezra Green's motives had been not to investigate but to destroy the Order from the start. *Good God—Beau. I have to warn him.* Bad enough he was facing this alone. Now she saw that the second Nick made his move, all their husbands would be doomed. And if Green was the one who had hired Nick, then he was in charge of when the assassination would take place.

He was in the perfect position. Ezra Green and his cronies could paint the killing as bloody proof that the Order was corrupt and too powerful.

All they had to do was catch Nick in the act, and if they were the ones giving him his instructions, where and when to pull the trigger, that part would be easy.

An even more terrifying question came to her.

Whom have they hired Nick to kill?

From what she had heard that day at Professor Culvert's lecture, the Radicals hated nearly everyone. There seemed to be a few choice villains in their minds: the Prime Minister, the royal family.

What am I going to do?

She knew in her bones that she was onto something. She had to see this place, find out more about this artist.

No! Forget it! If you go against his orders, Beau will never forgive you. You know full well he sent you here as a test. This was your second chance, and if you fail, you might not get another.

Very well, what if she merely wrote out her warning in a letter? she wondered.

But that would mean admitting how she had snooped earlier at the bookshop—which she had never told her husband about—because she knew he would be furious. He'd have been shocked to hear she had dared to go checking into the old mentor of the politician who was giving him such headaches.

After the huge quarrel they'd just had, if she confessed now to her earlier round of snooping, he would probably hand *her* over to the press gang.

Anyway, even if she dared explain to Beau in a letter what she had done that day, what she had heard—though she had thought it meaningless at the time—what if her letter was intercepted by Green's minions?

She knew the committee had Beau under surveillance. If she wrote a letter confiding her suspicions about who the real villains were, and they themselves got hold of it, that could spell serious danger for all of them.

No, she dared not put anything in writing. If she was going to follow up on this, she would have to do so in person. It was the safest way for her friends and their husbands—and her own.

Listen to me. You are not allowed to leave here! her better sense insisted. *Beau will* kill *you if you leave their protection. Besides, how could you possibly get past all these guards?*

Ah, but Sergeant Parker had just gone to great lengths to show her exactly how to escape in case of emergency.

It had obviously never occurred to the stalwart soldier she might be daft enough to try it on her own.

You mustn't.

Daphne would never do such a thing, she pointed out sternly to herself, her pulse pounding.

Well, Kate would, her more stubborn side responded. And a man's orders certainly wouldn't have stopped Madame Angelique.

She bit her lip, agonized with indecision.

She felt damned if she did and damned if she didn't pursue this. *What if you're wrong?—and you probably are. You could risk everything for nothing. If you slip away from here, and he finds out you disobeyed him again, Beau will probably never forgive you.*

She wished this theory had never occurred to her.

She did not want to go. It was frightening. She did not want to lose her marriage. *But what if I'm right?*

What if Beau and the rest of our men are being set up to be portrayed as criminals, and Nick is just to be used as an example?

That would be one way for their enemies to get rid of the Order.

Carissa stared unseeingly at the advertisement.

The private decision before her tied her stomach up in knots, especially now that she grasped the danger any mistake on her part could bring to all her friends—to say nothing of the destruction of her marriage.

But Sergeant Parker had said it all too well.

Order men don't marry namby-pambies.

She saw she had no choice. She was not sure which was worse—if she turned out to be wrong or right. But either way, she had to know. The question was too dire to leave unanswered. If ever there was a time for a lady of information to save the day, that night had come.

You had better be right about this.

If she could succeed, maybe then Beau would forgive her.

"Time for bed, Tommy," Mara told her son. "I mean

it this time, you. Come along, say good night to your aunties."

Thomas ran from Kate to Daphne, giving out hugs. He had only just met Carissa that day, however, so she had not yet earned one. But he must have decided he liked her, for he came over and offered her an alphabet block.

"Well, thank you," she replied, summoning up a smile. She tapped him on his little nose. "Good night, Thomas," she said, as Mara scooped him up and carried him off to his nurse.

"I think I shall retire, too," Carissa spoke up. "It's been a long day." She bade her friends good night, then took a candle and calmly walked up to her chamber, already plotting her escape.

*T*hat night back in London, Beau wandered restlessly from room to room. The house was much too empty with Carissa gone. Her absence left a gaping hole that he had not expected. Missing her with every nerve ending, he wasn't quite sure what to do with himself.

He did his best not to think about her, but there was nothing else to occupy him, waiting for the gunsmith's apprentice to return from making his rural delivery. Rather maddening, actually. He thought of writing her a letter to pass the time . . . but what was he to say?

He was still raw from fighting with her.

The automaton clock struck the hour of one. Beau leaned against the doorway in the dark and stared at it, wondering if he'd been too hard on her.

He knew she was only trying to help.

As the chimes ended, he leaned his back against the door frame, staring into space. The house seemed too big and hollow, and the thought of going to their bedroom alone made his chest ache vaguely.

He walked slowly into his office, poured himself a brandy, and sat down to drink it by the fire.

Just when he had started to settle his troubled mind, he heard an urgent knock at the front door.

He heard the night footman go and answer it. The door creaked. "Yes, can I help you?"

"Message for Lord Beauchamp!"

A courier.

Beau rose from his chair while the footman paid the messenger. When he stepped out into the entrance hall, his servant was just locking the door. Putting ceremony aside, Beau went and took the message from his footman rather than waiting for it to be brought to him.

He held it up to the candle; his face hardened as he recognized the hand.

He tore it open and read the letter from Rotherstone, his pulse pounding. *We have Drake. He's not a traitor, he's the bravest damned fool I've ever known. Wait till you hear what he did in Germany. We've landed at the coast and will be in London by tomorrow . . .*

"Sir, is something wrong?"

Damn it, they were already in England! His warning had obviously come too late.

"Nothing. My greatcoat." He went and got his weapons while the servant fetched his coat. "Listen to me very carefully," he ordered as he pulled it on. "I've got to leave for a while. Don't let anyone in while I'm gone, especially Mr. Green or anyone from the government."

The young man's eyes widened. "Yes, sir. Do you require assistance?"

"No. But thank you." Beau paused in the doorway. "I am not sure when I will return, but I am expecting a certain caller tomorrow from Mr. Schweiber's firm, Michael—the gunsmith's apprentice. Do let him in. In fact, if I am not back yet when he comes, send him to me down by the river. I'm not sure exactly where I'll be, but somewhere 'round the London docks. Tell him I said to come and find me. It is imperative that I speak to him. But don't tell anyone else—anyone—where I've gone."

"Yes, my lord."

Then he marched out, his sole concern to reach Max and the others before Green's soldiers did. He had to stop them from coming ashore, warn them at least to go to Scotland.

The Order's abbey headquarters in the Highlands would be the safest place for them, at least until he had all this nonsense with the panel sorted. If they set foot on English soil, Ezra Green had promised what would happen.

They'd be walking right into a trap.

Chapter
23

*T*he next morning, Carissa stood outside the odd establishment in Southwark, looking up dubiously at the sign. THE GALA OF HISTORY—A WAXWORKS MUSEUM.

She could still barely believe, herself, that she had come. It seemed like madness by the sane light of morning. Why would the owner of a waxworks museum want to hire an assassin, after all? Nevertheless, here she was.

Too late to turn back now.

She just hoped Sergeant Parker and his men did not get in trouble for failing to prevent her escape.

It really wasn't their fault. She had been as sneaky as she knew how last night. It had been difficult keeping her mouth shut—she had a feeling Kate probably would have loved to help—but she had not told the others where she was going.

She did not want her friends to be blamed for her decision if there were consequences. Nor did she think herself capable, frankly, of resisting all three of them together if they had opposed her plan, united.

So, resigned to go it alone, she had sought to buy herself more time, taking to bed as early as little Thomas had last night with complaints of the headache.

She had told Margaret to let her sleep in late the next morning, as she could use the rest after all of the strain of her tearful argument with Beau. She hoped the others would not be angry at her when they discovered her deception. It pained her to do it, but she had no choice.

Indeed, she was doing this for their own good and their husbands'.

When the house had gone silent, Carissa had risen from her bed and set out alone, creeping out exactly as Sergeant Parker had explained—a viscountess in disguise, sans jewelry. Dressed in a plain walking dress, sturdy half boots, a simple pelisse, and the most ordinary bonnet that she owned, she had walked through the dark woods to the coaching inn, where she had bought a ticket on the stagecoach back to Town. She had arrived within five hours.

It was only nine o'clock in the morning. She figured she had plenty of time to see the waxworks, then sneak back to the country estate the same way she had left, and wander back into the house in time for the midday meal.

She had already planned her excuse: that she had gone out on a long constitutional and had wandered off the property by accident. She had a book with her that she could claim she had sat down to read and dozed off.

Sergeant Parker might find her story odd, but he was tasked with keeping intruders out. The security he had put in place was not designed for locking his charges in.

At any rate, the moment of truth was at hand. She braced herself, opened the door, and went in.

As her eyes adjusted to the gloom inside a grubby receiving room, she recalled that many times, her cousins had wanted to come here, but Miss Trent, their governess, had said the place was vulgar. No doubt Miss Trent was right.

Morning sunlight coming through the dirty front window did no more than cast a rectangular glare of brightness on the floor. It could not touch the general heaviness of the place. An old woman greeted her, coming into the chamber with her broom.

"Are you open yet? I know it's early—"

"Oh, yes, come in, dearie. I'll never turn away a customer," she added with a toothless grin.

"Thank you." Carissa smiled back and went over to the desk to buy a ticket.

"Right through that door. Enjoy your visit!"

"Thank you." Carissa took her ticket from the old woman and stepped through the doorway into a maze of dimly lit corridors housing the wax historical displays.

Spooky place, she thought. It was clearly meant to inspire the visitor with tingling Gothic dread.

She saw the scenes Mara had mentioned . . . the Coliseum, with two rather mangy lions closing in on some early Christian martyrs. The animals looked like real ones that had been stuffed and mounted after being felled by some hunter's rifle, but the human figures were of wax.

The Inquisition made her wince.

The Gala of History had certainly not spared on the fake blood. Some of the figures even moved stiffly with various tricks of marionette strings and clockwork mechanisms. She shook her head. It really was a marvel of the macabre. The accused witch in the Inquisition scene was so lifelike that Carissa stared, half expecting to see the figure breathing.

She moved on through the hush, still the only visitor, since the place had just opened for the day.

There was much more to see. Anne Boleyn and her executioner. In the next scene, King Charles I was also preparing to put his royal head down on the chopping block, surrounded by Cromwell and his unsmiling Roundheads.

Another tableau featured fearsome Mohican warriors from the American wilderness trading pelts for guns with British soldiers. The trees in the scene looked as solid as any in the woods she had hurried through last night.

Each wax figure was carefully painted, rendered in life size, exquisitely costumed. You could almost hear the birds in the trees chirping and the babble of the artificial brook that wound past their feet.

Honestly, this required real artistry, she mused. Perhaps the talent behind the scenes was someone who had built sets for the theater.

At last, she came to the scene that had been the whole object of her visit here today—the Paris mob scene that Mara had told her about, with the guillotine. She gulped slightly, staring at the gleaming blade.

Her gaze traveled over the elaborate tableau. *Lord, those really* are *lifelike heads.* She looked more closely at them. *Egads.* The gory spectacle was meant to shock and cause the viewer to look away, glossing over details. But when Carissa forced herself to look more closely, good heavens, she recognized some of the faces of people in Society! Aristocrats. Royals. *I could swear that one's supposed to be Queen Charlotte . . . and the Regent's large head lying next to it in the basket. How horrid!*

How brazen.

It was hard to say for certain if she was right. But she had the queasy feeling she had stepped into someone's twisted fantasy. All of a sudden, an invisible door painted into the background creaked open, and a thin, rather gangly man in black started to step out of the back wall.

"Oh! Beg your pardon, ma'am," he mumbled, starting to withdraw. "I didn't know anyone was here yet—"

"It's all right!" She smiled, masking the flare of recognition in her mind.

He had a forgettable face, but it was absolutely he, the man she had seen that day at the bookshop. She was certain the second she saw him.

"I don't mean to intrude. I was just going to fix something, make a little adjustment—I'll do it later. I'm always fussing with them," he admitted with a self-deprecating little laugh. "I won't disturb you, Miss. Good day." He started to retreat backwards through his hole in the wall.

"Oh—I say, are you the artist behind all these magnificent scenes?" she spoke up quickly, her heart pounding. She was startled by her own daring, but this was her chance to try to find out what she could.

She just prayed to God he did not recognize her, in return. She did not recall him looking at her that day.

He had paused. "Yes, I am. Why do you ask?"

"To offer you my compliments, sir. Your work is simply excellent!" she flattered him with a nervous smile.

"Why—you are too kind, ma'am. Thank you." He

hesitated, blushing like a schoolboy. "Do you really like them?"

"They're incredible!" she exclaimed. "I've never seen anything like them!"

He stared, taken aback by her praise. "Thank you very much. W-we do try to give our visitors a unique experience."

"Oh, it's far more than that. It's educational, as well," she pointed out as she glanced at the angry mob figures. "You've truly re-created the spectacle of historical events. It gives such a greater impact to see it before one like this rather than simply reading about it in some dry old history book. Everything is so lifelike." She shook her head, laying on the praise as her best hope of coaxing answers from him. "It really makes you feel like you're actually there."

He stammered incoherently, as though he had never received a compliment from a woman before in his life.

Carissa was astonished that this shy, soft-spoken, mild-mannered, little milquetoast of a man could be the force behind these wild, violent scenes.

But if he was, then he might well be the 'disposable man' that others had sent as their liaison to Madame Angelique. *Keep him talking.*

She gave him her best smile. "Do you mind if I ask you a few questions about how you create all this? I'm the leader of a ladies book club, you see. I organize our events, and I was investigating your museum as a possible outing for our members."

"Your ladies won't find it all too frightful, I hope?"

"Oh, no," she assured him, and he laughed nervously. "I have them reading Gothics."

"Ah, Gothics. Well, I would be more than happy to answer any questions you and your ladies might have," he said, as if he were the most agreeable person on the south bank of the Thames. Not the sort of chap who'd ever go in for hiring assassins. "We don't get many visitors from the fashionable world," he added with a probing glance that scared her half to death.

That Charles should've already realized she was highborn brought her attention back to the risk that she was taking with her own safety. His perception of her rank was too much already for him to know about her. Especially since hers was a level of Society that he clearly didn't like.

Still, she held fast to her nerve, knowing that this would likely be her only chance to try to find out more information—details she could bring to Beau. She cast about for another useful question. "So, how do you choose your scenes?" she asked with a disarming smile.

He shrugged. "For their historical importance and the drama to be had from them, and of course, whatever might be entertaining to our guests. We survive by our ticket sales."

"I see. And how on earth do you make your figures look so real? They seem almost alive."

"Ah, that's my secret! No, I'm only jesting," he assured her with an awkward laugh. "I studied as a surgeon at the royal medical college," he admitted, "but medicine was not for me. I had too much of the artist in my nature. But I did stay long enough for the anatomical studies."

"I see. Then you have put your talents to good use." She smiled cheerfully, but a chill ran down her spine, for she knew that the anatomical studies at the royal medical college were made on real corpses.

If milquetoast Charles had not been too squeamish to

cut up dead people, then hiring an assassin ought to be a trifle for him.

It occurred to her presently that if he suspected the real reason she was asking all these questions, she could end up a corpse herself.

Groin, throat, eyes. Plus, she had the pistol in her reticule. *Thank God for Sergeant Parker.*

Glad that she had some defense, this did not change the fact that she was standing alone in a darkened space with a man who had once dissected dead bodies. A man who hired assassins and consorted with revolutionaries and Radicals. A man who probably thought that aristocratic heads belonged in baskets.

I want my husband.

Beau would throttle her if he knew the danger in which she had placed herself. Time to go.

Still smiling, she started backing oh-so-slowly away. "Well! This has been fascinating. My lady friends will love it."

"May I assist you in making arrangements for your group's visit, Miss—?" He walked through the mob scene and jumped up out of the dropped floor of it that allowed visitors to look down on the proceedings from a few feet above.

"Oh, yes, that would be most helpful. Do you have a card for your business so I know who I am speaking to?"

"Mother keeps them at the front desk. Have her check the book. I hope you will come back soon."

"I'm sure I will. Again, wonderful work. I've really enjoyed it." She kept walking backwards, past the Indians. King Charles seemed to eye her with a silent stare of baleful warning as she passed.

God, now this place had her well and truly spooked.

"I don't mean to keep you from your work."

"It's all right. My friends will wait. They're not going anywhere," he jested, laughing, but she had a feeling he spoke in truth. Odd as he was, those waxen people might be the only friends he had.

A disposable man. Someone that the people who sent him into the lion's den didn't care about. It had been fairly clear that day that Professor Culvert had wanted to brush him off and get rid of him as quickly as possible.

Oh, dear. Perhaps she had flattered Charles too much, for he was altogether attentive and obliging, walking her all the way out to the receiving room and making sure the old woman there attended her at once.

"Mother! This lady wants to bring her group. Will you help her make the arrangements?"

"Oh, that's very nice, dearie. I'm sure we'll be glad to have you. How many?"

"Um, ten."

"And when would you like to come?" the mother asked with a toothless smile.

Before Carissa could answer, the son chimed in: "If you know the date, I can make myself available to answer any questions your friends might have about my scenes. We could close for a couple of hours to all other visitors in order to accommodate your group."

"How kind!" Carissa said, wincing with guilt at getting their hopes up. She felt strangely sorry for the odd pair. "I'm sure I would not wish to inconvenience you, or deny others the pleasures of your museum."

"Not at all."

"Did you have a date in mind, Miss?"

"You know," she said, "I'll have to discuss it first with my group. I want to make sure everyone is available, so none of them will miss it. If you would be so kind as to furnish me with your card, I will most certainly be in touch with you to schedule the date and time."

"Excellent! Here you are, Miss."

As the old woman handed it to her, Carissa quickly skimmed the card: CHARLES VINCENT, THE GALA OF HISTORY. Then she looked across the desk at them with a smile. "Thank you so much for your time. You'll be hearing from me shortly." *When my husband comes back to arrest you.* "Good day!"

"You forgot to tell us your name!" Charles Vincent exclaimed as she fled for the door.

"Williams," she said absently, seizing the first name that popped into her head. "I am Mrs. Williams."

There had to be a hundred Mrs. Williamses in a five-mile radius of here. It wasn't as though she could say she was Lady Beauchamp. One hand on the door, she bade them farewell with a nod, then rushed out and sped to the edge of the street, flagging down a hackney.

She had to tell her husband what she had learned. Beau was going to have an apoplectic fit, but her information was dire enough to warrant the battle that this was going to lead to.

She had to warn him. He'd know what to do.

"Faster!" she shouted to the hackney driver, then she angrily told him through the window that she would pay him extra if he would gallop his horses all the way there.

At last, he brought her to her home. She jumped out and gave him a handful of gold coins, her hands shaking with her terror at her discoveries. A moment later, she burst through the front door of her own home.

Vickers, their butler, nearly jumped out of his skin. "My lady! What on earth—"

"Where is my husband? Quickly! Fetch him now!"

"His Lordship is not here," the flustered man replied.

"Where is he? I must speak to him at once!"

"My lady, what on earth are you doing back in London?"

She ignored him. "Beauchamp?" she hollered up the stairs. "Where is he?"

"My lady, with all due respect, I'm sure you should be in the country. There is serious business afoot—"

"Dashed right there is, and I think I've found out who's behind it. I have to see him!"

"Madam, I must strongly recommend you wait here for His Lordship to return."

"There's no time!" She waved him off, shaking her head. "Just tell me where he's gone, Vickers. Has something happened? Is something wrong?"

Vickers clasped his hands behind him and fixed her with a quelling stare.

She lost her temper. "If you do not at least tell me where my husband is, I'll have you sacked!"

His chin came up a notch, but he looked down his nose. "My lady, I have been with His Lordship's family for twenty-five years. I have not risen from errand boy to my current post by disregarding my master's instructions. You might like to follow suit, with respect," he added with a supercilious bow.

"Well, I never!" Carissa reached into her reticule and pulled out the pistol. She aimed it at him. "Talk."

"Good heavens, Madam!"

"I assure you, I do not wish to shoot you, Vickers. Head servants of your quality are extremely hard to find. But you must tell me where Lord Beauchamp has gone! I have learned the most alarming information directly concerning my husband and his more, er, mysterious pursuits," she said obliquely, though she was sure the loyal butler must know his master was a spy.

"Answer me!" she insisted just as there came a knock at the door.

They both looked over.

She narrowed her eyes. "No tricks. Go on, you may answer it," she muttered, waving the pistol toward the door and feeling like a proper highwaywoman.

Vickers was one cool customer. With his usual gravity, he marched over to the front door and peered out the sidelight window.

No one looking at him ever would have guessed he had a weapon aimed at him as he answered the door, though in fairness, he probably was very sure she had neither the will nor the ability to shoot him.

"May I help you?" he asked their caller.

"Sir, my master, Hans Schweiber, the gunsmith, sent me over. He said Lord Beauchamp wished to speak to me."

"Yes. Do come in." *And never mind the crazy woman waving a pistol,* his droll stare seemed to add as he widened the door.

A lanky, freckled lad of about nineteen stepped in, hat in hand. "Gor!" he exclaimed when he saw the armed viscountess waiting in the entrance hall.

"I'm sorry about this, but it can't be helped," she said.

"I-I can come back later," the boy started.

"No," Vickers interjected. "Lord Beauchamp is waiting for you, young man. Michael, is it?"

"Yes, sir."

"He is not yet back, but he wished for you to go and find him. Please do so without delay. You have important information for His Lordship, I believe?"

"As do I!" Carissa cried indignantly. "This stranger is allowed to see my husband, but I'm not?"

Michael sent her a puzzled glance, then looked at the butler again. "Where shall I go to him, sir?"

"Yes, do tell!"

"I am telling this lad, my lady. Not you—with respect. I humbly beg your pardon and hope you will understand."

"I understand you're a bounder," she muttered. But she stepped closer to try to hear what the butler said as he leaned toward the lad and murmured in his ear.

The gunsmith's apprentice nodded and turned back to the door. "Very well, sir. Good day, milady."

"Wait!" She dashed after him. "I'm coming with you!"

"My lady!" Vickers started, but she backed him off with her pistol.

"Stay out of this, you! Don't worry, I'll let your master know you tried to head me off." With that, she ran out after Michael, who was climbing into his heavy delivery wagon. "Where are we going?" she asked as she jumped up onto the driver's seat beside him.

"We?" He furrowed his brow and looked at her as if she were insane.

"You can tell me. I'm his wife, I'm Lady Beauchamp!"

"Er, the London docks, milady."

"The docks! Of course!" she whispered to herself. Max and the other Order husbands must have arrived!

This was excellent news. Beau would get some help. As long as Nick did not go trying to shoot anybody within the next hour or so. "Well, let's go, then!"

"I'm going," he mumbled.

She put the pistol back in her reticule as they lumbered off. "Can't you drive any faster?" she exclaimed.

But this was a foolish question for any lad of nineteen. The apprentice looked askance at her with a lively twinkle in his eyes. "Aye, ma'am. I was trying to be polite."

Lord, males and their chivalry. "Don't be! Just drive!"

"Hold on, then."

She did. He cracked the whip, and his powerful carthorses lunged against their harness.

"That's more like it!" she cried heartily, not caring who turned to look. She held on to her seat as the cart went rattling over the cobbled street.

They made a beeline for the docks.

The wind picked up as Carissa and Schweiber's apprentice neared the open breadth of the river. The London docks bustled with activity. The Thames bristled with countless masts. Fishing boats trawled the current, and watermen ferried people back and forth to the south bank.

Unfortunately the street was clogged with so much traffic around the fish market that the gunsmith's wagon barely progressed at a crawl.

"Come on, people, move out of the way," Carissa muttered under her breath. "Did our butler tell you why my husband came down to the docks?" she asked, as they inched along through the mob.

"No, ma'am, only where I was to go to."

"So much traffic! Are they having a sale at the fish market, for heaven's sake?"

"I think they've blocked off the road ahead."

He was right. Leaning forward, Carissa saw some

soldiers directing carriages away from a section of the docks. *Oh, no,* she thought.

"I wonder what's happening," Michael said.

Then she felt her heart lurch in her chest as she spotted Ezra Green crossing the empty space that the soldiers had cleared. He was marching toward the water.

As their cart neared the cordon where they'd be forced to turn, she had a fairly good view of what was going on from the height of the carriage seat.

There was some sort of a row going on down at the river's edge. Ezra Green was shouting at more soldiers he had brought, waving them on ahead of him . . .

Toward her husband.

She spotted Beau standing on the dock near a moored schooner, his coat and blond hair blowing in the wind. He turned to face the approaching soldiers, roaring at them to stand down. She drew in her breath, aghast, as a dozen soldiers of the King aimed their weapons at him. Beau, in turn, was trying to protect the small group of people who had apparently just arrived on the boat.

Lord Rotherstone, the Duke of Warrington, Lord Falconridge, and another man and woman she didn't know. "Stop the carriage!"

"But, ma'am, they want me to keep moving."

"I don't care! Look!" She pointed.

"What is the meaning of this?" Lord Rotherstone bellowed as the soldiers closed in.

The Duke of Warrington was more a man of action, however, and pushed two of the King's men into the water, one with an elbow, the other with a well-aimed kick.

"Seize them!"

Carissa stared with her heart in her throat as the

scene on the narrow wooden pier turned to barely controlled chaos. The soldiers went after Warrington first.

Beau yelled at his friends to cooperate. She did not know the young woman who had come ashore with the men—or why she was wearing trousers—but when the soldiers tried to lay hold of the black-haired man beside her (the infamous Drake? Carissa wondered), the girl whipped a bow and arrow off her back and smoothly took aim at the oncoming guards. "Don't you touch him!"

"Emily, no!" Jordan yelled. "They'll shoot you where you stand! Hold your fire!" he bellowed at the soldiers, holding up his hand.

The fierce girl's devotion to her man inspired Carissa, jolting her out of her own shocked inaction. Before she quite had any sort of plan, she jumped down from the gunsmith's cart and strode toward the docks.

"Milady, come back!" Michael pleaded.

She ignored him. Pushing through the crowd, she noted she was not the only one who had stopped to watch the standoff unfolding. Many onlookers had also stopped to gawk. *So much for avoiding scandals,* she thought.

Unfortunately, she was shorter than most of the big, sweaty roustabouts and wharf workers gathering to watch.

"Excuse me! Let me through!" She had to shove her way to the front of the rugged crowd, then she had to sneak past the soldiers keeping them under control.

But when she saw Ezra Green joining the soldiers on the dock—only after they had got the Order agents safely surrounded—she realized he would likely have them shot if they tried to escape.

Besides, knowing her friends' husbands, they would

certainly refuse to flee even if they had the chance. They were not the fleeing sort.

"Explain yourself, by God, sir!" Beau cried in fury as Green walked through the crowd of soldiers.

"*You* explain yourself, Lord Beauchamp! You were supposed to inform me as soon as you heard from them, but I had to find out from one of my men here. Did you think you all could slip away?"

"We don't run from fights," Lord Rotherstone informed him. "What's all this about?"

Mr. Green took out a scroll and unrolled it in front of the agents. "Your Grace; my lords; Miss," he said with a sneer at the pretty young woman, "I'm placing you under arrest in the name of the King."

"This is madness!" Beau exploded.

"On what charges?" Warrington demanded.

Green gloated while the soldiers held the agents at bay. "I am happy to answer that for you, Your Grace." He looked around at them, relishing his moment. "You all have been charged with seventy counts of murder."

Carissa nearly fainted hearing that. Seventy counts!

"We know about Bavaria," Green added. "You had to know there would be hell to pay. Or did you all think you'd get away with everything, as usual?"

The black-haired man stepped forward. "Take me. Let them go. It was all my doing—"

"Drake, no!" the girl cried.

He ignored her. "Do you want my confession? Very well. I did it; I acted alone. They tried to stop me—"

"He's lying! It was me! I did it. It's true. I'm the one who killed those filthy traitors, and I'm not sorry!" Emily cried in fury, a note of panic in her voice. "They were in the cave. I shot the flaming arrow. It was I who made the firedamp explode."

"On my orders!" Drake insisted, while Beau pleaded with all of them to shut up, to no avail.

"That's nonsense, it was all my idea," Warrington informed Green's men, taking the lead, as he was wont to do.

Carissa saw the grim glance Rotherstone and Falconridge exchanged, some silent communication passing between them.

"We are all responsible," Jordan declared.

"He's right. You either arrest all of us," Max declared, "or get out of our way."

"Why, that is an easy decision," Ezra Green replied. "Men!"

"No, let them go! It was me!" The girl, Emily, stepped forward and offered them her wrists.

Green merely looked amused by her plea. With a smirk, he nodded for his troops. When a soldier stepped forward and clapped the girl in manacles, Drake went slightly mad.

He lunged at the soldier, shoving his musket skyward to step in and punch him in the face.

"Arrest them all, now!" Green thundered, as Drake sent the man flying into the Thames.

Pandemonium broke out all around poor Emily. Carissa watched with a pang of sympathy. She could have told the girl her selfless offer was in vain. Even if her claim were true, it was not some odd girl in trousers that they wanted. Because of what she had learned, Carissa now understood this whole charade was aimed at one grand goal: Destroying the Order for once and for all.

Green seemed close to accomplishing his quest as the agents made the choice to stop fighting and let themselves be taken. It appeared their view was that if one was going to be taken, they all would go.

"You're making a huge mistake," Lord Rotherstone informed Green as he, too, was clapped in manacles before hundreds of watching Londoners.

Carissa was glad Daphne wasn't here to see it, or the other two women, as their husbands were likewise placed under arrest. At last, even Drake was subdued. "You're going to pay for this," he spat at Green.

"Is that a threat, Lord Westwood?"

"Drake, please," Emily murmured. He kept his mouth shut, but cast her a rather desperate look as they put the shackles on him. *Hadn't he been a prisoner of the Prometheans for months?* Carissa recalled. No wonder he looked so wild-eyed at the prospect of being put back in a cell.

"It's all right," Emily assured him as though she were soothing a wild animal.

The only one left with his liberty was Beau. "I'll get you out of this," he swore to his friends.

"No, you won't, Lord Beauchamp. If you are wise, you will continue to cooperate."

"God, Beauchamp, what else have you told them?" Jordan exclaimed.

"I didn't—" Beau started to answer in frustration, but he silenced himself as they started leading the others away. "Just—trust me."

"We do," Max murmured, giving him a communicative nod.

"Take them to the Tower!" Green ordered.

"The Tower?" Warrington uttered in outrage.

"That's right, Your Grace. A place reserved for traitors."

"Damn you, I've been serving this country since I was seventeen—"

"Enough, Rohan. He's not worth it," Max clipped out. "Beauchamp will get all this sorted soon."

Beau walked alongside his friends as the soldiers escorted them toward waiting prison coaches. He had not yet noticed her. "Don't worry," he was saying to them, "I shall go directly to the Regent. I promise you, this will not stand."

"The Regent?" Green gave him a quizzical look. "Who do you think signed the arrest warrant? The Home Office has not the authority to take such high-born warriors into custody, my lord."

Carissa stared, horrified. *The Regent already knew of this?* But the prince was the final authority. Their last hope.

"Beau, get Mara to talk to him! They're good friends. She'll find out what's really going on," Jordan called in a dark tone before they shoved him into the coach with the others.

Beau stopped Green as he was walking away, seizing him by his coat. He threw him up against the prison carriage.

Carissa took that as her queue. She rushed toward him to restrain her husband's fury before they saw fit to arrest him, too.

Of course, that seemed unlikely; she got the feeling that Green somehow needed Beauchamp free. Perhaps it made his claims seem more credible, if he could paint Beau as certifying the alleged crimes of the other agents.

Did he have some way to back him into a corner? Was that how Nick came in?

"The Regent would never agree to this," Beau was

snarling in Green's face as he pinned him against the carriage. Green merely held up the paper and showed him the signature with the royal seal. Beau glanced at it through narrowed eyes. "Then you manipulated him somehow."

"I, sir? Never, surely. Though I do hear it is rather easy to manipulate someone who's out of funds."

He slammed him again. "What's that supposed to mean?"

Green winced. "Why don't you ask your friend, Lord Forrester?"

Beau went stock-still. "You . . . ?"

"What?" he asked innocently.

Carissa stepped closer, her heart pounding. Beau's back was to her, but she could just make out their furious exchange. "What do you know about Nick?" Beau demanded.

"You'd better take your hands off me before I have you shot. I know you all are trained killers, but you answer to me now, Lord Beauchamp. Don't forget it. Unless you want something unfortunate to happen to your friends while they're in prison."

Beau was seething. "Tell me, Green. When did you join the Prometheans?"

He laughed. "I don't need such bedtime stories to know the Order has outlived its usefulness, my lord— along with most of the institutions your kind hold so dear."

"What are you talking about?"

"Wait a few years. You'll see. For now, heed me well. There is a new England coming, and those of us birthing it are going to make an example of your fine friends, so that everyone may see that from now on, even the highborn must answer to the law. Not your wealth, your

rank, your guns, not even the Crown you've so foolishly served all your life can save you from the coming
change." He glanced around at Beau and his fellows in
scorn. "You're a relic. Now take your hands off me."

Beau seemed so stunned by his words that he let him
go. Green cast him a smug look, righted his coat, and
walked away. He climbed up onto one of the prison
carriages. As it started to roll away, Green noticed her.

Carissa found herself looking into the eyes of a traitor. She shrank back when Green tipped his hat to her
in mock politeness. "Lady Beauchamp," he said, as his
coach drove off.

Hearing her name, Beau spun around and saw her
standing there.

His jaw dropped. Motionless, he stared at her as
though she had just stabbed him in the heart.

"What are you doing here?" Then he shook his head
at her with an icy look. "Never mind. I don't want to
know. I don't have time for this."

"Beau, wait!" she cried, as he brushed past her.

"Go home," he said, crisply enunciating the words as
he walked away from her.

Her very heart shriveled within her. But she had to
tell him what she had found out. She started after him
as the gunsmith's apprentice came pushing toward him
through the crowd. "My lord!"

Carissa was jostled this way and that by the throng
while the two conferred ahead.

When she cleared a knot of giant roustabouts, she
saw Beau marching toward his own coach, with Michael hurrying beside him. "Husband! I need to speak
to you!" she yelled after him.

But he didn't even listen. He climbed up into his
coach, pausing only to send her a cold, reproachful

glare over his shoulder—a wordless reminder that his sending her to the country had been a test—which she had failed. Michael jumped up onto the carriage. Then Beau threw the brake and drove off without even giving her a chance to speak.

Stubborn male! She knew he was angry about a thousand things—understandably so—and no doubt her arrival at that precise moment was the worst thing she could have added to his burden. But, blast it, the time had come to show him what she was really made of.

Her jaw set with determination, she rushed back to the gunsmith's abandoned delivery cart and commandeered it. The apprentice probably intended to come and get it later, but she would save him the trouble.

Because she was bloody well following them.

"Out of my way!" she hollered at the fishmongers and wharf workers milling about in the road.

At the moment, she did not care how unladylike she looked. Let the gossips report on it for all she cared!

She cracked the whip over the horses' backs, determined to catch up with her errant husband.

*I*n that moment, Beau felt pulled in a dozen directions at once, and going after Nick was the last thing he wanted to be doing. But of all the pressing matters crashing in on him at the moment, this one seemed the most dire.

If Schweiber's apprentice could show him to Nick's hiding place, then he still had a chance of stopping the ultimate catastrophe. If he failed, and Nick assassinated his target—and it had to be someone big for eight thousand pounds—Beau knew for certain the rest of them were headed for the gallows.

Every second counted now, but God knew, he would've rather been telling his wife in detail what he thought of her defiance, her inability to respect his orders as her husband. Maybe now she would see this wasn't a game.

At the same time, he wanted to be in the Tower making sure his friends' legal rights were being observed and nobody was treating them with undue cruelty. He wanted to be writing to the Elders up in Scotland, telling them to send the best lawyers they could find.

Most of all, he wanted to go tearing off to Carlton House, where Prinny was likely gorging his face, as usual.

How could their royal benefactor betray them like this? Somebody must have got to him. Beau did not know whether Green was part of the Prometheans or not, but even if he wasn't, the outcome was the same.

This little weasel of a bureaucrat had done more to damage the Order than the Prometheans had managed to inflict on them in a century.

As Schweiber's apprentice directed him into the East End, Beau tried to ignore his fury and focus on the task at hand. But he was still enraged about what Green had put his brother warriors through back at the docks. Damn it, any one of them would have been willing to die for the cause, but no one had ever suggested that their labors would be rewarded with public disgrace. How could this be happening? Had the world gone mad?

"Here it is, sir, the street I followed him to. The building's just 'round the corner."

Beau nodded, drawing his horses to a halt. Judging by the dodgy look of the surrounding neighborhood, he hoped his vehicle was not gone when they got back. "We'll go on foot from here."

They jumped down from the carriage. Beau murmured to his horses to stay. Then he nodded to the boy, and they headed for the corner.

The lad peered around the brick corner first, then looked at him. "The building on the right, sir. He went in that second door, toward the back, ground level."

Beau recalled Nick's telling him that he had been keeping Trevor in some sort of basement. "Good work, Michael. You stay here."

"I don't mind helping, sir, if you need me. I'm a good shot."

He smiled ruefully. "I'm sure you are. But my friend is on the road to his own personal perdition, and has already shown he doesn't care who he hurts along the way. I'll handle this. You can keep watch—and keep an eye on my carriage, would you?"

"Aye, sir."

With that, Beau slipped around the corner and began walking toward the building. Prowling closer, he took out his gun. His heartbeat quickened as he approached the second door. With every step he took, his instincts sharpened, homing in on the details of the tenement building. Nick would have left himself another exit. He'd have to look for it as soon as he went in; otherwise, the bastard might escape him yet again.

With his gun at the ready, he braced his back against the wall beside the door, listening. Silently, he tried the handle. Locked, of course.

Maybe Nick was not at home, he mused. But Trevor had to be in there somewhere. Hell-bent on stopping the one and saving the other, Beau gave himself a mental count to three, then he lunged at the door with a mighty kick.

Blasting it open, he steadied himself with a wide

stance and instantly swept the interior with his pistol drawn. No counterattack was forthcoming from the dark and dirty hovel. But he had to make sure the place was clear.

With that, Beau proceeded through the first room into the second, looking out not only for that bloody turncoat mercenary but for any sign of a trapdoor to the cellar, where Nick had boasted he was keeping Trevor "safe."

It had to be here somewhere. It was a tiny apartment of only two rooms. The front room was practically bare, except for a hutch of shelves with pots and pans on them and a battered table with four equally battered wooden chairs. He found a newspaper on the table along with the stump of a candle, an empty bottle of gin, the crumbs and uncleared plate from a sparse meal.

Beau checked the second room and found a moldy cot, but no one was sleeping in it. There was an old, scarred wardrobe by the wall, but he found nothing but a greatcoat and a few other items of clothing inside that seemed too fine for such surroundings. In the greatcoat pocket, he found Nick's lucky deck of cards. His lips twisted. At least he'd got the right place, then. But Nick wasn't at home.

He went back and shut the door he had kicked open in case Nick returned. Prowling back through the place, he scanned again in all directions, a little confounded. "Trevor?" he called. "Trev, are you here? It's Beau!"

That's when the low banging started. *Thud, thud, thud.* It was coming from somewhere under the floor, along with a very muffled voice.

"Damn it, down here! Beauchamp! Let me out!"

Beau dashed into the other room, following the

sound. His stare homed in on the stained, ratty chair with a low table beside it, arranged before the fireplace.

"Trevor!" he bellowed, his gaze trailing down to the filthy oval rug beneath the table and chair. It lay unevenly, and that could signify nothing, but he went over and pulled the edge of the grimy rug back.

A curse escaped him. "Trevor!"

His heart was pounding as he shoved the chair and table out of the way, exposing the full outline of the trapdoor. Unfortunately, it was padlocked.

The banging was coming from the bottom side of the planks. "Get me the hell out of here!" a furious, muffled voice demanded.

"Hold on, I'm here!" Beau's pulse pounded with fierce joy to hear his long-missing teammate's voice. "Move back from the door! I've got to blast the lock!"

He gave Trevor a moment to back away before carefully shooting the lock apart at point-blank range. He holstered his pistol, but before the smoke had cleared, he had pulled the broken halves of the lock away.

At once, he bent to grasp the handle and pulled the trapdoor up, flooding the space below with daylight.

Trevor lunged up the rough wooden stairs like a captive lion finally escaping its cage. He bounded out of the darkness below to freedom, he whipped around, rather wild-eyed, his jaw roughened with a beard.

"It's all right."

"Took you long enough!" he spat. "Where is he? I'm goin' to kill him."

"Easy . . . Good God, how long were you down there?"

"Too long," he growled. As he strode out of the room, Beau stole a quick glance into the hole and saw it had actually been rendered more comfortable than the dank hovel above. So, at least Nick had made sure their friend was comfortable. Nevertheless, it was still a prison.

Then Beau rushed after him into the other room. "What are you doing? Trevor, calm down!"

"Easy for you to say! You haven't been in a hole for the past few months." Tearing the kitchen area apart in search of any sharp object, Trevor turned to him and practically snarled at the question. "What the hell took you so long?" he growled over his shoulder.

"It's a long story. I've had every asset at my disposal looking for you."

Trevor growled in response.

"How are you?" Beau asked.

"How am I?" he repeated, his gray eyes blazing, his thick brown hair grown past his shoulders. "How. Am. I . . . Well, let me tell you, Beauchamp. Back in Spain, we had a massive skirmish with thirty Promethean hirelings. We killed them, of course, accidentally blew up a church in the process. Then I got shot. Spent a few weeks as an invalid, then realized my best friend had lost his mind when he tried to talk me into becoming a bloody mercenary.

"Oh, but that was just the start of the fun. Because then, when I refused, he took advantage of my weakened state to kick me into his own makeshift prison. Hell, I'm talking to myself down there in the dark. Whole conversations, and sometimes the furniture talks back! Of course, my dear old friend, Nick, will still come and talk to me through the door since the rat bastard has got no one else to talk to. Of course, most of the time, my only answer to his conversation is 'Bugger off, you snaky serpent shit.' By the way, he told me you got married."

"Yes."

Trevor harrumphed. "Nice you had the time to find a bride and court her, what with how busy you must've been looking for me."

"It was a short courtship," he said with a wince.

"Mine's probably ruined, you realize. Laura's probably written me off for dead. I haven't gotten laid in half a year, not that you give a damn. Do the Elders know about Nick?"

"Not yet."

"Because they probably think I deserted like he did. Don't ask me to run, either. Bastard kicked my knee out in one of our recent brawls when I tried to get out. I'll probably limp for another month yet. And to top it all off, I look like"—he gestured toward his long hair and bearded jaw—"the mad, bloody hermit living in the far corner of somebody's wooded acreage! So does that answer your question of how I am?"

"Quite," Beau replied. "I understand you're irked, but I'm glad as hell to see you alive."

"He wasn't going to kill me!" Trevor scoffed. "He's just abused my friendship and my trust past toleration and for that, I will make the bounder pay."

"You'll get your chance, I promise." Still stunned that Nick would do this to Trevor, Beau watched his friend lay hold of a kitchen implement that could easily do some damage in the hands of a trained Order agent. But Trevor tossed the roasting spit aside and put out his hand.

"Give me your pistol."

Beau stared at him. He was wearing a pair of Mantons in the holster belt round his waist. But he hesitated. "We need him alive, Trev."

"I know that! When I said I'd kill him, I didn't mean it literally, for God's sake."

"Are you sure?"

"Yes."

"Because it would be understandable."

Trevor took a deep breath and let it out, slowly beginning to turn back into the relatively civilized human being Beau remembered. "All right," he said at length. "I'm all right now. I just needed to get some of that off my chest."

Beau smiled. Then he handed him the gun. "Don't do anything stupid."

Trevor nodded, looking even more like his old self once he had a means of self-defense securely in hand. He tucked the pistol into the waist of his dusty tan trousers. "It's good to see you."

"You, as well, mate." He gave Trevor's shoulder a brotherly squeeze.

He was not sure he had the heart to tell Trevor that Rotherstone's team had just been sent to the Tower of London, though. One thing at a time.

"So, do you know where he went?"

"Where, no, but I do know *what* he was doing. Every day he goes to check the drop point to see if they've left him the name of the person they want him to kill."

"He'll be back soon?"

"Any moment." Trevor paused and looked at him.

"Good," Beau murmured as he reloaded the pistol he had shot at the door. "Then we'll be waiting for him."

*D*riving a delivery cart was harder than it looked, Carissa was finding. Her arms and shoulders ached from laboring to manage four very strong carthorses, and a whip, to boot. But she had seen the general route Beau's carriage had taken.

It took some searching to find his parked coach. She had got lost twice and had to turn around in a cramped alley, which had involved getting down from the driver's seat and taking the lead horse by the bridle.

She got under way again once they were headed in the right direction, and at last, she spotted her husband's glossy black coach-and-four parked on the side of the street.

The gunsmith's apprentice came jogging over with a look of alarm as she pulled up behind it.

"Where is my husband?" she demanded, but Michael quickly signaled for quiet, a finger to his lips.

"Milady, it isn't safe for you to be here."

"Well, I am here now, and I'm not leaving until I speak to my husband!"

"His Lordship is inside, but for your own safety, will you please stay out of sight?"

"We're near Nick's hiding place?" she asked dubiously.

"It's just around the corner. We're waiting for him to arrive."

"Then I suppose you're right. I'd better hide. He'll recognize me if he sees me and realize Beau's inside."

Michael nodded. "We can't let him see my master's name on the delivery cart, either. If you'll wait inside Lord Beauchamp's coach, I'll drive the cart around the block. You're going to be here by yourself, so you'd better stay hidden if he comes by."

"Very well." Remembering Nick's cloaked death threat against her, she slid down from the driver's seat of the cart. The lad steadied her with a polite hand as she caught her balance. Then he waved her toward Beau's coach.

As soon as she climbed inside, Michael ran back to

the delivery wagon and drove away, to keep it out of
sight.

His timing proved impeccable, for he no sooner
drove it around the corner than Nick himself appeared,
riding across the intersection on horseback.

Carissa ducked with a gasp as Nick rode by.

When the sound of his horse's hooves had clip-
clopped past, she peeked past the edge of the carriage
window.

He was out of sight. But she had to know what was
happening. She slipped down from the coach and
sneaked over to the corner, peering around it.

Her eyes widened as she watched the rogue agent
dismount, walk his horse into the mews, and then re-
appear a moment later, heading for a door toward the
back part of the building.

She ducked behind the wall, her heart pounding, when
Nick glanced around, looking back over his shoulder,
a man perennially on guard. But as he reached for the
door handle, he suddenly noticed something wrong
with it and froze.

In the next heartbeat, Nick backed away from the
door, and Carissa knew he was about to get away again.

"Beau!" she hollered as loud as she could. "He's just
outside the door!"

Nick whirled around to see where her shout had come
from, but the door blasted open behind him, and Beau
flew out, charging straight at him.

In the barest of seconds, she saw Nick hesitate, his
hand drifting toward the holstered pistol at his side.
Before he could decide whether or not to draw on his
boyhood friend, Beau plowed into him, tackling him
to the ground. *Slam!* They began to brawl: two trained
killers.

A tall, muscular man who looked to her like some sort of pirate with a shock of long, dark brown hair and a scruffy beard came racing out of the building right behind Beau. Despite slightly favoring one leg as he ran, he dove into the fray. *That must be Lord Trevor Montgomery!* Beau's other missing teammate.

Glad that Beau had freed him, she ran toward the fight, leaving the shelter of the corner, but she could not see clearly what was happening. Both men were on top of Nick, pummeling him and getting him under control.

Trevor pulled back his right fist while holding Nick's jacket with his left hand. He was perfectly aligned for a shattering punch to the face, but something inside him must have held him back, for he did not land the blow. "Damn you," was all he said. Roughly releasing Nick's jacket, he pivoted and took a few, uneven steps away, his chest heaving.

With a grim scowl, Trevor struggled to bring his anger back under control while Beau hauled Nick to his feet.

"Who's the target?" he demanded, holding fast to his arm while making the implied threat of his pistol.

Nick just looked at him.

"Search him," Beau said to Trevor.

"I already destroyed the message," Nick said wearily.

"No, you didn't," Beau clipped out. "Not when you know full well it's the only evidence that can exonerate you if anything were to go wrong."

"Did you hide it in your watch, as usual?" Trevor asked.

"You boys are really something else," Nick muttered.

But Trevor pulled Nick's fob watch out of his waistcoat by its chain and clicked the metal back of it open.

"Ah, what have we here?" he taunted, drawing a tiny, folded piece of paper out of the watch itself.

"You're getting predictable in your old age, man."

"Only to you," Nick replied dryly.

"What does it say?" Beau asked.

Trevor paled as he read the slip of paper. Then he lifted his gaze to Nick's in shock. "You son of a bitch. Were you really going to do this?"

Nick said nothing.

"Who's the target?" Beau repeated.

Trevor glanced at him. "The Prime Minister."

"Good God! You weren't really going through with this, were you?"

"I don't know!" Nick erupted in sudden fury. "I only got the damned thing minutes ago! You think I expected this?"

"You should never have taken the job in the first place!" Beau roared back in his face. "You don't even know who hired you!"

"I do," Carissa spoke up uneasily from several feet away.

This was the first the men noticed her.

Already furious, Beau turned at the sound of her voice; his eyes narrowed to angry slashes at the sight of her, but she held her ground.

"I found the artist," she informed him. "The 'disposable man' Madame Angelique described. If you can make him talk, you'll have your proof about who hired Nick."

"You found him?" Beau demanded.

"Yes!" she said. "And if you'll listen to me for once—just give me a chance—I can take you to him."

"*W*ho is this woman?" Trevor asked bluntly.

"Beauchamp's wife. Hullo, Carissa."

"Nick," she answered with a wry look.

"The wife!" Trevor exclaimed.

"How dare you ignore my orders once again?" Beau demanded.

"I didn't want to do it, believe me. Especially after all that's happened between us. But I had a sudden insight, and I had to check on it—for your sake. For all of us!" she insisted, refusing to back down. "And it's a good thing I did, because it turns out I was right."

Beau stared rather coldly at her. "I'm listening," he said.

"Mr. Charles Vincent owns the waxworks museum in Southwark, where all his bloody fantasies of revolution are on display for all the world to see. I know for a fact he is connected to the so-called Prophet, Professor Culvert, Ezra Green's mentor—"

"I know who he is," Beau snapped.

"I saw Culvert and this artist together with my own eyes at a bookshop in Russell Square. Culvert was giving a speech and I-I went to hear it, after you told me about him. I wanted to find out more—"

"You went to hear him speak?" he cried, throwing up his hands.

"I wanted to tell you!" she exclaimed, her cheeks flushing. "But then Nick paid his call on me and rather changed the subject. So I just let it go. I didn't think I had learned anything useful, anyway! And I didn't want you to be angry at me. Look, I'm sorry," she said impatiently. "But let's keep our minds on the problem at hand! If it was Culvert who sent the artist to hire Nick to assassinate the Prime Minister—who's to say that Ezra Green wasn't in on it from the start? You already told me you thought he was out for the Order's blood. What just happened at the docks proves that you were right." She glanced around at the agents. "You all are being set up. Nick was merely the tool with which they meant to destroy you."

His jaw clenched, Beau conceded this with a nod. "Back at the docks, Green did just say a few cryptic things to me about a new England coming. Together with what you've just told us, his words begin to make sense."

"Then what are we waiting for? If you can get hold of Charles Vincent and persuade him to reveal the names of those who sent him to France, then you can turn the tables on that odious lizard man. So, do you want to stand here fighting with me, or do you want to get to the bottom of this?" she flung out.

Beau and his friends exchanged a sardonic glance.

"You do know how to pick 'em," Trevor drawled.

Carissa scowled at him, but Beau eyed her dubiously. "You say he's down in Southwark? Whereabouts?"

"Come on, I'll take you to him. There's no time to lose." She pivoted on her heel and began marching back toward the carriage. Despite her outward show of confidence, her knees were shaking after she had made her stand before her outraged husband.

They had greater worries to deal with at the moment, but she was not naïve enough to think that this was over.

𝒰pon their arrival in Southwark, Carissa tamped down her anxiety, watching out the carriage window as Beau and Trevor went across the street toward the waxworks museum.

She told herself not to worry. Charles Vincent was no match for two Order agents. Yet from the second they went through the door and disappeared inside, every minute dragged.

"He'll be fine, Mrs. Beauchamp," Nick muttered, sitting across from her, his wrists bound with the very ropes he had previously used on Trevor.

Michael, the gunsmith's apprentice, was also in the carriage; sitting across from their prisoner, he was keeping Nick in the sights of his pistol.

Nick gave the lad a darkly mocking stare and seemed to be contemplating all the ways he could've bested him, a green, untried youth.

Carissa knew firsthand that Nick was a force to be reckoned with. Nevertheless, she sensed the heaviness of his utter remorse ever since Beau had related how their comrades had been arrested at the docks and thrown into the dreaded Tower of London.

"Quit staring at me," Nick rumbled at her in a low tone.

She tilted her head. "I'm sorry, I just can't stop wondering, would you really have shot Lord Liverpool?"

"I don't know," he muttered, gazing out the window in disgust.

"Would you?" she persisted.

He let out a sudden, bitter scoff. "What does it matter what I say? Even if I'd have refused, who'd believe me now?"

"You know who would," she answered softly. "Beauchamp."

"After I threatened his lady?"

"You didn't scare me," she replied.

As he gazed at her, a rueful half smile slowly curved his lips. "I've known Beau a long time, my lady. For what it's worth, I think you're exactly what he needed."

She gave him a wistful smile in spite of herself and lowered her head. "I hope you're right," she said. At the moment, she feared Beau was kicking himself for ever getting involved with a meddling lady of information.

"*B*loody hell," Trevor murmured, as they prowled through the dark, macabre labyrinth of the wax museum. "This is what he does in his spare time?"

"At least he's got talent. You've got to give him that."

Charles Vincent had employed every visual trick known to art and science to enhance his sinister scenes. He used mirrors and *trompe-l'oeil* painting like a magician; lighting techniques and clockwork mechanical devices borrowed from the theatre gave some of his figures motion and made them seem even more alive.

Beau scanned each new, gruesome scene they passed,

his gun at the ready, but concealed in his coat pocket to avoid alarming the other visitors at the museum.

Their presence complicated matters, but even so, he had to admit it felt good to be *doing* the sort of thing he was trained for instead of all those endless rounds of hostile interrogation.

"Your lady was right. There does appear to be a theme," Trevor remarked wryly, as they passed the waxen beheading of King Charles.

"I can't believe she came here by herself," Beau growled, but Trevor laughed softly, both of them watching everywhere, searching the shadows for the pale, lanky artist Carissa had described.

"So," Trevor said in amusement. "A redhead, eh?" He looked askance at him with a jolly glimmer in his eyes.

Beau ignored him with a huff.

"Never thought I'd see the day."

"What?" he retorted.

"You're madly in love with her."

He snorted. "At the moment, I'd like to wring her neck. She's completely impossible."

"Hmm, who does that sound like?"

"Uh, shut up."

Trevor laughed quietly as they both continued advancing, guns drawn. "So, Beauchamp's met his match. Well, when I think back to how you and Nick used to rail on me for being so smitten with Laura." He shook his head.

"How is she, anyway?" Beau asked, as they moved on through the dimly lit maze of corridors.

"No idea. She probably thinks I'm dead. So, how do you want to do this?" Trevor nodded at the corridor ahead.

Beau shrugged. "By the book, I think. If we get too rough, it'll only seem to prove everything Green's been saying about our organization."

"Good thing we left Nick outside, then. Speaking of the Inquisition—" Trevor nodded at the scene of a Spanish torture chamber.

"Charming. Let's find this sick bastard and put an end to his fun."

Trevor nodded. They split up, continuing their search.

When Beau passed the scene of Ann Boleyn kneeling for the axe man's blow, it tightened the knot in his stomach, reminding him afresh of his brothers in the Tower. The sight of the dungeon tableaux renewed his cold rage. What the hell was he going to say to their wives about all of this, anyway?

That reminded him. Jordan had told him to summon Mara, who had ties to the Regent. Prinny was a personal friend of hers, the godfather of her little boy.

Beau made a mental note to do that next. But he could not think about their wives right now and the female hysterics he was going to have to deal with. He had enough trouble with his own meddling bride at the moment.

On the other hand, Carissa had brought him this lead, he admitted, irked at his own surging pride in her. *Not so fast. We'll see if it pays off.* Their visit to the wax-works could still turn out to be naught but a dangerous waste of time.

Then Beau came to the French Revolution scene and stopped, taken aback. With a chill down his spine, he scanned the grim spectacle.

The wild Paris mob had been lovingly reproduced, down to the last detail—thanks in part, most likely, to Madame Angelique's firsthand account. Then he spotted the basket of heads Carissa told him to watch for. Beau lifted an eyebrow, spotting a possible likeness of Prinny among the waxen decapitated heads. Under normal circumstances, the artist's gall would have made him furious. In this case, however, it was a welcome sight: evidence. Tangible proof of their malice toward the Crown, and certainly a strong suggestion of their violent, revolutionary intents.

He glanced around, saw no one was coming, and vaulted lightly over the railing for a closer look. He lifted the Prinny head out of the basket by its shock of frizzy reddish brown hair. With an odd sense of graveyard humor, he held it up and looked at the waxen head, eye to eye, then laughed dryly under his breath. *Trevor needs to see this.*

He climbed out of the mob scene, taking the head with him. He found it rather hilarious to be carrying the Regent's head around, but the damned thing might be needed for evidence. Still on the hunt for its maker, he walked down the darkened corridor, his pistol in his right hand, the head tucked under his left arm.

But when he noticed a black curtain on the right and heard work sounds coming from behind it, he stepped closer, intrigued. Ignoring the sign that read KEEP OUT, he pushed the curtain aside a couple of inches and peered into the latest waxworks scene still under construction.

His stare homed in on the artist hard at work, clearly absorbed in his pursuits. The fellow matched the description Carissa had provided, but even without it, he could've known him by his theme—another king getting his comeuppance. In this one, the English barons were forcing King John to sign the Magna Carta.

Inspired, himself, with an interesting way to get the

man's attention and challenge him about his guilt, Beau rolled the Regent's head at its creator.

Charles Vincent looked over as Prinny's likeness came tumbling toward him. Beau stepped past the curtain, strolling toward the proprietor with a dark stare.

Vincent blanched and backed away from his figure. "What is the meaning of this?" he sputtered.

"I've been wondering that myself," Beau replied.

"You're with the Order," the man breathed.

Beau smiled.

Charles Vincent bolted, dashing out past the far side of the curtain. Beau chased him.

"Trev!" he shouted into the hallway.

Trevor was coming around the other corner and appeared just in time to head him off.

Vincent whirled around, saw Beau closing in behind him, Trevor blocking his path ahead. He darted sideways into the Coliseum.

"Stay back!" he warned, brandishing a sculptor's implement with a nasty little blade on the end.

Beau leaped over the rail into the scene and stalked him like a lion. Vincent dodged away again, running for a door in the background that had been painted into invisibility. "Go round the other way!" Beau yelled to Trevor as he set off chasing the man.

Beau knew he was at a dangerous disadvantage. This was Vincent's lair. He knew every nook and cranny of the place, while all the illusions and pitch-black passageways behind the walls were new to Beau. Even so, he pursued him through the hidden maze that gave the artist access to his sets, until, all of a sudden, they somehow burst out near the guillotine once again.

Passing visitors screamed at the sudden intrusion.

Waxen figures went flying: pitchfork-wielding revolutionaries in liberty caps, gendarmes, a hooded executioner.

Cornered, Vincent slashed at him with his wax-carving knife; Beau grasped his wrist and forced him to the floor.

"Cooperate, or I'll break your arm!"

He screamed. "No, please!"

Locating them by the sound of the visitors' shrieks, Trevor came hurtling over the front rail to assist, ignoring his injured knee though he cursed when he landed.

"Don't move," he ordered, training his pistol on their man.

"I've got him," Beau said through gritted teeth, his heart pounding.

"Who are you? What do you want with me?" the artist cried, aghast.

Beau crouched down slowly. "Oh, I think you already know."

By the time Beau and Trevor escorted Charles Vincent out of the wax museum, he had already confessed, confirming their worst fears. Professor Culvert had reassembled his coterie of young devotees, now powerful men placed here and there in the government, including Ezra Green.

Vincent did not know how many were taking part in the conspiracy, but he guessed their number at under twenty men. The group had hired the "assassin" to kill the Prime Minister and were even now, ready and waiting to pounce.

They would seize their opportunity in the crisis that they knew in advance would erupt once the Tory leader fell.

It was clear to Beau that this odd waxworks fellow had been specifically chosen to go to France and arrange the contract. He was expendable because, to start, he did not bring the kind of power the others had to offer.

More importantly, with the subtle themes of violent revolution on display throughout The Gala of History, the eccentric artist would seem unstable, even unhinged enough to have conceived the plot alone. They must have brought him in from the start as their unwitting scapegoat.

Unluckily for them, the conspirators had not counted on anyone's being able to trace the man to them, let alone getting him to confess. But when Beau had convinced him that his coconspirators meant to let him take the fall for all of them, he finally gave way.

The waxworks man had tearfully admitted that Culvert and Green had set out in secret to kill two birds with one stone: assassinate the hated Lord Liverpool and destroy the Order in the process.

But men who saw themselves as possessing superior intellect had, in Beau's experience, a fatal tendency to overreach. Arrogance and hatred got them every time. Once again, they'd gone too far. Destroy the Order? No, Beau vowed. Chivalry and honor would not be killed so easily.

Except perhaps in Nick.

When they returned to the carriage, he asked the others to step out of the carriage so he could have a private word with his errant brother agent.

"Listen." He stared hard into Nick's dark eyes. "We got our man, but coward that he is, I fear he's going to back out of his confession as soon as it's official. There's only one way this is going to work. We need your help."

"Figures."

"It's time for you to choose which side you're on, Nick. Here's my offer. I won't say anything to the outer world about this. The Elders can deal with you privately, later, as they see fit. I'm very sure you'll end up in the dungeon either way. But if you want to restore what's left of your honor, I'm giving you this chance. Come with me and we will make the claim that you were on a covert mission the whole time—as loyal as ever, an Order agent in good standing—sent to unearth this conspiracy."

Nick stared at him incredulously. "You're going to make *me* out as the hero? After what I've done?"

"Do you think I care who gets the credit?" Beau retorted. "Right now, my concern is for our brothers in the Tower. We need to present a united front now if we're going to get through this attempt to destroy us. Otherwise"—he shrugged—"these bastards are going to have us for breakfast."

Nick studied him with a dubious look. "So, you want to expose a conspiracy by telling more lies? I trust you see the irony."

"Order doctrine says liars don't deserve the truth," he replied. "Besides, you'd only be playing a role. It isn't as though you're off the hook. But help me now, and I'll help you to mitigate whatever punishment the Elders hand down to you. I'm willing to give you another chance to make up for what you've done because, frankly, I need your help. If there is any honor left in you, back me up in this."

"Of course," he murmured, looking stunned. "Of course I will."

Beau was a little stunned himself, but he could see no other way. His best strategy to save the others and nail

Green to the wall was to claim that Nick's few months as a mercenary had all been a counterploy.

One that their enemies had obligingly walked into.

The Elders could sort out the dark truth later in dealing with Lord Forrester, but it was best if this was handled internally by the Order.

"I can't believe you're giving me another chance," he said quietly, his gaze downcast.

"Neither can I. But you saved my life plenty of times. Don't get me wrong, you're a thoroughgoing bastard. But you're still my brother."

At Beau's simple statement, Nick could no longer disguise his remorse behind bravado. He lifted his stricken gaze slowly to Beau's. "I wouldn't have done it, you know. Lord Liverpool, I mean. I hope you can believe that."

"I know," Beau said quietly.

"I'll do whatever it takes," Nick forced out. "Just tell me what you want me to say."

Beau cut the ropes around Nick's wrists and filled him in on the details of his plan.

*W*ith the strength of the information they now had on hand, Beau made the decision to appeal directly to the Regent. The mood inside the carriage was tense as they rushed to Carlton House.

When they reached the corner of Pall Mall, a short distance from the prince's residence, Beau sent the gunsmith's apprentice on his way. "There's no reason to drag you any further into this than you already are. You did well. I'll be sure to put in a good word with the Elders for you."

If the Order survives.

"Good luck, sir." Michael jumped out of the carriage and jogged off, but when Beau glanced at Carissa, she shook her head at him in warning.

"Don't even think about trying to send me off, too."

He smiled in spite of himself. "I wasn't about to."

A few moments later, they drove up to the gates of Carlton House. The guards admitted them on the Order's credentials and looked at them with private admiration. But given the arrests of their brethren, they were parted from their weapons, and five palace guards escorted Beau, Nick, and Trevor inside, along with their prisoner and Carissa.

"We need to see His Royal Highness at once. This man has critical information for the prince." Beau nodded at the waxworks man, who cowered from the soldiers.

"I'll take you to the chamberlain, but I don't know if you'll get an audience," the lieutenant confided. "His Royal Highness already has some important visitors, including one who doesn't like you gentlemen very much, from what I hear."

Beau gave the man a discreet nod of thanks for this warning, but mentally, he cursed. Apparently, Ezra Green had beaten them there. The schemer must have anticipated that Beau's next move would be an attempt to appeal to the Regent personally. No matter. He was ready for him.

The only question was, how would Green react when he faced Charles Vincent's accusations. Would he give himself away? Was this even going to work?

There was only one way to find out. Striding through the opulent halls of the Regent's palace with their uniformed escorts, Beau and Trevor kept Nick between them though he was no longer bound; Nick, in turn, kept hold of Charles Vincent, who was.

The waxworks man had his wrists tied behind him. Trevor was keeping a close eye on him, while Beau walked beside Carissa.

As they strode down the interior colonnade approaching the large, glittering Throne Room where Prinny had been cornered by his royal responsibilities for once, they could already hear Ezra Green whining.

"Sire, the findings of my investigation are most dire! Something must be done! The Order has caused an incident the full ramifications of which we cannot yet know! Who knows what else they might have up their sleeves?"

"Yes, but to put them in the Tower? Seems rather extreme, what?"

"Your Highness—seventy dead! And every victim of this tragedy was either a representative of a foreign court or a member of some prominent European family! It is a black mark for all of England, what they've done. Moreover, they admit to it! The agents are all guilty, they said as much themselves! If they are not punished, the nations all these victims hail from will demand an explanation. If we do not make an example of these cold-blooded killers and subject them to the full fury of the law, then the Crown will be seen as endorsing their behavior. You, sire, could be personally blamed! Who knows what it could lead to? Trade tariffs, withdrawing of ambassadors—perhaps even to war!"

"Yes, but I've played cards with these men," Prinny said in annoyance. "They are not, as you describe, cold-blooded killers, Mr. Green."

"I am sure they would not show that face to you, Your Highness. And if I may be so bold, sire, one cannot afford to be blinded by personal feelings in such matters. Furthermore, if Your Highness will permit me to point out, if these men are proven felons, all their holdings revert to the Crown," he finished with a humble bow.

Beau fumed in silence, but beside him, Carissa faltered. He glanced at her and saw that, hearing this, her face had gone white.

He steadied her with a hand on her elbow, but he had a fair idea of what she must be thinking. If Max, Rohan, and Jordan all were hanged, their homes and holdings forfeit to the sovereign, then Daphne, Kate, and Mara would be left widowed and penniless.

But he was not going to let any of that happen. The time to stop it was at hand.

He stepped away from his wife and approached the chamberlain; after a moment's quiet conference, he procured the fellow's nod. The chamberlain slipped in discreetly.

The name of Viscount Beauchamp was obviously not unknown to Prinny, for they were promptly admitted.

Just outside the open double doors, Beau turned to the others. "Carissa, stay out of trouble here. Trevor, bring Mr. Vincent in when I call for you. We'll see how Green reacts when he's faced with our witness."

"Good luck," Carissa murmured.

He held her gaze with muted adoration and gave her a nod. Then he glanced at Nick. "Ready?"

Nick nodded back.

The chamberlain announced them: "Viscount Beauchamp and Baron Forrester!"

They walked in, both of them on guard.

The Regent sat on a throne beneath a velvet-draped canopy at the head of the room. A number of ministerial types had apparently rushed to the scene to find out why four of the ton's most notable peers had been thrown into the Tower.

"Ah, Lord Beauchamp," the Regent addressed him. "It's good you've come. Perhaps you can tell us the Order's side of the story."

"I would be honored, Your Royal Highness," he replied, as he and Nick both made the proper bows.

Then he and Nick split up, walking cautiously around Ezra Green, flanking him on either side. Mr. Green turned nervously, trying to watch them both from where he stood in the center of the room.

"I heard some of what Mr. Green was saying, but I'm afraid he left out the most important part of the story."

Green scoffed, but the Regent lifted his eyebrows.

"Oh? What's that?"

"Although the seventy men who died in that explosion in Bavaria were indeed courtier friends of various princes, and aristocrats from great families, they also happened to be the remaining leaders of the Promethean cult. Yes, our agents stopped them by killing every last one of them. But our men should be thanked and congratulated, not imprisoned for doing their duty."

"Ha! What else should we expect him to say?" Green countered in contempt. "Of course he would defend them. He is one of them. But do not be fooled by his smooth talk, sire. Order agents are trained to lie expertly, as much as they are trained to kill. This is why the panel has ruled they prove such a threat!

"Of course they give lip service to loyalty," he continued, "but what if that's just one of their lies? Why, their old handler could barely control them, arrogant as they are! With their skills, their influence, their power, fortune, and access to secret government information, think of the threat they could pose to all of us if they were to unite with some unknown goal of their own! They could pose a threat to this government!"

Beau laughed aloud. Green's face reddened as he whirled back to face the Regent. "It's not as though this would be a new skill for them! They've done it before, sire! In Naples! Some of the German principalities!"

"To limit the reach of Napoleon," Nick chimed in, qualifying that accusation.

"The point is, they know how to do it. And now that the war's over, and they're all here in England together, how will they keep themselves busy, I ask you, sire? War is all they know. If they become restless, such coups are already part of their repertoire!"

"I suppose you're right, we probably could, if we really wanted to," Beau drawled. "What, make a virtual prisoner of His Royal Highness? Control key members of Parliament? Maybe we already do," he taunted him.

"I say!" a leading Cabinet minister exclaimed. "Do you?"

"Of course not, Lord Eldon. We are loyal. That is the chief difference between us and Mr. Green and his shadowy friends."

"I beg your pardon!" Green uttered, drawing himself up in withering indignation.

"As a great student of human nature—which I must be, as a proper spy—I have learned that we are all hypocrites in some way. People generally accuse others most vehemently of the very fault they themselves are secretly prone to. And so it is with Mr. Green." Beau turned to the real traitor. "He accuses the Order of disloyalty. Of plotting to take over the country. This is absurd. If the Order had wanted to do so, it could've been accomplished decades ago, perhaps even centuries. But, you see, that would be going against everything we stand for, believe in. Not so with Mr. Green."

"How dare you?" the angry MP cried.

"We have unearthed the truth about who's really scheming to remake England, and it is not the Order, I can assure you."

"What? Is this true?" The old ministers in the room began murmuring among themselves.

"What are you insinuating, sir?"

"That you are the traitor, Mr. Green."

"That's a lie!" he shouted. "I will not hear this nonsense. Sire, this is the sort of manipulative slander in which the Order specializes, and any evidence he might produce to support this fiction is likewise manufactured!"

"Beauchamp, what is going on?" Prinny spoke up with a curious frown.

"Your Royal Highness; ministers; my lords, it is time we ended this charade."

Mr. Green was shaking his head at him but beginning to look nervous. "I have no idea what you can mean by all this."

"Then I shall enlighten you. I'm afraid my friend Lord Forrester here is the 'mercenary' you and your coconspirators hired to assassinate Lord Liverpool."

A gasp arose in the room.

"Who is alive and well," Beau hastened to add. "Don't be alarmed, gentlemen. The Prime Minister was never in any danger. For you see, Lord Forrester has been on a covert mission for months to draw out the traitors in our midst. We just didn't expect to find a Member of Parliament among them."

All the color washed out of Ezra Green's face.

"Nothing to say for yourself, sir?"

"This is preposterous! Sheer, utter nonsense!" he sputtered, backing away with a look of panic. "You see, Your Highness? You see how these men are out of control? Honestly, Beauchamp, how dare you come before the Regent and make such wild, unfounded accusations? Not that anyone here believes you—"

"I do," Nick offered.

"The word of a scapegrace and a libertine who has dallied with half your wives?" Green scoffed at the gentlemen, shaking his head. "I don't know what game you are playing, Beauchamp, but you have no proof, and so I will see you in court for this unforgivable libel."

"Hmm. Proof. Well." He folded his arms across his chest, rather enjoying this. "Perhaps your colleague can help to jar your memory. Montgomery! Bring him in!"

The door opened, and Trevor stepped in, escorting their frightened prisoner into the room.

When Ezra Green and Charles Vincent saw each other, the recognition on both faces was unmistakable.

Green briefly looked like he might pass out.

"Remember now?" Beau inquired.

Green looked at Beau, his expression hardening into an icy mask of rage. "I've never seen this man before."

"Of course you have. And he will admit it. Why should he not, when you were willing to let him hang alone for your conspiracy? The only question is, was it you or Professor Culvert who first hatched the plot to hire our 'assassin' here to kill the Prime Minister?" he asked with a casual gesture at Nick.

"Why would he want to kill Liverpool?" Prinny asked in astonishment.

"Why, indeed. Because he is a secret revolutionary,

following in the footsteps of his mentor, Your Highness. With one bullet, he could kill two birds with one
stone. Not only could he get rid of a man he and his
cohorts see as a tyrant, but he could have had the Order
condemned in the process by pinning the assassination
on us through Forrester. Fortunately for us all, and for
Lord Liverpool, it was an Order operation all along."

Ezra Green's jaw dropped.

Beau flashed a smile—and set him off.

"To hell with all of you!" Green snarled, bending to
whip out a small pistol he had concealed in his boot.
"Death to tyrants!"

Beau was already in motion, leaping through the air
as Green took aim at the large, easy target of the startled
Regent. Beau tackled him to the ground as the gun went
off. Around the opulent chamber, the ministers cried out
in shock, and Beau was dimly aware of Carissa rushing
in at the sound of the shot while he struggled to subdue
Green.

He knocked him out cold with a punch in the face
that, for him, was downright cathartic. Damn, but he'd
been wanting to do that for weeks.

Then, chest heaving, he glanced over his shoulder to
make sure Prinny was all right.

He drew in his breath at what he saw.

Nick was bleeding. While Beau had tackled the
gunman, Nick had rushed to shield the prince. The
bullet meant for George had ended up in the midsec-
tion of their would-be mercenary.

Nick fell to the floor.

Trevor abandoned Charles Vincent to the custody of
the palace guards who had come storming in. He flew
to Nick's side, sliding across the polished floor onto his
knees beside him. "You foolhardy—"

"Uh, shut up. Had to do it. He'll be King." Blood was flowing out from between Nick's fingers as he clutched his wound. "Trev," he rasped, "can you forgive me?"

"Hell, no, if you go dying on us now," Trevor retorted, choked with emotion. "Don't even try it, or I'm comin' down to the underworld to kick your arse."

Nick smiled weakly at the jest but closed his eyes. "Like to see you try."

*C*arissa looked on, stricken, as Beau joined the other two, shouting for a surgeon. She knew this was her beloved husband's worst nightmare, seeing his best friend bleeding his life out right before his eyes. *Please, God, let him live.* Nick might be a bounder, but Beau did not deserve this. *Don't make him lose another friend.*

The politicians in the room were all shouting at each other, while the Prince Regent looked horrified and shaken.

The palace guards took both Ezra Green and Charles Vincent into custody, while the royal physicians sped Nick away to try to save his life. Trevor accompanied him, but Beau turned, impassioned, to the Regent, and, to Carissa's shock, her husband let the sovereign have it.

"Do you see now? Can you see that we are loyal?" he cried, taking a step toward him, enough to alarm the soldiers, who came closer. "Confiscate our homes?" he wrenched out. "He just took a bullet for you! You don't even know, *sire,* you don't even know how many have died for your sake—for England's! They'd give their lives without a second thought—and you throw them in the Tower? Well, damn you, sir. Damn you, I say. When will it ever be enough?"

The Regent stood with a look of such offended wrath on his ruddy face at being addressed in this manner, that Carissa feared her husband had just signed all the agents' execution papers, including his own.

She ran to him, taking his arm, seeking to quiet him. "Forgive my husband, Your Royal Highness, please!" she pleaded, heart pounding in dread. "Lord Beauchamp would never presume to rebuke you. He is overset to see his friend fallen."

Beau pulled his arm free of her grasp. "Rubbish. I meant every word." And he held the royal stare without averting his eyes, without bowing, without backing down, his chin high.

He stared at the monarch, man to man, until finally, it was the prince who faltered slightly. "And what would you have Us do?"

"Show some damned backbone," he replied. Then he bowed his head, though his eyes still blazed. "Your Royal Highness," he added obediently—through gritted teeth.

Carissa stared at him in disbelief. Now, for certain, he would hang. He had not just yelled at the future king. He had cursed at him, too. She was beside herself.

We're doomed.

The Regent turned slowly to the Captain of the Guard and gave his judgment: "Release Our agents from the Tower."

"What?" she breathed, glancing over.

Beau lifted his head again.

"Well, don't dawdle, man! You have your orders!"

"Your Highness—" One of the ministers from the Treasury attempted to belay him.

"Do not question me!" George bellowed, sounding almost like a king. "Beauchamp's right. I should have

never let the matter go this far." He fluffed out the tails
of his coat and took his throne once more. "Demmed
impertinent, though, I say! You get away with that once
with me, sir. Once!" He held up a chubby, jeweled
finger. "For your friend's sake. But don't worry about
him," the Regent muttered. "Lord Forrester does not
have Our permission to die."

"Thank you, Your Royal Highness. Thank you."
Beau closed his eyes as Carissa slipped her arms
around him. He leaned his head against hers and let
out a long, shaky exhalation.

Chapter
26

"Well, I stand corrected," Beau announced, as they walked out of Carlton House, his arm casually draped around her shoulders. "You, my little lady of information, are a better spy than some of the agents I've known."

Carissa beamed at him. "Really?"

"It's true. We owe you a huge debt of gratitude. You did the right thing. I'm man enough to admit it. If you had not come through with that crucial piece of information, who knows where we'd be?"

"Does that mean you forgive me for disobeying you, then?"

"Of course. But it wasn't because of your heroics today." He stopped and turned to face her, taking her gently by the shoulders. "You were already forgiven when we parted ways, my darling. Didn't you hear me say so?"

"Maybe not. I was too busy feeling awful." She

searched his blue eyes. "What I didn't hear you say," she ventured, then lost her nerve.

"Yes?" he prompted tenderly.

"Well—when I told you I love you, Beau, you didn't say it back."

"Cowardice."

She searched his face uncertainly, her heart still feeling bruised and vulnerable.

He tilted his head, staring wistfully into her eyes. "I do love you, Carissa."

"You don't have to say it if you don't want to—"

"But I do." He captured her chin on his fingertips and lifted her head, forcing her to meet his stormy gaze. He took her hand and placed it on his heart. "This is yours, my love. When you said you loved me that first time, I was just . . . taken aback by everything that had just occurred with Benton. Under the circumstances, I wasn't sure how to react. I wasn't even sure you weren't just saying that to manipulate me, so I wouldn't be angry at you. Trying to wrap me around your finger."

She shook her head. "I said it because it's the truth. I'm always going to tell you the truth now, Beau, however hard it might be. I've learned my lesson, believe me. I'm not going to let any more secrets come between us. You have my word on that. If you'll give me another chance, I'll show you that I *can* be honest with you from now on. I would never risk losing you again."

"Sweeting, you've got all the chances you need, and I hope you'll give me the same, because I'm probably going to need them."

"Of course," she whispered gently, a lump in her throat. Then she stepped closer, hugging him. He wrapped his arms around her. She laid her head on his chest. "After all, that's what love's about, isn't it?" she asked softly. "Forgiving each other. Finding the courage to trust."

He kissed her head and nodded as he held her. Then he lapsed into a thoughtful silence for a moment. "You know, I bear some responsibility, too, for choosing not to bring up your, er, situation after our wedding night," he said discreetly as they stood, embracing tenderly, in an empty, gleaming corridor of the Regent's palace.

She looked up at him.

He gave her a distracted half smile, lost in his thoughts. "I thought I was only being kind, doing you a favor by not bringing it up. But, in another sense, it was my way of keeping a safe distance between us." He shook his head. "Perhaps I was afraid of getting too close, afraid of what you could do to me if I really let you in. But I don't want that anymore," he whispered. "I'm done holding back. I want to see where this love can take us."

The first place it would take them, to the surprise of neither, was home and straight to bed to make up properly. One kiss decided the matter.

They stared into each other's eyes in mutual understanding, then left the Regent's palace and rushed home in pulse-pounding eagerness to reaffirm their bond.

Two hours later, the sound of the musical automaton clock awakened them.

Beau groaned and buried his face in the pillow. "Oh, why did I ever give you that thing? It never shuts up."

Laughing softly, Carissa ran a caress down the supple curve of his bare back. "Because you love me," she purred, thoroughly sated by his lovemaking.

He turned his head on the pillow and gazed at her, his blue eyes shining softly. "Yes, I do."

"I love hearing you say it."

"I love you," he repeated.

She smiled with a glow from her very heart and kissed him. "I love you, too."

He captured her fingers, curling his own around them. He pulled her hand wearily to his lips and brushed her knuckles with a kiss. Then he sighed, rested their hands against the pillow, and closed his eyes. "I'm so glad all that's over."

"Me, too," she whispered, stroking his golden hair and savoring in awe the memory of how brilliant he had been today. How he had looked the future King of England in the eyes and given him what-for.

The way he had taken Ezra Green apart using Green's own favorite weapon—words—though Beau was no lawyer but a warrior, a man of action.

As for Nick, it seemed that Order agents were remarkably hard to kill, especially when the weapon that Green had shot him with was a small-caliber pistol that gave up power for ease of concealment.

Deadly enough at point-blank range, Beau had told her, the pocket pistol could have killed Beau when he had tackled Green if Green had been aiming for him.

Instead, the Radical had opted to target the prince, who had been sitting some fifteen feet away. As a result, the royal surgeons did not have to dig deep to retrieve the small, flattened ball from the hard muscle layer of Nick's abdomen. Thankfully, the bullet had not pierced any internal organs. He'd make a full recovery, and would have, as Beau put it, another scar to brag about.

Meanwhile, Lord Rotherstone and the others had been freed from the Tower. They had sent word that Beau and Carissa should meet them later at the secure estate where the wives were waiting.

No doubt they were still angry about their unjust arrest. Ezra Green and Charles Vincent had been taken into custody, and the Regent sent out soldiers to detain Professor Culvert and his circle of devotees.

The Prime Minister was advised of the thwarted assassination plot against him; ironically, his wrath at this was sure to bring about a fierce new reactionary crackdown on all the Radicals in England that was the very opposite of what Culvert had hoped to achieve. A good number of the conspirators behind the plot were already being arrested.

The only real hitch in how it all worked out was that they had been unable to hide the commotion from the professional snoops: the newspaper reporters.

Usually, Beau had told her, they were able to keep all news pertaining to the Order out of the papers. But thanks to the very public manner in which Ezra Green had chosen to have the returning agents arrested at the docks, the better to disgrace them, there had been many witnesses, and now all London was abuzz. In short, the true purpose of the Inferno Club had been exposed.

Now the Order was going to have no choice but to talk to the reporters.

Poor Vickers and the rest of the staff had already chased away a dozen journalists lurking outside their house. So much for avoiding scandal, Carissa thought wryly. Instead of alarming her, however, she found it rather amusing. Beau, on the other hand, was extremely annoyed.

"We should escape tonight to the country house with the others," he remarked.

"Maybe it's for the best that the big secret about the Inferno Club is finally going to come out. Maybe you'll finally get the credit you deserve."

"Ugh," Beau replied. "Virgil must be turning in his grave."

"No. I'm sure he'd be very proud of the way you've handled this. I know I am." She rested her arm across his back and patted him in affection.

"Well, what do *you* know?" he retorted in a cheeky drawl. "You're in love."

She let out an indignant huff, but, of course, the rogue was perfectly correct in his teasing. "So, what if I am?" She leaned down and bit him lightly on his shoulder.

"Hey!" He lifted his head from the pillow in surprise. "You bit me!"

"Serves you right." She grabbed his shoulder and rolled him onto his back. "Look at you. All tousled and inviting. You'll be lucky if I don't eat you all up in one bite."

"I rather like the sound of that," he purred, as she knelt astride him.

She laughed, feeling his arousal stir anew, for they were both naked, but for the swathes of linen sheets that veiled them here and there. "I daresay you do, my lord."

"Redheads! You are growing even more saucy than when I first met you," he remarked, running his hands up her bare thighs. "And I, for one, find it utterly enchanting."

She lowered her lashes and ran her fingers lovingly down his chest, stroking his splendid body.

As he curled upward to give her a soulful kiss, she felt his breathing deepen. She inched her hand sensuously farther down his sculpted body. He captured her fingers and kissed them, then placed them on his member.

Pleasuring him in a blissful trance, she began to kiss

him in a variety of interesting places, until he rolled her onto her back and moved atop her.

Soon, the playful music of the clock's dainty chimes mingled with the rapturous cries of lovemaking coming from their chamber.

Only this time, knowing they had all the days, hours, and minutes of their lives together, neither of them paid the least attention to the melody, too busy delighting in each other.

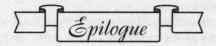

$\mathscr{I}$t couldn't be helped. The Order had been hopelessly exposed. With the true purpose of the Inferno Club known throughout the land, the Crown had no choice but to make heroes of them.

All of the covert actions and diverse missions that Ezra Green had wished to expose in order to hang them had, instead, awed the English public. Perhaps the shocking revelation suited that ironic, British sense of humor, that all the time the world at large had believed the rakehell lords of Dante House to be the most depraved libertines, they had, in secret, been valiantly protecting the nation. The story grew. Minding their own business, the agents were cheered in the streets. At White's, they were surrounded, in various ballrooms, mobbed. They couldn't go anywhere or get much of anything done because after all their faithful service, they now had to endure the maddening punishment of becoming celebrities.

Not even their wives were spared. It was a good thing Carissa had come to terms with the possibility of some notoriety as a natural part of being married to her scandalous viscount.

All the wives were interviewed by the ladies' fashion magazines about what they were wearing on any given day. Daphne, patient creature, handled it all, of course, with her usual unflappable serenity. But the nonsense came to such a point where Kate, the "Divine" Duchess of Warrington, shrieked a few choice words she had learned as a child among the sailors on the decks of her father's ship and slammed the door in their faces.

Emily, Countess of Westwood, was even more direct; she resorted to her bow and arrow when the journalists had the nerve to bother her and Drake at their country house—a threat the papers interpreted reported as "charming." Meanwhile, the progress of Mara, Lady Falconridge's pregnancy became a general obsession, and she was consulted for her expertise as a parent. During this interview, of course, little Thomas ran about the drawing room, pell-mell, like a wild Indian. It didn't matter. All faults were forgiven. Everything they said was clever, for the moment.

All England was in love with them. There was talk of a statue of St. Michael the Archangel to be erected in the middle of some Town square in their honor. But when a new musical pantomime based on their adventures was announced at Vauxhall, and advertised with posters everywhere, claiming "The Most Dramatic Spectacle with Fireworks, Explosions, and Breathtaking Feats of Daring," Prinny threw up his hands in despair.

This story was bloody well not going away quietly as His Royal Highness had hoped. Something had to be done about this mess. Then, perhaps, he need not face daily reminders of how he had wronged the bastards. He was already unpopular enough.

With a sigh, he had called in the Archbishop.

Now the day had come when they were to be honored with all pomp and ceremony at Westminster Abbey.

After this, God willing, the world would (from Prinny's point of view) shut up about them already, and (from theirs) leave them alone to enjoy, finally, the peacetime they had helped to bring about.

The men, fully uniformed, stood in a row across the front of the magnificent church, the Elders of the Order seated off to the side.

The ladies, dressed in their finest, looked on from the front pews, beaming with pride in their husbands. Everything that had happened had only strengthened the bond among the women. They had become like sisters. Carissa sat between Kate and Daphne, who squeezed her hands as they all watched, teary-eyed, as the future King of England pinned medals on each man, in turn.

Even Nick had been allowed to participate today.

Indeed, even trusty Sergeant Parker was awarded with special distinctions. While the music played, the Abbey's great organ and the choir interspersed with the noble tunes from Scottish bagpipers, representatives of all the elite branches of the military were on hand to pay their respects. Countless parliamentary leaders attended, including a grateful Prime Minister, Lord Liverpool.

Ambassadors had also been sent by the various crowned heads whose thrones the Order had helped to protect over the years.

Amid all this fanfare, they had discussed privately among themselves some uneasiness about all their identities being exposed after all the things they had done, all the enemies they had made. But what could they do? Their cover was blown; the cat was out of the bag.

They could do naught but assure themselves and one another that the Order took care of its own. They'd all be looking out for each other, as always, and nothing could ever change that. That went for the ladies, too.

From the corner of her eye, Carissa saw Kate blow a kiss to her Beast while Daphne dabbed at her eyes with a handkerchief.

After the Regent had walked along the row of men, congratulating each one, the ceremony was over.

The men tried to rejoin the ladies, but their progress was slowed by the sea of well-wishers and grateful admirers surrounding them. As Beau worked his way through the crowd, Carissa saw his parents, who had been sitting together for the ceremony.

Perhaps it was not just pride in their son that had inspired the Earl and Countess of Lockwood to unite for today to show their support. They seemed to be getting along better ever since she and Beau had announced Carissa's pregnancy.

Beau had forced them to come into the same room to hear the news, then had sternly informed his parents that if they wanted to spend time with their coming grandchild, they were going to have to set a reasonable example and not act like children themselves. It had been surprisingly smooth sailing ever since. The older couple seemed to be tentatively getting acquainted once again.

As Lord and Lady Lockwood headed down the long, lavish aisle toward the Abbey's giant doors, Carissa also saw Uncle Denbury and his family in the mulling throng.

Aunt Jo was walking in between the girls, Lady Joss

and Lady Min. Having learned her lesson, the glamorous Comtesse d'Arras wasn't about to let another niece go astray. She had stepped forward to begin finally putting some teeth into poor Miss Trent's efforts to keep the formidable beauties under control. After all, the girls' own mother wasn't about to do it.

Carissa smiled as her relatives shuffled out. She'd be seeing them afterward at the reception for the conquering heroes.

Nick, however, was not going to be permitted to attend that part of the day's festivities. The brawny bagpipers from the Order, who had played during the ceremony, doubled as guards. They'd be escorting the wayward Baron Forrester back up to the Order's headquarters in Scotland to put him back into his cell.

Two years, minimum, in the brig.

His large, kilted escorts did him the honor of not shackling him in front of the world, but Nick paused a short distance from where Carissa stood to bid his mates adieu. The three former team members conferred in low tones nearby.

She could not hear much, besides which, she was trying not to eavesdrop. But she could tell by the looks on their faces that Nick was apologizing to Beau and Trevor one last time.

"Good luck in prison," she heard Beau say ruefully to his black-haired friend, at last. "Don't worry, we'll write often. We won't forget about you."

"Thanks. That would mean a lot to me in there."

Handshakes and bear hugs were exchanged.

"I'm going to miss you, man," Trevor admitted. "Take care of yourself."

"You do the same. Be happy," he replied. "And both of you, take good care of your ladies." Nick gave them a roguish wink, and with that, the Order guards led him away. Beau put his hands in his pockets with a wistful look as he and Trevor watched the soldiers escort their teammate out. Then they exchanged a glance.

"Do you think he'll be all right?" Trevor asked.

"He's Nick," Beau said. "He's fairly indestructible. He'll be fine." Then he nudged his friend. "What about you?"

"I'm going home. There's a lady who's been waiting for me. New house is nearly completed. My real life can finally start." Trevor smiled, his gray eyes gleaming, and Carissa, eavesdropping in spite of herself, found him quite handsome, especially now that he'd shaved off the scruffy beard. Interestingly, however, he'd kept his hair long, which made him look rather dangerous and slightly wild. Presently, it was tied back in a queue.

Beau clapped him on the back. "Well, I won't keep you, then. Go find your Laura. But I expect to be the best man at your wedding."

"Of course. Provided she'll still have me."

"What?" Beau protested. "Can there be any doubt? Of course she will. Especially now that you're a famous hero," he drawled, punching him in the arm.

Trevor shrugged his broad shoulders. "She hasn't heard from me in a long time, that's all."

"Don't worry, my friend. I'm sure you'll find her waiting for you right where you left her. And here is a lady I see waiting for me," he greeted Carissa. He put his arms around her and gave her a doting kiss.

"You were splendid up there, all of you," she congratulated them.

"Yes, we rather were, weren't we?" Beau drawled, as they headed out.

The spring daylight glowed through the stained-glass

windows as the whole group of them filed out of the sacred twilight of Westminster Abbey into the bright open air.

The endless sky that wrapped around the spires was a blazing blue. The resident flock of doves lifted off the church and flew free over the city. Watching them, Beau felt his throat unexpectedly tighten.

He and his brother warriors stopped on the threshold of the Abbey and watched their scattering flight. When the birds had flown away, the men glanced at each other in silent, stoic comprehension. It really was over—the struggle. At least for them. They had done their duty, and it had taken some doing to clean up the aftermath, but at last, they were truly free.

A tension they had been carrying since they were little more than boys had started to ease from them. They still had scars from all the battles they had faced, all the tests they had somehow passed. The day had finally arrived that they had only dreamed of. The day they had come out on the other side.

Beau had almost stopped believing it would ever really happen. But here it was, upon them. They were going to have to learn a whole new way to live.

As they glanced around at each other in mutual understanding, a spark of curiosity about the life ahead shone in the eyes of each, a glimmer that seemed to wonder if perhaps the adventure had only just begun.

Then Kate's jovial command broke their thoughtful silence. "Come on, you scurvy lot, look lively! We're going to miss our own party!" Then she fluffed her skirts and marched off ahead of them, organizing the carriages.

A few of the fellows smiled at Rohan.

"Not very duchesslike, is she?" Max observed.

"Pirate's daughter," Rohan murmured to the others with a guarded smile.

"And he wouldn't want her any other way," Jordan supplied, and the Beast nodded in full agreement.

"Max is the one who wanted a fine lady. And you got one," he added, nodding over at Daphne.

Max clapped him on the shoulder. "My friend, my 'fine lady' has a side to her that you cannot imagine. And I don't suggest you try."

Rohan laughed. "Wouldn't dream of it, brother."

Then Mara brought little Thomas over, reaching for Jordan. The two-year-old launched himself into his stepfather's arms. Jordan set him up high on his shoulders so Thomas could see over all the people, while Drake and Emily walked out arm in arm, as inseparable as they had been since childhood.

Max glanced at the sky again as they waited for their carriages. Beau had a feeling he knew what the other team leader was thinking.

If only Virgil were here.

The old Scot's absence had left a hole in their midst. But at least his death had been avenged when the men had gone to Germany.

"I'm sure he's watching," Jordan murmured with a meaningful glance as he held his stepson.

Beau smiled wryly. "Then I guess we'd all better be on our best behavior."

"Such as it is!" Carissa piped up, coming back over to his side.

"Aye," he murmured, smiling, "such as it is." He kissed her head as he put his arm around her. Then they all went off together to start the celebration.

Bonus Scene!

*Read on to find out what happens next to
Lord Trevor Montgomery,
as the Inferno Club continues . . .*

The Homecoming

Lord Trevor Montgomery clutched the flowers behind his back so hard that he nearly snapped the stems. "Is Lady Laura at home?" he asked again, for the Bayne family butler just stood, staring at him as if he'd seen a ghost.

"I-I-" The poor servant shut his mouth abruptly, then opened the door for him with the air of a man who did not know what else to do.

When Trevor stepped inside, heart pounding with eagerness, he got his first inkling that matters here were not as he had left them.

First he heard a bouncy tune being played on the pianoforte upstairs—the instrument sat in the drawing room upstairs, if he recalled correctly.

This was accompanied by a peal of girlish laughter; the familiar sound brought the start of a smile to his face. That was the beauty of Laura. So carefree, untouched by all the ugliness he had seen.

And then a deeper voice—male—joined in her laughter.

Trevor froze, his upward gaze homing in on the staircase. *What the hell?*

The butler blanched and gazed at him apologetically, flinching a bit as the two voices from upstairs began harmonizing in a merry duet.

A love song.

Trevor went very still. "Who is that?" he asked in a tone of murderous quiet.

The butler gulped. "I'm so sorry, my lord. That would be, er . . ."

He narrowed his eyes, waiting.

"Lady Laura's new betrothed," the terrified servant blurted out.

"*New* betrothed?" he echoed in a shocked whisper.

"I'm sorry, my lord, the poor girl thought you were dead! We all did," the butler whispered. "I'm sure she was going to tell you very soon—"

Trevor barely registered anything after that.

As their duet rambled on playfully from upstairs, he couldn't help but notice that if, indeed, Laura thought that he was dead, she did not sound all that upset about his demise.

Good God.

The betrayal nearly took his breath away. He suddenly felt ill. He shot his hand out and stopped the butler from fetching her, mainly because he did not trust himself not to rip out her new fiancée's jugular on sight. "Who is he?" he asked in a low growl.

The butler told him the name, but Trevor had never heard of the man.

The next thing he knew, he was standing out on the pavement in a daze.

The world spun, and it wasn't due to the large quantity of liquor he had drunk at last night's reception following the ceremony at Westminster Abbey. He had been riding high with his mates, the conquering heroes.

He had expected the victory to continue today as he came to claim the sweetest reward of all. But this was a rude awakening, to say the least. How could this be happening? Everything he had so meticulously planned . . .

The new life he had awaited for so long . . .

His chance at a normal, orderly existence with a pretty wife in a nice, new house . . .

Gone.

Poof.

All for nothing. He couldn't believe it. First Nick had locked him in a cellar, then the Crown had all but thrown him and his fellow agents to the wolves. And now even Laura had proved faithless.

He had a thousand questions about when exactly she had decided to give up waiting for him and get on with her life. But he was too shocked and angry to ask them now. Besides, he had the darkest, bitterest feeling that it simply didn't matter.

The vision that had held him together through these past few brutal years of war lay in pieces on the ground. "New fiancé?" he whispered to himself.

Unsure where to go or what to do with himself, he just started walking blindly down the fashionable Mayfair street, pausing when he realized he was still holding the flowers. He was in such a state of disbelief he could barely remember how they had come to be in his hand.

Harlequin roses: silly things. Gaudy. Bright pink and white striped.

Her favorite.

How carefully he had removed the thorns so they would not hurt her delicate hand!

He suddenly tipped his head back and let out the bitterest, most cynical laugh. *Fool!*

He started to throw the damned things into the street.

Let them be trampled, shit on by carriage horses, he thought in rage, but from the corner of his eye, he noticed the sad figure he had just passed. An impoverished-looking old woman wrapped in a threadbare shawl. She looked like she had been scrubbing floors for the past few hours. She was leaning on the wrought-iron fence, likely waiting for the omnibus.

He stopped. Turned around. Went over to her and offered her the flowers without a word—and shocked her to the core, apparently. "For me? Oh, oh, my goodness! How kind of you, dear boy!" the old, frail grandmother exclaimed, lighting up. Tears sprang into her eyes.

It humbled him somehow, jarred him out of the focus on himself. He could not quite manage a smile, but he gave the old woman a respectful nod, then walked on.

Heading where, he had no idea.

And yet, strangely, he felt lighter the moment those roses were out of his possession.

If the woman he'd meant to make his wife could care so little about him, then maybe he had just dodged a bullet. Maybe Laura had served her purpose as naught but a figment in his head to keep him going. Perhaps it had been a delusion all along. What now? he wondered, at a loss.

What now, indeed.

Author's Note

*D*ear Reader,

Thank you for reading *My Scandalous Viscount*. Before we part, I thought you might like to know about some of the real historical inspiration behind this story. The "bad business" among the villains in this tale came from the 1812 assassination of Prime Minister Spencer Perceval, who was gunned down in broad daylight while he was walking into the House of Commons. I combined the assassination of the Prime Minister with the Cato Street Conspiracy of 1820, in which a group of would-be revolutionaries plotted to blow up the full Cabinet of King George IV (AKA Prinny, in his first year as king). A few of the Cato Street Conspirators were the last men to be sent to the Tower of London as traitors, interestingly enough.

Also, anyone who has visited Madame Tussaud's Wax Museum in London will no doubt recognize it (and its famous, ghastly Chamber of Horrors) as the inspiration for the waxworks in this story. Madame Tussaud herself first learned how to make wax models in

1770s Paris, and later became an art tutor to the sister of Louis XVI at the Palace of Versailles. This put her right in the middle of the action when the French Revolution broke out. She was forced to make likenesses of guillotine victims, including making copies of the decapitated heads of the more famous unfortunate souls (like the royals), so that they could be displayed on pikes at various locations—proof of their deaths.

No doubt the artist was glad to make a new life for herself upon her arrival in England in 1802. For the next thirty-three years, her waxworks exhibit was a traveling show, until the Baker Street location in London opened in 1835, where it still stands today—allegedly containing the actual guillotine blade that beheaded Marie Antoinette! Go figure.

On a happier note, many readers have written to ask me if there will be more Inferno Club tales to come. As you have probably guessed by now, the answer is yes!

The story you've just read acts as a bridge between the previous four installments and the final set, focusing on the members of Beau's team. (If you missed them, the first four books in order are: *My Wicked Marquess,* featuring Max and Daphne; *My Dangerous Duke,* with Rohan and Kate; *My Irresistible Earl,* Jordan and Mara; and *My Ruthless Prince,* featuring Drake and Emily.)

With those nasty Prometheans sewn up in Drake's story, the rest of our heroes are now free to turn their attention to matters of the heart. Trevor's book will be next, although the last we left him, things were not looking too bright for him, poor fellow. Bad boy Nick will be our grand finale, but I'm afraid he's got to do some time in the Order's Scottish dungeon first.

I don't have titles or release dates for either story yet, but if you'll visit my website (www.gaelenfoley.com), you can sign up for my monthly e-newsletter and be the first to hear my news as it happens. You can also find Chapter One of all the previous books available there for your perusal.

Thank you again for reading. I hope you've enjoyed Beau and Carissa's story. It's always a joy and a privilege to entertain you.

Best always,

Gaelen

At Avon Books, we know your passion for romance—once you finish one of our novels, you find yourself wanting more.

May we tempt you with . . .

- **Excerpts** from our upcoming releases.

- Entertaining **extras**, including authors' personal photo albums and book lists.

- Behind-the-scenes **scoop** on your favorite characters and series.

- **Sweepstakes** for the chance to win free books, romantic getaways, and other fun prizes.

- Writing **tips** from our authors and editors.

- **Blog** with our authors and find out why they love to write romance.

- **Exclusive content** that's not contained within the pages of our novels.

Join us at
www.avonbooks.com

*G*ive in to your Impulses!

**These unforgettable stories only take a second
to buy and give you hours of reading pleasure!**

Go to *www.AvonImpulse.com* and see what we
have to offer.

Available wherever e-books are sold.

AVONIMPULSE